SECRET LOVERS

THE TAYLORED MEN SERIES- BOOK THREE

J R GALE

J R GALE PUBLISHING LLC

Editing: Britt- Paperback Proofreader

Proofing: Brooke- Brooke's Editing Services

Cover: Sarah Paige- The Book Cover Boutique Cover

Photographer: Wander Aguiar

ISBN: 979-8-9885905-1-4

"To love is nothing. To be loved is something. But to love and be loved, that's everything." — T. Tolis

AUTHOR'S NOTE

Please check the author's website to find the content warning for Secret Lovers.

SECRET LOVERS

PROLOGUE

Las Vegas

Annabelle

DRUNK. It's the only word to describe us right now.

Disorderly, even. But who cares when we're having the time of our lives.

"Bloody hell, Jack!" I squeal as my best friend's brother tumbles on top of me, both of us rolling around the filthy ground of the Las Vegas strip. "What are you doing?" I laugh, letting an unattractive snort slip through my nose.

I have no control over myself in my drunken state.

"That was the worst wedding of all time." He groans, throwing his head back.

He's not wrong.

It was bloody awful. Hence the drunkenness.

"Why the hell did you drag me to that?" I ask, unsure why he would have wanted to be there.

It was clear the bride and groom hated each other from the second they locked eyes at the altar. You could feel the disdain from across the room.

"And why the hell did they get married in Las Vegas when they're both from New York?"

He rolls his eyes. "Who knows? If we ever get married, it will be so much fucking fun."

I brush off his marriage comment. I know he's only kidding around, yet his words still make my insides twist with excitement.

"Come on, B." He jumps up, trying to pull me with him, and we instantly fall back over.

Unable to contain myself, I burst out laughing.

What must we look like?

"Oh, hell!" I say, crossing my legs. "I've peed myself! Now you've done it, Jackson Peters."

"Uh oh, she's using my full name. I must be in trouble." He rolls back on top of me, still snickering to himself, as he takes his tie and runs it along my face, pretending to be an elephant.

Fuck's sake, we need some water and a bed.

With no luck, I swat him away and try to push him off me. He's dead weight. "By the way, where are your mates?"

His eyes widen. "Fucking shit, I forgot about them." He goes to grab his phone, then groans dramatically with something that sounds like "oh no," before falling to his side.

"You lost your phone, didn't you?" He doesn't answer, confirming my guess.

I'm not even going to try to help him look. I know it's not here because he doesn't have his tuxedo jacket on, where his phone was placed inside the pocket.

I close my eyes for a second. It feels like heaven on earth, I could stay like this all night. "Jack," I call. "Jack," I call again when he doesn't answer.

"Mmm?"

I look over. He must have given up looking for his phone and is lying there with his eyes closed too.

We really need to get off this disgusting floor.

"Go look for your mates. Nate and Seb seemed like they were looking for a good time tonight. You don't have to babysit me. I've had too much tequila and should go to sleep anyway."

"No, and no," he shouts, my statement suddenly waking him up.

He jumps up with a new burst of energy and grabs my hand, succeeding this time in pulling me off the ground.

"What do you mean, *no, and no*?"

"I don't care about going out with anyone but you, sweetheart. I'm staying with my best girl." He pulls me into his body, and my stomach drops.

What is he going to do?

My eyes are wide as I whisper, "Jack."

His infamous cheeky smile slowly creeps across his face, causing his dimples that I hate—*that I love*—with a passion to pop.

He leans in and kisses my lips.

Shit, he feels amazing, except he pulls back all too soon. "Ready to do something crazy, B?"

"Umm… no, not really," I answer, my voice getting louder as he starts dragging me down the Las Vegas strip.

"Well, too bad. Tonight's going to be a night to remember."

"Ah!" I cover my ears when the alarm goes off at six in the morning.

Our groans of protest are loud enough to wake the neighbors, and on instinct, my arm shoots out and quickly shuts it off. *At least I remembered to set one after the night we had.*

My eyelids feel as if they weigh one million pounds, I can barely open them, and I'm in major need of hydration.

My mouth is drier than the Sahara. I'm bloody knackered, and I need more sleep.

Fucking hell.

Instead, I force them open, because if we fall back to sleep now, we'll never get up.

Sadly, we have a flight to New York early this morning to support our friend testifying in a court case, so we have no choice but to get up and suck it up.

Jack is spooning me from behind, our legs intertwined, his hand splayed across my exposed stomach. It's not unusual for us to share a bed, and he's always been a cuddler.

Only this time, I'm entirely naked… and so is Jack.

I think hard about last night. Did we have sex? I flex down below a bit and… fuck. I'm sore.

I probably wouldn't be able to tell if it were anyone else. But with the size of Jack's penis, there'd be no doubt.

"What happened last night?" he asks.

I attempt to turn my head to look at him, though the pounding in my temples causes me to quickly drop it back down on my pillow.

"What do you mean?" I whisper, acting dumb, afraid of letting any emotion show.

It was only a few hours ago. Do both of us truly not remember anything?

Could we both have been that drunk?

"I can only remember bits and pieces." He snuggles closer. "Fuck, that feels good." He pushes his groin into my arse. "Did we…"

"Mmhmm. I think so."

He moans. "You're kidding me. And I don't remember?"

He trails his hand up higher to cup my breast, and I close my eyes at the tingly feeling that courses through my body.

"I think maybe we need a re-do," he whispers darkly against my ear, sending shivers up my body. Then, he stiffens. "Annabelle?" Worry laces his tone.

"What is it? What's wrong?"

There's an extended silence…

"Why the hell am I wearing a wedding ring?"

What?

I glance down, and holy fucking shit. This can't be happening.

I hold my hand to his face. "I think… for the same reason I'm wearing one too."

1

One Year Later

Annabelle

For the fifth time, I dare myself not to look at the clock. However, I can tell by the burning sensation rapidly growing in my eyes that more time has passed than I would like.

My anxiety is through the roof, and I can't kick the nervous feeling I've had all week.

Owning a PR firm at a young age is hard enough. Waiting to hear about the biggest deal of your life? That's more stressful than you could ever imagine.

Always trying to compete with well-established companies while showing your worth as a young female entrepreneur is a daily struggle, but today's meeting will be life-changing, and I have no idea which way it will go.

My client has been pleased with our performance over the last year; of that, I'm sure.

The looming question is whether they want to extend our contract or not.

I've been working with the DeLuca family in Tuscany to help rebrand and rebuild their image throughout Italy after one of their sons almost drove their winery into the ground by gambling away everything they've worked so hard for.

Our deal was that we start small.

A year long face-lift in Italy, and if they were happy with my company's performance, they would extend to a three-year contract where we would work alongside their California-based family to bring their brand to the States.

Which, in turn, would make Hughes Agency a worldwide company. A dream I never thought would happen so early in my career.

I turn over and finally look—three *in the morning.*

This is ridiculous. I'm getting up.

I'm stressing myself out more about my sleep than the actual meeting. I was planning on getting up at five anyway, so I might as well start my day two hours earlier to prepare. Surely if they didn't want to keep us on, they wouldn't have suggested lunch or flown from Italy to meet me.

Right?

"Okay," I say into the darkness, shaking myself out of my thoughts. I know I need to stop before I drive myself insane, so I pull out my favorite purple yoga mat—because, obviously, outside of black, purple is the superior color—and turn on the light. Then, I start the flow I do every morning to calm my nerves.

For so long, I thought this was a joke of an exercise and a waste of time.

When I work out, I want my heart pumping and music blasting as I run in the park or sweat my arse off at SoulCycle.

After being told a few times—okay, maybe more than a few—that I'm "too high-strung" in the office, I relented, taking up yoga to start my mornings with the goal of a calmer and clearer mind.

I must admit I'm addicted, and it doesn't hurt that I'm more flexible than ever. Which is something I've never heard anyone complain about… especially in the bedroom.

After yoga, I lean against my bed and email Lola. My former-assistant-turned-good-friend is now my chief operating officer.

She is a jack of all trades and helps with everything in the office. There is absolutely no way I could ever do any of this without her.

I ask her again, for the millionth time, if she wants to attend today's lunch meeting with me, knowing she's going to shoot me down again.

Lola is more introverted and feels most comfortable behind the scenes, but I'm slowly trying to break her out of the awkward shell she keeps herself in. She lacks the confidence needed in our industry, even though she's still young.

My phone pings instantly. I'm not surprised.

She's a nervous nelly on the best of days, and there's no way she's sleeping, either.

The response is short and sweet:

No.

Love you lots.

Unable to hold back my laughter, I reply with a sad face, even though I never expected her to respond any differently.

I guess I'm doing this alone today.

Well, fuck it… that's how it should be, right?

I didn't work my way up to need the support of others. There is only one name on my office door:

Hughes.

And you best believe Annabelle Hughes can handle things all by herself.

Just a spritz more hairspray to ensure the curls hold throughout the day, and I'm done. Challenging, when you have long, thick hair that is hard to tame on a good day, let alone when you need it to behave most.

I tuck my pearl silk cami in my trousers, then shrug on my black Prada suit jacket.

My power suit.

I bought it for my first big client pitch and wear it to all my important meetings. It's been good luck ever since.

Not that I need it, I remind myself. Luck shouldn't be a factor today, my team and I worked day and night on this project, and we deserve the contract.

Just as I'm about to exit my bedroom, I turn around for one last look in the mirror.

A slight smirk graces my face.

Fuck yes, I look good, and I'm ready to be the badass businesswoman I know I am.

No more doubts.

I'm Annabelle Hughes, and I got this shit in the bag.

I grab my phone to call for my car, but it buzzes in my hand before I can dial.

Huh?

I glance at the clock. It's ten to four. What the hell?

"Hello?" I answer as I pack up my work bag. People are screaming in the background, and I can hardly hear. "Hello," I yell into the phone.

"I'm sorry, B. I need you to come and get me."

Shit. "Jack. Are you fucking kidding me right now?"

"I wouldn't call if I could ask anyone else, you know that."

"Or how about don't get yourself in these situations, and you wouldn't have to call at all," I respond dryly. "Time's up, Peters. Get off the phone."

"Annabelle." He rarely uses my full name, so I know I have no choice.

"I'll be right there," I mutter.

Then the line goes dead.

I wave my hand dramatically, trying to get the attention of the dismissive policewoman so I can finally get out of this dreaded place… *for the second time this week.*

"Hello, I'm here to pick up my husband," I call again, yet I'm completely ignored.

She types away on her keyboard, not lifting her head to look at me even once, before she finally says, "You and all the others. Sit. I'll call you when I'm ready."

I'm in no mood to deal with this nonsense.

"You see, that won't do. John Porter called in a favor, and my husband is ready now and will not wait another minute back there in that cell."

Don't fuck with me today, lady.

She finally lifts her head, eyeing me suspiciously, then huffs loudly, visibly annoyed. She doesn't say a word as she picks up her phone and makes the call.

Of course, hearing me mention John's name, she knows I mean business.

He's my best friend Sadie's driver, and his brother is the chief superintendent.

I hate to throw his name around… actually, who am I kidding? That's a lie. I'll use all the help I can get to make this process move along more efficiently.

The sad thing is she doesn't even have to ask who I'm here for.

Lately, I've been a frequent visitor.

The side door opens with a loud click, and I rush to the exit to get out of here as quickly as possible. Something about being here freaks me out, especially at this time in the morning.

I don't look back when I hear him creeping up behind me. I'm fucking livid. He knows today is a big day for me.

Though, I suddenly have a vision that it's not who I think, and that a strange man is following behind me instead, so I turn quickly to make sure.

Yup. Even though the sky is dark and the stars are dull, I can see clearly.

It's *him*. The major pain in my arse.

My "husband" and best friend's brother, Jackson Peters.

I shake my head at my unfounded paranoia. I need to cool it with the missing people documentaries I've been watching lately. They're fucking with my head.

The other day I was sure my taxi driver was trying to kidnap me, so much so that I made him pull over in the pouring rain with no umbrella while I was on my way to a meeting.

"You mad, B?" Jackson calls from behind me.

I don't answer.

Then the pounding of his footsteps gets faster, echoing through the night as he tries to catch up with me. I'm quicker and make it to the car first.

Perks of having sky-high legs.

I'm not dealing with this in public. I have a reputation to uphold in this city, and I've always tried to keep my private life just that.

Private.

Jackson jumps in behind me and slams the door. Not sure what he has to be mad about when I'm the one who had to get out of bed to come here.

Even though I was up already, he doesn't need to know that.

"Fuck," he mutters, realizing who's driving. "Why couldn't you just pick me up in a taxi?"

"Jackson Peters," I grit, so angry I could scream, but keep my voice down so I don't make a scene in front of John. "You're lucky I even came at all. You should be thanking John for having your back and always bailing you out."

"John, I appreciate it, but you can't tell my sister. Sadie will kill me this time since I promised no more fights."

John's eyes flicker to me in the rearview mirror, then back to Jackson, "This is the last time, Jackson. I won't tell your sister, and not because you asked me, but because I don't want her to be any more stressed than she has been recently. You're almost forty years old. Grow the hell up."

Jackson flinches, likely knowing John's right.

On both accounts.

Sadie's been overly stressed lately with finalizing the last-minute details of her Paris wedding.

On top of that, her dad has tried to reach out, and with them being estranged for many years, it's not been easy. Though if he's trying to contact her, I'm more worried that it might mean her mum could reach out next, ruining all the progress Sadie's made to heal and build herself up over the years. Jackson and Sadie's mother is the Wicked Witch of The West and an abusive fucking cunt.

I've never hated someone more in my life.

From my peripheral vision, Jackson nods his head to John. I can see he's clearly embarrassed, even through the darkness of the car.

Which doesn't surprise me. This isn't Jackson.

I don't know what's gotten into him. I've repeatedly told him that he needs to calm down. The first time he laid a hand on someone was a couple of years ago when he punched Wills—his future brother-in-law—which is a story for another time. But other than that… he doesn't fight people.

He's similar to his sister in that respect.

Somehow even with fucked-up parents, they both think with their hearts, and despite his boyish charm and good looks, Jackson is sensitive and always means well.

He may go about it the wrong way at times, but I know who he truly is deep down, which is what makes this hard.

"Belle," he mumbles. "You know I hate when you're mad at me. If you knew what he was saying this time. He—"

"No." I take a breath to prepare myself. Did I mention his fights are to defend my honor when my toxic, wanker ex runs his mouth? Let's face it, what girl wouldn't swoon over that?

Still though, it upsets me, because he turns into someone I don't know. *Someone I don't like.* "Don't even go there. I've told you time and time again that I don't care what that lying, cheating, piece of shit ex of mine has to say about me, and neither should you. He's a loser cokehead and can say whatever he wants because I won't let his words get to me anymore."

I've done it for too long.

I pride myself on being a strong, independent woman, and I let that arsehole get to me for too long.

I'm done.

Jack turns his body toward me and takes my hand. "I'm proud of you for that, but the words still get to me, and as one of your best friends and husband—"

"Shh!" My eyes bug out. Is he kidding me right now?

I raise the partition so John can't hear Mister Big Mouth.

"Let's not use that word loosely. You're my husband on paper and nothing more, so don't use that as an excuse."

He narrows his emerald eyes and rolls his lips, annoyed. Whenever I remind him of this, he gets visibly aggravated.

When we made the drunken mistake of getting married in Vegas, we both had a lot going on and realized what a hassle it would be to get an annulment. So, considering we've known each other our whole lives and trust each other implicitly, we agreed to keep it legal, while still keeping it a secret. The deal is, if the time comes when one of us wants to settle down with someone, then we'll take steps to end it.

"Regardless of that, besides Sadie, you're the most important person in my life, and I won't sit around and listen to him disrespect you time and time again. Whether you like me sticking up for you or not… I won't be sorry for it."

I stay silent.

There's no changing his mind.

He needs to learn how to deal with his anger better. The problem is, I'm not sure he knows how, considering he's never really been an angry person until now.

Trey, my lowlife ex-boyfriend, turned into a raging alcoholic coke addict who can't keep his mouth shut about me when he's out on the town, even though he's the one who cheated and left me.

A blessing; trust me, I know.

He thinks because he has family in high places, he can get away with murder. Unfortunately for him, Jackson couldn't care less who his family is and somehow is always around him—same pub, same club… wherever it is, Jackson hears all the vile words Trey spews.

I love Jackson for always sticking up for me, he's done it most of my life, but I don't want him to fuck up *his* life because of it.

He's also a business owner with a reputation around this city, and I don't want any of that tarnished because of me. It took a long time for this community to trust some American bloke, so I won't let him jeopardize that.

Truthfully, I've been worried something more has been going on, wondering if Sadie might have mentioned their dad's messages, but if it were that, I'm sure he would have told me.

Shitty dads are our common ground, and because of it, we've been each other's sounding boards since we were kids—something else I'll never take for granted.

Jackson's sister might be my best friend, my "sister soul mate," as we call one another, but I could never share all the parts of my life with her.

I know now it's something she notices and might even resent me for, since she has shared every integral part of her life with me.

But even as a young girl, I somehow knew Sadie wasn't strong enough to handle my issues on top of hers, and if she knew I had more going on than I let on, she would have made it all about me. She would have put herself last, and what Sadie needed was for someone to put her above all else for once. To care for her, as her parents should have.

That's how Jackson and I found one another, we sought comfort in each other, and to this day, she doesn't know that Jackson and I have this kindred type of friendship. Only thinking we're close because we all grew up spending every summer together since she and I were five.

It's the type of thing that we've kept from her for so long that if she found out now, I know my sensitive Sadie would blame herself for not being strong enough to help us both. Let alone navigate her brother's issues.

Though it's times like this, his hand in mine, reminding me we're still married and sticking up for me even if it lands him in jail, that I wish I had my best friend to talk to.

For her to tell me it's normal that I wish this were all real, that he were truly mine.

While we may be good mates, Jackson and I, it goes beyond that for me.

I've secretly been in love with him since I was a teenager.

When we were younger, I thought it was weird that I was crushing on my best friend's brother. They look so much alike, but where Sadie is softer, giving her that gorgeous girl-next-door look, Jackson was blessed with sexy, defined features.

The chiseled jaw, structured nose, perfect cheekbones, and piercing green eyes. His skin that stretches over his tall, lean but built body is always the perfect color tan.

Despite his best attributes, being together is not in our cards.

Don't get me wrong. The chemistry is there, like full-on, I-want-to-rip-your-clothes-off-right-this-second chemistry.

But it ends there.

Jackson is a perpetual playboy and always will be.

I have my fun, I go out, and I don't let defining names stop me from meeting men if I choose. Only for me, it's to pass the time.

I want to settle down. I want a partner to thrive with, to talk about work at night, and bounce ideas off.

However, it's been a struggle so far. All the men I've met are too threatened by my success, afraid I'll strip them of their masculinity.

Wankers.

Despite Jackson's nighttime activities, on paper he would be the perfect partner. He is among the hardest-working people I know, and has only ever celebrated my success.

I look past his possessive, dominant side because he's considerate and loves his sister and nieces to death. He would give the skin off his back to help someone in need.

However, sometimes, that's not enough… because his overshared dick negates all of it.

Well…

Maybe not all of it, but most of it.

Lately, though, our relationship has been slightly strained. I'm not sure Jackson sees it, but since our Vegas ordeal, something has shifted for me personally.

I'm not mad per se, but I've realized how much I want a happy ending with someone, and how much I deserve it. I resent the fact that I had a drunken wedding I barely remember, and that Jack sure as shit doesn't.

Once we came home, it hit me. It was like a big *fuck you, Annabelle*. Teasing me that I can't actually have him.

He's not mine.

My heart drops at the thought, slowly breaking, knowing he'll never truly be mine.

Jack's my *fake* husband, and to be honest, it's made me feel like shit ever since.

"B!" Jack's raised voice snaps me out of my thoughts.

I turn my head, and those cheeky dimples are on full display.

"I asked why you look so fucking hot right now?"

And then there's that. Jack is a complete flirt. He's been like this his whole life, which has never bothered me. *Until now.*

I slide my hand out of his and turn toward the window. "I'm going to the office early. Today's the DeLuca lunch."

I can feel the air change as he sucks in a deep breath. "Oh fuck, B. I'm so fucking sorry. I forgot. God, I'm an asshole."

"Yeah, you are." I won't sugarcoat it to make him feel better.

He unbuckles and slides closer, and I hate that I love the feel of him pressed up against me.

He puts his arm around me, and I can't help myself as I lean my head against his shoulder.

I love this feeling.

"Well, so you know, I'm sure you'll be happy to hear I've already received my punishment tonight." He huffs and squeezes me around my shoulders, bringing me closer to his chest.

"What are you talking about?"

"That fucking lunatic was back tonight, the same guy as last time.

Making eyes at me. Only this time, he kept inching his way toward me. I couldn't even fucking move away because the other guy next to me kept trying to jerk off in the corner."

"What?" I burst out. "Are you kidding me?"

"No, I am not." He shivers with disgust, "What fucking shit luck do I have?"

I shake my head in amusement and say, "This would only happen to you." I laugh again, and snuggle into this side.

One laugh and the black cloud over us is broken.

The partition lowers slightly. "We're here, Annabelle," John calls from the front.

Bloody hell.

As upset as I was with Jackson, I'm thankful he distracted me from the day ahead.

"Thank you, John. For everything," I say, and he tips his hat in response.

"Hey," Jack whispers, and I turn back toward him. "I would never do anything to hurt you. You know you're my best girl, and I'm always looking out for you."

I cup his cheek. "I know, my darling Jack. But I need you to stop the violence. I'm not sure what's gotten into you lately, but I need you here, not in jail. Because eventually he's going to press charges, and John won't be able to help. Then what? You leave me, your sister, your mates, and your two beautiful nieces behind when you go to prison?" He looks down, forlorn, which is so unlike his usual happy-go-lucky self. "But you know I will always appreciate all you do. Don't you? You're the best, Jackson Peters. Your heart is always in the right place. Sometimes, though, your execution is lacking."

A slow smile creeps across his face. "I am the best, aren't I?" He laughs, and I playfully hit his arm. Of course that's what he picks to zero in on.

Before I exit, he grabs my hand to stop me and says, "You're the most hardworking person I know, and you deserve this today. I have all the faith in you."

I smile, kiss his cheek in thanks, exit the car, and hope he's right.

His encouraging words perk up my attitude, making this the perfect way to head into the office.

A loud whistle echoes off the city buildings just as I'm about to step inside. When I turn back, Jack has half his gorgeous body out the window as John begins to pull away. "Knock 'em dead, sexy!" he screams, blowing me a dramatic kiss before they turn the corner.

I can't help the smile plastered on my face.

You know what? I *am* going to knock 'em dead.

I'm going to show the DeLuca family that there is only one right answer to today's meeting.

2

Jackson

THE SECOND BELLE'S out of view, John lowers the divider the rest of the way down.

Great.

I blow out a sigh of annoyance; I know exactly what's coming.

I respect John. He's a good guy, has helped me out a few times, and I know he means well. He's become close to all of us, especially my sister and her family, but I'm not in the mood for a lecture right now.

I haven't slept, I smell disgusting, and I'm sick of hearing advice from anyone with a voice.

People forget I'm a grown-ass man. I know what I'm doing, and I know the consequences. If I thought they outweighed the fight, I wouldn't have done it. But I'm also a grown-ass man who cares deeply for a person who's been verbally attacked countless times.

I dare you to show me anyone who would have reacted differently. Because if they wouldn't react, they're cowards without an ounce of loyalty in their bodies.

Trey's lucky he's dealing with me and not one of Belle's brothers.

Especially Theo.

I've known him most of my life. He's always been into working out, but in the last five years, he's taken it to another level, becoming a beast.

Working out at the same boxing gym has given me a front-row seat to his transformation, and I can count on one hand the number of guys who can beat him.

If I didn't think he could kill Trey with one hit, I would have told him what was happening when it started. I won't risk it though, because while I might push Trey around a little, there's no doubt in my mind that Theo would end his life.

Leaving her brothers out of it means it's my job to protect her. If that ends with an arrest record, so be it.

We stop at a red light as John's eyes flicker up to mine, glaring at me through the rearview mirror, and I must admit, he's scary as fuck.

John is ex-military.

I cross my arms. "I like you, John, but god damn… you weren't there, so don't fucking judge me."

"Explain it to me, mate."

I shake my head, feeling my blood boil from last night's theatrics.

I'm no stranger to growing up with money, and I'm well aware two types of people arise from that lifestyle.

There are people like me and my friends, both in New York and London, who use our connections to grow our businesses, working our asses off to make a name for ourselves.

Then there are the people I hate most in the world.

The Treys.

Born privileged and with a "spoiled brat" mentality, always relying on mommy and daddy, knowing no matter what happens, they'll clean up their messes.

Running their mouths, thinking they're the fucking kings of the world.

Not on my watch, and I'm happy to put this one in his place.

I might have moved out of New York years ago, but no one loses the "don't fuck with me" New York attitude. You're born with it, and it stays with you forever.

Trey is messing with the wrong guy, especially in my soon-to-be club. It's why I was out late to begin with.

I was checking out the scene, and when things escalated with Trey, the bouncers called the police, not realizing I was the potential new owner.

Wills and I, alongside our best friend Declan Buckley, own the number-one members-only club in London as an investment.

There is only one other club in town that rivals our popularity: The Social Club.

We're currently in negotiations to purchase it, and I would be lying if I didn't say a big part of me was looking forward to the day we sign the contract just so I can ban Trey for life.

I don't care about his family's status or how much money he has. It means nothing to me.

He's banned from Charlotte's, our first club, and you can only imagine how it dented his ego when some of his friends continued their membership with us.

Once we sign on that dotted line and The Social Club becomes ours, his social life will be nonexistent because, unfortunately for him, there are two places to see and be seen, and we'll own both.

Resting my head against the seat, I sit back and try to think of something other than Trey. With the only other thing being my busy schedule, I close my eyes to try and quiet my thoughts.

Only it's no use when I can feel John's eyes on me as the silence lingers in the air.

I know he won't let this go, except I feel sick repeating what Trey has been spewing this last year.

Gulping down my unease, I give in, telling him the facts.

Explaining the way Trey has drunkenly stood on tables yelling, calling her every vulgar name in the book, describing every intimate detail—down to how much hair is on her pussy, for fuck's sake.

I take a breath before I fly off the handle just from talking about it. It's sickening what he does with no consequences.

This is all because Annabelle picked herself up after the initial shock over their breakup and hit the dating scene running. Clearly, Trey was not happy about his ego being bruised.

Last week he went into detail about the people he'd cheated on her with—sometimes in her own flat, and even on occasion when she was sleeping in the next room.

This is a massive trigger for Belle, and I'm glad she hasn't been around to hear any of it.

Because what Belle saw as a kid scarred her and has kept her from trusting men. Which brings me to what Trey was saying last night.

"This is the first time I've heard him bring up her parents and how Belle watched her dad have an affair with her aunt." John's eyes fly to mine, obviously unaware of that little fact.

It's not a secret, but it's not something we openly discuss, and for good reason.

"He was spinning it like Belle is a sick freak. He was screaming to anyone who would listen that she stood there and watched because she enjoyed it." I punch the back of the passenger seat, my voice raw from shouting.

My stomach turns at the thought of him and the words he said about Annabelle. He took it to another level this time, and I couldn't hold back.

He deserved it.

She wasn't *watching*, she was in shock, and I know this because I was there and saw it firsthand.

Annabelle was maybe thirteen years old, spending her summer in the Hamptons with her family. This particular year, Belle's mom had to fly back to London early, so it was only her dad, aunt, and brothers.

They came every summer and stayed at their aunt's estate, which happened to be near ours— convenient as kids.

It was one of the last days of summer. I remember walking right in and running up the steps toward Belle's brother's room. As I turned the corner, there Annabelle stood, tears running down her ashen face.

On instinct, I'd run to her, dragging her away as fast as possible the second I saw what she was looking at.

Her brothers handled her dad and aunt... I'd consoled Belle.

When you care for someone as much as I care about Belle, their pain is your pain.

I drop my head in my hands. God, I hate this for her.

"I'll take care of it," John says.

"What are you talking about?"

John's clearly aggravated. His foot pushes heavier on the peddle, his knuckles turn white from gripping tighter on the steering wheel.

"Don't lay another hand on him, don't speak a word to him. Do you understand? Leave this to me."

I narrow my eyes with incredulity.

"I may not be in the military anymore, but I still have many connections"—he pauses, takes a deep breath—"in high places, and I think it's time we put our mate Trey in his place, don't you think?"

I nod.

"You should have come to me sooner. Or even Ethan, one of us would have handled it."

He's right. I didn't even think of Ethan, one of Declan's good friends who owns his own security firm. He's ex-military as well.

Some time passes, and I think we're finally done with the chit-chat since we're almost at my place, but he breaks the silence.

"Can I ask you a personal question?"

I shrug. "Sure, of course."

"Why aren't you and Annabelle together?"

Not what I expected him to say, but I don't hesitate, because it's an easy answer. "I'm not good enough for her."

"What shit are you talking about? You love that girl."

"Of course I do. She's one of my best friends. Sadly, 'friends' is all we are, because I've never had a girlfriend, and Belle should be someone's queen, not someone's test run."

It's why I've never pursued her, petrified of ruining our friendship. I'm not deluded. I know how well we'd get on, how the chemistry between us is off the charts. I've felt it since I was a teenager. Annabelle was always the girl out of reach for me, never letting my mind wander there because I respected her too much to fuck it up.

But I know deep down that if I took a different path in life, she would be my future. The few times I've ever let myself feel more, she was the only one to make my chest ache, in the best way possible.

Though, ever since Vegas, something's been different. The connection and bond we have has been taking up my mind more often than not. Wondering… *what if.*

"You stupid boy," John says, shaking his head. "Annabelle wouldn't be your test run. She'd be your first and last lap. That sounds like the perfect win to me."

"Life isn't always fairytales, John. We live in the real world."

"Don't be stupid. I see how you look at her."

I shouldn't be stunned at his observation, but I am. "How do I look at her?"

"Like I look at my wife." He holds my stare. "We're here."

"Thanks," I mutter as I get out of the car.

John calls my name before I get to my door. "I was just like you, Jackson. Out with the lads, a different woman every night. Then I realized it wasn't enough, and I deserved more. My wife was my 'more,' and when I finally got my head out of my arse, I almost lost her. Don't lose Annabelle."

"Thanks." I pause. "Hey, John?"

"Yes, Jackson?"

"Theoretically… if I ever decided to take the next step. What happens if I fuck it up?"

Because I'm petrified of doing just that.

"You won't."

"You're so sure?"

"When you find the one, you do everything in your power *not* to fuck it up."

My office door swings open. I look back and see Declan pause as he takes up the entire doorway. "You look like fecking dog shit, mate."

I flip him the bird and mumble, "Fuck off, Dec." Before turning back to my floor-to-ceiling windows, taking in the view of London and contemplating life.

He walks over and feels my head before I slap him away. "What the hell are you doing?"

"Feeling your temperature, I can't remember the last time you called me Dec."

I do love pissing him off.

"Awe, do you like my little term of endearment, Bucks?"

He rolls his eyes. "I shouldn't have mentioned it. Come on, what's up with you?"

I walk over and slump back in my chair, rubbing my temples in frustration.

Where the hell do I even start?

There is a ridiculous amount of work I need to get done, and considering I'm on three hours of sleep, I'm exhausted. John's words are playing on repeat in my head, and I can't seem to turn them off.

As the seconds tick by, the idea of being with Annabelle makes so much sense to me.

I'm not a fucked-up teenager anymore… The only reason I haven't let myself go there in the last decade, or two was to protect Belle. I pushed the feelings aside with such force earlier in my life that they were hidden even from myself.

I already love her as a friend, our compatibility and attraction is off the fucking charts. Why wouldn't we try to see if this could be more?

And I'm not blind… I know she feels the same way.

Now I can't figure out if I'm overthinking it because I'm in a delirious state of exhaustion, or because I genuinely think it would work out.

People think I want to be a lifelong bachelor, but that couldn't be further from the truth. I've always wanted more, only I've never allowed myself to try. Without a doubt in my mind, I would put my all into it with Belle. I respect her too much to let her down.

Because trust me, letdown is something I'm sorely familiar with in my life, and I wouldn't wish that feeling upon anyone.

I let out a sigh of frustration because, still, almost thirty years later, the memory of my abandonment by my father haunts me.

And I hate him and myself for it.

I sit forward, back, then swivel in my chair from nerves.

Internally, I'm starting to freak out. Am I really letting my feelings for Belle finally come to fruition?

Feelings I've never mentioned, burying them deep down years ago because I knew I wasn't boyfriend—let alone husband—material.

But am I?

Am I letting my past dictate my future?

Do I mention this to Declan? He's the one I would confide in if I had to…

"Can you stop being a drama queen and spit it out already? Watching you silently freak out over there is driving me insane."

I bite my lip and stare at him, contemplating. I need someone who knows me well enough to tell me I'm not crazy for considering this… Of course, he doesn't need to know we're already married, only that I'm interested.

He crosses his arms, unimpressed. "Jackson."

"I'm asking you this in confidence. No mention of this to Nora or anyone else. It can't leave this room until I figure out how to proceed."

His face drops as he gives me an indignant look.

"Aye, you don't even have to mention that. You know I'd never repeat anything private." I know, he's right. I trust him with my life.

Declan is an ex-rugby player—ginormous and covered in tattoos. One look at him, and you know he could break you in two.

But it's all a facade. He's a gentle giant and has the soul of a saint, always wearing his heart on his sleeve.

I rub my hands together while I feel my leg shake a mile a minute. Why the hell am I so nervous?

"Jesus, Mary, and Joseph."

"Okay, okay. Umm… I'm just going to come out and say it."

His eyes widen. "Aye, probably a good idea, mate. Just spit it out."

"Do you think Annabelle and I would make a good couple?" I mumble it so fast, I'm unsure if he understood me. He's staring at me, not saying a word.

His phone rings and it's his wife Nora's ringtone, so he picks it up, bringing it to his ear painstakingly slowly, his unblinking eyes still on me.

"Hi, angel. Everything okay?" He pauses. "Aye, sounds good. But, listen, I really need to go, something monumental is happening right in front of my eyes. I'll talk to you later. Love you, Pip."

He brings the phone back down, eyes never leaving mine, and not a second later, he rolls his lips, his mouth tips up slightly on one side, and then he loses it.

Full-on hysterics.

"What the shit, Bucks?" *What is so funny about my question?*

He goes to open his mouth, but nothing comes out.

"What?" I demand. My irritated reaction seems to amuse him, and he can't hold back his shit-eating grin any longer.

He takes deep, meaningful breaths, trying to calm himself down, and when he finally does, he apologizes.

"I haven't had a good laugh in a while. Thank you for that." He smirks.

"Just leave," I huff, and turn to pour myself a drink, even though it's half past ten in the morning. I need something to take the edge off.

I know I'm always the group's jokester, but I can't say it doesn't sting when I ask him something serious and he laughs in my face.

I don't need it this morning.

He puts his hands up in defense. "I'm sorry, truly. I'm not laughing at you, Peters. I'm laughing because I was taken so off-guard. I've been waiting for this very day… everyone has. Of course I think you'd make a great couple. It's the two of you who don't see it."

My eyes go wide. What is he talking about? "Seriously?" I nod toward my drink, and he shakes his head.

"Yes, seriously, and it's the fecking morning. Why are you drinking?"

"Don't ask. I've already had the wildest day ever. Please, explain."

"I mean, isn't it obvious? You guys are meant for each other."

I lean back in my chair and sip my scotch. I'm in complete shock.

John, now Declan.

"Sadie's always said Belle's had a crush on you since she was a kid. You seriously didn't know?" He frowns.

"A crush is different. That means nothing."

"Come on, Jackson. I see how you gaze at each other when you think no one is looking. Honestly, the first day you met Nora… you remember, at the restaurant? She even picked up on it. She still says to this day that you two will get married."

I choke on my drink and hit my chest from the burn. God, if she only knew.

"You good, mate?"

I nod.

Shocked is what I am, so I change the subject. "How is my favorite redheaded beauty? Ah, excuse me, my redheaded *beauties*." Declan recently had twins, and they are the spitting image of their mom.

Whom I happen to adore. The day I met Nora, we clicked instantly.

"No changing the subject, but they are all good. Great." He smiles and puffs out his chest.

He's so proud to be a dad.

A tinge of jealousy hits me in the chest. I'll miss out on that if I never settle down.

Of course, I have my nieces—including Declan's girls—though it's not the same. I've always wanted kids of my own.

I want to show them the life my sister and I were never lucky enough to have.

"I have to ask, so don't take offense—"

"Anytime someone says that, the other person instantly takes offense, Bucks."

"Fair enough." He shrugs. "If you're serious—"

"I am," I say, cutting him off.

He puts his hand up. "If you're serious, are you ready to leave your old life behind? Because Jackson, this is Annabelle we're talking about. She's one of us. You feck her over, and you'll have hell to pay."

I take a deep breath in and feel my nostrils flare. I would never intentionally hurt her.

Ever.

It's the exact reason why I haven't pursued her, but I'm not a teenager anymore, nowhere close to one.

"I'm not trying to upset you, Jackson; I'm only trying to be realistic. You've lived a colorful life, to say the least. I once walked into your house and found a girl tied to your bed… then that night, a different girl. Are you okay with giving that all up for one woman? No more one-night stands, no more threesomes—"

"All right, I get the fucking point, Declan," I yell and stand up in a rush. My chair flies back, hitting the bar, glass smashing behind me, but I could give two shits right now. "Annabelle Hughes is not some random fucking girl! It wouldn't be a sacrifice to give that up for her. It would be a goddamn honor!" I heave, trying to catch my breath as he smirks.

He fucking smirks.

Oh, that bastard. "That was a test, wasn't it?"

"Uh-huh. One you passed with flying colors."

I pick up my chair and sit back down, slightly embarrassed. I'm all out of sorts lately.

"You don't think this is all too sudden?" I have to ask to confirm I'm not losing my goddamn mind.

Because somehow, to me, it all feels right.

"No, mate. I think it's always been there, and I reckon she's already there as well."

God, this could be a disaster… or it could be the best thing to ever happen to us. Because if this works between us, if she's on board, we could be all types of epic.

"What do you like about her?"

"What's not to like about her? She's so naturally beautiful. Anyone with eyes can see it. She loves her family, and mine, which you know is important. She's generous, smart, and hardworking. She listens to Queen without complaint." I smirk, thinking about when we were younger, and how my sister would die of embarrassment when I would blast it while driving in the car, but Belle would smile and go along with it, throwing her hands up and dancing along.

"She's fun, loves to travel, she—" I keep the last part to myself, not wanting to share that she's sexual and can keep up with my appetite.

I love sex, lots of it, and Annabelle is right there with me.

"And… she's one of my best friends."

"And that, mate, is the most important of them all. Being best friends with the one you love elevates your relationship to a whole new level that others will never understand."

I grin. "All right, all right. Enough of this sappy, pussy shit so early in the morning." *Or ever.*

My phone has been buzzing continuously in my desk drawer, so I grab it, then throw it back in disgust.

It's like a bucket of ice water was thrown in my face, and I'm instantly brought back to reality.

This is what I would be bringing into a relationship.

Drama.

And it's the last thing I want for her. I was fooled for a second into thinking I could do this.

"What the hell was that?"

"A reminder."

"Elaborate, you gobshite."

"Twelve missed texts, five different girls. It won't ever stop. I set a precedent that I'm available whenever, wherever, and it's like I'm on a fucking hamster wheel."

"So change it."

I stare at him, confused, and he rolls his eyes. Without a word, he walks over to my desk, pushes me out of the way, takes my phone, and smashes it to bits.

"What the fuck, Declan!" I cry.

"Step one of Operation Belle: get a new number," he says as he goes to leave.

This is why Declan's the smart one. It never once crossed my mind to get a new number.

"Hey, Peters?"

"Aye?" I fake an Irish accent, imitating him.

He smirks. "You're an eejit."

"I know." I laugh.

"In all seriousness. I know you have hang-ups, but you deserve to be happy too. You won't let her down."

"You're so sure?" I call, repeating what I asked John.

"Aye, without a doubt. I see you for more than you see yourself, Jackson. You're good people, and you'll do right by the lass."

I watch as he walks out of the office, then stare at the door in thought long after he's gone.

If only I had the same confidence everyone else had in me, this would be a lot easier.

But for once, maybe I need to give myself a chance.

"You're sure everything will transfer to the new phone?" I ask the sales guy for the tenth time. This kid definitely wants to kill me.

"Sir, you have the cloud. It's all going to transfer." I open my mouth and am quickly cut off. "Yes, all your notes and all your pictures will be saved. I know you have important things in there."

I nod dutifully. "Okay, sorry. I had to check once more. Thanks for all your help."

He doesn't answer; he walks away. I guess I deserved that.

So what if I asked a lot of questions?

I walk out of the store and check my phone to make sure again he's not lying, and he's right. It's all there.

My special notes, my saved photos.

Good.

I put my hand up to hail a cab to return to the office but stop mid-step.

Trumans.

I grab my phone and open my email. That little shit! My email isn't synced yet.

I call my assistant quickly.

"Hello, Mr. Peters."

"Millie, I know you're new here, but please stop calling me Mr.

Peters. Jackson will do."

If she says it one more time, I'm going to rip my hair out of my head. *Mr. Peters* is my father, and hearing that name infuriates me.

"I'm sorry. I keep forgetting. What can I do for you?"

"Can you look in my email? Under the file marked "Annabelle," there should be an email from last week with where she was having lunch today. I think she sent it on Friday."

"Sure, hold on." I hear her clicking away as I wait.

"Mr—I mean, Jackson, it says here she will be at Trumans for a one o'clock lunch meeting."

"Okay, thanks, Millie. Change of plans, I'll grab lunch while I'm out; no need to order me anything. I'll see you later this afternoon."

I hang up and hustle across the street, zig-zagging to dodge the cars. I have five minutes until her meeting starts, and I'm hoping I can grab her quickly to apologize for this morning and wish her luck again.

Not that she needs it. If anyone deserves this, it's Belle. She's put her all into this deal, and I would be shocked if they said otherwise.

Annabelle Hughes is a force to be reckoned with.

Except, looking back on our car ride together, her usual confidence was lacking, and it's been bothering me that I played a role in her stressful morning.

I walk through the bar and see I'm too late. She's approaching the table when an older gentleman embraces her in a hug.

"Ciao, Bella." He greets her with a warm expression, which is promising. If you were going to let someone down, you wouldn't be so kind. Or is he trying to soften the blow?

A woman holding his hand, maybe his wife, says hello next, complimenting Belle on her favorite suit.

"You ordering, mate?"

"Can I do takeaway?" I ask, not moving my gaze from Belle.

A second later, my proud feeling turns into something entirely different.

My stomach sinks, feeling a wave of unease wash over me as I watch a younger, good-looking man step up, kissing her and allowing his lips to linger longer than appropriate for a client.

What is this shit?

"*Sei troppo*, Bella." His seductive voice is low, yet loud enough that I hear it from my hidden spot.

I know that fucking voice. I use that fucking voice.

Excuse me, I *used* that voice.

No more, because there are no other women for me besides Belle.

He holds her cheek and kisses her again, and I can see Belle blush down her neck onto her chest.

Who the hell is this clown? And what the hell did he say?

I quickly Google what I heard… "*You're too beautiful.*"

Bastard.

All I know is he better get his hands off my wife, or he won't have hands by the end of this meeting.

"Ready to order?"

I turn to the bartender. "I'm going to stay and eat if that's okay."

"No problem." He points to a stool, and I ask if I can sit somewhere more private, trying to explain that I don't want my wife to see me without sounding like a creep.

Then for the next hour, I sit there and watch her, *my beautiful B*, in awe of the successful businesswoman she's become.

It's a serious turn-on to watch her in her element. She radiates confidence.

From where I'm perched, I can hear her pitch how she plans to expand their wine into the States. Her timeline and strategy are flawless, and I can see her plan for press releases impresses them.

I take one last bite of my burger and pay the bill. I don't need to see the rest.

It's clear on all three of their faces. They're beyond captivated by Belle, and from what I've heard, they wouldn't have changed a thing she's done for them so far.

There is no way she isn't getting this contract extension.

And don't ask when I decided to refer to her as *my beautiful B*.

It was sometime between Declan smashing my phone and that Italian dickhead touching her, but it's happening.

Although I think Queen B might suit her better.

3

Annabelle

"ANNABELLE." Mr. DeLuca sighs, resting his chin on his steepled hands.

My entire body tenses.

His words linger while I sit on the edge of my seat, waiting for my future to unfold in front of my eyes.

Because that is what this is: my big break. So I cross every finger and toe, hoping I wowed them with my presentation.

For the last hour, I've walked them through our new proposal for the upcoming three years.

Outlining immersion trips we would take throughout Italy and the States, experiencing everything firsthand.

I could tell they were impressed with my connections to the press and through social media. Although Mr. DeLuca, set in his old ways, wasn't keen on it initially, now he's seen the power of what it can do, and I've barely scratched the surface.

"Annabelle, Annabelle, Annabelle," he says again. "*Hai fatto un lavoro fantastico e sei un talento incredibile*," he sings in his beautiful Italian language. He smiles broadly and takes my hand in his.

"I'm so sorry. Could you please repeat that in English," I ask.

"Si." He smiles. "You've done a great job, and you're an incredible talent, is what I said. Brava, Annabelle. You're an impressive young lady, and we would be honored to have you stay on with us. Although we think three years is not long enough, we would like to sign a contract indefinitely with you. To be our PR agent… How do you say? All the time? Si?"

"You mean on retainer?"

"Si, on retainer, as you say."

"What?" My eyes widen in shock. My thoughts are scattered, too excited I can barely think straight.

A silent scream of excitement slices through the fog in my brain. It's taken me a second to register his words. The moment I do, I shoot up from my seat and hug them, thanking them profusely for putting their faith in me.

Hugging clients probably doesn't fall into appropriate etiquette, but they're Italian. They do affection in their sleep.

"Mr. and Mrs. DeLuca, Romeo"—I address them individually, making eye contact one by one—"thank you so much for this opportunity. On behalf of everyone who's worked on this at Hughes Agency, we thank you for giving a small boutique agency a chance. I promise we won't let you down." I say the words earnestly, trying to hold my tears back.

If I could pat myself on the back right now, I would.

I instantly feel lighter after carrying around the weight of this meeting on my shoulders for weeks.

"It was never a question. We were always picking you. I wouldn't trust my family's business with anyone else," Mrs. DeLuca chimes in, which surprises me.

For a long time, I wasn't sure if she even liked me. She rarely smiles. Her serious mode is turned on at all times.

"Especially over that other woman," Mr. DeLuca mumbles.

"Oh, I hadn't realized you were interviewing other candidates." My face drops. I'm not sure how I feel about that.

"No, no." He waves his hands dramatically. "We were always

working with you. Some woman had just called and called, pestering us. Si, Romeo?"

"Si. She is called Victoria. I don't recall her surname. I'm sorry."

"Victoria Palmer?" I ask, already annoyed.

"That's her name. She said she heard we were looking to sign with someone, and that someone should be her, not you."

My eyes narrow. That little… She can sod right off.

Romeo's dark, mysterious eyes sparkle. He can see I'm trying to hold back my anger. "Don't worry, bella. We told her we are loyal only to you."

"I appreciate that." I felt another weight of relief lift off me, but still, this woman needs to stop trying to interfere with my business.

Victoria Palmer is my biggest competitor.

She also happens to be an ex-hook-up of Wills's, even going so far as to cause issues for Sadie and Wills at one point. Ever since, she's been bitter and putting in extra effort to be a pain in my arse.

"Where has the time gone? I'm so sorry, my wife and I must call for our car. We are meeting our friends while in London, and we'll already be late."

"Oh, please don't apologize. I'm meeting a co-worker here soon, so it works out perfectly. Again, thank you for signing on with Hughes Agency. I promise you… you won't regret it, Mr. and Mrs. DeLuca, Romeo."

Mr. DeLuca shakes his head. "No, No. You don't call us Mr. and Mrs. anymore. Please, Lorenzo and Luciana."

I smile warmly at them. "Such beautiful names that sound so lovely together."

Luciana sports another rare smile. Hmm, maybe she's warming up to me after all.

"One last thing before we leave," Lorenzo says. "I almost forgot the most important part."

"Lorenzo, I doubt anything is more important than working for you." I laugh.

He smiles and pats my cheek, ignoring my compliment.

"You love Italy, it's a beautiful place, si?"

"Of course, are you kidding? It's a dream location."

"Ah, *perfetto*. The new job won't start until September. You will stay in one of our properties for the rest of the summer. As a thank-you for all your hard work."

What?

They own at least four houses throughout Italy, not counting their private residence. Two in Tuscany, one in Sicily, and one on Lake Como.

I'm shocked into silence. It would be a dream to stay in one of their luxurious homes, but I'll never be able to make it happen.

We're inundated with work as it is, and I need to prepare for the DeLuca expansion. So, unfortunately, an extended holiday is not in the cards for me.

A week or two maybe, but the rest of the summer?

It's only the beginning of July. It won't happen, even in my wildest dreams.

I extend my gratitude and explain my predicament, but he won't take no for an answer, making it even harder for me to turn down.

"Think about it for a couple of weeks. We will talk again when you return from Paris, si?"

How can I say no to this sweet old man? "Okay, we will talk then."

I love how he remembered that Sadie and Wills are getting married there. Mr. DeLuca is a great listener. While I visited them in Italy during a work trip, we often sat with our cappuccinos in the early morning, sometimes quietly, but most of the time, he liked to hear about my life.

He's a good man.

After kissing them goodbye, I look at my watch and see it's much later than expected. Lola should be here any second. I asked her to meet so we could have drinks no matter how the meeting went.

I had preemptively taken the rest of the day off just in case.

"Annabelle," Romeo calls after me as I head to the bar. His beautiful, silky Italian accent makes my name roll off his tongue like magic.

"You will join me for a drink, si?"

Yes, yes, yes, you beautiful, sexy man, you. But only in my dreams.

Romeo is all things amazing about an Italian man. He's tall, dark, and handsome, with the biggest brown eyes I've ever seen.

Full lips, strong hands, sexy accent.

I could go on forever, but I need to get myself together.

He's my client's son, who will be working alongside us now, more than he has in the past.

I won't go there.

Even though it's clear that every time Romeo looks at me, it's as if he wants to eat me alive.

"Bella?" He smirks with a knowing look.

"Annabelle?" I whip my head around to see Lola wide-eyed, staring between Romeo and me.

I kiss Romeo goodbye again, you know, for good luck. "Maybe next time. I'm meeting with my co-worker about another project. I'm so sorry." I point to Lola.

"Ah, okay, Bella. Don't worry. I will see you soon," his deep voice says with more meaning than it should.

His eyes linger, glancing down at my lips once before turning and walking away.

"Holy crap! Who. Was. That?" Lola dramatically fans off her face. "And why can't I ever meet anyone who looks like that?"

I bite my lip and cringe. "That was Romeo."

Her eyes widen. "Oh hell."

"I know," I whisper as we watch Mr. Hottie walk away, snapping us out of our Italian Stallion-induced fog.

She assesses me carefully. "Sooo?"

The second she switches the subject, I let down my guard. I extend my arms out to her, and as soon as she gets close enough, I pull her into me and let the tears come.

I needed this.

"Are we drowning our sorrows, or are these tears of happiness?"

I lean back and smile. "We did it, darling. We did it!" I cry, grabbing at her again.

She's screaming in my ear, and I have no idea what she's saying, but we did it.

What is this life?

At thirty-six years old, I'm a successful CEO with a company that now works internationally.

"Belle, this is bloody brilliant!" she yells, matching my enthusiasm. "How do you feel?"

"Fucking knackered."

"I know the whole office has been stressed. I don't think anyone slept last night. This is so big for us."

I pull back, holding her shoulders to look her in the eye. "You, my darling Lo, are an invaluable member of my team, my right-hand woman, and I could have never done this without you."

"Annabelle," she whispers, wiping the tears now instantly falling from her eyes.

"And I don't mean *this*, as in this job with the DeLuca family. I mean this business we've built together. You've been with me since day one, and I couldn't have done a single thing without you. I'm so blessed to have found you."

"I love you," she cries, dragging me back in for a hug.

"Looks like you two could use this?" The bartender holds up two shots of Jameson, and Lola's eyes nearly pop out of their sockets.

"You'll be fine. We're not going back to the office today, and we have a lot to celebrate."

"To the Hughes Agency," she toasts.

"And to the badass bitches who run it!"

"I'm drunk," Lola states.

No shit, we're both drunk. Who knows how many hours later it is, but we're still sitting at the bar, having had a few pints, taken several more shots, and maybe even mixed some spritzes in.

The drunker we get, the harder Lola tries to convince me to go to Italy for the summer. She's insisting I deserve it, considering the only time I ever take off is with Sadie on our annual girls' trips, and since she's getting married this year, we're postponing until autumn.

"I miss your curls." I run my hands through her now straight hair.

"Oh god, you must be drunker than I thought if you miss the frizz. It took you five years to convince me to straighten them. Either way, I'm never going back to curls again, I have a newfound hatred toward them."

She's right, her hair is a disaster when she doesn't straighten it, but it's so Lola that I miss them.

"And don't change the subject. If you don't go to Italy, I'm going to take your spot and elope with Romeo, because no one else wants me," she slurs. "Hmm, so sexy. The things I would do to him."

My eyes widen, then so do hers.

"Did I say that out loud?" She covers her face as I bend over, laughing.

My quiet little Lola always shocks me with her candor.

I take a big sip of my drink and murmur, "Trust me. Eloping isn't all that it's cracked up to be." Then I take another gulp.

Thud.

What the?

Lola's on the floor, her mouth wide open and her eyes blinking rapidly.

"Wh-what did you say? How the hell would you know about eloping?"

Oh fuck.

My drunk mind has a mouth of its own.

"Just what I heard." I shrug it off, but even to my drunk ears, I hear the lie clear as day.

"Help me." She tries to get up, only to keep falling back. She looks like a fish out of water flopping around.

"You look ridiculous down there." I chuckle. I put my hand out to help her, not even batting an eyelash at her clumsiness causing her to fall off the stool.

"I know you're lying." She glares at me.

"I am not, thank you very much." I take another sip so she can't see my tell.

She says my lip twitches when I lie, which made for an awkward friendship in the beginning when she would ask me about her wardrobe.

"Don't be daft. I know you better than you know yourself. If you don't tell me the truth, I'll call one of the two people who will know."

"Oh yeah, and who's that?" I ask.

"Sadie or Jackson, duh," her drunk, high-pitched voice sings.

"I-I… I… Oh, fuck." This is when my brain decides it can't make coherent sentences. I know we drank a lot, but get it together, Annabelle.

"You better start talking." She crosses her arms with gusto, causing her to almost fall back again.

I roll my eyes. "Yeah, real tough."

"Annabelle Hughes," she warns.

I gulp down my fear, then gulp down another shot. I pass Lola one, knowing she'll need it when I tell her about Jack. After all this time, I'm finally telling someone. Even though Jackson and I agreed to keep it a secret, I need this.

I feel lighter as the words come out fast and in a ramble.

Every other second, Lola has another exaggerated reaction. Gasping, arms flailing, fake hyper-ventilating.

She's a very dramatic drunk.

"Lately, though, I've been thinking, for my own mental health, it's time we finalize the end. It probably isn't the best idea to stay married to your lifelong crush."

She takes my hand. "No. No. You can't end it. Jackson's your One. You're meant to be together."

"I don't think he would agree," I admit sadly. And even if he did, I'm not sure it would ever work with his lifestyle. I would always be questioning his past.

Childhood trauma will do that to you.

"Although I don't remember much from Vegas, I can assure you the two times we've been together were magical. So we know we're a fit in that department."

"Twice? I thought it was just on the trip."

I cringe at my slip. What the hell is wrong with me tonight?

No one knows about the time when we were younger, and I never wanted anyone to know.

I was going through the toughest period in my life at the time it happened, and it's not something I like to share.

Though, now that it's out there, I'm sure it won't hurt to tell her just about that one night, since I'm just letting all my secrets free today.

"The summer before Cambridge, Jackson and I may have had a night together while I was in New York."

Lola's mouth gapes open in shock, then she tries to hide it with her palm. It's her signature move today.

"Oh my god, what did Sadie say?"

"She doesn't know, and she won't find out because she will be so hurt that I never told her."

"You never told her! You tell her everything."

Not everything.

"Sadie is a romantic, and she's always had the idea in her head that her brother and best friend would ride into the sunset and live happily ever after. She won't find out about that, or that we're married now."

"She doesn't know that you're married now?" she screams.

I roll my eyes at the dramatics. Jeez.

"Lo, get with the program. I said no one knows, and I mean it."

"I don't even know what to say."

"Yeah, you and me and both, Lola. You and me both."

Lola goes to the loo, and I think it's time we head out. Unfortunately, our happy, celebratory moods have taken a turn for the worse.

I grab the bill as my phone buzzes, and just like that, my mood has changed back to cheerful at the speed of light.

It's from my older brother Matthew; he always has that effect on me.

Matty: Hello, my beautiful baby sister. Mum told me the good news about the Italy job. CONGRATULATIONS!! I'm a little hurt you didn't at least text your favorite brother, but I'll let it slip this time.

Matty: In all seriousness, I want you to know I'm so proud of you. Always remember that you're strong, capable, and intelligent. I love you and miss you with all my heart. Talk soon xx

Such a simple text and yet I have to wipe the rapidly falling tears.

God, I miss him.

He's currently in Africa with Doctors Without Borders, and I rarely see him. Before Africa, he was in Yemen, and before that, Haiti.

Every year, he promises it's his last and that he'll come home to London, but it never happens. And although his surgical skills are needed there, I selfishly need him too.

It's been six years without my big brother living in London, and I want him home.

Hughes Agency celebrated its five-year anniversary a little over a week ago, which he was due to fly in for. But of course, the second he landed, the chief-of-staff at his old London hospital called, granting him privileges for a high-profile surgery he couldn't turn down.

Luckily, we were able to catch up during the week, but it wasn't the same. I miss him by my side.

Matthew is one of my biggest supporters. Has been since I was a little girl full of wild ideas and aspirations. He constantly told me I could be whatever I wanted. One year, it was an actress, then a model —which didn't last long… I have the height, except once my D-sized boobs came in, that idea went out the window.

I'm not sure he would have been the biggest supporter of what I could model with those.

He wanted me to do what made me happy and always said I would be the best at whatever I chose, which is why I am the way I am today.

Ambitious.

Something I've learned from him. All three of my brothers, really. Each of them are strong-minded and independent.

I wipe my tears and shake off any sadness.

Get it together, Belle.

Belle: Mattyyyy, don't make me cry. I love you!

My phone rings with a rare video call from Matthew. "Hi! Oh my god, I'm so happy to see your face."

"Why are you crying?" No hello, nothing. Always concerned for me.

I shrug, embarrassed. "I just miss you, that's all."

His body deflates. "Please, don't. Especially when I'm not there to hug you, I can't stand it." Then his eyes narrow. "Are you drunk? It's…" He looks down at his watch. "Barely five."

"Celebratory!" I'm all too happy to change the mood of this call. Today has been a lot of ups and downs. "Oh, you have to meet Lola finally. She's walking back from the loo now. Hold on."

His eyes bulge. "I'm in no state to meet anyone right now."

"Oh, it will just be a quick—"

"Dr. Hughes, you need to scrub in for your last surgery," a nurse says, cutting me off.

"Saved by the bell. Sorry, Annabelle, I need to go. I love you so much."

"Love you!"

"Who was that?" Lola asks.

"My brother, Matthew. I was hoping the two of you could finally meet, but it sounded like he had to head into surgery."

"Oh." She drops her head, and… is she crying?

"What's wrong with you? This is the fifth time you've started crying out of nowhere this week."

What is going on with her lately?

If she isn't deep-diving into work, she looks like someone killed her cat.

She shakes her head and wipes them. "I don't know, I'm drunk." She dismisses me and then points at my phone ringing, so I let it go.

"Hey, Sades!" I yell, just as I hear Lola chirp, "Hi, Sadie," over my shoulder.

"Hello, my drunk little friends." She laughs.

"How do you know we're drunk?"

"You only call me Sades when you're drinking, and I'm sure you pressured my sweet, innocent Lola."

"She did, she really did." Lola sighs, and I roll my eyes.

"I was calling to see if you two wanted to come for a celebratory dinner. I'm cooking your favorite, Lola."

"Chicken Milanese?"

"Yup."

"We'll be there! Especially because I'm starting to feel a little sick. I just realized we haven't eaten anything."

"Oh, you two better sober up. I'm so stressed about the wedding. I need your help, and Charlie is driving me insane, and I also want to—"

"Sadie," I say, cutting her off, "if you don't stop waffling, we can't leave."

"Oops, you're right. I'm so excited to see you both." She giggles, then hangs up.

Jackson

"Look, it's my best girls," I whisper as I kiss a sleeping Annabelle on the forehead. Turning to my sister, I ask, "How did I get so lucky today?"

"I don't know. We're pretty amazing, aren't we." Sadie smiles, kissing me back.

"Hey! What about me?" Charlie, my niece, asks as she enters the room.

"Ah, now it's confirmed… best day ever. I have my best girls and now my bestest niece."

Charlie squeals and runs into my arms.

"Shh, Auntie Belle is still sleeping," Sadie says.

So similar to my sister, Charlie scrunches up her nose. "She's been sleeping forever, Mommy."

"Forever?" I question Sadie.

"It's been an hour. She's sleeping off her day of drinking. She and Lola went out for a celebratory drink that turned into ten. I was going to wake her up soon."

"I'm up," Belle grumbles from the sofa.

Charlie smothers my face with kisses. "Bestest means better than Chloe, right?"

I suppress my laughter when Sadie corrects her.

This kid was made to be an only child. One year later, and she still hasn't gotten over the fact that she isn't the center of attention anymore.

"No, babygirl, the same as Chloe. I love you both equally." Her face falls, so I add, "But guess what?"

"What?"

"You are special in another way because you're my goddaughter, and that's extra special."

"And mine," another grumble comes from Belle.

"Oh, goodie, I like being extra special!"

Sadie shakes her head and covers her eyes.

"Ohhhh, we know you do." I laugh.

"Charlotte Rose!" Wills screams from down the hall, and Charlie's eyes go wide.

"Uh oh." She jumps off, running in the opposite direction of Wills.

Sadie jumps into action after her. "Charlotte Rose Taylor! What did you do?"

"Nothing!" I hear, and then her bedroom door slams shut.

I can't wait to find out what she did. It's going to be funny as shit, at least to me, the non-parent. Wills rarely raises his voice at her, so it must have been something bad.

I turn my attention to Belle, who's closed her eyes again, allowing me the opportunity to take her all in. Her platinum hair is wild and stuck all over her face, her makeup slightly smudged, yet she's still more beautiful than ever.

"Stop staring and come cuddle me." She holds out her arms, and I don't think twice; I'm up and moving closer in a heartbeat.

Belle and I have always been close, but she started keeping a bit of a distance between us after Vegas. Now that the opportunity is right in front me, I have no intention of missing it.

Especially when Operation Annabelle is in full swing.

Her lean, slender frame molds seamlessly against my body as she wraps her arms around my neck, kissing my cheek.

Within a second, my body reacts, and I feel the swell of my cock pressed into her.

She wiggles against it, waggling her eyebrows, knowing the exact effect she has on me.

I don't manage to hold back my grin. She has no idea of my inner thoughts, though since we've been teasing each other like this for as long as I can remember, it's nothing new.

I've always been attracted to her, and it's like my head finally caught up to my dick. That *head was clearly the smarter of the two.*

"I got it. I got the job," she whispers in my ear, and leans her head back to look me in the eyes, her crystal blues sparkling with happiness. "Can you believe it?" She bunches up her shoulders in excitement. I love that she's proud of herself.

"Never doubted it even for one second." I lean in to kiss her cheek, close enough to her lips that I'm sure she can feel mine brush against hers.

I remind myself I can't jump the gun here. I need to ease her into the idea.

"I tried to call you a few times," she says with a hint of dejection.

"Hmm." I brush her thick, silky blonde locks out of her face and tuck the strands behind her ear. "Sorry, B, I got a new phone at lunch. I'll give you the number."

"Why would you need a new number?"

I shrug, not yet ready to tell her, so I go with a semi-truth. "Ready to switch things up in my life, and I only want the people I care about to have my number. Done with a lot of my past."

"Oh. Okay then," she says, confused.

"Funny story from when I was getting my phone. I realized I was near Trumans, and I wanted to stop in to say sorry about this morning before the meeting started." I wasn't going to mention anything. Only, her interaction with that Italian guy has been fucking with my head all day.

"You should have." She rubs her hands up and down my arm,

making it hard for me to concentrate. Not from her touch, but from how my brain is paying attention to all the little things it never has before.

"Well, I did go in. Your meeting had just started, and I happened to see something I didn't enjoy watching."

"What are you talking about?"

I wrap my arms around her waist and pull her into me as tight as possible. My jealousy is in full force just thinking about the guy.

I lean in, nose to nose, so no one else in the house can hear. "I saw another man touch my wife."

Her eyebrows shoot up at the bite in my voice. "Is that jealousy I detect, Jackson Peters?"

I ignore her, making her connect the dots. I figure if I start leaving little hints, she won't be so shocked when I bring *us* up to her.

"I saw someone touching you, and his lips lingered a little too long for my liking."

"Oh please, he's no one, just a very handsome Italian man." She winks.

"B," I warn.

"Jack, he's Italian. Being touchy-feely is in their DNA. Plus, he's a client."

I clench my jaw, trying to keep my mouth shut. I don't give a shit if he's a client. He wants her. I saw it in his eyes.

"I don't know what is going on with you, but I kind of like this jealousy thing." She tickles my side in the one spot that always gets me.

"B!" I laugh, trying to wiggle away from her.

"Soz not soz." Belle winks.

Sades groans as she enters the room. "Can you be any more British? *Soz not soz*," she mocks.

Belle pulls her shoulders back as she sits up. "I cannot, as a matter of fact. My lineage has been traced back to Great Britain, generation after generation," she states in her posh English accent, then bursts out laughing.

Annabelle was raised to be a polite, rule-abiding English daughter, who went to the best private schools, studied at Cambridge, and didn't raise her voice above a certain octave.

Then her dad did what he did, and all hell broke loose. The Hughes kids rebelled against his archaic rules.Their mom, understandably, went into a bit of a depression, and at that time, there wasn't much structure in the house.

Thank god for her brother Matthew. He's the only reason they all still have their shit together, and all happen to be very successful independently.

"All right, you two, dinner's ready. Lola just woke up, so it's perfect timing, because Wills wants to talk to you all together."

"Me, Jackson, and Lola? What ever for?"

Sadie wrings her hands, a clear indication that she's nervous.

"What's going on?" I question.

"Um, all I'm going to say is that it wasn't my idea," she mutters, then runs into the dining room.

"What the hell was that?" Annabelle questions, turning toward me, concern written all over her face.

"I guess we're about to find out."

4

Annabelle

"WHY WOULD you need us to go to Paris a week early?" Jack questions Wills.

Wills takes Sadie's hand and kisses the back of it. It's clear she's uncomfortable asking us to do this.

"I'm taking Sadie and the girls away, and then we'll go straight to Paris for the wedding. It's been stressful, and I want to give Sadie her wedding present early. It would really help if you could both help with preparations."

"Wills, you know I don't need a present, baby. Marrying you is the best gift I could get."

He cups her cheeks and beams the rare smile he only uses for her. "I know, but this is special for both of us and our growing family. I promise."

She will be shocked when he shows her the holiday home he's bought her and the girls, especially since the house we're sitting in now was only finished this past year.

She'll think it's excessive, but he can easily afford it, and I think it's sweet he's buying a house in the place they first fell for each other all those years ago.

Wills may be an overbearing, jealous jerk a lot of the time, causing us to bump heads constantly, but he loves Sadie to no end. He always has her best interest at heart, and he's surprisingly romantic.

Wills is not the kind of guy to ask for help, and they're family, so it's almost impossible to say no.

Besides, Jack and I would both do anything for Sadie. Though deep down, I won't deny I'm a bit gutted knowing that because of this time off, there's no chance I could go to Italy with the DeLucas if I had wanted to try to make that work.

Even if it would have only been for a week or two.

I glance at Jack to try and gauge his reaction, and his look of apprehension quickly changes to something I can't decipher.

He almost looks… excited.

Which is surprising, considering both of us are extremely busy with work. Just the other day, we were saying that even taking off for the wedding would be a struggle.

Jack, on top of the businesses he invests in, works for Wills at The Taylored Group as an Independent Advisor, helping Wills's athlete clients invest smartly, and business has been booming, keeping them all busy.

He's still staring at me when I look back again.

"What's with that face?" I whisper.

His bright green eyes sparkle, a lopsided grin gracing one side of his face. He stretches his arm across my lap, squeezing my thigh, as his thumb rubs small circles on the inside.

Instantly, my body is on fire from the heat of his light touch, making it impossible to hide the hitch of my breath, and by the way his eyes darken, I know he's heard it.

Jack leans in slowly, brushing his soft lips against my cheek. "I'm just happy to spend time with you, sweetheart," he whispers, then pulls back, not breaking eye contact.

I have to look away.

The energy radiating off him is not something I'm used to. I don't understand what's going on with him, and honestly, it's freaking me out.

Our flirting has always been innocent, but lately, and especially today something is different.

His jealousy.

His lingering stares.

This feels like more, and I'm unsure what to make of that.

I rip my eyes from his, and find Lola wide-eyed, practically drooling.

"Stop," I mouth so Sadie doesn't see.

She's probably dying inside after my drunk slip-up about our accidental nuptials.

"Listen," Wills continues. "Of course I could ask any one of our friends to go, including my sister, but you're Sadie's brother." Wills glances at Jack and then at me before adding, "And you're practically her sister. You know, 'sister soul mates,' or whatever shite you two always say."

Sadie smiles softly in my direction as she bounces Chloe on her knee. "She *is* my sister."

I blow her a kiss, then look back toward Wills and ask, "Why isn't the wedding planner handling this?"

Sadie chokes on her laugh, trying to hold it in. "My very loving but insanely paranoid fiancé thinks she has an ulterior motive and might be the one who sold the pictures of us to the paparazzi. He was two seconds from firing her, but at this point, it's done, and she's the one with all the connections. So, I insisted she stay, and he agreed as long as someone is there to supervise, more or less."

"It's not that I don't want to help, but work is hectic, to say the least. I need time to organize the office. I'm not sure it's possible for us to leave right away," I say.

He shakes his head. "I've done it all already. I knew you would use work as an excuse, so I set it up with Lola. You leave in two days."

I stare at her, and she shrugs. When did she become so good at keeping secrets from me?

Usually she's foaming at the mouth to tell me everything.

"Plus"—he points to Jack—"he needs to get the fuck out of London before he kills Trey, and you need a holiday away, Annabelle. You work too damn hard. You're going to burn out. Take it from someone who spent his life at work. A step back won't make business stop. If anything, taking time for yourself can only help. Trust me on that. Going home at a reasonable hour these days has made all the difference."

I lift an eyebrow. "Interesting use of words, considering you're the least reasonable person I've ever met."

"That's for fucking sure," Jackson mutters, and a deep chuckle comes from the door as Declan walks in.

He fist bumps Jack, leans over to kiss me and Lola hello, then continues over to embrace Sadie, taking Chloe out of her arms.

"What is this shit all over Chloe?" Declan asks, confused.

Wills ignores everyone and keeps going. "Declan is going to hold down the fort while we're gone until he leaves to meet us. It's all under control. I've learned to delegate." He smirks.

Because he knows we will do anything for his fiancée, meaning neither of us will say no.

"But Wills, a whole week is a little crazy, no? They won't even set up until a few days before."

He crosses his arms, unimpressed.

"Don't even waste your breath, lass." Declan laughs with amusement. "You know our mate is crazy and wants to ensure everything is perfect."

"I don't think—" Sadie tries to cut in.

"You will not fight me on this, Sadie. We're going on holiday. End of."

"You will not fight me on this," I mimic. Lola and Jackson chuckle while Wills shoots daggers at me, so I playfully stick out my tongue at him.

It's a life mission of mine to annoy him; he gets riled up so easily.

"I have a checklist, but most importantly, supervising the flower delivery and meeting the jazz band that's playing at the welcoming party are most important. Sadie will, of course, be in contact with the florist all week. However, I still want both of you on top of it. I want it to be perfect."

Jackson has a cheeky smile plastered on his face when he says, "We have it under control. If not, we have in-house entertainment, no need for the jazz band."

We all look at him with questioning faces, and then he points to Declan.

"Our own personal Riverdancer, as he lives and breathes. Declan Buckley: millionaire extraordinaire, aka Bucks, and one-of-a-kind rugby-playing Riverdancer."

Declan looks like he's going to rip off Jackson's head, and we all burst out laughing at the memory of Declan dancing.

Wills is trying hard to hold it in, but it's impossible not to let it go. "That was the best day of my life when Nora played the video of him dancing. I'll never forget the image of you in tights. It's all I ever think of when someone mentions your name."

"I'm going to kick both of your arses, you gobshites, then I'm going home, because Nora is in big trouble for ever showing you eejits that video."

"Can I come downstairs now?" Charlie yells from upstairs.

"Are you sorry for coloring your sister's face with a permanent marker?"

"Um. Yes?" she questions, and all of us except Sadie and Wills find it amusing.

Wills groans, covering his face. "What are we going to do with her?" he says to everyone and no one. "Poor Chloe was trying to take a bloody nap. I walk in to wake her up, and her whole face is covered."

"Come here. I need to speak with you," Sadie calls.

Charlie stomps her feet down the stairs, their dog Buddy following behind her as always. Those two are inseparable.

Her arms are crossed, already on the defense. Whoever made up the saying "terrible twos" never had kids, because she was an angel at two. Now at five, she's a complete terror.

Her attitude is permanently out in full force, yet to me, she's still the best kid of all time.

"Can you tell me why you did it?"

She looks at Wills for help, but he shrugs. It's funny how the roles are reversed here. Sadie is quiet and sweet, without a mean bone in her body, whereas Wills couldn't be any more different. Yet, with parenting, they've entirely switched roles, causing Sadie always to be the disciplinarian.

"If you don't answer me, there will be no movie tonight, and you'll go straight to bed," Sadie threatens, although her words have no effect on her.

Charlie shrugs. "I don't like how her face looks, so I colored it to be better."

Sadie takes a deep breath. "That is a very unkind thing to say about your sister. You're lucky she doesn't understand, because it would really hurt her feelings. I know you've hurt mine."

"Why?"

"Because it makes me sad when you're not nice to Chloe. She loves you very much. Sisters and brothers are meant to be nice to each other and love one another. They're supposed to be best friends. Like I am with Uncle Jack."

"But she's always crying and pooping. I don't like that."

"Because she's only a baby. You did that once too."

She crunches up her nose. "Ew," she says, and we all laugh.

"Will you come here and apologize to your sister, please?" Sadie says. I know it upsets her that Charlie still hasn't warmed up to Chloe even after all this time.

"But I'm not sorry."

"Charlie," Wills threatens.

"You're not sorry?" Sadie cries.

"No." Charlie recrosses her arms with fury.

Sadie ducks her head to hide her tears.

Wills stands up and points to the stairs. He's mad. "Go back upstairs now, Charlotte, and think about how it would make you feel if someone said they didn't like your face. Or if Mummy, Daddy, or any of your aunts or uncles"—he points to the three of us—"were mean to you."

"You're mean!" she yells as she runs for the staircase. "And I'm not living here anymore with you meanies."

"Okay, then move out," Wills yells.

"Fine! I'm moving to Uncle Decs's tonight!"

"Good luck, they have two babies, not one."

"Well." She thinks about that for a second. "They're my cousins, not my sister. That's different," she yells and slams the door.

My sensitive Sadie starts crying, and Wills pulls her in for a hug then cups her cheek, pressing his lips to her forehead. "She's going to grow out of it, I promise," he whispers.

"You said that last month, and for the six months before that."

Wills looks at us, his eyes pleading. "This is why I want to go away. It's been stressful here with the wedding and Charlotte. On top of that, work has been crazy for both of us. Going away just thc four of us will give Charlotte a chancc to bond with Chloe in a more relaxed atmosphere. And it's the only week that works since we're going on our honeymoon soon. It would be nice if they got along for the wedding, and I don't want Charlotte to be a nightmare for my mum and sister while we're away."

I don't even have to look at Jack. I already know the answer. "Of course we'll do it." Although, the thought of being alone with Jack doesn't necessarily excite me. It petrifies the shit out of me.

The last time we were alone in a foreign city, we ended up married, which didn't turn out so well for us.

A door slams upstairs, followed by the sound of crying echoing from Charlie's bedroom.

"I think that's our cue to leave. Unless you want me to talk to her?" Jack asks Sadie and Wills.

Wills considers it, but Sadie shakes her head. "No, you go, it's fine."

He slaps Wills on the back and kisses his sister. "She's going to grow to love Chloe. Who wouldn't?" He blows a raspberry on Chloe's tummy, and she giggles, hiding her face in his neck.

"I hope so." She turns to me. "Have fun on your date tonight."

I furrow my brows, unsure of what she's talking about. Then it hits me like a ton of bricks. "Fuck. I was so wrapped up with my meeting that I completely forgot."

"What date?" Jackson growls.

Sadie hits his arm. "Leave her alone. You probably have three dates tonight."

"I don't have one fucking date, let alone three, thank you very much. I'm going home after I drop off Lola and B… By myself," he tacks on.

"Are you being serious right now?" I question.

"Yes." He narrows his eyes. "I don't need meaningless dates to fulfill my week."

"Since when?" I prod. He's *always* out.

"Since I said so," he huffs, annoyed.

This is different from Jackson's normal overprotective side; just another thing to add to the subtle changes between us.

Declan squeezes his shoulder and whispers something in his ear. Jackson gives a curt nod, then takes a deep breath.

What the hell is that all about?

Little footsteps come to the end of the stairs when we're about to walk out. Tears track down Charlie's face. "No goodbye?" She sniffles.

I open my arms, and she runs down, throwing her body into mine. Then she leans over, draping one arm around Jack's neck to hug us both.

"You hurt Chloe's and Mommy's feelings, Charlotte. You're my precious angel, but you can't act like that," Jack whispers.

She nods into his shoulder, turning her head toward Sadie. "I'm sorry Mommy. I'm sorry, Chloe."

Sadie walks over to kiss her. "We forgive you, but we need to be kinder to one another. Chloe loves you very much."

"Okay, Mommy. Can Uncle Jack read me a book?" she begs with a pouty lip.

"Uncle Jack needs to take Auntie Belle and Auntie Lola home. Maybe another time."

"I'll stay," Lola chimes in. "I need the distraction. I have no plans tonight, and I don't want to sit at home." She puts her arms out, and Charlie flings her body into Lola, almost knocking her over.

Which leaves me with my unpredictable friend for a car ride alone.

We finish our goodbyes and then Jack and I walk out to his car. I feel as if we're in a silent war; one that's clearly one-sided.

He's power walking to the car, leaving me in the dust, which is very unlike him. Once we're in, he starts the car and zooms out into the road, barely checking traffic.

"Bloody hell, slow down and cut the shit, Jack. What's wrong with you today?"

"I'm just perfect, don't worry about it." He smiles, looking deranged.

Fine, I won't. I can't deal with his crazy right now. I'm too tired after my stressful day and the pounding headache from all the afternoon beverages I consumed.

I must have dozed off, because I'm woken up by the slamming of his brakes in front of my place.

"Thanks for not killing me on the way home." I get out and slam the door, annoyed he's put me in a sour mood.

He rolls the window down. "Have fun on your date!" he snaps.

I freeze, and my whole body deflates. "*Jack*," I whisper, too low for him to hear, but before I can ask if everything is all right, he pulls away, leaving me on the sidewalk, stunned.

Is that why he's being such a bastard? Because I'm going on a date? I go on dates multiple times a week—one's he's privy to, most of the time—and I've never seen him act like this.

I'll ring him tomorrow and get to the bottom of this newfound jealousy, especially before we head to Paris. Jack and I rarely bump heads about anything, so it's quite off-putting that he's acting a fool out of nowhere.

Something's going on in that handsome head of his, but right now, I can't take the time to figure it out, because if I don't hustle, I'm going to be late.

"Tell me what you like most and least about your business?" Logan asks from across the small cocktail bar that separates us.

I smile, answering easily. "I'm a people person, and I love the excitement of the city. So the events, traveling, and meeting new people is all a thrill for me. My least favorite part is taking on a client I don't necessarily vibe with. Since we're a young company, I don't have the privilege of picking and choosing. We're not at that stage yet."

"Give me an example," he urges.

Logan has been highly attentive all night, genuinely interested in knowing everything about me and the Hughes Agency. I have to say, it's nice for once. I'm enjoying myself way more than I ever thought I would.

"One of my best mates owns a sports management agency, so I've partnered with him, taking on lesser-known athletes. They probably account for half of our earnings because they're constantly up to no good. Our crisis management team director handles them mostly, but a few clients are my personal responsibility, and to be straight with you, athletes can't keep it in their pants. They get caught up with mistresses, prostitutes, sex clubs, strip clubs, you name it, and most of them are married or in serious relationships. I hate being the one trying to cover it up. I despise cheaters with a passion, and I feel I'm failing my fellow women by not outing their husbands." I say all of that in a rush and am slightly embarrassed for rambling.

Logan grins. "I'll be rooting for your company's growth and success so you can finally turn the arseholes away. I also hate cheaters. My dad cheated on my mum when I was younger."

My eyes widen, and I apologize that he and his mum went through that. I don't mention my dad did the same bullshit, because I'm worried that the second the disgust slips through my lips, I'll ruin the night.

It's just another thing we have in common—probably the tenth of the night—and I would normally be elated because of how hard it is to find a decent guy in this city. Unfortunately, it's been hard to concentrate on Logan when bloody Jack has been on my mind all night, driving me insane.

I haven't been able to appreciate the man before me, which I plan on doing now.

I lean back, sip my martini, and give my date an easy smile. "I have to say, Logan, this is the first date I've been on in a long time where the guy is interested in me and my business. Most of the time, it turns them off and sends them running."

Confusion crosses his face. "Why? Being with a strong, independent woman is a turn-on. I've always wanted to be a power couple with my significant other."

I lift my glass and cheers him. "You're a good person, Logan. Thanks for taking me out. This has been the best blind date I've ever been on."

He lifts one brow and smirks. "I thought I was your first and only blind date."

"Touché." I cross my legs and lean in, not missing his eyes scanning the length of my long legs up to my chest, which of course, I did on purpose. I crook my finger so he comes closer, and whisper, "I'll let you in on a little secret. This date has been more riveting than all the others I've been on this year."

He gulps down the rest of his drink. "I couldn't agree more," he says, then takes my hand in his. "This is forward, I know, but what are you doing this weekend? I would love to take you to a new sushi place I've been dying to try."

Eager is not always a turn-on, but with Logan, it sure as hell is.

I grab my phone. "Let me get your number. Unfortunately, I'll be away for the next week or so, but I'd love to see you again when I get home."

My phone buzzes in my hand, and fuck… Bubble burst. *Thanks, Jack.*

I try to ignore it, but it buzzes again.

Jack: Get his number and see what happens.

Bloody Hell. I look around the cocktail bar and don't see him anywhere. So how the hell does he know I'm getting his number?

"Everything okay?"

"Sorry, I just got a crazy text. Just give me one minute, please."

Me: Where are you?
Jack: Bathroom. Now.
Me: What the hell are you doing here, Jack?!!!!!!!
Jack: Bathroom, Annabelle. I'm not joking.
Me: It's the fucking loo. You're not taking a bath.
Jack: You have one minute.

Oh, he can fuck right off with this demanding, domineering shit. I'm finishing my date. If he suddenly wants to be some crazed lunatic, he can wait until I'm done.

I look up and smile at Logan. "Sorry, where were we?"

"I was trying to give… Do you need to get that?" He points to my phone that will not stop vibrating.

"No, just ignore it." I open my contacts so I can enter his name.

"I still can't get over how someone as beautiful and successful as you doesn't have a boyfriend. It blows my mind."

"No need for the sweet talk. You'll still get my number tonight." I wink playfully.

"You're right. She doesn't have a boyfriend. She has a fucking husband." A deep growl vibrates my body from behind.

Fuck.

"Jackson." I fake a smile. "What a surprise. What are you doing here?" I'm gritting my teeth like a wild animal, ready to attack him.

"Husband?" Logan chokes.

I wave dramatically. "He's only kidding, don't listen to him." Turning my head so Logan is out of view, I mouth, "What the hell?"

Jack ignores me. "I'm not fucking kidding. You better get going," he states, standing wide-legged with his arms crossed, his chiseled muscles bulging in his tight Henley. A power stance if I ever did see one.

"Yeah, I'm not into drama. I'm out of here." Logan stands. He's tall, taller than me at five foot eleven, but shorter than Jackson.It's apparent he's trying to bypass him, but Jack doesn't even attempt to budge.

"I didn't get your number," I call after him.

"I'm suddenly unavailable." He pushes past Jackson and leaves in a rush. Not that I'm surprised, but he's the first bloody bloke I've liked in forever.

The waitress comes by holding up the check, but not before smiling softly at Jack as she passes. He doesn't even see her since he's glaring at me with intensity.

"What a guy," he snarks. "Leaving you with the check. A real gent, let me tell you."

"Oh, because you gave him a bloody chance, you… you…" Ugh! I can't even get my words out. I'm so mad at him.

I sign the check, then rush past him as fast as my feet will allow in my heels. I don't know where this all came from, but in the last twenty-four hours, I've been madder at him than I have been in the past five years.

I storm out of the hotel, and Jackson, following closely behind, grabs my hand and squeezes tight so I don't run off.

A dozen people are standing around, and he knows I won't make a scene. I try to snatch my hand away discreetly, finding his grip deathly, not allowing me to move. He throws the valet some money, thanking him for holding his car up front, and escorts me into it.

"Great, another ride with the lunatic. This time, let's not almost kill us. Thanks," I mutter, crossing my arms, annoyed I'm stuck in this car.

We almost *always* get on brilliantly. Then occasionally, he lets out his possessive arseholeness, and I want to cry in annoyance, but I usually don't, knowing he's coming for a good place.

But this time feels different…

I still can't believe he followed me.

"Did you have fun with your pretentious banker bro?" he growls.

"Yes, actually, if you must know. It was one of the best dates I've been on in a very long time, so thanks for ruining it. Since when do you care who I go on a date with?" I yell.

"Since always," he yells back.

What?

I'm stunned into silence. *What did he say?*

The quiet in the car is deafening, but not enough to miss Jack's ragged breathing. He leans back and closes his eyes, taking a deep, labored breath to calm himself, rubbing his hands up and down his face in agony.

"Jack?" I whisper. "What's going on, darling?"

He reaches over, cupping the back of my head, rubbing small circles, all while his eyes remain closed. His pain is palpable, and I'm not sure what to do.

"I'm sorry," he breathes, then turns to me. Those green eyes shine bright, despite his misery.

Turning my head an inch, I kiss his wrist, then lean back, letting his touch calm and connect us.

"You need to talk to me. What's going on with you?"

"I—" A knock on Jack's window startles us, breaking up our moment.

"Sorry, Mr. Peters, are you able to move? Or at least pull over to the side, please."

He gives the valet a curt nod, and then we're off.

"I promise we'll talk. But, B, give me some time to process everything that's going on with me. It's a big deal."

"Okay, if that's what you want."

"It is, but I won't keep you waiting for long. And I'm sorry again for today. For all of it."

I've been tossing and turning all night. You would think I'd have passed out quickly, considering I've been up since the early hours. Only, I can't get Jack's words out of my head: *It's a big deal.*

What's a big deal, goddamnit?

I hate waiting, and I wouldn't say I like surprises.

Only… I could tell by his vulnerability that he needed my acceptance of giving him this time with his thoughts.

So, while he's contemplating life, my mind is in detective mode, and the only moving parts I have so far lead me to one thing.

The big deal is about… *me.*

5

Annabelle

"HEY, I'm leaving for my flight soon. Fancy a quick cuppa before I leave?" I swing my head into Lola's office and freeze on the spot when I see the tears running down her cheeks. "Lo," I say, lowering my voice. "What's going on, darling?"

Startled by my sudden appearance, she doesn't have a chance to wipe her tears to try and hide the evidence.

It's too late. I've seen it, and I'm not giving her a pass like I have all week. "Can you please talk to me? You've been upset, and I don't know how to help you. I can't leave you like this."

"I'm a good person, right?" she questions.

"The best," I quickly reply, confused as to why she would ask such a thing.

"Then why can't I find someone who wants to stick around? I want the happily ever after and the two-point-five kids. I don't want this crazy city life if I'm all alone. I'm not happy, Belle."

Sorrow tears my insides apart, my heart breaking for my sweet Lola.

I've known she's been struggling for a while, but I wasn't sure how to help her. I never want to seem insensitive, because Lola and I have very different views on the outcome of our lives, so I thought not saying anything was best.

Where she would have been happy marrying her uni boyfriend and having kids before twenty-two. I, on the other hand, cringe at the thought of settling for anything less than everything.

Don't get me wrong, I want that. Maybe not the kids, but the husband… the partnership. The difference is that I wanted to establish my life and business first so I can stand on my own two feet if needed.

I never want to be in a position where I'm forced to rely on someone else.

Luckily my mum comes from money, because when my dad left, he took everything. He was spiteful and manipulative, even though he was the cheater.

But I can't help but think… what if she didn't?

What if my mum didn't have the money, the security, and the support of her family when she went through what she did?

Would her depression over the situation with my dad have spiraled into something far greater than it was? My mum didn't have much of an identity besides being a dutiful wife and mother, and because of that, I knew I never wanted to be in that situation.

I sit down and pat the seat next to me. "I love you and want you to find whatever you're looking for. But you can't push it, Lola. You're young, not even thirty yet, and have so much life ahead of you. You'll find the one, I promise. You're worth someone extraordinary. Don't force it, don't settle. When you least expect it, you'll find what you're looking for."

She cuddles up next to me, and I wrap her in a tight hug.

"That was wise advice from someone who is usually more cynical about love," she mumbles.

"I'm not cynical. I'm realistic. I'm not in search of some grand love story. Would it be nice? Of course. I've always wanted it. However, if I end up surrounded only by my friends and family, I'll be happy with that too. I don't need anything else to be fulfilled."

"I wish I was that confident."

I tutted, pursing my lips, annoyed she would say such a thing. "You are confident, and I love that you're searching for what makes you happy. Just because happiness looks different for everyone doesn't mean you're wrong. I don't want you to force it or talk down on yourself."

She sits up, shaking out of her current slump. "You're right, and I'm sorry for pouring this all on you right before you leave. Are you all ready?"

"Never be sorry, and I am ready. Wills is sending a driver to get me since John is picking up Jack on the other side of town in about"—I glance at my watch—"five minutes, so raincheck on the tea, but I'll see you in a week, and we'll have the best time in Paris. I'll treat you to a new bag as a special bonus." I pull her in for another hug. I know it's only a week, but Lola is part of my everyday routine, and I'll miss her.

"You're not buying me another purse and calling it a bonus. You already overpay me."

"I'm the boss, and I'll decide when I give a bonus or not." I kiss her cheek and squeeze her tight one more time.

Sometimes I can't help but treat her like the little sister I never had, spoiling her like crazy.

"I'll be okay running everything, right? I don't think you've been out of the office this long and left me in charge."

I narrow my eyes, confused. "I leave you every summer when I go on my girls' trip with Sadie. What are you going on about?"

"That's different. The office is practically a ghost town. Everyone, including our clients, is on holiday for a whole month."

"I'm not even entertaining this conversation. We already know you're the brains and I'm the beauty of this operation," I say, laughing when her eyes bug out.

Putting one hand on her hip and narrowing her eyes, she says, "Are you saying I'm not pretty?"

I slowly exit the office, trying to hold back my smile. "Nope. I'm just saying I'm prettier," I yell and run back to my office, dying of laughter when I hear Lola's shrieks.

She knows I'm kidding, but I knew I would get her out of her head if I said it.

Now… if I could only get out of my own head about my upcoming flight with Jack, that would be helpful.

Why am I nervous right now?

I cross my legs, then uncross them just as fast, wringing out my hands to try and expel some of my nervous energy as I watch Jack jog down the tarmac toward the jet.

He's in a fitted navy-blue suit, tie gone, and his crisp white shirt is unbuttoned enough that his tan, muscular chest peeks out with every swift movement. Simply watching him move toward me is causing my heartbeat to do that dumb pitter-patter rapidly against my chest, wondering what's in store for us today.

Walking up the small set of steps with his usual swagger, I can't take my eyes off him.

Not that I usually can. I've always had a strong pull toward Jackson Peters that can't be explained.

He ducks his tall frame through the door, instantly searching for our usual seats, and when our eyes meet, he pops those dimples and shoots me a cheeky wink.

Our eyes don't waiver, and the ferocity of his passion seeps out as he strides over to me.

He's already so intense.

"My beautiful B." He leans down, kissing me on the tiny spot where you're unsure if it's your cheek or lips he's aiming for. "What's wrong?" He reaches up and smooths the tense lines creasing my face.

The words don't come after he calls me his. *My beautiful B*. Jack has always had a way with words, but the "my" part is undoubtedly new.

Trust me. It's something I most definitely would have taken notice of.

I stare up, getting lost in his green eyes, like a forest with no way out, stuck in all its beautiful glory.

Feeling hypnotized with his mere presence, the knot of anxiety deep in my stomach grows quickly when the words still don't come. Jack's the only person in the world that could leave me both speechless and awestruck within seconds. It's been like this my whole life.

"Hey, Peters, you ready?" Captain Miles thankfully interrupts us, breaking me out of the spell I was bound to. "Hey, Belle." He maneuvers his head around Jack, who is blocking his view, to shoot me a playful smile.

Jack lets out a slight growl in warning, not that anything Jack does would stop Miles from being flirtatious. It's second nature for Mr. Playboy Pilot.

This is the fine line that Jackson and I often teeter because that growl is nothing new, but today it seems more.

Protectiveness is one thing Jackson has never let up on, not for me or any of the other women in his life. On the contrary, the domineering shit is what drives me nuts. I will never fault him for being protective of the ones he loves, but him being a controlling arse out of nowhere makes me want to kick him with my heel.

Deciphering this new behavior of his is proving to be more difficult than I could have imagined.

Finally coming to my senses, I swat Jack away to greet Miles with a proper hello. As I approach him, I can feel the heat radiating off Jackson as he presses up against my back in warning.

Miles, of course, finds this amusing. He's never understood our relationship, but he does understand Jackson since they're mates and hang out often enough. So pushing his buttons is something he enjoys.

Jackson clears his throat. "Don't you think we should take off now?"

Hesitation crosses Miles's face, probably wanting to rile him up a bit more, but he ultimately agrees since we're already behind schedule.

The plane Wills recently bought is huge, and even though it has plenty of seats, Jack and I always sit together. It's only natural, even with no one else on board, that we would still choose to sit next to each other.

I scooch over to my preferred window seat while Jack takes the aisle. We sit in uncomfortable silence—*or at least it is for me*—until the plane starts to taxi, and the stewardess comes out to give us a safety demonstration.

"What the fuck is she wearing?" I whisper to Jack.

I've seen her the few times I've been on the new plane, and never once has she looked like this.

I watch her do the demonstration, her eyes never leaving Jackson, and ever so slightly, she pokes out her chest to enhance her boobs.

Are you kidding me right now?

"Have you hooked up with her?" I growl, taking a page out of Jackson's book.

He freezes, and I think he considers lying or making an excuse for a second. "No, but almost."

"Almost? What the fuck does that mean?" I hiss, immediately annoyed.

Do I like to hear about Jack's conquests? No, most definitely not.

Not even after all these years have I gotten used to the pang of jealousy that courses through me every time we're out. But am I able to usually move on from it undetected, knowing a future together is not for us?

Yes.

I'd rather be friends than ruin everything because of my ongoing crush, so I'm not sure why I'm being so vocal right now.

He doesn't answer the question, but assures me he doesn't even have one ounce of interest in her.

"Well, what a joke. Why even wear clothes at all? If Sadie saw her working on her plane dressed like this, she would lose her shit."

When the plane starts to rumble, indicating it's about to take off, I throw my arm into Jack's lap and he intertwines our fingers like always.

No matter how often I fly, the take-off and landing get me right in the gut with that free-falling, out-of-control feeling.

Once we're up in the air, Miles lets us know it will be about an hour and twenty minutes until we land, and it should be a smooth ride.

Little does he know there will be no smooth riding back here, and I wish I meant it in the way it sounds. I can see Jackson already champing at the bit to talk, and from how he acted the other day… I have no idea what he wants to say and it's freaking me out.

Jackson's phone buzzes a million times once the Wi-Fi kicks in. "Fucking shit," he mutters and types away furiously, mumbling a million curses as his typing gets faster.

The upside is that his attention is elsewhere, and since I'm like a baby with motion, the rumbling on the plane has me quickly falling asleep.

"B?" Jack whispers.

I turn and lean my head against the headrest. "Mmhmm." I don't even attempt to open my eyes. "I just fell asleep. Why are you waking me?" I groan.

"You've been asleep for forty-five minutes, sweetheart. I want to talk to you."

My stomach drops, worried about what he has to say. I should have kept my mouth shut and pretended I was still asleep.

Jack leans over and pushes my bedhead out of my face and behind my ears as best he can.

When I'm awake enough to open my eyes, I see he looks extremely nervous.

"What's wrong, Jack? You look weird—wait, is that a Freddie Mercury sticker on your laptop?"

He lifts his chin proudly, smirking. "Yes, Charlotte gave it to me… well, I bought it for her to give to me, but I was showing her the record shop near my house, and she wanted to buy it for me since I love Queen. It was the proudest moment of my life when she recognized who Freddie was." He sighs.

"You're ridiculous, you know that, right? I can't believe you go to meetings with that on there. It takes up the whole length of the laptop. It's a little extra, no?"

"Excess is part of my nature. Dullness is a disease," he states, as if I should know what the heck he's trying to say.

I stare at him like he has ten heads. Wait. A. Minute. "You just quoted Freddie, didn't you?"

"Of course I did, baby." He laughs, and I can't help but grin in return. How does he even know these things?

Giving his hand a quick squeeze, I tell him, "You are a special type of person, Jackson Peters." And I mean every word.

I may kid around about him loving Queen so much, but it was an essential part of our childhood that I would never give up—even the part where I'd sneak around, watching him pretend he was a member of the band.

It was even better when Sadie quickly ran to tell all my brothers that Jackson was at it again. It left me alone to bask in all my Jackson glory without having to hide my goo-goo eyes from Sadie.

"B," he whispers smoothly, waiting for me to give him my full attention. He runs his thumb across my cheek, and if I'm not mistaken, a slight tremor racks his fingers.

I stare into his eyes, and I'm shocked to see them clear, sparkling with a deep determination.

"Have you ever thought about us giving it a go?"

I hesitate, blinking in bafflement, wondering if I'm in the same universe as him right now.

Of course I have… my whole damn life. Though, those thoughts stay only in my dreams.

As much as I love and respect Jack, he isn't made for relationships. He's said it so many times before, which is why I've never expressed my feelings toward him.

"Jack," I mumble with a shaky voice. "Where is this coming from?"

He swallows hard before getting his words straight. "It's coming from years of pushed-down feelings because of my relationship issues. But I've realized the life I want to live is not one alone. And if I'm putting it all out on the table, I want you to know I've always had feelings for you, and not the fun flirtatiousness you see, but true, meaningful feelings. I just never let them boil into anything more than that. You're the only one I've ever felt anything real for."

"Years?" I choke.

Years?

"Years," he confirms with resolve, never once breaking eye contact.

His large hand takes my face and holds it gently, smiling softly as I run through all my thoughts, which is not an easy task.

"I don't understand what changed. I thought you loved your bachelor life."

"When we got married—" I open my mouth to interject. "Let me finish, B. When we got married, sham or not, I came home, and something was missing. I had a wife who wasn't by my side, *you* weren't by my side. We both know my parents fucked me up for life in the relationship department, so I didn't think anything of it. As time passed though, an instinctual and overwhelming feeling of want came over me. And not until recently did I realize I could separate myself from my childhood trauma to be the person my wife deserved. And if you weren't my wife already, I'd still pick you, Belle. It's only ever been you."

His words send my pulse racing. I've wanted this my whole life, but I never put myself out there, afraid of rejection and the pain it would cause.

But the man in front of me is so different from the Jack I know, and he seems so sure of his decision. It also makes so much sense now why he's been acting jealous and possessive.

"How recent?" I ask, and it's clear he's confused. "You said not until recently did you realize, so how recently?"

"What does that matter? I've always had feelings for you. I never pursued it because, at the time, I knew I couldn't treat you the way you deserved, I wasn't going to risk ever hurting you, but now I know for sure I never would."

Although his words hit me deeply, I don't let up. "How recently?"

He sits back and crosses his arms, annoyed. "It's irrelevant. What matters is that I'm ready."

I blow out a loud, frustrated breath. "Jack," I chastise. "You can't just decide one day you want a relationship, and then bam, it happens."

"Are you not hearing me? I'm telling you I purposely kept my feelings for you a secret all this time because I didn't want to hurt you. I'm not going to fuck that up now. If I'm saying I'm ready, I mean I'm all in."

Split in two. That's how I feel.

One side of me is squealing like a teenager, happy her first crush is paying her attention. The other side reminds me that I'm fragile in this department and shouldn't rush into anything.

Even if it's Jack.

I hesitate. How do I say this without hurting his feelings?

Because, fuck.

I've dreamt of the day I could be his girlfriend for most of my life, so I can't even believe I'm fighting him on this. But my insecurity with men is getting the best of me.

"Jack." I sigh. "You're not exactly boyfriend material."

His eyes grow wide. "What the hell are you talking about, B?"

"You're a man of many women. You may think you want to settle, but down the road, one woman won't be enough. You're forty years old. You don't just decide you suddenly want a relationship out of nowhere after pushing them away your whole life."

"So you're judging me, is that what I'm hearing? Because I have a past? You are aware that people are allowed to change, right?"

"No, Jack. I'm protecting my heart."

He crosses his arms, annoyed. "I never knew you to be so judgmental, Annabelle."

My stomach drops. I am being a judgmental cow, I know I am, and it's fucked up. It's not what Jack deserves at all.

"If you need me to prove it, I will." He adds it with such reverence, it's scary.

"What does that mean?" I ask in a rush, only he ignores me, putting on his headphones and closing his eyes for the ten minutes we have left.

I'm still in shock, sitting here staring at him after this discussion, completely confused as to what just went down.

What I do know is that I really upset Jack in a way I never knew I could. I saw it the second he said I was judgmental, the disappointment that I would be so critical of his so-called past life.

And although I'm trying to protect myself, knowing my insecurities, I've just broken a little bit of my heart because hurting Jack hurts me like nothing else in this world.

Could Jack honestly be ready for a relationship after all these years?

And do I want to be his first one?

Because I can tell you right now, if I'm his first… I'll also be his goddamn last.

"*Bienvenue au Ritz. Quel est le nom de votre réservation?*"

"Bonjour. Annabelle Hughes et Jackson Peters."

She clicks away on her computer and glances up at us. "*Alors, comment était votre vol?*"

I give her a friendly smile. "*Très bien, merci.*"

"English would be nice, B," Jackson mutters. It's the first thing he's said to me since the plane.

I shake my head, forgetting he doesn't speak French. "She welcomed us to the Ritz, asked for our names on the reservation, and ensured our flight was okay."

"Pardon me. I should have asked if you spoke French, Monsieur. Ah, yes, I see your reservation. One prestige suite."

One?

"How many bedrooms does the suite have?" I quickly ask.

She narrows her eyes, probably wondering why I would ask after she surely assumed Jackson and I are together. "One bedroom, but the space in the common area is quite large. I can assure you of that."

"Sorry, can you hold on one second?" I turn and face away from Jackson's glaring eyes and dial Wills's number.

"What's wrong?" He answers my call quickly.

"Did you only book one room for us?"

"Yeah?" he drawls. "You've always shared rooms, plus they didn't have any left besides what I booked. I figured you'd prefer to share a suite at The Ritz rather than having to switch hotels next weekend for the wedding."

Of course, this makes sense. I'm the only one freaking out over here, worried that being so close to Jack will confuse me even further.

Not wanting to stress Wills out over this, I tell him it's okay and hang up, but then open my booking app and, big surprise, there are no nice hotels in the area with rooms left for both of us.

"Are you being serious right now?" Jack growls from over my shoulder. "You can't suck it up and stay with me for the week, so much so you're over here in the corner, hiding, trying to book another hotel? Un-fucking-believable. I'm staying here, in one of the nicest hotels in Paris. You do what you want." He marches back over to the front desk to finish checking in, and once again, I feel like shit, acting like a bloody drama queen.

"Is everything okay?" the receptionist asks.

I smile politely. "Yes, I'm sorry. I'm ready to head to the room."

Two men appear to take our bags and escort us to the room, and although I've been here many times before, the grand opulence never ceases to shock me with the wow-factor.

I take in the handcrafted molding, marble pillars, and blue velvet curtains that hang from the ornate windows.

Paris elegance at its finest.

I make a promise to myself to fix things with Jack and enjoy this time with him because we don't usually get time away without it being work-related.

Stepping into the elevator, I take Jack's hand in mine and don't hold back my smile when he squeezes it instead of pulling away. I should have known that he's most likely already forgiven me and I won't have to fix anything.

"Oh, Jack, look, let's do this cooking class. It says they do it every other day." I show him the paper the receptionist handed me. "Oh, and they have a champagne brunch this Sunday."

He kisses my forehead. "Whatever you want, sweetheart, you know that."

My stomach sinks at his words, because he's right. Jack would do anything and everything for me, no questions asked.

Have I been taking him for granted all this time without realizing it?

I think, maybe, he has been showing his feelings toward me all these years without either of us even knowing it.

"B, stop staring at the bed like it's going to blow up in flames." Stepping up behind me, his palms encase my waist and he pulls me back into his body, resting his head atop mine.

A low and pleasant hum warms me like usual, but after Jack's words from earlier, now more than ever.

"Last time we shared a bed, we got married," I whisper.

"Mmm," he purrs. "Who knew I would be thanking my lucky stars for that day."

I spin around, coming face-to-face with him. "Jack…"

His dimples pop as he pulls me tighter into his body. I hastily bury my head into his neck when his eyes darken, knowing full well that if I keep eye contact, all of my resolve will falter.

"Maybe tonight you can sleep on the sofa?" I mumble into his chest.

"Not happening, so don't even ask again."

It's not like I expected him to say yes… I'm not sure I even meant it.

We stand there for a minute in silence before I push back and head into the en suite to get myself together. I need a minute alone without Jack breathing down my neck.

Literally and figuratively.

"Annabelle," he calls. I turn back, those green eyes holding me hostage. "I'm not giving up, my beautiful B, so you might as well get it through your head. Not now, not ever, not until you realize you can trust me. We could be something so fucking amazing if you let me show you… Something that's been brewing for two decades."

I clench my jaw and turn around to hold back the tears that instantly spring up, because he's not wrong, except for that it hasn't been *brewing*. It's been full-force exploding secretly inside me for as long as I can remember.

I close the door and sag to the floor, holding my head in my hands as all the words from today swirl through my mind.

At first, I was worried he was rushing a new feeling he had, but I should have known better. Jack contemplates and analyzes everything. He would never come to me with this if he weren't entirely ready.

Now, I'm confused about how to move forward, because I want everything he's been saying.

Every surprising word that came out of his mouth made so much sense to my heart.

I want us to be fucking amazing together, as he said. Because I know we would be, and if I'm being honest with myself, I do trust him. I'm just so screwed up after seeing my dad cheat that this invisible wall I put up to protect my heart keeps holding me back.

If I wanted to psychoanalyze myself, it would take two seconds to realize that I've been dating wankers my whole life because I knew it would never amount to anything. Never caring enough if they did hurt me.

When my ex, Trey, cheated on me, of course I was gutted, but it lasted all of one day. I got back out there and moved on without any regrets.

So, it's frustrating and irrational, even to me, that I would ever imagine, for one second, that Jackson could do something so hurtful.

Jack is more of a man than my dad or Trey could ever be. He would cherish and respect me with every fiber of his being.

So why can't I let go and do this? To finally put my past to rest?

If I'm going to spend the week with the one person I've ever truly loved, with him confessing his feelings, I need to finally release my insecurities. Because if he continues to break down my walls, wouldn't it be easier to let him in?

6

Jackson

THE ESPRESSO I ordered for Annabelle has arrived. I place it on the large mahogany table she's turned into a makeshift desk before stepping back and pausing against the doorframe.

I watch her with rapt attention as she ambles back and forth, listening intently to a work call she's been on for the last hour.

It's damn near impossible to take my eyes off her gorgeous figure. It's always been like this, but now that my blinders are off, it feels like so much more.

A low and pleasant hum warms me as I continue to watch her long blonde waves swish through the air as she picks up speed, becoming more and more passionate about what she's explaining to her client.

My eyes sweep up her killer legs to where her tight, black, designer, knee-length skirt runs over every perfect curve of her body, with a slit so high that when she bends over, I get a glimpse of her purple-and-black lace panties.

The things I would do to be able to run my hands up the inside of her toned thighs, to trail my fingers over her sensitive area, teasing and taunting, except, instead of granting her any pleasure, I would continue my journey, grabbing her plump juicy ass until she begs for more.

Fuck.

I adjust myself before she catches me *again* since I've been perpetually hard, watching her work like the badass boss she is.

My Queen B.

Once I admitted my feelings—that were regrettably locked away for far too long—something unraveled inside of me. Every feeling I have suppressed over the years is coming out in spades.

I'm utterly obsessed with this woman and am not afraid to admit it.

And to be honest, even before I confessed my feelings, I see now that I might have been obsessed with her all along.

No matter where we are—my sister's house, the club, literally anywhere—I'm constantly tracking her, needing to know exactly where she is in the room at any given time.

Forever craving to know what's going on with her, the yearning to spend as much time together as possible has been constant throughout the years.

It's almost embarrassing that neither of us realized it before, because as much as Annabelle puts on a front, it's the same for her, I can feel it.

Now that my eyes are open, I see us both, not just me.

And according to Bucks, it was only *us* blind to it all.

Annabelle spins toward me and places a hand on her heart, blowing me an exaggerated kiss, whispering a "thank you" for the espresso she wasn't expecting, and the next moment mouthing "one more minute," and rolling her eyes at whoever is on the phone.

She's been nonstop business, all day.

Earlier, she met with one of her big-time clients who happened to be in Paris this morning, hence the work attire, then met up with the wedding planner to make sure everything was in order. Now she's on a call with another client until we leave for our cooking class.

She didn't understand the assignment that we were supposed to be taking a few days off.

"Yes, we'll have our crisis PR team handle it. Make sure your client keeps his dick in his pants next time." She slams the phone down on her desk and mumbles a bunch of curses. "Fucking piece of shit, it's endless." She slams her phone again for good measure. "I fucking hate athletes. We got the lucky trifecta this time: cheating, drugs, and a divorce." She turns her venom toward me. "And why are you standing there staring at me like that? I saw you tracking my every move. You were making me nervous the whole call."

Ignoring her question, I cross my arms, sweeping my tongue over my bottom lip, taking in the rise of her chest and the outline of her perfect breasts against her silk top.

"*What*?" she asks curiously, with a tilt of her head. "What's with you?"

"It turns me on watching your dominant CEO side. The tone of your raspy voice and the confidence you exude makes me rock hard." I adjust myself, *again*, this time not trying to hide it.

She smirks, biting her lip, letting her eyes linger longer than she would probably like to admit.

When she finally snaps out of it, she turns, pretending to straighten up her work.

I let her have this. I told myself I wouldn't push her. *Yet.*

"Two of your best friends are athletes, by the way."

She whips her head around, confusion gracing her face. "Huh?"

"You said you hate athletes."

She huffs and slams her bag down. "They're the exception. You know I hate this part, cleaning up the messes of married men. If not for Wills, I would have already backed out of the relationship with The Taylored Group. I can't stand the cheating and pompous insolence anymore, and it seems like a common denominator with all these bastard athletes." She pauses and narrows her eyes. "Why aren't you working? You're usually glued to your phone at all times."

"I decided to embrace my time off. I would much rather watch you than be bogged down with my own work all day."

"Creep." She chuckles.

"Won't deny it, sweetheart." I wink, then stride over to her.

In a few steps, I make it to her… needing to touch her, desperate to feel her under my palm.

I've waited all day for even a simple pinky hold, so I wrap my arms around her waist, startling her when I bring her close, causing her to fall exactly where I want her. "Hi," I whisper against her smooth skin, letting my lips linger, breathing in her woodsy floral scent I crave.

Goosebumps scatter across her skin as I skim my lips along the sweep of her cheek, having no plans to stop unless she tells me to.

To myself, I promised I wouldn't push her. Though, that doesn't mean I'm playing this cool, either. I'm putting it all out there until she realizes I'm not giving up. Especially since there is no doubt in my mind that she wants the same things I do.

Over the last two days, I've seen it in her eyes.

It's impossible for her to hide it from me, yet still, she's holding back the best she can, and soon enough, I'll wear her down.

Her insecurities are aimed toward the women that have come in and out of my life and, unfortunately, only time will prove that my bachelor days are in the past. They're so far gone that it feels as if there's only ever been Belle to see.

And in some ways, that's true.

For now, I'll do whatever it takes to prove to her that she's my one and only girl, the only person who's ever made me feel *more*.

"Jack." Belle sighs softly, squeezing my bicep when I run the tip of my nose up the sensitive side of her neck.

I pull back slightly. Wanting… *needing*… her eyes.

The second our gazes catch, the world stops around us. It's as if the universe was waiting for this very moment to click it all into place.

My eyes widen.

Her breath hitches.

The air crackles.

A strong, electric feeling, something beyond our control, pulls us together, and it's this moment, this very second, that I know I will remember forever.

Unable to hold back, I lean in and press my mouth to hers, savoring the feeling of her soft, plush lips. Desire burns a hot spot in the pit of my stomach as I slowly open my mouth and let our tongues intertwine.

Belle's arms tighten around my neck as my hand runs up and over her back, snaking my fingers through her hair, tightening my grip to maneuver her head at the perfect angle, letting our tongues seductively explore each other.

This isn't our first kiss, but it's the perfect one.

The one we will always remember.

I hoist her up around her waist and unsteadily walk us forward, seeking out something to keep us upright as our kiss turns frantic.

Finally, we slam into the wall, groaning as our bodies crash together. I grind my dick against her, needing to relieve some pressure before I lose my mind.

Her fingernails scrape up my neck, and as she presses her body into mine, she releases a loud whimper against my mouth.

Her knees give out; she's unraveling. I'm there to hold her up but not stop her because, finally, we're in this together.

I release my grip on her hair, letting my fingers glide down her side and around the curve of her breast. My thumb brushes over her nipple, which instantly hardens from the light touch.

Our tongues are tangled with deep, frenzied movements. As though lost in a trance, we haven't stopped for even one breath—too enthralled in one another.

Again, I cup and squeeze her breasts.

I will never get enough of how they spill over, too gloriously large to fit in my hand, and if they aren't my favorite thing ever… I don't know what is.

Her mind, strength, and beauty may bring me to my knees, but my dick has a mind of his own, and his favorite things are these firm, luscious tits.

I can't blame him for even one second; they're fucking magnificent.

"Oh god," Annabelle whispers against my lips, pulling back, pushing my chest to create distance. Her eyes widen, stricken with a look I'm unfamiliar with. "Jack."

"Annabelle," I whisper, unsure of myself for the first time in forever. I can't read her. "Are we good, sweetheart? Are you okay?"

She nods her head, still in a semi-state of shock.

Shit.

Did I fuck this up?

She was right there with me. I know it.

I stand there, breathing heavily, wide-eyed, waiting for her to say something. Hoping whatever she says won't diminish the moment and the best kiss I've had in my whole life.

"B," I whisper, unable to take the silence any longer. This time though, my voice breaks her out of her daze.

She reaches out and squeezes my hand, letting a small, lopsided grin curve up one side of her face. "Yeah, Jack… we're good," she says, biting her bottom lip, still grinning when she leans in and kisses my lips once more. Keeping her eyes locked on mine, she backs away until she turns abruptly and closes the door behind her, leaving me alone.

I stand there for what feels like hours before it hits me… *we're good.*

I send an invisible fist pump in the air. *Fuck yes!*

This is our moment of clarity. Her resolve is melting, and soon, she'll be mine.

Because that's what she is—mine.

Every goddamn inch of her is *mine*.

Annabelle

I lock Jack out of the room to jump on the bed and scream into *his* pillow to feel like he's right there with me. Allowing my teenage alter-ego to take over—she needs a split-second to relish in what just happened.

I wish I could go back in time to tell myself that it's finally happening, what I feared most yet still wished for every time I closed my eyes, every time I blew out a birthday candle. Jackson Peters may finally be mine.

What my younger self would never understand is why I've been the one holding back, but after that kiss… *that perfect kiss*. I'm not sure I have the strength to hold back any longer.

Our first kiss, we were young and careless.

The second was drunk and forgetful.

The third one was everything… *meant everything*.

The third one's undoubtedly the charm. I feel it deep in my bones —things are changing.

Jack's been trying to tell me all weekend, showing me through the real and raw emotions he never once hid.

Ones that he didn't shy away from, practically forcing me to see what he sees in us, and it wasn't until now that I'm finally allowing myself to open up and see it too.

Every emotion poured into that kiss came from somewhere deep within me. The energy was electrifying, and I know he felt it; I could see it in those beautiful eyes of his.

I won't pretend I'm surprised it happened.

We were forced to share a room, and the air around us had been thick and full of arousal since the moment we stepped on French soil. If I had opened my eyes to the reality of it all, I would have seen it coming a mile away.

What I'm more shocked about is how I'm allowing myself to finally give in to a possible future of happiness with the one person I've yearned for my whole life but was always too afraid to take the chance with, knowing he's never been a one-woman type of man.

Am I ready to jump in and open up my whole heart?

No, I don't think I am.

Though, I *am* ready to give Jack a fighting chance.

A knock at the door startles me. "B, I want to call and check in on my sister and the girls. Meet in the lobby when you're done, okay?" His voice is hesitant and unsure.

I hate that I did that.

He doesn't sound like my strong, confident Jack, so I swing open the door and stand tall, shooting him a panty-dropping smile that I know he won't mistake for anything else.

"Sounds good." My lips stay curved as I tell him, "I'll be down once I change out of my work clothes. Tell Sadie I'll call her later."

His eyes lower to my mouth, and I think he might kiss me again, but instead, he runs his thumb over my bottom lip with a soft caress. My breath hitches when the sparks ignite my core, and his gaze cuts to mine, desire burning deep in his eyes.

He takes a meaningful step toward the door. I can tell it's taking all his might to hold back. "Meet you downstairs, B," he rasps, then high-tails it out of the room.

Exiting the lift into the pristine, marble-adorned lobby, I spot Jack, standing and talking to someone in the corner.

I take the opportunity to run my eyes over his tall, lean frame. I hadn't noticed earlier that he had changed, too focused on our kiss.

He's wearing dark jeans, hugging his bum in all the perfect ways. When Jack was younger, he played baseball, and I've heard through my American friends that they have the best behinds. Now I can concur.

He's wearing the navy checkered blazer I gifted him for Christmas, with his light gray Brunello Cuccinelli loafers I bought him the year before.

Did he wear them for me or because he loves them… or both? The thought of it makes me excited that he enjoys what I've picked out for him.

Jack's always been stylish without the help from others, so it's a compliment if he appreciates the gifts I've picked for him.

I look down at my silk jumpsuit and new Chanel heels, realizing we're both entirely overdressed for a cooking class, but it's Paris, and I only packed the most stylish clothes I could find. I can only hope they have an extra-large apron to cover everything.

I walk out from behind the column to take in the rest of Jack. His dark, pushed-back, perfectly styled hair. The—

I stop abruptly when I see the wedding planner's hand on Jack's forearm.

Nicole laughs an exaggerated cackle at whatever he's said, which doesn't seem funny at all, considering his face is void of all emotion, and his dimples are nowhere ready to pop.

Jack seems uninterested, but jealousy still rears its ugly head at the thought of her touching him, and I absolutely hate this feeling. It's only been thirty minutes since our kiss, and I'm already an insecure cow.

"For the third time, please get your hand off me, or I will remove it myself."

Nicole giggles, thinking he's joking, but I pause, stunned at the venomous tone I've never heard Jack use before.

He must sense me, because he snaps his arm away and turns swiftly in my direction. His worried green eyes catch mine, and I conjure up whatever I can to show him it's okay, that I know he tried to get away.

He shoots me a small smile and holds out his hand. "There she is, my beautiful B."

I stand tall and flip my hair over my shoulder, not letting this Nicole chick ruin my day.

"Hi, darling." I grab Jack's outreached hand, and he pulls me tight to his side, kissing my cheek.

"You're together?" Nicole sneers, eyes narrowing.

He kisses me again and smiles. "We are." This time, the dimples pop. "And we're late for our cooking class, so if you'll excuse us."

He doesn't wait for her to respond. Instead, he pushes past her, then interlocks our fingers.

"I'm sorry, B—"

"Don't even waste your breath. I saw her and her man hands all over you," I huff.

He tries but fails miserably to hide his laughter. "*Man hands*?"

"Oh, shut it. Let's go." I pull him forward.

"Here it is." Jack lifts our intertwining fingers and points to the massive sign that says "Cooking School."

I chuckle and pat his cheek with my free hand. "You're so smart sometimes."

My phone dings, and I stop outside the door to check it quickly in case Lola needs anything before we head in.

The agency picked up a few unexpected clients recently, and I hate the idea of leaving her hanging.

Lola: You wouldn't bloody believe what happened. The building manager came and forced everyone to ejaculate! Including the clients. It was a huge mess!

What?

I can't hold myself up from the silent vibrations quickly racking my body, even with Jackson holding on to me. I can't do it, so I lean against the wall and suck in a deep breath, wheezing from my trapped laughter.

This is the best thing anyone has ever sent me in my whole life.

"What are you doing? We're going to be late."

"Can't. Breathe," I try to say, but the air gets stuck in my lungs.

I hand Jack my phone, and his instantaneous laughter is so loud and boisterous that the haughty-taughty hotel patrons shoot us nasty looks as they walk by. His chest is vibrating more than mine.

"I took a screenshot and sent it to the group. She's never going to live this down… my poor Lola." I feel like I'll never get a handle on myself, but I need to respond before she realizes what she said.

Me: I can only imagine what a sticky mess that would make, with the manager AND the whole office coming! Did everyone have to go home to get changed?
Lola: OH. MY. GOD.
Me: Was it simultaneous?
Me: Was there moaning or just silence when everyone shot their loads?

Lola: I meant evacuate!!!!! The freaking hell, I meant E V A C U A T E!!!!!! Damn auto-correct.
Me: HAHAHAHAHA… I hope you know I will never let you forget this. Jack already sent it to the group. K BYE… LOVE YOU.
Lola: HATE YOU BOTH!!! Ugh!!!!!! Why me…

My chest is still bouncing as we walk into class. "Well, it's official, today is the best day of my life."

Jack stills, his eyes holding mine, prolonging the minute before he picks up my hand, pressing his lips to my fingertips.

"Mine too, sweetheart." He cups my cheek with his other hand. "The best day, my beautiful B." He smiles, gulping down his emotions when I try to hold back the tears filling my eyes.

I knew that kiss was everything and more.

"You must be Mr. and Mrs. Peters," an elegant, older Parisian woman with rosy cheeks says as she greets us, breaking us out of our bubble.

I whip my head toward Jack at the mention of his surname. A cheeky, irresistible smirk is plastered on his face. "Yes, that would be us"—he throws his arm around my shoulder—"Mr. and Mrs. Peters." He bites his lip, knowing I'm about to burst.

"I'm Jackson, and this is my wife, Annabelle."

"It's lovely to meet you. I'm Chef Odette. Please come in so we can go over today's menu."

"Jack," I chastise through gritted teeth.

He shrugs. "I would rather not start the day on the wrong foot. I despise liars. Are you not my wife?"

I give him an exasperated look. "What are you playing at, Jackson Peters?"

"Just want to test it out on my lips is all," he says, then follows the chef like he doesn't have a care in the world.

Test it out on his lips. Why? Why would he need to do that?

7

Annabelle

OF COURSE, Jack is the star of the class. He's one of those people who excel in everything they do, and cooking is no different.

It's never bothered me until now.

I hate failing, and I can't cook a goddamn thing right, for fuck's sake.

And, of course, every woman is fawning over him like he's God's gift to the world, including the chef, since he's "the star of the class."

"I keep burning everything. How are you such a good cook? Have you been hiding this talent from me?"

First, he looks down at my burnt baguette, then tries his hardest to hide his smile as he eyes my burnt éclairs.

Great.

"Believe it or not, I remember a lot of what Mrs. Morales taught us as kids. It's why Sadie's such a good cook."

"Your mate Sebastian's mum?"

"Mmhmm," he mumbles around a piece of cheese he popped into his mouth, then cuts another, making sure it's perfectly sized against the cracker.

It's my weird quirk. The portions have to be perfect for me to enjoy it.

He presses it to my lips, so I open wide, and my eyes nearly roll back in my head when I bite down.

The French truly know cheese. It's one of the hundred things they do well. But cheese is life, so it tops anything else.

He takes another bite, then continues, "After school, all the guys—and Sadie, of course—would meet at the Morales house since their mom was the best cook around. She always had something waiting for us. When it was time for everyone to go home to their families, Sadie and I often stayed since there wasn't much to look forward to at our home." He pauses, shaking his head at the memory. "Leo—I don't know if you remember him; he's Seb's younger brother. He would help Sadie with her homework while Seb and I would help his mom make dinner. It just stuck with me."

"I remember. That was before Sadie and I had phones, so I would learn from her letters, often weeks later, what she learned to cook. I know it will never make up for shitty parents, but it was nice you had a familiar place to go," I say as the timer goes off.

"Can you grab that while I take the demi-glace off the stove?"

I bend over to get the mini Madeleine's out of the oven, our second dessert that Jack picked, knowing it's my favorite. He's always been thoughtful like that, remembering all my favorites and putting them first before thinking about what he wants.

My thick, unruly hair keeps falling in my face, making it hard to see, and of course, I didn't wipe my hands clean, so anytime I try to push it back, it gets filthy.

"Stand up. Let me fix your hair, B," Jack says from behind me, and I freeze on the spot, instantly taken back to a memory from my childhood I haven't thought of in a long time.

"J-Jack? What are you doing?" I stutter, then scrunch my face up in embarrassment at the crack of my voice.

God, act cool, Annabelle.

It's so hard, though—my stomach flutters like crazy whenever Sadie's brother, Jackson is around, but this time he's touching me, and I decide here and now I love the feeling, and I never want it to stop.

He's hugged me before, but only when I'm sad, so I don't really pay attention, but now... now it feels different.

He's only touching my hair, except his fingertips keep accidentally sliding across my neck, shooting tiny sparks through my body, making me feel warm and fuzzy inside. I'm not sure I've ever felt something so pleasant.

I've always had a secret crush on Jack. I think sometimes Sadie can tell, or maybe not.

I think I'm good at keeping it to myself because I would die a mortified teenager if Jack ever found out. I'm only thirteen to Jack's sixteen, and even though it's only three years' difference, it's like dog years when you're a teenager. Plus, he turns seventeen at the end of the summer, and that seems so much older! He would probably laugh in my face if he knew how much I liked him.

Well, that's not true.

That's something my brothers would do, but Jack is kind. He wouldn't laugh at me, though I would still want to crawl away and hide if he ever found out.

It's just a silly crush... but sometimes... I see him watching me, smiling more than he does at the other girls. That could mean something, right?

No... no. I'm just a baby to him: his sister's best mate, his friend's little sister.

"Belle?"

"Huh?" Did he just say something?

He chuckles, and I melt on the spot at his dreamy laugh. I wish I could turn around and see if his dimples are out.

They're my favorite.

"Don't you like your hair braided, B? Let me help you so it's not in your face. I saw you almost fall before because of it."

"You know how to do a braid?" I ask, surprised, but it's clear he does as I can feel him making fast work of it.

He doesn't answer but pats my shoulder. "Okay, all done." He leans over, kisses my forehead, and my eyes nearly fall from their sockets.

Holy crap, I just felt a kiss from his lips!

And not just a "hello, it's good to see you" kiss... this was a kiss with his lips fully on my skin.

Oh. My. God.

Besides thinking about the kiss, I wonder...

Did Jack learn how to braid for me? Sadie prefers a regular ponytail, so he didn't learn for her.

I all but squeal at the thought of it... Maybe he has a crush just like me?

"There you go. I still got it." He pats my bum, and I couldn't hold back the onslaught of tears if I tried."B." He frowns. "What's wrong, sweetheart?"

"You haven't braided my hair in so long. It just brings up so many memories. Sorry." I smile and wipe my tears with the back of my hand.

What a crybaby I am today.

"Good memories, I hope."

"Oh god, yes. The best memories." I beam. "Spending my time in New York, in the city or the Hamptons, were the best days of my childhood. I spent the whole year looking forward to leaving England to visit you guys and..." I pause. "I feel like it's time to confess something." I grab a Madeleine when Chef Odette isn't looking and have to suppress a moan. "Holy shit, these are good, Jack. Like really good, better than some I've had from bakeries."

He dusts his shoulder off and takes a bow. "Chef Jackson at your service, Madame."

"You're an idiot." I laugh, then take another bite.

I wasn't kidding. These are beyond, and trust me, I know a good Madeleine.

"So, what are you confessing to me?" He leans back against the counter, crossing his arms and legs, giving me his full attention.

I bite my lip to hold back my smirk, knowing he'll think I'm ridiculous. "I may or may not have purposely left my hair messy at times so you would come braid it. I knew after I fell off my bike that one time, you would always braid it." I chuckle, thinking about how clever I thought I was.

His eyes widen. "You did not."

"I did." I widen mine right back. "When did I ever walk around with anything out of place? You never picked up on it? I would mess it all up before I saw you."

He shakes his head like he can't believe it. "I'm not sure if I should be impressed or not."

I nod my head enthusiastically. "Impressed, definitely impressed. Come on, I was a kid, thinking outside the box. It was genius. Brilliant, even."

He rolls his eyes playfully. "Whatever you say."

I reach out and wipe a bit of sauce on his gorgeous face. He grabs my wrist and pulls me forward so I lean against his chest. "Hi." He smiles.

"Bonjour." I wink.

He looks cute right now.

Not that *cute* is a word I would typically use for Jack—more like devastatingly gorgeous—but with his dirty face and dark, messed-up hair, not to mention his pink apron… he's looking freaking adorable.

"We have time before the duck is ready. Tell me about the rest of your day," he says, wrapping his arms around me tightly, keeping me close to his chest.

I sigh, thinking about my morning. My meeting with my client was unproductive and a waste of my time, which could have been spent in bed next to Jack, pretending I was asleep while he cuddled me.

Then there was *her*, Nicole. "I hate to admit anything Wills says or does is right, but after meeting with the wedding planner"—I narrow my eyes at the thought of her hands on Jack—"he was right to have someone keep an eye on her. Something about her screams *shady* to me."

His brows furrow in concern. “Is this because you were jealous, or do you honestly think that?”

“I was not jealous,” I lie.

One side of his lip curves up in a cheeky smirk. “Oh really? So why did your lip just twitch?” He pokes at said lip. “Liar.” He laughs.

I hate that I have a tell.

“Whatever.” I ignore him. “I would never make something like that up. Even before the whole lobby incident, she gave me a bad vibe. I would have mentioned it to you, but it slipped my mind.”

His body goes rigid. “I want to come with you the next time you go. I will not have my baby sister’s wedding fucked up because of Nicole or anyone else. Period, end of story.”

“Shh.” I glance around to make sure no one is looking at us, squeezing his hand in a way to calm his impending freakout. “Your sister appreciates you in every way, but remember she has a new protector in her life, and as much as it pains you, you have to let the reins go and pass them on to Wills. If something’s going on, we should tell him.”

“Yeah, not happening,” he says in a dismissive tone while he pushes away from me to tend to his next task.

“Jack,” I warn. “It’s what you do when you walk her down the aisle. You pass the responsibility off to her husband.”

He stares at me, dumbfounded, as if he’s never heard such a thing in his life. “Well… she should have John or Mr. Taylor to do it then, because there is no way in hell I’m giving up the responsibility of my sister after all these years. It’s been only us all our lives until Wills came along. He’s gotten used to me thus far, and he’ll have to figure out how to deal with it forever.”

“I know, I was there. We were all taking care of one another,” I say as I take the duck out of the oven, then turn back toward Jack when he doesn’t answer. “Hey.” I lower my voice. “What’s going on?” I cup his cheek when I see his pain-stricken face.

“I’m so incredibly happy for both of them… and my nieces. Sades deserves this more than anyone in the world, especially after what they've been through." He takes a deep breath. "I guess I just never thought about how that might impact my role in her life."

I shake my head at my stupidity. "You're right, don't listen to me. You can both be there for her."

"No, you're right, B. I need to step back and let Wills be there for her. If they need me, they'll ask," he says, gulping down his emotions.

"Let's get out of here, okay?" I turn off the oven and grab his hand. When he doesn't resist, I realize how upset he is.

Wills has been in the picture for a while now, but I think with the permanent role of husband, it's finally hitting Jackson that after years of being Sadie's only protector, he's not her number one guy anymore.

"Monsieur Jackson, Madame Annabelle, we're not finished," Chef Odette calls when she sees us packing up to leave. She must see the look on one or both of our faces, "I'll box it all up. Come back later for it." She smiles kindly and rubs my arm.

"Merci," I whisper, then leave quietly before making a scene.

Pressed against Jack's chest in his crushing hold, I move us to a hallway that's out of sight from the hotel patrons.

I curse myself for not anticipating Jack's feelings of "losing his sister" sooner when I feel his wild heartbeat pumping against his chest, answering my anxious thoughts about whether he's okay.

He's stressed out to the max.

We coined Sadie with the Sensitive Sadie moniker, but what outsiders—anyone besides me, Sadie, and maybe Declan—don't realize is that she took after her brother in that department.

Only, Jack doesn't wear his feelings on his sleeve like her. He's a professional at hiding his emotions from the world.

But one look past his long, thick lashes into those deep green eyes would show you a whirlwind of emotions, and without him even uttering one word, I already know what he's going through.

Jack turns his attention toward me when we sit on the bench we find around the corner. "I'm well aware it's beyond ridiculous to have these feelings about my thirty-five-year-old sister getting married, except I never truly stopped to think about it all, how impactful all the changes would be."

Grabbing his hand, I interlock our fingers, squeezing tight to get his attention.

I want his eyes locked on me when I speak.

"Not one person in this world would fault you for your feelings. The two of you have a unique relationship that most will never experience or even understand." When he nods in agreement, I continue, "Since the day you were old enough to realize your parents were non-existent in your lives, you stepped up and took care of your sister in ways other siblings never would. You were the mum, dad, brother, best mate, and protector. You comforted her when she was sad, building her up in every way possible. The two of you are each other's number-one fans. It was always the Peters duo, and now you feel like the band is breaking up in a way. What you need to remember is that Sadie loves you more than life; she'll never be far from reach. Although she has Wills and a changed surname, there is no doubt in my mind that she'll never completely stop relying on her brother. It might not be the way it was years ago, but there are some things that only family can help with."

I reach up to wipe the rogue tear that escapes his watery eyes, letting my hand glide along his chiseled jaw, cupping it to bring his eyes back to me.

"You are a good man, Jackson Peters. The best. Someone I often say I'm proud to know. You have changed my life for the better, and I've never admired someone as I do you. I've always looked up to you, especially as a young girl. I could tell you were different, even then."

Startled by my admission, Jack's mouth opens and shuts a few times before I press my finger to his lips.

Shaking my head, I will him to stay quiet. "There is no need for more words. I only want you to remember that just because your sister is getting married, she will always need you, and you will never be inconsequential in her life." I hold his stare. "Or mine, Jack. I will always need you…" I gulp down my emotions, not realizing how sentimental I've gotten.

He smiles softly, then leans in for a quick peck to my lips.

I have to hold myself off not to deepen the kiss.

I'm the one who said I didn't want anything between us, but now, he's all I see.

"Thank you, sweetheart," he mutters, running his hand along my long hair, fingering a loose tendril that's fallen astray.

He leans in again, this time kissing my forehead, holding his lips for a beat, letting our heightened emotions pass through us.

I can tell he wants to say more, so I'm grateful when he resists.

Sometimes silence speaks so much louder than words.

I take a deep breath and smile when he pulls back, playfully hitting him in the chest. "Stop with all this emotional crap, will you? This is supposed to be a fun day, not a cry fest," I jest, waving my hand in front of my face to stop any lingering tears from escaping, plastering on a broad smile to help lighten the mood.

He chuckles, then stands, holding out his hand, demanding me to take it. "Come on. I think we could both use a drink."

I stand up in a rush, happy to put all the crap I just word-vomited behind us.

"Yes! Brilliant idea, Jack. I could go for a glass of crisp champagne right about now."

There is no more room for depressing or sappy thoughts today.

"The salon was a good choice over the bars. It has an intimate feel, with red and gold velveteen sofas and wood-paneled walls. Very Downton Abbey-like," Jack states as he looks around, appreciating the room.

What the hell did he say?

Regarding him with a questioning look, I ask, "Um, come again? Did you just say *velveteen sofas*?" Widening my eyes, I can't help but wonder who this bloke is in front of me. "What are you, my ninety-five-year-old grandfather?"

His words are a vast contradiction to the manly specimen sitting in front of me, with his long muscular legs spread wide while he carelessly drapes his strong arms across the back of the sofa, all dominant, gorgeous, and perfect.

His eyes twinkle as he shrugs unapologetically. "I binged it with Sades when Charlotte was born. Remember? You called a few times during."

"Yes, I thought you watched it a *few times*, not studied the terminology of the grand décor. Plus, Downton Abbey is English, not French."

I'm confused… Why are we even talking about this shit?

He shrugs again. "Same time period. I looked that guy up when we arrived—" He points to the oval portrait beside the impressive bookcases. "Marcel Proust, Parisian novelist. This room is named after him, and his popularity reached its height in the same time period. So, they're one in the same in my head."

Thank god the waitress chooses this moment to walk up and serve our drinks, interrupting our *riveting* conversation.

Her hands shake as she places each one in front of us, flickering her eyes to Jackson, completely awestruck.

The poor girl, I know exactly how she feels.

Jack's presence has always been compelling to all, even in a crowded room of beautiful, well-put-together people, like today.

Luckily, when I was younger, around the waitress's age, I had my shit together and pretended he didn't affect me.

Not that I had a choice.

If my brothers knew how I felt about Jack back then, they would have killed me, Jack, or both of us.

Her eyes widen in horror as some of Jack's drink spills over, quickly trying to clean it. She looks like she's going to burst into tears at any second.

I flicker my eyes toward Jack, trying to get his attention since he's closer. When he realizes, he jumps in to help her.

"*Je suis vraiment désolée, monsieur*," she cries.

"She says she's very sorry," I mutter under my breath, loud enough for only Jack to hear.

He places his hand on hers to stop her vigorous wiping, then takes the cloth and finishes it himself. "There is no need to be sorry." He winks, and I practically roll my eyes out of my head.

I wanted him to help her, not give her a heart attack… but Jack, ever the flirt, can't seem to help himself.

"*Merci pour la boissons*," I say, thanking her for our drinks and rubbing her back when she seems stuck in place.

"*Tout le plaisir était pour moi.*" She smiles, embarrassed when she tells me the pleasure was all hers, right before her eyes go round at the sight of Jackson's dimple popping.

Then she's off, fleeing the scene. I'm doubtful we'll see her again.

"You're terrible." I shake my head.

He smirks. "I did nothing wrong."

"Uh-huh." I hold up my champagne. "*Levons nos verres*, let's make a toast."

Jack follows suit with his glass.

"To us, to Paris, and all the memories we'll make over the next week in this beautiful city. *Santé*."

"*Santé*—now that I know. Cheers." He clicks my glass but continues to hold it up. "And to taking chances."

On us… and to taking chances on us, is what I know he really wants to say.

I hold his sparkling eyes because, in France, you never look away while you cheers. It's bad luck.

Then decide to give an inch. "And to taking chances." We clink glasses again, sipping our drinks in a brief moment of silence.

"What's that look for, Jack?"

He takes a long sip, eyes penetrating mine over the glass, before he responds. "I'm not sure you want to know."

The air around us seems to thicken as I hold his stare, not answering, silently begging him to go on without me asking.

"I'm thinking that kiss wasn't enough, and I need more of you." I raise my brows at his brazen remark, but he doesn't stop there. "I want to feel your skin against mine and listen to the little moans and whimpers you don't realize escape you whenever I so much as brush against you."

I want all of that… right this second.

"A-A kiss is all you'll get," I lie.

"We'll see about that," he mumbles, knowing full well I hear him and that I won't fight him on it.

Jack usually gets what he loves when he wants it. And what he loves are women—beautiful, intelligent women.

And I'd be lying if I didn't say I know I'm both.

Suddenly, I'm broken out of my thoughts when I hear the chant—"Glory Glory Tottenham Hotspur"—of Jack's favorite football club.

"Jackson," I hiss, looking around the room when everyone turns to glare at us. "Are you freaking watching football on your phone right now?"

His chest vibrates at my embarrassment. "*Football* starts in September, B, but no, I wasn't watching *soccer*. I checked the score earlier and accidentally pressed it again."

As he goes to put the phone away, it buzzes in his hand and his body stills. A look of shock crosses his face. "Holy fucking shit, it happened."

"What? What is it?" I cry.

His eyes snap up to mine, then widen in astonishment. He tries to speak, but his words get stuck in his throat.

"Jack! What's going on?"

Glancing down at his phone one last time, he shakes his head, then passes it to me.

My eyes snap up to his to confirm I'm reading this right.

He bites his lips and nods ever so slightly.

I'm out of my seat, flinging myself on his lap in a second, kissing him hard on the lips.

Fuck my rules. He deserves a million and one kisses right now.

I pull back, grabbing his face and squeezing his cheeks hard, then kiss him again. "Holy shit, I'm kissing a billionaire."

He chuckles. "I think I'm in shock."

"You didn't know this was happening? How could you not know? Tell me everything!"

He laughs at my eagerness. "A second ago, you were mortified by a two-second clip from a soccer game. Now you're okay with straddling my lap, kissing me, and yelling in excitement?"

"Yes, bloody hell, Jack, when have I actually cared what people think? This is more important than their judging glares."

He adjusts me on his lap to make us more comfortable. "To answer your questions, when I was younger and first started investing my money, the guys from New York and I invested in a start-up tech company, before tech was all the rage. Over the last year or so, they've been in the process of going public, and voilá, as the French like to say, they did it, and I made a shit ton of money. So yes, I knew it was in the process, but anything can happen with the markets changing, so I put it out of my mind until it was official."

He makes it sound like nothing. This is huge!

"Who was that email from?"

"Oh, that was just Seb congratulating me. He knew if they went public that it would put my finances in the next tier."

"The next tier, meaning billionaire," I whisper, and he nods to confirm. "You need to call Sadie and the lads."

"Nah, I'm going to wait. I need to see Declan in person to rub it in his face." He chuckles, and I follow, laughing alongside him.

"You two are the worst." They're like two little kids, annoying the shit out of each other at all times.

"He's going to kick himself in the ass since he declined to invest when I told him there was an opportunity. Sucks for him now." He laughs.

"Congratulations, Jack." I throw my arms around his neck, cuddling him close. "I'm so proud of you. We need to celebrate."

"Mmm," he purrs into my ear, then thrusts his groin into my bum. "I know the perfect way to celebrate."

I hold on tighter and giggle into his shoulder, ignoring his advance. "You know, you don't really fit the bill of a billionaire. You don't look the part."

He pulls away and looks at me, deadpan. "What part?"

"You know." I shrug. "You're"—I wave my hand in front of his face—"Mr. GQ."

"And?"

"And aren't most billionaires all stuffy and stiff?"

He inhales sharply. "Oh, trust me, sweetheart, I'm fucking stiff." He thrusts up again. *We need to get out of here.* "Stiff as a fucking board."

"All right, you sexed-up maniac, let's go."

He chuckles dryly. "Sexed-up maniac?"

I roll my eyes. "Oh, bugger off."

He leans over and kisses the curve of my neck. "I can't help it when I'm around you, B. I have no control over myself."

What is he saying?

He drags the tip of his tongue along my collarbone, up my neck, and I inhale sharply. "You don't get it, do you?" he whispers.

"Get what?" I rasp.

"This is happening, so you better break down this makeshift wall you put up. Because after today, I'm not waiting any longer." He sucks, marking me on my neck.

A wave of arousal sweeps through my body, and I grind my teeth to hold myself back.

This man is making me forget everything I've ever worried about when it comes to Jackson Peters.

Because all I want is him.

I've never wanted anything more in my life.

8

Annabelle

"JACK?" I call.

His eyes shoot up to meet mine and he smiles softly, causing my heart to somersault at the affection shining back at me.

"I'm going to sit outside on the terrace and call Lola back while I answer work emails if you need me."

"Okay, sweetheart." He smiles before turning back absentmindedly to watch his program.

I pause, teetering in the door frame, stealing a moment to take him in.

He's lying on our bed, stretched out and comfortable in low-waisted gray sweatpants, looking like every woman's wet dream—shirtless and abs rippling.

He's watching one of the crazy shows I got him hooked on. This one is about the serial killer "Son of Sam" who operated out of New York, and he's totally addicted.

Soon he'll be like me, thinking everyone's out to kidnap him.

He doesn't even realize I'm staring, so I take another minute to admire him.

Over the last few hours, his words from earlier have been playing on repeat. *Because after today, I'm not waiting any longer.*

I haven't told him that I'm ready for more between us. I sense he's figured it out, with the small kisses and touching, more than we usually do.

It all makes me nervous, and if I'm being honest, it's not in the way I thought I would be.

It's more because this is all feeling too normal.

Why does it seem so easy?

My phone buzzes, so I pick it up quickly and head outside. "Hey, Lo. What's going on, darling?"

"Not much, just working. I missed you and wanted to say hi and see how it's been going.

You know, with Jackson." She whispers the last part like he can hear her through the phone.

I glance at the clock and realize it's getting late back in New York. "Why are you still working? I've seen the nonstop emails all day. You need to rest."

"I'm fine," she says, but I can still hear the rapid clicking of her keyboard in the background.

"Shut it down, Lola," I demand.

She'll be up all night knowing her. She doesn't have an off button for work—even worse than me at times.

"Fine, only if you give me good news."

"Like what?"

"Ah, don't play dumb. Give me the gossip."

I chuckle at her weak demand, trying to be authoritative, which is adorable, and decide not to hold back. "It's been incredible, Lo."

"Oh god, I knew it would be," she squeals. "Tell me more."

I lean back and put my feet up, closing my eyes as I think back on the memories we've made so far.

"We kissed and—"

"You kissed?" she shrieks, "Like, *kiss* kiss?" I can hear the smile in her voice.

"Mmhmm." I beam. "It was everything… He's been everything."

"Of course he has. He's Jackson. He always treats you like a queen. So what now?"

I sigh. "Without sounding like a love-sick fool, everything's starting to feel different. His kiss was a promise of more. I could feel it deep down."

Silence.

"Darling?"

"Yup?" She sniffles.

"Are you okay, Lo?"

What's going on with her lately?

She blows her nose into the phone receiver, so I pull it away slightly. "Ahh, the lovely sound of boogers."

"Oops, sorry," she mutters. "I'm so happy for you. I just want to make sure though… are you ready for more, Annabelle?"

"Yeah, I think I am. It's strange because, from the outside, we're still just Jack and Belle; not much has changed. We've always been close like this. I'm telling you, though, it's different. I feel it. Things are good."

I hear her rustling in the sheets to get comfortable.

"I'm so happy. Tell me more," she whispers.

"Not much more to tell." I sigh. "It's only been a couple of days. I'm only hoping I don't fuck this up with my insecurities."

It's always been a worry of mine.

I've dated on and off for years and, of course, long-term with Trey.

However, even before he became a lunatic, I never let him in enough to make a future together.

Not that he noticed. He comes from a loveless family, so it worked perfectly that companionship was all it was—guaranteed date nights and sex at the end was exactly what I was looking for.

Nothing more, nothing less.

"You won't screw it up," she says sternly. "Don't let yourself. You're stronger than you give yourself credit for. You won't let your mind take over."

"You're too young to be so wise."

"This will be his first relationship, so you'll work at it together.

Who cares about all the other stuff? Your past is in the past. Keep it there."

She's right.

It doesn't matter if we start later in life or have had many partners. If we're both committed to making it work, it should be all that matters.

"Shit. Shit, shit, shit," Lola grits, breaking me out of my thoughts.

I instantly sit up, on high alert. "What's wrong?"

"Not that I want to burst your Jackson bubble—trust me—but I should tell you, Victoria is sniffing around again. I just got an email from one of our clients who I'm close with, and she said Victoria reached out to her."

"What the actual fucking fuck!" I snap. "What is wrong with this girl? I know she's a lot younger and needs to learn the business, but I'm so sick of her unprofessional shit. People are going to catch on soon. And why is she singling me out? I've never done anything to her except be her competition."

This is exactly what happens when you're barely thirty and running your own business without knowing zilch about how to do so. She only started it because she had nothing else to do with her inheritance.

"Do you think it's because of Sadie?"

I crinkle my face, confused. "What do you mean?"

"You know Victoria has always wanted Wills. So, maybe because of the upcoming wedding, her jealousy is at an all-time high, and the only way to act out is to hurt Sadie's best friend if she can't get to Sadie herself."

I think on it for a second."That would be so insane. What respectable adult would do something like that?"

Lola huffs. "Can we even call her respectable?"

I look down at my phone. "Aha, coincidentally, Sadie is beeping in on the other line. I haven't spoken to her properly since we arrived. Investigate more, and we'll speak soon."

"You going to tell her about Jackson?"

I pause. "No. This needs to stay a secret. Who even knows what *this* is yet? Just because we're best friends doesn't mean we're compatible. I'll talk to you later."

Lola snickers and says, "Yeah… okay, *Mrs. Peters*," and ends the call before I can protest.

I'm going to kill her, I think as I answer Sadie's call.

"You're on holiday. You're not meant to call me, my darling girl," I answer in greeting, both of us knowing it's a joke. This weekend is the longest we've gone without speaking on the phone in our whole lives, and it's only been a few days.

"I know." She sniggers. "So… I'm assuming you knew about the house?"

"I did. Do you like it? Are you there now?"

"Do I like it?" She yells it so loudly, I might have permanent hearing loss in my right ear.

"All right there, killer, take it down a notch."

"Oh shh, I can't help but be excited. I don't *like* it. I freaking love it. It's beyond amazing, and I didn't expect this even in my wildest dreams."

I can't help but laugh at her surprise. "You're telling me you're surprised? The man is utterly infatuated with you, and his love language is giving, so you better get used to it. It seems like you may have a lifetime of them coming your way."

She breathes a deep sigh. "I know. I never want him to think that I take any of it for granted."

I take off my heels and pull on the folded blanket Jack had placed outside for me earlier during dinner, getting comfortable. All the while, I talk to my soul sister and take in the most beautiful city and Eiffel Tower views.

"I don't know how I got so lucky, but I can't wait to marry this man. I know he's already mine, but I want to take the last name of my girls officially, and—" she cuts herself off.

"Are you crying?"

"Uh-huh." She sniffs. "I can't help it. You know that," she mumbles.

Everyone in my life has been so sensitive lately. Including me.

Maybe Mercury is in retrograde, because I can't explain it any other way.

"Oh, trust me, I know it, my Sensitive Sadie. But, hey, I'm going to hang up and FaceTime you. I want to see you."

"Good idea."

The phone cuts off, then rings once before her beautiful face fills the screen. God, she looks so freaking happy right now. It's filling my heart up to the max to see my girl so fulfilled.

"Oh my God, Belle, why are you crying now?"

I wipe my tears and grin, taking in her happiness once more. "These are good tears, darling. You look so happy, and as much as I give Wills a hard time, I knew from that first night that you were meant to be together, and that's saying something because I don't believe in that love-at-first-sight crap."

She rolls her eyes. "Please, you wanted me to have a one-night stand, not marry him."

"Okay, that's a fair point. You were coming off a breakup, and you know what I say—"

"Yes, yes, I know. To get over is to get under," she says, faking a British accent.

I shrug unapologetically. "I mean, it's the only way. Sex is good—no, better than good. It's the best, most exhilarating feeling in the world, and it's the only way to get over a man, in my opinion."

She grins and looks at me warmly. "I love you, Annabelle. You and your slightly slutty ways."

"Oh! Look." I turn the screen around so she can see the view of the Eiffel Tower sparkling. It does this on the hour, every hour, starting at dusk. "Doesn't get old, does it? No matter how many times we see it."

"No, it doesn't," she says dreamily. "I can't wait to take pictures this weekend with it in the distance."

I flip the screen back around, and the second it does, Sadie's eyes are wide with amusement. She slaps her hand over her mouth, letting an uncontrollable giggle spew out.

"What the hell is going on?" I ask.

She points above my head, so I turn around, gawking at him in disbelief.

"B? What the fuck is this?" Jack holds up my huge vibrator by the suction part meant for your clit.

His face is priceless.

"A vibrator, obviously."

"No shit, Sherlock. Why do you have this massive thing with you here… in Paris?"

I shrug.

Isn't it obvious to him?

I probably won't need it anytime soon with how things are going between us, but you always need to be prepared.

Sadie's laughter finally stops enough for her to speak. "Don't you know her motto?"

Jack looks at me, then back to Sadie. "Enlighten me."

"An orgasm a day keeps the doctor away," Sadie sings, but her tune quickly changes to horror when Jack turns it on. "Okay, that was in her vagina. Can you put that down?" She shivers in disgust.

Jack looks at me, smirking and wiggling his eyebrows.

"Okay, you two," Sadie yells. "Enough."

"Prude," I snort.

"I am not a prude. I don't see the need to put it all out in the open… or for my brother to play with something you stick up your private parts."

I smirk. She's flustered, and I can't help but egg her on. "I don't stick it up, I only use it on the outside. I've never had an orgasm from penetration. I only—"

"Okay! Shut the hell up or I'm hanging up," she cries, placing her hands over her ears.

I glance up at Jack and see that his jaw is snapped shut, his hungry eyes glaring at me.

"What?" I whisper, putting the phone on mute.

Wordlessly, he walks over to my side of the sofa and sits down, pulling my feet onto his lap.

In a punishing grip, he grabs my ankle and grinds my foot against his cock.

It's rock solid.

"At least I'll get one of your firsts," he mutters darkly, seemingly lost to the feeling of me practically wanking him off with my foot.

Why is this turning me on so much?

Nerves dance in my stomach. "What first?" I breathe.

He gives me a slow, cheeky smile. "Your first orgasm from penetration. You haven't experienced Jackson Peters to his full potential, and I'm going to fuck you so good you'll forget what it was like before."

Fuck.

"Hello!" Sadie yells.

Jeez, I forgot I put her on mute.

"Sorry," I squeak, all breathless.

Jack laughs sardonically, knowing the effect he has on me while he looks cool, calm, and collected—even with a raging hard-on tenting his sweatpants.

I take a deep breath in.

Calm the fuck down, Annabelle.

God, all I'm thinking about is climbing in his lap and letting him do exactly what he wants with me.

Jack lets go of my ankle, grabs my phone, and smiles at his sister like everything is normal.

Nothing is normal.

Luckily, though, over the next hour, we're easily distracted, talking to the girls before bedtime and listening to Sadie prattle off details of this weekend as if we haven't been part of the planning all along.

Jack tenses below my feet, and I turn a questioning look toward him.

Sadie must realize it too. "What's wrong?" she calls, panicking at his stricken face.

He silently hands me his phone, and my stomach drops when I read the texts.

"Mum fell," I say, reading Theo's messages.

I can't believe it. She was doing so well.

"Oh my god, Belle, is she okay? I'll have Wills call for the jet. We'll be there first thing, and then you can leave in the morning. There might even be a late train you can catch now if you wanted."

"I-I…" I feel uneasy, not sure what I should do. Theo says to stay here and he'll take care of it, but I should tend to my mum. "Okay, yeah… I'll go in the morning."

Jack shakes his head, then takes his phone back, typing away. "I'm talking to Theo and Oliver. You're going to stay and enjoy yourself. She's already leaving the hospital; there's nothing you can do now."

"Jack," I caution lightly. He just doesn't understand.

Wait, did he say *Oliver*?

Oliver, my youngest brother, is typically MIA, so I'm surprised he was there to help.

"I get it, B, but your brothers have it. They aren't kids anymore; let them take the responsibility for once. It can't always be you and Matthew. If they say it's bad tomorrow, or you feel like your mom needs you after you call her, I'll get us home to her as fast as I can."

I nod, mollified for now.

He's right. If it's just a fall, she should be okay.

"She's drinking again?" Sadie whispers hesitantly.

It's not something I want to admit, but Sadie understands my mum's heartache and that I'll never blame her for the path she took, knowing all the pain she has been through.

She truly loved my dad. She often said he was the other part of her soul.

"She hasn't in a long time. She's been coming to yoga with me and even on runs in the park. It took her longer than she would've liked to get her life together, but she's been truly happy lately." *Until today.* "Theo said they were out to lunch and my dad walked right by the table… with my aunt. I guess we finally got our answer after all these years that they stayed together. I can't blame her. Can you imagine what she was feeling?" God, my poor mum. "You know, Theo was the one that took her drinking the hardest. He said he didn't even try to stop her. Almost wanted to join her."

Sadie's eyes go wide, covering her mouth to hide her shock. "Did your dad see your mom?"

"Theo said he was positive they both did. I'm more shocked that he stood by my mum's side and didn't cause a scene. You know what a hothead he can be. He's worse than this bloke's been—" I motion to Jack but he ignores me, still talking to my brothers on his phone.

"God, I'm so sorry, Belle. Can you tell your mom I'm thinking of her? I can have Eleanor stop by, if that would make you feel better. Did you know they had lunch together recently?"

I shake my head. "Mum didn't mention it. That would be nice if she did. I'll let you know tomorrow if I head back or not."

"Okay, whatever you need."

It's wonderful that Eleanor and Mum went out together.

Eleanor is Wills's mum, a badass, strong, independent woman. I think it'll be good for Mum to hang around her, considering it was hard for her to meet new friends that didn't know my dad after the affair.

"All right, I hear Mr. Grumpy downstairs calling my name. The girls must have gone down easier for him than I thought. I'll get going." She pauses and looks back and forth between where Jack and me are cuddling. "You guys look good together."

"Sadie," I scold.

She smirks. "Love you guys, bye."

And this is why I told Lola to keep it a secret for now. Too many people would be invested in our relationship, and that's not how I want this to play out.

I want no interference.

If I'm going to take a chance on this, we need to do it without a million voices in our ears.

Jack hugs me closer to his chest. "Hmmm," he purrs. "We do look good together, don't we?"

Jackson

It's been four days since we arrived in Paris, and I'm not wasting another day without Belle as mine.

This past weekend was the icebreaker… Sure, we've known each other our whole lives, but once you speak up and cross the line, everything changes. We needed time to adjust.

Our usual flirtation means so much more now.

Yesterday was our first kiss, our first *real* kiss, and today I plan on making it our first date.

I've been patient, but I'm done waiting. Finito. Finished.

My dick is also done.

Sleeping pressed up against the sexiest body in the entire world with my arms wrapped around my favorite pair of tits every night is sending my poor guy into a frenzy.

I've never had so much restraint in my life.

Nora once told us how Declan was perpetually hard and couldn't get it down no matter what he did, so I texted him asking if I could die of blue balls.

All I got was the middle-finger emoji.

Declan Buckley… a man of few words.

I have the best night planned, so hopefully I'll be able to resolve my dilemma down below.

We're having dinner at her favorite restaurant, one that's almost impossible to get a reservation at. After that, I have tickets to an underground jazz club, followed by dancing, since that's usually all she cares about.

She could dance for hours, given the opportunity.

I'll let her think I'm giving her a choice, but either way, the date is happening; she wants it just as much as I do. So if she's not going to come right out and say it, I'll decide for both of us.

The answer is yes, one way or the other.

I crawl onto the bed, climbing in behind her as she naps after her busy morning. More drama is going down with the wedding planner, and she's trying to handle her without alerting Wills and Sadie—or me, for that matter.

"I know you're up, sweetheart. Roll over," I whisper against her ear, silently thinking I need to buy Wills a thank-you gift for forcing us to stay in the same room this week.

She rolls over and yawns, her hair wild like Medusa and her face scrunched in fury. “I wasn’t awake until you crawled on the bed,” she rasps, then cuddles into my chest.

I wrap my arms around her toned stomach, resting my chin atop her head.

“B?” I whisper.

“Mmm?”

“Will you go on a date with me tonight? I’d like to take you out to dinner and then for some live music.”

“Oh—” She hesitates.

Hearing her question my proposition instantly annoys me, considering she’s on one every other night with strangers.

She tries to get out of bed. However, I’m not letting her leave my sight until I have the answer I want.

“Jack!” she squeals. “I need to use the loo.” I ignore her and crawl on top of her, trapping her in with my arms so she can’t go anywhere.

“Will you please go on a date with me, sweetheart?” I lean down and kiss her lips softly. “I’m not asking for anything more. Just some time with my best girl. Give us a chance, Belle.”

She gulps down her unease, her eyes flickering to my lips every few seconds.

She leans up, and just as her lips brush against mine, the little minx tickles my side, using the opportunity to slip under me.

“Annabelle!”

She pauses at the bathroom door and winks, adding a small smile of defiance. “Of course I’ll go out with you, Jack. I only wanted you to work for it a little.”

The night has been nothing short of incredible.

After the rain stopped, we strolled hand in hand down the Seine, then through the small streets of Saint Germain toward the restaurant.

At first, I was surprised at Belle suggesting the walk, considering she’s wearing heels tall enough to bring her up to my height.

Though that didn't stop my fierce queen B, strutted down those Parisian cobblestone streets like she owned them.

She insisted we see the city like this—right after it rains when the water glistens from the city lights.

We laughed, we talked, we kissed.

So carefree and easy, though it's not a surprise. It's always been like that with Belle.

It still amazes me that it took us as long as it did to get our heads out of our asses and put our insecurities aside to make this work.

Over the last few days, I've had more time to think about a future with Belle and why I'm so adamant now.

For one, I don't see a reason to wait. Ever since it clicked with me, it's all I can see.

We're older and know everything about each other—the good and the bad. The foundation is there.

Not to mention, this last year has had my head spinning like crazy since we got "married," and although I'm well aware it was a drunken accident, the idea of Belle as my wife has always felt right.

I wasn't lying when I told her I felt like something was missing when we came home from Vegas, and I'll do whatever it takes to prove it to her.

My phone vibrates inside my suit pocket, snapping me back to the present.

I should check it to ensure it's not Belle's brothers or my sister, but I don't have the will.

I've yet to tell Belle my dad's been emailing me, after twenty years of no contact aside from maybe five words when Charlotte was born.

And if I'm being realistic, we probably said five words the twenty years prior.

When my dad checked out of being a parent, it did a number on me, and it will only worry Belle if she knows.

I can't have that.

I need everything to go in my favor so that when we leave here and head home to London, we can genuinely make a go at this with no distractions.

"How did you know I love this place?" Belle smiles and takes a sip of her pinot noir. I note the way her eyes flutter in pleasure and make a mental note that it's her new favorite and preferred choice of wine.

I look at her, confused. "You've told me many times, and I remember everything you tell me."

"Oh." She blushes innocently, and my dick jumps at attention.

This is a side of Belle I don't often see, and her little innocent act turns me on like never before.

"Well, thank you, it was delicious. Did you enjoy yours?"

"Mmhmm." I lean back and cross my arms, my gaze never leaving her face. "Not the only delicious thing here tonight."

Her eyes brighten with interest, and it feels like time stops as we stare at each other.

I push her water toward her. "Drink," I demand. We've had too many drinks as it is, and the night is still young."

She pops her brow in disbelief at my tone but drinks it anyway. The fact she actually followed a command from me only causes my dick to swell even more, pressing uncomfortably against my pants.

"You're beautiful, B." I rake my eyes along her body and over her face.

She's going for the sex-goddess look tonight. Her long blonde hair is pin-straight, parted down the middle, and her eyes are dark and smokey, making her baby blues beam across the table.

My heartbeat hammers in my ears as she slowly stands up.

What is she doing?

Our eyes are locked, and arousal pumps through the air with each step she takes.

"I'll be back," she whispers seductively, then runs the tips of her fingers along my forearm, trailing them up my bicep.

She leans down, and I almost miss her full lips pressing against mine because my hungry eyes are glued to the deepened V of her blouse.

Why the fuck did I plan anything after this dinner?

My priorities have changed, and I need to get her back to the hotel and into bed.

Taking a deep, tortured breath to calm myself, I shift my focus to the spectacular floor-to-ceiling windows and away from ravaging Belle right here in this restaurant.

We're lucky enough that the restaurant is on the top floor of a hotel, giving us 360-degree views of the city. I might as well take it all in while I can.

To my left is the Eiffel Tower, and I can make out the gold-leafed dome of l'Hôtel des Invalides, where Napoleon is buried. To my right, the French flag flies high on top of the Grand Palais.

Straight ahead is… You've got to be kidding me right now.

God dammit.

Out of all the places he could be, Trey walks into this restaurant with a massive group of people.

I watch them get seated, hoping they won't be in view, but luck is not on our side tonight, so I flag down the waitress and pay before Belle gets back.

God, I hate that fucking prick.

I promised Belle and John I wouldn't let him get to me anymore, so we need to get the hell out of here as quickly as possible.

Of course, Belle times it perfectly, walking back to the table just as I'm settling up.

Her brow furrows. "We're leaving?"

I stand and take her hand, pulling her toward the exit. "Yes, sweetheart. It's getting late. We can grab dessert at the jazz club."

She narrows her eyes and pulls me to a stop. "What's the real reason? I can tell when you're worried. Your eyebrows always dip down when you are."

Do they?

I nod toward the corner. Her body tenses for a brief second before she pulls back her shoulders and stands tall, getting into character.

This is the Annabelle the world sees, completely different from *my Belle*.

"We can stay." She looks back at me. "We should. Why does he get to be here?"

I shake my head, not agreeing. "Honestly, B, I don't want to be here. If you want to stay, we can, of course. But I'd rather leave."

"Jackson?" I turn and am shocked to see Anna, a girl I've occasionally hooked up with, walking into the restaurant.

Someone who Belle hates with a passion.

9

Jackson

*F*UCK.

Belle grips my hand, cutting off my circulation as she stands as tall and still as a statue.

What I thought started out as the perfect date is slowly turning into a nightmare.

It takes a lot for Annabelle Hughes to get rattled, but Anna has always gotten under Belle's skin.

It all started when we were younger.

Annabelle's nickname used to actually be *Anna*, only sometimes using Belle. But the day I kissed this Anna for the first time in the pool was the last time we were ever allowed to call Belle by that name.

I only realized it because I overheard my sister talking about it, which of course made me feel like a piece of shit. I brushed it off as a small crush from my sister's best friend.

What the hell did I know back then?

I barely realized I had a crush on Belle myself until I got older, and it was then that I realized Belle's never went away.

It didn't help that my kiss with Anna didn't stop there either. It became an every-summer occurrence when she came to the Hamptons from Italy.

She was an easy hookup, and as a teenage boy who only wanted to fuck around, it was perfect.

Then when I moved to London, she lived there as well, and we quickly realized we ran in the same circles.

I never wanted monogamy or a commitment; she was happy with that for a while.

Until she wasn't, and that was the end of it.

Though, she was the only woman I ever kept around for longer than a month, and now I see that's what Belle hated the most.

"Hey." I plaster on a grin, trying to be polite.

She startles me by leaning in and hugging me tight, and by the time I pull back, Belle has already ripped her hand away from mine.

Anna looks between us, and her face grows serious. "Are you two together?" I don't miss how she doesn't say hi to Belle.

"We are," I state confidently, hoping Annabelle doesn't fight me on it.

Instead, it's worse. She doesn't say a word. She just looks between Anna and me and then turns to leave.

I don't get a chance to say goodbye to Anna as I instinctively turn and run out of the restaurant after Belle.

The ride in the lift is silent and uncomfortable, filled with tension I don't know how to handle.

When we step out onto the street, I take Belle by the hand and pull her toward our waiting car. "Let's just forget about her and continue our night. I have lots planned." I smile and try to shrug off the last ten seconds.

"Not happening," she deadpans.

I stop walking and pull her so she faces me. "Belle." I sigh. "You make it seem like I planned to run into her; I don't want this to ruin the night."

She rips her hand from mine again and crosses her arms. "Consider it ruined, and you might not have planned it, but this is our *first* date, and we aren't even in London. The second we're back home, we'll be swarmed by all the women you've fucked," she snaps.

Fuck this. Now I'm pissed.

"Did you forget your ex was there too, someone I want to kill? Someone you dated for *three* fucking years. And you're worried about my ex?"

She stills, and her face drops. "Ex?" she whispers. "You've told me multiple times you and Anna were nothing more than a hookup."

God dammit, this is so fucked. I rub my hands down my face in frustration. "Wrong choice of words. I've never been in a relationship before. I've never wanted to be in one until you, but you can't blame me for what happened back there. Because *nothing* happened."

I've done everything to show her how much I care for her, and with one quick run-in, she freaks out.

What the hell is that about?

"Fuck, Annabelle. What do I need to do? I can't go back in time. If I could, I would. I would forgo all my bachelor days if I knew we would be together in the end. But I can't. Are you going to be able to get over the fact that I have a past? And I'm not trying to be a dick, but so do you. There could be a good chance we run into one of your hookups, too, not just Trey. So before you judge me, think about it for a fucking second. Please!" I can't catch my breath… The more I think about how she fled the scene, the angrier I get.

I wanted tonight to be perfect, to show her I could be the person she's always wanted.

How the fuck do I do that if she won't let me in?

I look up and can see my words have affected her. "Let's just go." I sigh.

She doesn't move toward the car with me. Instead, she looks like she's fighting some internal battle with herself.

I don't have the energy anymore. "Come on. I don't want to be standing on the street any longer."

She shakes her head vigorously. "No. Let's forget all that. I would really like it if you could take me on the rest of our date now, please?" She holds out her hand in a gesture of… hope, maybe?

I know I should say yes. She's asking for a clean slate from tonight. But, honestly, I'm tired.

I'm tired of trying to prove myself—not just now, but in general. It's felt like an uphill battle my whole life.

I'm done.

I smile sadly. "Another time. I'm not feeling up to it anymore."

Holding the car door open, I motion for her to get in. She hesitates, then nods, knowing I won't change my mind.

We're quiet the whole ride back to the hotel, and once we get back in the room, you could cut the tension with a knife. I know she's champing at the bit to talk. I can see her brain racing a million miles a minute, but I'm done talking for the night.

While she gets ready for bed, I turn off my lamp and close my eyes, wishing for it to be tomorrow so we can start again.

I'm not mad at her, I'm just disappointed she gave up so quickly.

And it hurts.

The bed dips, and I feel her cuddle close to me. Usually, I'm the one turning to cuddle her.

She slips one arm under my neck and places the other around my chest, squeezing me into a tight embrace.

She kisses my neck and whispers, "I'm sorry. Goodnight, Jack."

Unable to help myself, I wrap my arms around hers and intertwine our fingers. Then I lift her hand and kiss the inside of her wrist.

"Night, sweetheart."

Annabelle

Jackson's arm shoots out, trying to find me in his sleep. When he comes up empty-handed, he slowly opens his eyes, first scowling, then confused when he sees me sitting there wide-eyed, waiting for him to wake up.

He turns his head toward the clock and whispers, "What the fuck," when he sees it's half past five in the morning.

"What's going on? Why are you awake, staring down at me like that?" His voice rasps, low and deep.

"Can you sit up please?" I whisper.

He quickly obeys, and from the concerned look on his face, he's aware of the vulnerability in my voice. So, without questioning my odd behavior, he sits up, letting the blankets fall to his waist, causing me to stagger slightly at his exposed chest.

God, get it together, Annabelle. We have more important things to talk about.

I walk into the other room, grab a robe for myself, and pick up the tray with Jack's coffee and croissant that I ordered a little while ago, knowing his cranky arse needs breakfast before we talk.

And we have *a lot* to talk about.

Last night should have never happened as it did, and I couldn't sleep a wink because of it. I acted like an immature fool, and I hate myself for ruining our first date.

A date I have waited my whole life for, yet still let my insecurities get in the way of.

I'm the bloody CEO of a successful business, yet I'm emotionally stunted in every way.

Although I'm grown, mature, and confident in almost all areas of my life, my level of security when it comes to relationships is where I struggle, and that's what I'll try to remember as I explain myself to Jack this morning.

The sun is starting to peek up through the horizon as I place the tray down and open the curtains to let the tiny sliver of light in.

Crawling across the bed, I throw my hair into a messy bun and sit criss-cross in front of Jack, ready to apologize for last night.

He eyes me suspiciously but stays silent while he drinks his coffee, so I take it as an opportunity to begin.

"Jack… I screwed up last night," I mutter, rubbing my hands up and down my thighs. *This is harder than I thought, and I've only said a few words*. "I couldn't sleep at all once we got home, knowing I might have ruined everything we haven't even had a chance to explore yet. What amazingness could be between us, and I'm so sorry for that. I was wrong in blaming you, to take away a real fighting chance for the two of us. It wasn't fair to you. It wasn't fair to us." I take a deep breath in, then exhale to calm myself.

Jack's face is impassive as he listens, and he hasn't said a word, which is concerning since I can't read him.

I can always read him.

I bite my lip and look toward the window to gather the rest of my thoughts, hating myself for being so weak when it comes to expressing my emotions.

Without looking back, I continue, "We've both been through so much in our lives already, yet this is a first for me. Caring for someone enough that it scares me half to death… enough that I'd sabotage it, even though it could possibly be the best thing to ever happen to me." I pause. "I'm not just scared of this. I'm bloody prettified, Jack. I don't want this to fuck things up between us, because I need you more as my mate than as a lover. The thought of not having you at all is terrifying. It's one of the reasons why I've never tried for more with you in the past… well, besides—"

I hear rustling around on the bed and break off, watching as Jack places the tray of food on the floor.

He sits back up, still wordless, and startles me as he leans forward to grab me by my waist. He pulls me in and maneuvers me, turning my body so I can face him.

His eyes lock on mine fiercely. "Besides what?"

As casually as I can manage, I explain that I'm nervous about his life catching up to him… to us.

"Jealousy with this much intensity is new to me. I won't lie and pretend that I haven't been a bit jealous of the women you've been with ever since… Anna." I shrug, embarrassed. "But it was manageable. And I'm not sitting here trying to say I think you'd cheat or deceive me in any way. I trust you, Jack. Although, sometimes, that's not enough when you have deep-rooted issues like I do. And I hate that for us. We're too old for bullshit, and I should be stronger, but I don't know how to control it."

He leans forward again, this time pulling my legs onto his lap. "My beautiful B." He cups my cheek, holding my stare for a beat before he whispers, "I'm not your dad, Annabelle. You can trust me. If you remember that, we can get through anything together. I promise you with all my heart that I will never hurt you, I will never leave you, I will always be your friend. I will do all I can to be the person you deserve. Someone I wish I could have been for you many years ago."

I cast my eyes down, breathing deeply as immense emotions run through me.

He knows how much those words mean to me… I've always needed reassurance and stability.

The world only sees one part of me—the outgoing, party-loving Annabelle. But Jack knows it all… well, almost all. There's still one thing I keep close to my heart, hidden from sight.

But besides that, he's been there for it all.

"Hey, look at me," he murmurs.

I slowly lift my gaze, taking in his beautiful face. After all these years, I'm still awed by the feeling I get deep down whenever I'm around him.

"I know you're not my dad, Jack. I do, and I loathe that he's still impacting my life in these ways. Why did he have to fuck me up so badly? Why couldn't it have been anyone else to have seen him in bed with my aunt?" I cry.

His face drops at my words. "I don't have the answers you're looking for, sweetheart. I wish you hadn't watched it. I wish that upon no one, not even my worst enemy. It's a terrible thing to have witnessed, especially at a young age, but don't let his deceit dictate your life." He wipes away the few tears of frustration I've let escape my eyes before he continues.

"I know I'm not one to talk. I've let my parents, *my dad*, hinder my life as well. After being rejected as a son, I never wanted to feel let down again, so I went without a meaningful romantic relationship because of it. My parents and your dad are the screwed-up ones, yet we're paying the price. It's not fair, but many things in life aren't, so from here on out, let's try to move on and consciously make decisions for our future that will only better us."

He stops to stare at me for a second while I sit here speechless.

"Let's choose better… let's choose us. After years of thinking I was broken and unfixable, I see now that I was only waiting for you to put me back together. Two people with broken, jagged souls finding their exact fit to become whole again is pretty rare and unbelievable, don't you think?"

My heart stops and my eyes fill with tears as I throw myself onto his chest. "Oh my God, Jack," I croak, snuggling in close, needing the comfort of his arms.

His words are beautiful, and although I can't express my feelings right now, I hope that with my touch, he can feel everything I'm trying to say.

"We both probably need to see a therapist. Who the hell knows? We're pretty fucked up." He chuckles, trying to lighten the mood, and it makes me smile the way he can always turn a situation around.

After composing myself and my wildly beating heart, I lean back and look into those mesmerizing green eyes. "You're so special to me, Jack. I should have trusted that when you said you wanted to give this a try, you would give it your all."

His face perks up. "What are you saying, B?"

This is all new to me, but I'm letting go of all my inhibitions and allowing my fractured heart to lead the way… Jack has all my pieces in the palm of his hand. What he does with them next is one of my biggest fears in life.

But it's time to start trusting.

Otherwise, it will never work between us, and if he can let go of his past, the only way I have a fighting chance to do the same is with him by my side.

"I'm saying… I choose better. I choose us." I gulp down my emotions. "I want you to take me on a date tonight. I want a redo of last night. I—" I break off, knowing the next thing I say will drive him insane in the best way possible. "I want my husband to take me on a proper date."

"Oh, thank fuck!" He pushes the covers aside and hauls me onto his lap. Smooshing my face with his hands, he presses his lips against mine, kissing me hard and relentlessly.

His hands trail down my body, gripping my waist to grind my core against his impressive hard-on.

"Take your shirt off," he mutters against my lips.

"What's the rush," I pant. "Shouldn't we at least have one date, try to give it our all before we"—I waggle my eyebrows—"you know what."

"Not happening. I don't do things in halves, B. Well, I might bend you in half while I fuck the shit out of you, but my *all* includes my dick that's been hard for days on end now." He smirks.

"Put those dimples away, you cheeky bastard." I shake my head, trying to hold back my smile. "You're a born romantic, Jack."

I still my hips—*or try to*. He's too strong and on a mission. "You didn't let me finish before. I have something else to say."

He rolls his eyes. "We can talk later… less chatting, more kissing."

I swat at his hands, deflecting them as they attempt to cup my boobs.

Horny wanker.

"I want this to work between us, Jack, so because of that, I don't want to tell anyone about us."

His eyes widen in surprise. "Why the hell not? We're perfect for one another, and I want to shout it to the world."

"Jack." I sigh. "First off, I don't want to bring this up during Sadie's wedding weekend. She deserves all the attention to be on her and Wills, no one else. Plus, there will be so many expectations, questions, and concerns around our relationship, and you know it. Don't you want to figure this out together, you and me… no one else in our ears asking how things are going every two seconds? I know I want that. I only want to do this if it's you and me. Then after we get home to London, we can reassess."

"I should let you know that Declan knows I'm pursuing you."

"Pursuing me? More like railroading me." I laugh so he knows I'm kidding.

"More like railing you." Then he mutters, "Or about to," and we both laugh together.

"Well, I guess then I should tell you that Lola knows, too." I smirk, and he rolls his eyes.

"So what you're saying is everyone knows except my sister and Wills?"

"And Nora, Marco, and Evelyn."

He squeezes my hip bones a few times, thinking. "All right, it's a secret *for now*. Once we get home though, we're figuring this out, because like I told you, I don't do things in halves. If we're together, we're together."

I lean over and press my lips to his. "Okay, deal," I say, and not a second later, I'm crying out as Jack has me in the air, flipping positions so I'm on my back.

"Now, no more talking unless it's you crying out my name. Got it?"

So bossy. "Got it," I moan as he grinds himself into me, only teasing, and now I'm feeling as crazed as him.

Jack rips open my robe and stills. "Who wears this much clothes under a robe? I need them off, right this second," he says, pointing down at my pajama set.

After he leans back, I shimmy out of the robe, and he undoes the buttons of my pajamas, letting the top open and fall to the sides. His eyes widen and roam every inch of me, licking his lips in appreciation.

"Annabelle… *fuck*," he whispers to himself, then reaches forward with both hands, cupping and massaging my breasts with such rapt attention he seems lost in awe. Jack's been a boob man for as long as I can remember.

With each caress, it sends a deep shiver through my body and sparks of arousal straight to my…

Oh god.

He pinches my nipple, then leans over to drag his tongue along the tips of each one. I've never felt anything like this before.

"Belle," he growls. "These tits are fucking amazing. God, I could hold them like this all day." He runs his hands back up and over my boobs, rubbing the heel of his palm with deep pressure along my already hard nipples before cupping and squeezing tight.

Oh. My. God.

That feels amazing.

"I'm going to make you come like this one day. Playing with these pert pink nipples for hours until you can't take it anymore," he mutters, "Jesus, I feel crazed thinking of all the things I want to do with you, every way I want to have you."

I look down and see the head of his swollen, angry-looking dick is poking out of his briefs. "Naked, Jack, you need to be naked," I croak.

He stills. The air crackles around us, deep arousal thick in the air, as our eyes meet. "This is happening."

I nod with wide eyes, biting my lip. "It is."

He's so sexy. It's unreal.

When he stands up to take his briefs off, my eyes roam his tight and toned muscular chest, which is sculpted to perfection from his intense workouts. Tiny beads of perspiration begin to form against his skin, and all I can think about is licking each one off of him.

I let my eyes linger for another second before glancing down, and *holy shit.*

Was he always this big?

So fucking big… and hard.

He wraps a hand around his dick and slowly strokes himself, and with each labored breath of mine, his pace gets faster, working himself up like no tomorrow.

"Like what you see?" he asks through gritted teeth.

"So, so much," I whisper, then run my hands up my body, needing to be touched. I'm itching for Jack… desperate for him. "What do you want me to do?" I say through a labored breath.

He smiles darkly. "What I really want is for you to crawl over here and suck my cock. I've been dying—"

I cut him off with my eager nod. "God, yes, let me suck you off."

He shakes his head. "Trust me, sweetheart, all I've ever wanted was those plump lips on me, but I'll blow in zero point two seconds, so for now…" he trails off as he crawls on top of me. "I'm going to need you to get on top and ride the fuck out of me because I won't be able to hold on any other way."

"Okay." I melt into the bed when he licks up my clavicle, sucking at the sensitive part of my neck.

"So submissive," he says as he bites down.

"I submit to no one," I moan, letting the lie split through my lips, knowing I would do anything Jack wants right now.

He pushes my legs apart, then teases the inside of my thigh as he slowly creeps his fingers up toward my center, causing a wave of goose bumps to scatter along my skin before he swipes his fingers through my swollen, wet flesh.

"Ahh," I cry. I'm so sensitive.

"Oh, sweetheart, I beg to differ. You're made to be submissive, but just for me, do you understand?"

"Yes," I breathe without hesitation. *I'm all his.*

"Your body is in charge now, baby. Just how I like it," he growls, then impales me with two fingers. I cry out in pleasure as my back arches off the bed, and my hips begin to rotate with every pump of his hand, chasing a high that's coming on too fast and too quick.

He adds a third, then his thumb reaches over to rub my clit, and that's it.

I'm done for.

Looking at Jack, touching Jack, him touching me…

It's all too much, and with his thick fingers rubbing along my G-spot and his other on my clit, my body starts convulsing, shaking in the bed as my orgasm rips through me.

"Jackson," I scream.

Holy shit… this man. *He's everything.*

He smiles broadly, pleased with himself, as he withdraws his fingers from my soaking core. Then, he places them in his mouth, slowly sucking off my arousal.

That shouldn't be as hot as it is.

"Delicious," he moans, then rolls over, pulling me with him.

As I straddle him, his eyes darken with an appreciation only Jack could give me.

I go still… taking it all in before I make a move.

His brows draw together in concern. "What's wrong?"

I shrug, embarrassed. "I know we've done this before, but it's finally hitting me. This time is different."

His lips curve up. "So different. Come here and kiss me, sweetheart."

I lean over, shuddering slightly as my sensitive clit rubs against his dick, and press my lips to his.

Jack reaches around and rubs soothing circles along my back as his tongue slides through my parted lips, caressing me with perfect strokes.

Our kiss turns frantic and desperate as he grabs hold of his dick and places it at my entrance. He leans back, lifting a brow in question, and I know he's asking if we should use a condom or not. Jack would never even entertain it if he hadn't been recently tested, so I shake my head, and his nose flares. "Put me inside of you, baby," he grits out.

He holds it up for me, so I wrap my hand around his thick, long cock, and guide myself down onto it, and… oh god.

The burn.

"Wiggle side to side," he growls.

"Jackson," I moan as the head of his dick slips inside me. "This isn't my first rodeo. I'm well aware of the practices of easing a big dick inside me."

A deep growl rumbles from the depths of his chest. "Mention another dick inside of you—no, scratch that. Mention another dick at all, and you'll pay."

"Don't be such a caveman." I laugh.

He grabs my hips and halts my movement. "I'm not kidding, Annabelle. It makes me fucking murderous. Not another mention of it, or I'll stop this all right now."

I look into his eyes and clearly see he's not kidding. "That would punish both of us."

"If punishment is what I need to remind myself what a fool I was that I didn't get my act together sooner to have you and this hot as hell body, then yeah, I'll easily punish myself."

He takes my hips and pulls me down, impaling me in one movement. "Fuck!" he cries. "Not another word."

"Oh my god, Jack," I breathe heavily, mouth gaping open as I try to adjust to him. "Are you kidding?"

He gives me a cocky shrug. "Punishment," he deadpans.

Oh, he's in big trouble.

I give myself a second to adjust, then without easing into it, I lift my bottom and roll my hips, picking up the pace in a hurried speed. I can tell by his labored breathing he's already close, and if he wants to punish me… it might be fun to do it right back.

"So tight… shit, go slower," he cries, but his hands on my hips are saying something completely different, grinding me down hard against him. He scrunches up his eyes, biting his bottom lip.

"I've never felt anything better than this. Do you know that?" he grinds out. "Look at me."

I glance down so our eyes meet, and my heart flutters at the intensity.

Something new passes between us, a look, a feeling of the deeper connection we're building together.

"I do know that," I whisper. "This is amazing, Jack. It's everything."

His grip on my hips tightens, moving me up and down, gliding his shaft along every sensitive area inside me.

His mouth is open in pleasure and his eyes continuously move between me and my boobs. Our breathing is loud and labored, and if he reached up to touch me right now, I would shatter in a split second.

"Fuck, I can't see straight right now." His eyes roll back in his head, then he picks me up and slams me down again and again. *I'm no longer in charge.* Although I'm not sure he is either; we're both losing it. "Your big, beautiful tits are out, bouncing around, making me lose my goddamn mind. I can't even look right now. Otherwise, I'm done for."

I giggle at his dramatics. "Are you kidding?"

"No, I'm not." He thrusts his hips up. "Not even a little bit."

I lean over, pressing them into his face. "You can see them up close if you want… suck them, touch them," I whisper seductively and feel myself clench around him.

I'm so turned on, it feels as if I might combust at any moment.

He moves his head to the side and bites hard on one of my nipples. I throw my head back, yelling aloud at the pain that instantly turns into immense pleasure. He moves his legs up so his feet are placed on the bed and starts bucking into me with deep, powerful thrusts.

He's unrelenting, talented… a complete sex god. And I'm here for all of it.

"You need to come, B. I need you to come again," he grits, then picks up his pace—*if that's even possible*—knocking the air right out of me.

From the position I'm in, my boobs in his face and him pounding into me, I'm able to rub myself against him, and within seconds, a deep burn creeps up my body. I'm debilitated; I can't move. The delicious burn takes over everything.

"Fuck, you're sexy. Look at you," he grunts.

My eyes are closed tight in pleasure and I'm gripping his shoulders as I cry out, feeling the most intense orgasm I've ever had rip through my body. He thrusts up, holding deep each time, and I feel the jerk of his cock and his warm come filling me up as he releases inside me.

My body falls forward, completely slack, unable to move.

That was… everything.

He kisses the top of my head and holds me tight against him, both of us silent for a moment, relishing the moment.

My thoughts are jumbled up; I can barely think straight. All I know is that I'm completely and utterly addicted.

I lean my head up and kiss his jaw. "You're the only one that's ever been inside of me like that," I whisper.

His eyes cast down, confused.

"Without a condom. We didn't use one when we were younger… who knows about Vegas… and now. I've never let anyone else do that."

He squeezes me tight and smiles against my forehead. "I like that much more than I should."

For some reason… I do too.

"And, B." He pauses. "Husbands don't use condoms."

Oh, bloody hell… why do I like the sound of that even more?

10

Annabelle

EVEN THOUGH IT'S only half past eight in the morning, Jack said I had one hour to get ready, claiming our date is a fun-filled day. So I'm in the en suite doing just that, beyond excited.

Of course I'm excited about our date, but more so to spend a day with Jack as *mine*. He has been using the word nonstop, but I can feel it too.

Jackson Peters… mine.

Who would have thought it?

I bounce my shoulders a few times in excitement as I put the finishing touches on my makeup and shimmy around the room to the beats of Swedish House Mafia.

It doesn't matter what time of the day it is. If there is music on, my body is moving to it.

Pulling back my hair, I slick it into a tight ponytail since I haven't washed it for days and fix the flyaways with some of Jack's hair wax.

Perfect.

I walk out into the bedroom, and the music changes to "We Are

The Champions" by Queen. Jack grins at me when my face scrunches up in confusion.

He's lazing on the bed with his arms behind his head, not dressed whatsoever for our date.

"Don't you want to know why this song is on?"

I narrow my eyes. "Not particularly, no. Especially because it's a terrible song."

He scoffs. "The dance music you've been blasting for the last hour is terrible. This is a work of art." He throws his hand up and points to the speaker.

"Okay, Jack. Why are you playing "We Are The Champions"?" I ask dryly, not really caring one way or the other.

I do like Queen, in moderation, but I like to get under his skin about it more… because *who the hell cares about Queen as much as he does?*

He turns up the volume and starts to sing the chorus and… yep. I'm pretty sure he just pointed to his dick.

Oh. My. God.

He did not.

My eyes widen in horror. I think I might die of secondhand embarrassment.

"Turn it off right now." I cover my eyes. "If you ever want me to have sex with you again, stop it. Stop it right now. How you think this is normal is beyond me," I cry from behind my hands.

I shake my head, trying to rid my brain of the last sixty seconds. "Tell me… Why? Actually, don't tell me why. Please don't ever do that again. That was beyond embarrassing. The fact that you just referred to you and your dick as 'we' is semi-alarming."

There must be a handbook somewhere where they tell you *not* to date your best friend, because you skip right over the shy, get-to-know-you stage and start right in the comfortable, don't-hold-back, stage.

If I'm being honest, it's also one of the things I love about Jack. He can easily turn on and turn off the different aspects of his life.

From stoic, hardworking businessman to fun-loving jokester, not afraid to play tea party or get his nails painted with his nieces.

Newly a billionaire, yet doesn't give a crap what anyone thinks, dancing around the room, singing along to 80s rock bands.

He shoots me a cheeky smirk, then slaps my arse. "Anything to do with Queen is not embarrassing. Now get dressed properly. We have a long day ahead of us."

I stop and look down at my outfit. "First off, it's not the song. It's that you pointed at your dick, singing 'we' are the champions."

"*We* got the girl, didn't we?"

My eyes widen in horror. "Stop talking right now. You're digging your grave deeper and deeper as you go on. Secondly, I *am* dressed properly. You said dress casually."

He looks me up and down. "You're wearing a shoe with a heel on it. How do you think that's casual?"

I shrug. "It is for me. You should know this."

He shakes his head, baffled."Do you have any extra workout clothes?"

"You're taking me to work out on our date?" I narrow my eyes, not liking the sound of that.

Our little session this morning was enough of a workout, especially after yesterday when he made me do some crazy boot camp in the gym. My body is still beyond sore.

"Can you stop asking so many questions and answer mine? Do you, yes or no?"

"Yes," I huff.

I like the idea of surprises in theory, however in actuality, they stress me the hell out. I want to know what we're doing at all times. Striding into the walk-in closet, I look to my right into the walled mirror and stop dead in my tracks when I see a mark on my neck.

How did I not see this before?

"Jack!" I yell.

"What?"

"I have a fucking mark on my neck. Are you kidding me!" I peek my head out the door, and I don't think I've ever seen him look happier.

"Do you expect me to be sorry? I already told you. I want everyone to know you're mine."

I bite my lip. "I hate that I love you calling me that."

He waggles his brows. "Good… you didn't have a choice either way." Then he swats my arse again.

What the hell has gotten into him?

"You're lucky my bridesmaid's dress has a high neck," I tell him, thinking maybe the idea of the wedding will give him a reason not to mark me.

But, of course, it doesn't.

If anything, I think I see a small sparkle in his eyes as he turns and walks away.

Jack hands me my to-go cup of coffee, then gets in the car beside me. "Mmmm, this is pretty good. It tastes like the coffee you loved that was close to your old place."

"Ugh, can you believe they closed down? I was so upset. I go to Midnight Mocha now, right off Campden Street, and I hate to say it because I loved the family that owned the other place, but Midnight might be better. They even do this seasonal latte that's lavender honey, and I'm semi-obsessed."

He picks up his phone and starts typing, ignoring me. "What are you doing?" I stretch my neck to see, but he closes his notes app and pockets his phone.

I eye him suspiciously. "What are you hiding?"

"Nothing, give it a rest. How is your mom doing?"

I glare at him another second, then decide to give him a pass, knowing I'm being nosy. "Better. I'm mad she didn't let me come home, but she's in better spirits. I hope Theo can convince her to come to the wedding," I say, and it reminds me. "Speaking of the wedding, how long will we be gone for today? I don't want to leave the wedding planner alone longer than necessary. I think Wills's paranoia is rubbing off on me."

"Sadie will understand either way about your mom, but I'm glad she's doing better. As for the wedding planner, today was the bellhop's day off, so I hired him to keep an eye on her. After you told me it seemed like she was scheming on the phone yesterday, I didn't want to leave her alone either." He pauses. "To be honest. I think that when we get back, we fire her before they arrive. I was able to get the names of all the vendors, so I'll handle it myself if I have to."

I lean back and sigh, knowing he's right. I don't like the feeling that she's doing something shady, but I hope that if we fire her, it won't screw everything up. "Did you know what Wills did for Sadie's flowers?" I ask.

He smirks. "I did, that big softy."

When Wills and Sadie hit a rough patch a few years ago, he apologized in what he likes to call his "apology tour." For one of his apologies, he hired Sadie's favorite florists to fly in to work with her since she had just opened her floral design business, Sweet Pea Blooms.

As a surprise for the wedding, he's hired the same guy to do the florals. Sadie, of course has no idea, so the florist she has been speaking to for the last year, was all a ruse.

It's bloody brilliant, if you ask me. She's going to freak out, she'll be so happy. "He really is a good bloke, that Wills, isn't he?" Jack leans back, nodding, and I pat his leg. "Everything's going to be okay, Jack."

He picks up my hand and kisses my wrist. "I know."

"Oh my god, are you taking me on a helicopter ride for our date?" I bounce up and down in my seat like a little kid as we pull onto the helicopter pad. "I've always wanted to do this but have never had the guts."

Jack looks at me deadpan and states matter-of-factly, "I know. I told you, I know everything about you, B." He leans over and kisses my lips. "It's only part one. Hopefully the second part of the date is something you still want to do. It's not exactly something you can force on someone."

I waggle my eyebrows playfully. "The second part sounds a lot like anal. The date should be better than that."

The driver coughs, and my eyes go wide in embarrassment. I can't believe I just said that, completely forgetting where we were.

Jack chuckles. "Come on, crazy, the pilot is waiting for us."

"Mmm, is it Pilot Miles?" I tease and smirk when he turns to me with a pinched expression.

"Don't even play around like that. I don't find it funny one bit, Annabelle," he grits out, grabbing my hand with force, pulling me toward the helicopter.

I hate to say it, but I'm starting to like this jealous side of his.

I look out the helicopter window, then back to Jack, then back to the window. I'm on such a high right now, and it's all because of the man sitting next to me. "Holy crap, Jack!" I cry through our headsets. "Where are we right now? It's beautiful down there." I grin like a fool, so full of happiness I could explode.

His dimples pop, and his infectious grin has me smiling even wider. "We're landing soon, right near Soulac-Sur-Mer." He points down toward something resembling a town.

"Is part two of this date better than this? I don't know how you're going to top it, because I've always wanted to ride in a helicopter."

He gives me a look. "Again—*I know*."

I laugh at my own enthusiasm, knowing I'm acting ridiculous, but I couldn't care less.

It's a unique and special feeling when you cross items off a bucket list you've had since childhood. In a way, it feels magical, like you've made life that much more remarkable.

Jack takes my hand that's intertwined in his and kisses my wrist, palm, and fingertips. "I hope you think part two is better or equal, because I never want to see that smile disappear. Knowing I played even a small part in making it happen makes it all worth it."

I roll my lips, trying not to get emotional. How does he always manage to say what hits just right?

"You didn't play a small part, Jack. You've starred in making all my dreams come true."

The warmth of his gaze echoes in my heart when he kisses my wrist again.

After getting lost in his emerald depths, he breaks our daze by leaning in and cupping my cheek. "Belle, I—" He pauses, and I see him struggling with his words.

I did that to us, I put up a roadblock, and now he's afraid to cross it.

"You what?" I ask eagerly, hoping the sound of my voice gives him the strength to continue.

I'm almost positive he wants to tell me he loves me. I can see it written all over his face, and I would say it back in a heartbeat.

Am I still scared? Yes.

A part of me is petrified that when we go back to London, this will all fall apart like we're living in some French love bubble. But even if that were true and it doesn't work out between us in the long run… will I be broken? Same answer, yes.

Will I still love Jack with all my heart? Like I have most of my life? Without a doubt in my mind.

He gulps down his words. *He'll say it when he's ready*, I think, as he leans in to kiss me hard against my lips. I try to deepen it, but he pulls back too quickly. "Look, we're landing." He points out the window.

I breathe a long sigh of contentment, trying to remember the last time I felt this way. I'm not sure I ever have. It's a new feeling for me, one of equal parts euphoria, contentment, and gratitude. A feeling I hope is a new constant for me.

"Is that the Atlantic Ocean?" I ask, sticking out my neck as far as possible to see down.

"Yeah, and that's the Gironde, right there—" He points to a small river. "It's the river that passes through Bordeaux."

"This is spectacular," I whisper.

We're about to land, and Jack instinctually grips my hand tighter like always, remembering I hate take-off and landing.

"Thank you," I tell him as we walk to the waiting car to bring us to the next part of the date. "You didn't have to do more than the helicopter. Hell, you didn't even need to do the helicopter. It was amazing, but I'd be just as happy sitting in the room, having tea, and watching a serial killer documentary with you. Whatever time I spend with you makes me happy."

He raises one sarcastic brow while he puts me in the car, leaning over to buckle my seatbelt—which I try with all my might not to roll my eyes at.

"So you're saying you would rather watch a show on Jeffrey Dahmer than go on a helicopter ride over France?"

"Well, when you say it like that, it sounds a little crazy." I laugh.

He shakes his head and gets into the car on the other side. "It doesn't *sound* crazy. It is crazy. I think I have to ban those shows until we get home. You're starting to freak me out."

Little does he know how freaked out they get *me,* even at home. He would come over and rip my telly off the wall if he found out.

"How much longer?" I ask.

"What are you, five? We just got in the car." He chuckles. "Be patient; it's only a few minutes away."

The few minutes feel like hours, and I practically fall out of the car when we pull up to part two of the date, trying to get out so fast.

"Merci!" I call to the driver, then run off toward the entrance.

"Jesus, B, wait up!"

I stop at the front door and wait for Jack, practically jumping out of my skin.

"Bloody hell, Jack. How do you remember all these things about me?" My heart drops to the pit of my stomach, but the exhilaration coursing through my body won't let me think about anything other than the fact that I'm crossing another thing off my list.

"Are you surprised?" He wraps his arms around me, pulling me into his chest.

I kiss his neck, jaw, lips, cheeks… all the places. "You could say that." I laugh. "It's not everyday someone takes you on a skydiving date."

I've wanted to do this my whole life. My brothers and Sadie were always too scared to do it and I could never muster the courage to do it alone. It never even occurred to me to ask Jack because he never offered when he knew I had asked Sadie multiple times.

I lean back and look him in his eyes. "Do you want to do this? It's okay if we skip it. I know it's not for everyone."

"It's funny you think I would do something I didn't want to do," he says playfully, knowing he's completely lying and would do anything for anyone he loves, even something as crazy as skydiving.

"Come on, then. Let's not waste any more time." I go to move but he pulls me back into him.

"The instructors are meeting us out here in a few minutes. I won't let you miss a minute of anything." He leans down and his lips take mine, kissing me tenderly.

I wrap my arms around his neck, pulling him as close as possible, then sweep my tongue through his open mouth. This time he lets me deepen our kiss when I part my lips, allowing our tongues to dance together in urgency.

Sparks fly through my body, all the way down to my toes. It's like this every time Jack's lips touch mine, each time better than the last.

His hands travel down to my behind, squeezing tight, subtly pumping his hips into me, letting his hard-on press against my lower half.

I lose control at the feeling, gripping his shoulders, then run my hands up through his hair, pulling every which way with each deep swipe of his tongue.

"Oh, Jack," I moan, and his lips turn up against mine. "What?" I breathe, leaning back to look at him.

His grin is broad, stretched wide as he shakes his head. "I don't know." He chuckles. "It keeps hitting me at random times that we're really doing this."

I smile softly. "I know, it's crazy. Have you ever thought about how we've known each other for at least thirty years? Isn't that insane?"

"Yeah, it's pretty crazy, but makes for a good story to tell our kids one day."

I still in his arms and go to respond, only to be cut off by the skydiving instructors. I need to talk to Jack about the kid situation since I know he's always wanted them.

Unfortunately for me, that ship has sailed.

I think he'll understand when I explain my reasons. Still, it won't be an easy conversation, and now that I think of it, it's probably best to talk once we get home, not when we're about to go skydiving a couple of days before Sadie's wedding.

Oh shit.

"Umm, do we think this is a good idea, considering your sister gets married in three days? What if something happens? What if we die jumping out of the plane?" I whisper, feeling petrified all of a sudden.

"The odds of that happening were way more likely in the helicopter, not skydiving," Jack says, and my eyes widen in disbelief.

"What do you mean?" I cry.

He shrugs. "Statistics."

"Well, now we're taking the train home. No way I'm getting in that death box again."

"All right, you two, let's stop all the death talk. You're going to scare off the others," the one instructor says.

"Oh! Are you Australian?" I ask excitedly, pushing the dying part to the back of my head for a second.

"Born and raised in Brisbane. We travel all over for skydiving. I'm Billie." He sticks out his hand for me to shake, then offers his hand to Jack. "And this here is my mate, Oscar, but he's Kiwi, clearly inferior." He laughs, and Oscar rolls his eyes, probably used to his mate's antics.

They seem like a fun duo.

After we've gone through the video and lesson, we start getting suited up. Billie looks between me and Jack a few times.

"Jackson, you're with Oscar. You and I are too big together with the equipment, Oscar will be a better fit for you, and I'll take the gorgeous Annabelle."

The second he says it, I bite my lip to hold back my chuckle when Jack freezes beside me. "One second," he says, before turning us away. "No fucking way are you going with that creep. We'll come back another day."

"Why, because he called me gorgeous?" I roll my eyes.

"Don't roll your eyes at me, Annabelle. I don't want you going with him, and I'm not kidding. I'm going to lose my shit," he grits through his teeth.

"Well, you set this up, and we don't have another day." I put my hands on my hips, ready for battle. I finally worked up the nerve to go, and now he wants to back out.

"All right, you two, we gotta go. Ready?"

"Yup!" I call and walk away from Jack, knowing I'll pay for it later… hopefully in the bedroom.

I won't lie. Usually I hate this possessive, jealous shit from men, but again, for the first time in my life, knowing because it's Jack, it's turning me on.

Not that I'll ever admit it to him. That's a tiny little secret I'll keep just to myself.

The small prop plane takes off, and my eyes widen in horror.

This is some scary shit.

Maybe I'm not as ready as I thought.

I turn toward Jack. "I'm scared," I mouth, wishing I wasn't attached to Billie so I could sit with him. I don't like being unable to hold his hand right now.

"You can do this," Jack yells over the engine. "Or we can turn this plane around and go home. It's up to you, B. I'll be happy either way."

"This is the point almost every person wants to turn around," Oscar chimes in. "Have you ever gone off a diving board?" When I nod, he says, "No matter how many times you go off the high dive, you always get that sinking feeling in your gut, but once you jump, you're wondering why the hell you were scared in the first place. It's the same thing here. I promise."

I look at Jack, then back to Oscar when he speaks again. "You've already paid, so it doesn't matter to us," he says, laughing. "But, I could see how excited you were to do this, and I'd hate for you to miss out on the feeling skydiving gives you. I promise the second you're out of the plane, all of this anxiety washes right away."

I look back at Jack, his face neutral, not giving away anything because he wants me to make this decision all on my own. "Okay, yeah. Let's do it!" I yell, trying to pump myself up.

"Perfect timing. It's go time," Billie says, and everyone laughs when my jaw drops.

He propels us toward the opening, and I do everything but look down.

We have to go first since we're the lightest, or at least that's what Billie said. Apparently Jack and Oscar will fall fastest because of their weight distribution.

I glance back at Jack one last time. "You okay?" he mouths, and I nod, trying to swallow my fear.

I want to do this.

With a wave, Billie pushes us out of the plane, and we're off. And just like Oscar said would happen, my anxiety disappears within seconds.

I've already forgotten the free-falling part, which was over quickly. Now I'm getting to enjoy this gliding motion, and it's so freeing, it feels like flying.

The wind whips around us, but I barely register the sound. My adrenaline is pumping vigorously, coursing through my body, and all my senses are alive in all their glory.

The view is breathtaking… white, fluffy clouds, land, and the ocean. It's hard to take it all in, so I'm trying to live in the moment and let this feeling of peace overtake me.

Billie gives me a thumbs up, asking if I'm okay, and I give him one back since we can't talk to one another.

Seconds later, Jack and Oscar are right in front of us, and it's the most exhilarating feeling.

We're both smiling big goofy grins, and I can see it in his eyes, he loves this as much as I do.

He gives me a thumbs up, like Billie, and I give him one back to let him know I'm all good before we descend toward the ground.

This is a core memory I will always remember. Flying high at ten thousand feet in the air, with Jack by my side, living life to its absolute fullest.

"Wow, that was incredible," I say in awe as I face Jack, who's landed closeby. "I'm not even sure incredible is the right word. I even think that might have been worth dying for, after all."

"You have a wicked sense of humor." Billie laughs, and Jack gives him the death stare.

It looks like he hasn't warmed up to him, so when we can stand, I run into Jack's arms to give my man some love and attention.

"Thank you so much, Jack. I had the absolute best day. Do we have to go back to Paris now, or do we have time to eat somewhere?"

He laughs. "Hungry?"

"Starved, that worked up an appetite."

"We have time to eat. And if you want, we can sleep over. I packed us a bag, and know some people around here who have an extra room."

"Who?" I ask.

"You'll see." He smiles.

11

Jackson

"It was so good to see you guys tonight. I've loved going down memory lane." Belle sighs happily, leaning back against my chest while sipping her wine.

I squeeze my arms tightly around her, needing her close.

Everything seems right in the world with her here like this.

I don't know what it is, because even though she's still the same Belle as last week and the week before that, it feels different.

It feels… *right.*

And I love seeing her like this—carefree, wearing my Harvard sweatshirt and oversized sweatpants, free of makeup and any worries, while we sit here with some of my best friends in the world.

We met Seb, Nate, and Leo—my New York best friends who are more like brothers—for dinner near their rented chateau right outside Soulac-Sur-Mer and have come back for a nightcap around the fire.

Although I get to see them while traveling for work and vice versa, I haven't spent quality time with them like this in forever, which reminds me to make more of an effort to do so because it's me that's avoided it.

They often invite me—and Sadie—out to their Hamptons houses or Nate's Aspen ski house, and I've always had an excuse, which was nothing more than me trying to separate myself from New York.

"I still can't believe the two of you are together." Leo laughs, shaking his head. "Wait until Mason gets wind of it." He says about one of our other friends.

I narrow my eyes, confused. "Why the hell would Mason care?"

Seb, who has barely spoken a word all night, chimes in, "He had a serious crush on her when we were younger."

My eyes widen in horror, and I squeeze Belle closer to my chest in a protective hold in response to his revelation.

How did I not know this?

The thought of him and B together turns my stomach in unease and makes me feel slightly murderous.

"Jack, Jesus, I can barely breathe," Belle mutters, and I quickly loosen my grip.

"Sorry, sweetheart." I lean down and softly kiss her behind her ear.

Nate chuckles. "So possessive. I've never seen Jackson like this before. I can't wait to see how the two of you hide this at the wedding. You haven't been able to keep your hands off each other for even a second tonight."

Belle shrugs. "We've kind of always been like this. Well, maybe without Jack's *lover boy* eyes." She laughs.

"Lover boy eyes?" I raise one brow. "What the hell does that mean?"

"You know when you give me those *all I want is to rip your clothes off* eyes."

I chuckle. "Oh, those eyes. Yeah, I definitely have those. Like right now, I would love for these idiots to go inside so I can fuck you out by the fire."

She hits my arm. "Oh my god! You're such a bloody wanker. Ignore him. He's uncouth and suddenly forgets how to act in public."

Nate's eyes sparkle in amusement, and he mouths *lover boy* to piss me off. I know it now; he'll be calling me that for the rest of my life.

I turn toward Leo. "Did you ever get in touch with Wills's sister,

Evelyn? She'll obviously be there this weekend if you want me to make the introduction."

He tips his scotch toward me. "You, sir, are very smart. I didn't even think of that. I'd love an intro. I haven't had a second to breathe, and we need to get moving on the project."

Leo and Nate are highly sought-after architects in New York and have been recruited to design buildings all over the world.

"Oh, are you thinking of hiring Evelyn for one of your projects? I'm not just saying this… she's truly one of the most talented interior designers I've ever seen. She has a keen eye and can switch to your preferred style without hesitation," Belle says.

"Yeah, we're building sister buildings in New York, Miami, and London, and want a seamless design that works for all three places. Jackson said she travels all over the world, so I'm hoping it's a good fit. We don't have much time to look for a designer otherwise."

"You'll love her. You won't have to look anywhere else," I tell him, then turn toward Nate to make sure he gets my drift.

If she didn't get the job, I would be pissed, because I know she could do this with her eyes closed. At times, Leo can be a pain in the ass about who he hires and trusts.

"Ready to go upstairs?" I lean down and whisper in Belle's ear.

"Nope." She leans forward to smile up at me before kissing my jaw. "I need the gossip." She turns back toward the guys and says, "Tell me something good. I know almost everything about Jack, but you lot must know something juicy."

Seb's eyes light up, but he doesn't say a word. He's a vault.

Nate laughs out loud. "Did Jack ever tell you about how he lost his virginity?"

Belle jolts back, then turns to narrow her eyes at me.

Fuck.

"I've asked him, and he told me he barely remembers," she says slowly, still glaring at me, then turns back toward Nate. "I need to know." She rubs her hands together like a cartoon villain.

"This is a good one," Leo mumbles.

"Heidi from Germany." He sighs. "The hottest camp counselor on the face of the planet."

Belle shakes her head. "Of course it was a camp counselor. How old were you? Or better yet, how old was she?"

"I was fifteen, and she was twenty. I told her I was a senior about to leave for college." I smirk, remembering how slick I thought I was.

"Oh my god." Belle laughs. "Of course you did."

Nate continues, trying to contain his laughter, unlike Leo, who's dying in the corner. "They have sex, and then she finds out his real age a few weeks later, just as camp is ending. So, knowing she'd never have to see us again since she was going back to Germany, she told all the girls in our grade that she heard Jackson Peters had herpes and that his dick was so small that when it got hard, it was no bigger than her thumb."

Belle spits out the wine she'd just gulped and widens her eyes. "Sorry," she says, wiping up her mouth as her chest starts vibrating with laughter."This is not a joke, right?" she cries.

Seb shakes his head, confirming.

"That is the best story I've ever, ever, ever heard in my life, and I'm keeping it in my back pocket for when I need payback for something. You just gave me the best ammunition of my life." She chuckles.

I roll my eyes. "It wasn't even that bad."

It was fucking terrible.

Seb smirks. "Oh please, you went into hiding and attempted to dye your hair before school started."

Belle leans back, her body still shaking from laughter.

I bend down and bite her ear. "Keep laughing, sweetheart. See what happens."

She wiggles her behind, and I have to suppress a moan. I've been hard all night with her in my lap. "What are you going to do, *lover boy*?" she whispers. "Or should I call you *little dick*?"

"Oh, that's it." I take her glass from her and place it on the table, then stand and throw her over my shoulder. "Goodnight, assholes. I'm about to remind my girl of the real size of my dick."

"Oh my god, put me down, you Neanderthal," she cries, slapping my ass in protest, but I can hear the laughter in her voice.

"Your dick?" Leo calls, and I hear Seb's deep laughter echo through the space.

Shit.

"You mean, Snake?" Nate calls, laughing alongside the other two.

Belle stills in my arms. "What. Did. They. Just. Say?" she yells in excitement.

"Don't fucking listen to them." I run into the house. When I see them again this weekend, they're fucking dead.

"We'll tell you Saturday," Leo screams to Belle.

Over my dead body. She'll never let me live the nickname down once she hears the story.

I'm keeping her far away from those fuckers this weekend.

"This was a very embarrassing day for you, Jack. First Queen, now this. What's next?" She chuckles, squirming around.

I slap and grab hold of her ass. "Shush it, you, or you're going to get it."

"Mmm," she moans. "I was counting on it, Jack."

Of course she was… my beautiful, perfect, B.

"Morning, sweetheart." My eyes still closed, I moan, taking in the burning sensation running through my body.

Belle's plush lips are wrapped around my cock, drinking me down the back of her throat. Sucking hard but slowly, twisting her hand in rhythm with her mouth. I can already feel my balls tightening, ready for release.

She does this to me every time, and for once, I want it to last longer than two seconds. Never has this happened in my life, except this week with her. I'm a crazed man, obsessed with my beautiful B.

My queen B.

She releases me with a pop from the tight suction she had around me. "Good morning, Jack," she purrs, then extends her tongue to swipe up my shaft and around the head of my cock.

"So good," I moan.

"Stand up, Jack." Her breaths are labored, letting me know she's just as turned on as I am.

My eyes snap to hers. "What, why? Don't stop."

She bites her bottom lip then flattens her tongue, licking my whole length before pulling back again. Her eyes flick from my dick and then up to me before she leans back and scrambles to the floor, kneeling with her baby blues shining up at me, patiently waiting.

No more words are needed, and I stand without hesitation.

My rock-hard dick stands straight up, swollen red, glistening with her saliva, begging for her mouth again.

I caress her face tenderly and run the pad of my thumb over her rosy cheek. "So beautiful," I mumble, then gather her wild, blonde hair up on top of her head.

She leans forward, licking my balls, then trails her tongue up my shaft, continuously teasing me to no end. The amount of pre-ejaculate beading on my tip makes it look like I've already come.

I tug her hair hard and she lets out a low groan, squeezing her legs together, rocking back and forth to ease her ache. The sight of her so turned on is making me feel wild and out of control.

"Now," I growl. "Suck me now."

Her eyes hold mine. "Fuck my mouth, please," she whispers, then parts her lips wide.

Fuck.

I push past her swollen lips and suck in a breath as her hot mouth engulfs me to the base, gagging slightly but not letting it hold back her mission of taking me all in. I slide in and out, pumping fast and tightening my hold on her hair. Each time she moans, she sends vibrations around my dick.

"God, yes," she whimpers around me, then lifts her hand to cup my balls. I fall forward, shooting my arm out to hold myself up. I slam in, fucking her relentlessly just like she wanted, watching her eyes water as leftover mascara runs down her face.

"You good?"

Her eyes sparkle excitedly, groaning around me.

There's no way I can hold back now.

I pick up my rhythm, tipping my head back and closing my eyes. My loud, deep moans echo throughout the room as I shudder in her mouth, filling her throat full of my come.

I glance down in time to see her swallow, and I have to take a second to remember to breathe.

God, she's sexy as hell.

I lean over and pick her up, wordlessly laying her back on the bed. Then, I press my lips to hers with a deep, meaningful kiss before traveling down her body.

I've already told her I don't like coming before her, but I'll let it slide today since we fell asleep right after I ate her pussy until she came three times last night.

I run my hands up and down her lean, milky thighs, taking in her pink center.

"Fuck." I lean back. "Look what you do to me."

Her lips turn up as she glances at my already hard dick. "That's because you're a horndog."

I raise a brow. "*Horndog*?"

She giggles. "It sounded very American when I said it in my head."

I bend her legs and bring them down on the bed, giving me complete access to her as I swipe my tongue, licking through her soaking-wet sex.

Her arms fly to the side, grabbing at the sheets in desperation as I twirl my tongue around her clit, not stopping even when she begs. Instead, I continue to eat her with deep strokes, moving my head side to side, completely losing it when she screams my name, quivering beneath me.

"I need you to come, Belle," I growl, then really let her have it.

"Jack," she moans. "Please."

"Please, what?" I mumble against her clit, which causes her to buck wildly into my face.

"Come up here. I need you," she cries.

Yeah... well, too bad. I need her to come on my face like I need air to breathe, and nothing will stop me until she does.

I pick up my pace, feeling her body shake when I flatten my tongue against her clit. Her knees buckle beneath my hold, and her screams get louder and louder with each thrash of my head. She cries out, whimpering my name as her orgasm rips through her body, and I lick and suck every drop from her until the very last quiver.

I kiss her softly on her clit, around her sex, and along her inner thighs. I love her body, her smooth pale skin against my tanned olive hands, restraining her like this.

"I don't think I can breathe anymore." She sighs in happiness. "Now, please get up here."

I sit up, then lean over to kiss her pouty lips. "Mmm, I do like it when you beg," I say, and she smirks, playfully hitting me in the arm.

When she looks up, her eyes catch mine, and we both still.

A shared feeling of contentment passes through us. I can tell by the way her lips part ever so slightly and her eyes dilate that she feels whatever this is too. "Kiss me again, Jack," she whispers.

I push her legs apart once more. A sense of urgency drives me to slide home in one hard thrust before I lean down and give my girl what she wants.

Our kiss starts sweet and tender as I slowly pump in and out of her, relishing in the way she's squeezing around me.

Belle breaks our kiss to press her lips against my heart. "Mine," she whispers, and I freeze, letting the emotions hit me right there where her lips press again, *my heart*.

"I'm yours, my beautiful B, just as you're mine. You do know that, right?"

Her eyes lift to meet mine. "I do, Jack."

I pull out, then slide back in, again and again, never blinking. I don't want to miss even the slightest breath she takes.

Our bodies rock in sync, our breathing loud and desperate as we work together, chasing our release. I reach down and press slow but deliberate circles to her clit, watching as her body reacts and slowly starts to shake sooner than I anticipated, gripping me tight like a noose.

Her mouth gapes and her breathing picks up, but no sound escapes as she comes around me, and I follow her only seconds later, falling against her when I can't hold myself up anymore.

When I feel like my body has even an ounce of its strength back, I lean up, kiss her hard on the mouth, then roll over on my side to take her all in.

"You seem relaxed. I think you need to start taking more holidays with less work. It suits you," she says.

"It does feel nice. Although I won't lie, it's still semi-stressful thinking about all the work I'll have when I return."

"Declan will have handled everything. He won't let you come back to a mess."

"Some things can only be handled by me. I have new tennis pro clients of Wills's that recently retired and want to invest in athletic wear, but other than that, I guess I could get used to this. Maybe we'll come back every year to France—" I cut myself off when a thought comes to me.

"What is it?"

I chuckle, thinking how mad I'm going to make Wills. "I'm going to buy the house next door to the holiday home Wills bought just to piss him off. I don't care how much I have to pay the owners."

"Oh my god, he would die." She laughs. "But it's also genius."

"I know, it's so easy to rile him up. I feel like I can't *not* do it now."

"You really have to," Belle says as she turns on her side, mirroring my position.

I look her up and down, eyeing her crazed hair and smudged makeup she forgot to take off.

"What's that look you're giving me?" she asks.

"Just admiring your Medusa hair."

She narrows her eyes playfully. "You're supposed to tell me I look like Sleeping Beauty when I wake up."

"You're the most gorgeous, sexy woman I have ever met in my life. Someone I cherish and would never lie to," I tell her truthfully.

"I'm missing the point here, Jack."

I lean forward and bite her neck playfully. "The point is, I can't possibly call you a Sleeping Beauty when you're more like a sleeping train wreck."

Her eyes widen in surprise, and I can't hold back my deep rumble of laughter.

"What the hell, Jack!" She hits my hand, making me drop the piece of hair I'd been holding between my fingers.

I shrug, still laughing. "You're a one hundred out of ten. But you drool when you sleep, your face becomes swollen, and your eyes get crusty." I bite my lip, trying to contain myself, deciding not to point out how her hair is a sweaty, knotted mess.

"This is the one time you could have lied to me. Haven't you ever heard of a white lie?" she grumbles.

I cup her face "Why? It doesn't make me like you any less, and I can't help that not everyone can be perfect like me."

"Jack. Oh my god, stop talking." She pushes herself off me, and I let her go willingly, laughing my ass off.

It's so easy to ruffle her feathers sometimes.

When I hear the shower turn on, I follow her into the bathroom. I suddenly hate showering alone after forty years on this planet.

"I'm showering alone," she says, and I smirk, knowing how to get on her good side.

I pull her into my chest before she can step into the shower. "I'm sorry." I kiss her neck. "How about we take a bath instead."

She excitedly whips around. "You hate baths."

"I know, they're the worst," I grumble. "But you love them."

"Should we go downstairs first?"

"The guys left. They had an earlier start to their wine-tasting tour. They texted goodbye and said they would see us Saturday."

"Okay." She smiles. "Bath time it is, *lover boy*."

Annabelle

"The bath is almost ready," I call, peeking my head out to find Jack.

His phone buzzes on the nightstand where it's plugged in, then buzzes again. This happens three more times.

"Jack?" I call again.

"I'm here, sweetheart." He lifts a tray of breakfast pastries, a bottle of champagne, and some orange juice.

I momentarily pause as he walks past me, quickly giving me a chaste kiss, completely naked and so fucking gorgeous. My breathing picks up as my eyes stay glued to his flawless body, especially his arse… *God, I love his arse.*

I feel crazed thinking how I want to run my hands along the hard plains of his body, smooth and dusted with the perfect amount of hair.

He turns back, seemingly thinking the same as he drags his eyes slowly up my body, pausing at my breasts that pucker under his electrifying stare.

The breakfast tray tips to one side as we get lost in a daze, and the strawberries topple onto the floor, snapping us back to reality. "Oops." He shoots me a cheeky grin, dimples popping.

This is all so new to us. It's still shocking at times. "Your phone has buzzed a few times."

"Can you check it for me," he mumbles, trying to concentrate on not dropping the rest of the food as he sets it down next to the bath.

I type in his password and don't see any new texts, but there are missed calls from a 917 area code, which I know is New York because that's what Jack's and Sadie's old numbers used to start with.

I'm about to place the phone back down, but it sends a buzzing reminder, so I pick it back up and see an email pop up.

When I open it, the room sways around me, and I drop to the bed in complete shock.

Dear God, why didn't he tell me?

Bloody hell, Jack... you need to talk to me about this.

"Jackson…" I call. He steps into the room, his face full of concern when he sees my expression. "Why didn't you tell me your dad's been emailing you?" I whisper.

I don't miss the way his face drops at my words as he tries to recover quickly. "There's nothing to tell," he mutters dismissively, walking toward the bath.

I sit back against the headboard, waiting for a second before joining him.

This is huge.

I already knew their dad texted Sadie, but it's different for Jack.

Their dad wasn't always the arsehole he is now, and from what Jack remembers, he cared at one point.

I walk into the en suite, then hold onto Jack's shoulder as I lower myself into the rose and gardenia-scented bath.

I kiss him softly on his chest, then turn around and lean back between his legs as he wordlessly pulls me closer, wrapping his arms around me.

I can sense he's thinking about it as he runs his hands up along my breasts and down the side of my body.

When enough time has passed, I give in and ask, "Why didn't you tell me? We tell each other everything, especially about that."

He shrugs.

"This is what relationships are about, Jack, sharing our burdens so you don't hold all the weight yourself. We've been doing this almost our whole lives. But now, it's more important than ever. I want to help."

He sighs and leans his head back against the tub.

"I don't have anything to say. I never answer him."

His hands run up to my shoulders as he massages me.

"How long has this been going on?"

"A few months."

I frown.

Shit, that's longer than I thought.

"Are you not even a little bit curious as to what happened and why he's suddenly reaching out?"

He huffs. "Are you curious about your dad?" he counters in a tone I don't appreciate.

"No," I snap. "And don't be a bloody jerk. You know my father and what he did. It's different with your dad; we have no clue why he suddenly started acting like you don't exist."

"You're right, sorry." He squeezes me tight. "I'm all worked up now."

"Explain to me, in your eyes, what happened with your dad. Maybe we can make something out of it since we haven't discussed it since we were younger."

He moans his annoyance but doesn't hold back. "My mom has always been a nightmare, we all know that, so there's no real shock that she was the worst mom on the planet. Until Sadie was a toddler, and I was maybe seven or so, my dad was present like any other good dad." He pauses. "I don't remember everything, but I remember the small things that suddenly stopped."

"Like what?"

"He stopped showing up for my baseball games, no more ice cream dates or movie nights. He didn't bring me to the first day of school, leaving Maria, our nanny, to do it. He would dismiss me without looking at me. He—"

His voice catches.

I take his arms and hold them tight around me. "It's okay, Jack."

"H-he stopped saying he loved me, and I'm not sure I ever heard him say it to Sadie."

My heart drops. This is the worst story.

I lean my head back against him, taking a deep breath to calm myself. Needing to be strong for him.

"I remember trying so hard," he whispers. "No matter what I did, it was like I never existed… like I was nothing more than a burden."

"It's why you never wanted a relationship before."

"Ha, yeah. I don't need a psychologist to tell me that one. Jackson Peters: fear of commitment. Check."

I turn to face him, straddling him as best I can in the cramped tub. "Do you feel better after talking about it?"

"No."

"When was the last time you saw or spoke to him?" I ask, because as much as I hate this for him, it still seems so out of the blue.

"I saw him briefly after Charlotte was born. You know, when my mom disowned Sadie? Before that, who knows."

I shake my head in disgust. "I hate that woman."

"Yeah, you and me both, B."

"We may be fucked up in the relationship department because of our dads, but maybe that's part of why we're meant to be together. Maybe our trauma cancels one another's out. I was always scared of another man ripping my heart out of my chest like my dad, and you have commitment issues, afraid to be left behind again."

"I don't have issues anymore." He holds me close, taking a deep breath. "I won't rip your heart out, I promise, sweetheart, and I trust you."

My heart freefalls.

"That means more to me than you'll ever know." I kiss his lips, but before he can deepen it, I pull back.

"Don't get mad," I say, and he narrows his eyes. "But maybe you should hear him out. You don't have to talk, only listen to what he has to say. Maybe you'll get some closure out of it if anything."

He shakes his head, not wanting to hear it. "Nope. No chance, I'm fine."

"I know that he hurt you deep down, Jack." I cover his heart with my hand. "So even though you think you've finally moved past it, I'm sorry to tell you, you haven't. Not after this long holding onto all the resentment. I know you better than anyone else; it will always be there until you get your answers."

He doesn't respond, and I know I've pushed him.

He lifts me off his lap and gets out of the bath. I dry off and watch him pace back and forth, soaking the bedroom floor.

I hand him a towel, and he chucks it at the bed, then runs his hands up and down his face in frustration.

"I'm sorry, I just… I don't want to think about this shit while we're here. I want to spend my time uninterrupted, appreciating you… appreciating that we're finally doing this. And that my baby sister is marrying the love of her life in two days."

"You're right." He is. I shouldn't have pushed him today. "Let's forget this for now and go back to Paris. Tomorrow, all our friends and family arrive and we can start the celebration of our favorite girl. No need to take this on right now," I tell him.

"Yeah, okay," he mumbles, then walks into the closet to get clothes.

When he walks out, he looks better. "I forgot to tell you, Declan, Nora, and their army of a family arrived earlier today. Declan took care of firing the wedding planner and is handling everything until we get back."

I smirk. "You mean Nora fired her?"

"Yeah, probably." He chuckles. "My fiery ginger that she is."

"Brilliant, let's move on for now. Everything's already shaping up for tomorrow and the rest of the weekend."

Or let's hope...

12

Annabelle

"Can you warn a girl before you step out here looking all hot and gorgeous?" I grin, taking in Jackson's tailored suit-clad body.

His dark, slightly waved hair is styled to perfection, and his newly grown beard has been shaved down to nothing.

He puffs out his chest and brushes his shoulder off. "Not too bad, aye?"

"No… not at all, Jack. Not. At. All."

He chuckles, leaning down to kiss me and lacing his hands through my hair to pull my mouth closer. Without fail, a zap of warmth shoots through my body from his touch.

I pout playfully when he pulls away too quickly. "Where are you going?" I call when he walks back into the hotel suite, but I get no answer.

It's early morning and the city is still asleep, so when Jack woke up early to get ready, I came out to the terrace wrapped in my cozy robe to appreciate the quiet.

Unfortunately for me, though, I'll be appreciating one of our last mornings here all alone.

Jack has clients flying in from Germany for a meeting that popped up and he can't miss it. His clients were given an opportunity for a last-minute investment and must decide by noon today, otherwise the offer's off the table.

So, what was going to be our last morning together before everyone arrives in a few hours is cut short, and I'm left alone to think.

Which is not good.

There isn't even much to help with for the wedding. When we returned to Paris yesterday, Evelyn, Wills's sister, had already arrived and taken charge, putting everyone in their place.

Jack steps back outside and sits down next to where I'm lying. "Here you go, sweetheart." He hands me a latte, and I pause, confused. He typically orders me an espresso. "What is this?"

"A latte. What does it look like?"

I look down and... *Oh.*

This man is too perfect for his own good.

I take the sprig of lavender out and place it to the side. Just as I take a sip of my lavender honey latte, a gust of wind travels up the balcony and blows my hair in my face.

"Sit up, B." Jack takes my coffee and places it on the table, then turns me on an angle so he can braid my hair.

I smile inwardly at the sweet gesture that he picked up so easily after all these years.

I love it.

"Thank you, Jack." I grin when he's finished. "What's all this?" I nod toward the food.

"I need to feed you before I go," he mutters, cutting french toast and pouring massive amounts of syrup on top—*my favorite.*

"Thank you, but I'm capable of feeding myself," I say, my words falling on deaf ears as he tops the stack with fresh berries. "I'm not hungry. I'll eat later when Sadie gets here," I add.

"Eat, Annabelle," he demands, pressing a forkful to my lips.

This is it...

This is my chance to put him in his place and stop all this domineering shit right now.

Instead, I open my mouth and let him feed me.

The bastard has me wrapped around his little finger, and he knows it. I can tell by the way he's smirking at my submission.

"Don't be cheeky, Jack," I mumble around my food.

He cuts another piece, and I put my finger up. "If you're going to feed me, you might as well get it right. I want a taste of each thing in rotation: French toast, yogurt, croissant, fruit, a sip of my latte, then back to the beginning." I smirk. "Please and thank you."

He raises one brow. "There are two things you left out of rotation that are on the menu: cock and balls," he deadpans, and I laugh, choking on my food.

"God." I chuckle. "Is this all you think about it?"

"Yeah, pretty much." He shrugs. "It's taking every ounce of restraint I have not to fuck you into the lounger you're lying on. Every time you move, I get a glimpse of your pert pink nipples, and I'm about to blow in my goddamn pants."

"Mmmm." I reach down and playfully whip my robe off, shimmying my breasts out in the open. "You mean these nipples, Jack?" I tease, closing my robe stealthily when his hand shoots out to grab one.

"No, no… Your girl is hungry, and you said I need to eat." I wink, and he barks out a laugh.

"You'll pay for that later. You don't get to deny me what's mine."

"And like I always say, I look forward to it." Smirking, I take a bite of croissant. "But by later, you mean tomorrow, right? Don't forget we're not staying together tonight."

He pauses mid-bite, then places his fork down. "What are you talking about? Why the hell wouldn't we stay together? And don't give me that *We're keeping it a secret* shit. We always stay together. Way before we became a couple."

I roll my eyes at his dramatics. "I already told you, I'm sleeping with Sadie tonight."

"You were being serious?" he murmurs. "Why do they need to keep that crazy tradition? They have two kids together and aren't some innocent couple that needs to spend the night away from one another."

He's right, but Sadie's dreamt of her wedding her whole life and deserves the whole package. "Leave your sister alone. She wants the full experience. Kids or not… and speaking of keeping it a secret—"

Jack's phone dings and he looks down, seemingly not paying attention.

"You're not listening," I huff, annoyed.

"You're about to tell me some bullshit about our relationship that I don't need to hear, which proves I'm listening, so keep going."

"It's not bullshit. We need to figure out what to do about our marriage once we get back to London and leave our fairytale Parisian bubble."

He drops his phone and narrows his eyes. "What do you mean 'figure out what to do'? There's nothing to figure out."

"Jack." I sigh. "Marriage is so much more than what we've been doing. We went from being best friends, to married, to lovers. We did the last two backward. All I'm saying is I want to set us up for success, that's all. Maybe we start from the beginning, like normal couples."

"No—" he starts, then looks at his watch. "Shit, I have to go, B."

"Wait. What do you mean by *No*?"

He leans down to kiss me and I can tell he's holding back from deepening it. It will be a while before we can kiss like this again, and we both know if he does, we'll be starting something he has no time to finish.

He traces his tongue around the fullness of my mouth, biting on my plump bottom lip, groaning loudly in frustration… *I know exactly how he feels.*

I almost forgot what we were talking about, I'm in such a Jack daze, but I force myself to snap back to reality and pull back. "Jack, what do you mean *No*?"

With apparent reluctance, he stands, adjusting his tie—and his hard-on—and gives me a deadpan look. "I mean just that. *No*. There is no discussion." He leans down again and takes my chin between his fingers, applying a light pressure so I lift my eyes to his. "I told you, my beautiful *wife*. I'm all in, and there's nothing to worry about anymore. I've got you, B. This is our future… you and me, forever."

He squishes my lips together, kisses me hard, then turns and leaves without another word.

You and me, forever.

Only last week I was telling Lola that maybe I should move on and officially end the marriage for my own sanity, and now we're talking about forever.

Maybe finally talking about it with someone, putting it out there in the universe, shifted something for Jack and me.

Maybe the stars have finally aligned, and we'll both get our happily ever after.

And for the first time in my life, the word *forever* doesn't scare me when it comes to a relationship. If anything scares me, it's the overzealous feeling I have at the idea of a life with Jack.

Wills: Landed and on our way to the hotel. Sadie's fucking mum texted her about the wedding. They haven't spoken a word in five years, and she picks today of all days to screw with her. Sadie seems okay, but try to distract her when we get there.
Me: ARE. YOU. KIDDING. ME?!!!!
Wills: UK *Daily Mail* posted the location and other info this week. She must have learned from there. She texted saying all this bull-shit. I'm fuming.
Me: Or from the shady wedding planner. You were right to be wary.
Wills: Did you just say… I was right?
Me: Oh, shut it, arsehole. See you soon.

When the ding of the lift announces its arrival, I already know who will step off. We may not be sisters by blood, but I have a deep connection to my sister soul mate, deeper than most, and I can sense she's here.

"Annabelle," Sadie calls as she dives out of the lift, wrapping her arms tightly around my neck. "God, it's so good to see you." She pulls back, then kisses my face a million times.

"This is where Charlie gets it. She kisses the same way." I laugh, "I've missed you, darling. How was the rest of your trip? How are the girls? Tell me everything."

"Come, let's talk outside." She takes my hand in hers, squeezing it a few times in excitement, and guides us through the doors leading to the garden where they're beginning to set up for the ceremony.

"*Oh.*" Her gasp is loud enough that the workers turn around. "Sorry." She cringes, then turns to me, her eyes startling me for a second. They do that sometimes, since they are so much like her brother's. "Annabelle, this is incredible. Isn't it?"

"It's beautiful. Everything you've always wanted." I put my arm around her shoulders and pull her into my side, staring over the garden with her as they set up the chairs and altar.

Understated elegance is how I would describe it all, and it fits Sadie to a tee. All whites and creams, her dress, our dresses, the linens, and most of the flowers.

The only pops of color are from the foliage's greenery, and small accents of a blush rose from the sweet peas and carnations—Charlotte and Chloe's birth month flowers, which is something near and dear to her heart that will be placed in all our bouquets.

She hasn't been inside to where the reception will take place yet. She's going to flip when she sees the floral designer. I have to text Wills to get his arse down here because I don't want to wait much longer to show her.

I squeeze her tighter against me. It truly is so good to see her.

For much of our lives, we lived in different countries, and we didn't know a life of anything different. Now that we both live in London though, I could never imagine a life without her or the girls by my side.

"I'm excited about the rehearsal tonight," I tell her. They've booked a boat ride down the Seine for the bridal party and close family and friends.

"Oh, me too. Well, I'm excited about everything." She laughs. "It's going to be magical. Champagne at sunset, the Eiffel Tower sparkling, and Pierre, our favorite chef in the whole world, passing around his delicious and unique creations. It's a real dream come true, and I get to do it with all the people I love most. I can't believe it's all finally happening. I'm a lucky lady," she mutters, trying to hold back her tears.

"We all are," I say truthfully.

It's something I love about our found family: we may all be extremely different, but our values in life align perfectly, and that's what matters most. None of us take anything for granted.

As I watch Sadie soak it all in, I think about my future with Jack and instantly feel guilty about keeping our relationship from her. Though, I stand by my decision. Now is not the time; this weekend is about her and Wills.

I can't help but wonder, if Jack and I worked out, would we have another wedding? I think if we did, I would choose something small and intimate. Not that this isn't beautiful, it's absolutely stunning, but considering grand affairs and over-the-top parties are part of my work life, I would appreciate something smaller for my personal life.

Sadie leans her head on my shoulder and sighs again.

"You're loving yourself sick over all of this, aren't you?" I tease.

Her chest vibrates in silent laughter. "Yeah, pretty much." She takes my hand in hers. "Thank you for helping and staying here this week. I know it was hard with work. I truly appreciate you taking time off, and I have to say it was wonderful to spend some time just the four of us. And Buddy, of course."

"Is The Ritz even dog-friendly?"

I already know if Wills wants something, he'll get it, or he would have moved the whole wedding somewhere else to ensure Buddy was involved. He's no less one of their kids than Charlie and Chloe.

"They are, but only up to ten pounds. Wills told the manager that since our guests have booked all seventy-one rooms and seventy-one suites, we're allowed up to one thousand four hundred and twenty pounds of dogs." She laughs. "Can you believe it?"

"Of course I can. It's bloody genius." I laugh, because it's something I would do. "So, how did the rest of the trip go?"

"It was amazing, Belle. It's the first time the four of us have been away, and it was honestly the most magical feeling in the world." She smiles, her whole face glowing at the memory. "I did come to a conclusion about some news I wanted to share with you." She wrings her hands—Sadie's tell when she's nervous.

"What is it? You're making me anxious."

"I'm going to step back and let Marco take over the floral design business for a while. I'll still focus on Amelia's Angels Animal Rescue, but that's it."

I frown, confused.

Besides Charlie, Chloe, and Buddy, Sweet Pea Blooms is her pride and joy. It was the first thing she did for herself when she finally left New York, something she dreamed of her whole life.

"I don't understand."

She swallows hard, and if I know her as well as I think I do, she's trying to hold back tears, not wanting to get emotional again. "The girls were perfect. Charlie was my sweet angel, the best big sister I always dreamed she would be. And I can only assume it was because we were all together. I feel guilty for being a working mom and not spending enough time with them. It's not like I'm giving it up completely, trust me. Sweet Pea Blooms is my baby, and I'm only stepping back. I want to pick up Charlie from school, go to her drama classes, and bring her to play dates. Take Chloe to the music class I used to attend with Charlie when we had more time. All the things I wish my mom did for me." She sighs. "Being the boss of your own company should afford you at least that. It's not permanent, but for now, it's a decision I feel comfortable with. And as soon as I made the decision, it was as if a weight had lifted off my shoulders and the guilt I'd been carrying around dissipated."

I'm shocked, but I'll always support whatever she wants. "If you're happy, I'm happy. You should know, though, that being a working mum doesn't make you any less perfect." She smiles and hugs me tight.

"I appreciate that. I still run one of London's top animal rescues, don't forget." She winks, proud of herself. "I think focusing on that, for now, will keep me busy enough. And the girls love helping, especially since Maeve is there often. Charlie wants to go more than she ever has."

She's probably right. Charlie has a special bond with Declan's sister Maeve and has always been obsessed with animals like Sadie. "What did Wills say about all this?"

"I asked for his input, but for once in his life, he wouldn't tell me what to do." She smirks. "He actually told me he would take some time away from work to be with the girls if I wanted to continue working full-time."

I smile softly. "Of course he did. He would do anything to make you happy. You know that."

"He really would, and before I start blubbering like a baby again, I just want to say another thank-you… for accepting him. I know you don't always see eye to eye with Wills—"

I stop her mid-sentence. "Don't finish that. Just because I disagree with him sometimes doesn't mean I don't see how perfect the two of you are together. Someone hand-made that man just for you, and he was waiting in the lobby of that Antibes hotel for a reason. I like to bust his balls because he's like a brother to me, but believe me when I say, I appreciate what a good father he is and how he treats you the way you deserve." I pause. "I never told you this, but before Wills proposed, he called Jackson and me to ask for your hand in marriage." I smile at her surprised face.

"I thought he proposed on a whim."

"He asked us a few weeks prior, since he knew he wanted to do it soon, but the time and place was on a whim."

"Oh." She places her hand on her heart and takes deep breaths. "That means a lot."

She leans in and hugs me again. No words are exchanged—we don't need them. This is perfect the way it is.

A few minutes later, I see Lola over Sadie's shoulder in the distance, walking hand in hand with Evelyn, and I start waving my arm like a crazed woman trying to get her attention.

"Gahh, you're so embarrassing. Can you stop?" Sadie whispers and steps aside so as not to be seen with me.

We've always joked that she should have been born in England and I, in New York. Sadie is prim and proper, never curses or raises her voice, and I couldn't be more different.

"I can't help it. I've missed my sweet Lo."

I throw my arms around Lola the second she's within reach and hold her tight to my chest. She lays her head on my boobs like she always does as a joke since she can't reach higher. "I've missed you," she mumbles.

I playfully narrow my eyes at Sadie. "See, she missed me too."

I lean over and kiss Ev hello, then turn my attention back to Lola. "You're in a much better mood than when I left you back in London."

Sadie pushes me out of the way to wrap her arms around Lola. "Maybe it's because she's bringing a mysterious date."

I pause and glare at my friend. "What date? You never told me you were bringing someone."

She smiles awkwardly. "Well, it was sort of a last-minute decision."

I eye her suspiciously. "I thought you were done with the curls," I say, fluffing up her hair. She's done it beautifully, the frizz is gone, and the top is blow-dried, leaving the bottom voluminous and curly.

"My love for my curls is back." She smirks, looking past me.

"Not that she had a choice. She's done with straight hair. I like it natural," a familiar voice booms from behind me, and the way Sadie's eyes practically fall out of her head, I know I've heard right.

"W-what's going on?" I cry and fling myself at my brother Matthew. "Matty, what are you doing here?"

He ignores me and leans over to kiss Sadie on the cheek. "Sadie-girl is all grown-up. I can barely believe it. Congratulations." Sadie's in shock and hasn't said a word.

"Hello! Can someone tell me what's going on? I thought you said you couldn't make it to the wedding."

Wait…

I look between him and Lola. What did he just say about her hair?

"Can someone explain what's going on?" I glance up at Matthew, who walks over to Lola and embraces her from her behind.

"Hi, baby girl," he murmurs, then leans down and kisses her forehead.

Both Sadie and I freeze in shock… *What the actual fuck*?

Matty turns to Sadie and apologizes. "It was never our intention to bring this up today, but we knew you would see us here together and wonder."

"Our intention… here together," I mumble to myself, then turn to Lola, who is doing everything in her power not to make eye contact. "Lola, look at me," I demand.

"I-I…" Lola stutters.

"Shh, I got it," Matthew whispers to her softly. "This'll probably come as a surprise, but Lola and I are together. We met when I was in London a few weeks ago, and what was supposed to be some fun turned into so much more. We fell in love."

"*This will probably come as a surprise*?" I shout. "Um, yeah, I would fucking say so… Wait, did you say in love?" I look between them. Lola is white as a ghost, standing there like a statue, mute.

"What's going on over here? Why are you yelling, B?" Jack asks as he enters the garden cautiously, taking in the situation.

He throws his arms over Sadie and me, kissing us both hello before turning toward Matthew and Lola.

"Hughes, I didn't realize you were coming. Neither Theo nor Belle mentioned it." He takes his arm off me quickly to shake my brother's hand.

"He's here with Lola," I interrupt. "Like, together as a couple."

Jack freezes, and I see it in his face he's just realized something. "This is who you were with all week when we spoke?" He directs his question to Lola, and she nods, still no words.

"Okay, I'm losing my mind. Someone start from the goddamn beginning. Now."

Matthew's eyes hold mine. "Lola and I met the day of your five-year anniversary party and we had an instant attraction. She knew I was leaving and I was sick of dating, so we agreed to have a week of fun while I was in town. We ended up developing feelings for one another instead."

I turn toward Jack. "What did you mean before when you said you two spoke?"

"You were looking for Lola, and her phone location she shares with us hadn't moved much from the hotel, so I called to check up on her."

"She was with a man all week, hiding out, and didn't tell me?" I bite out.

He leans close to my ear. "Don't be a hypocrite. Considering you're not coming clean about us, you're *still* keeping it a secret."

I narrow my eyes. "Fine, fair point." I hate when he's right. I turn back toward Lola and our eyes finally meet for the first time. Before I can think twice, I ask, "Are you sure about this? Don't you think he's a little too old for you?"

"Annabelle," Sadie and Evelyn chastise at the same time.

"Shut up, Belle. What's wrong with you?" Sadie mumbles next to me, and I have no clue what's come over me.

"I don't know. Brain slip," I whisper, then peek up at Lola and Matthew. Just as I'm about to apologize, my brother jumps in, cutting me off.

He flexes his one hand, and his nostrils flare.

He's angry—*fuck*.

"I love you more than anything, but with all due respect, shut the hell up, Annabelle, and mind your own damn business. I thought I taught you that if you have nothing nice to say, don't say anything at all. Though, I shouldn't be surprised, considering the woman standing in front of me is *not* my fucking sister. When Lola was worried sick over telling you, I promised her *my* sister would never care. *My* sister would only be happy that two of her favorite people are together."

"Oh, sod off, Matthew. Don't be so dramatic, I didn't mean it like that, and I was about to apologize before you so rudely cut me off. Being away from England for so long has been detrimental to your manners."

"Okay, Jesus. Both of you, calm the hell down," Jack yells, pulling me to his side.

"Annabelle," he warns when he sees my mouth open. "Enough. You're upsetting Lola." He whispers it low enough for only me to hear. "Why are you so angry about this? I don't understand… Look, she's crying, B."

Shit.

"I'm not angry. It's not that." I shake my head and pull away from Jack, walking over to where Matthew has whisked Lola.

I freeze when I see her hysterically crying into my brother's chest. "Lo, darling, I'm so sorry. Please forgive me." I rub her back. "I should have never said that. Let's start over, okay? Let's talk," I plead.

"No," my brother snaps.

"She has a voice, Matthew. Let her speak," I say as calmly as possible.

Lola steps back and pats his chest while smiling up at him through her tears. "It's okay, Matthew, just give us a minute, okay?"

He looks between us and nods. "Fine. I'm coming back in two minutes."

When he's gone, I reach out and pull Lola into my chest. She instantly wraps her arms around me, and we stay in our embrace for a moment before anyone talks.

"Lo, I promise you with all my heart that I didn't mean the age thing. It's not that, it's just…" I pause, trying to tread lightly. "My brother is damaged goods when it comes to women. He doesn't want the happily ever after like you do, and he has more trust issues than me. I don't want to see you get hurt because of it. My outburst before was about that and that alone. Well, and a bit of shock, but mostly because I'm worried."

"I know about all his baggage, Belle. He's told me everything."

I look at her, shocked. "He told you about Emma?"

She nods. "I only recently learned her name, but he told me when we first met how she cheated on him and all the drama that came after."

Wow. He never tells anyone that, so maybe he is serious.

Not that I would be shocked.

Lola is the most endearing, kindhearted person I know, though I sometimes worry she's too naive for her own good.

I wipe a few stray tears from her cheeks, place her hair behind her ear, and smile. "I love you, Lola, and I can't help but worry. So please be careful, because you're young, and your life, in many ways, is still untainted. I only have your best interest at heart, regardless of whether or not he's my brother. I would react the same way if you started dating anyone seriously."

I'm not mad, honestly.

Why wouldn't I want Lola to be with my brother? Putting his issues with women aside… He's strong, selfless, successful, and not to mention handsome.

He practically raised my brothers and me after my dad left, then jumped right into uni and medical school. It's about time he finds his happiness; he deserves nothing less.

I just hate the idea of Lola being his first relationship so many years after his ex-fiancée cheated on him, especially since they live so far apart, because if it doesn't work out, she is going to be crushed, and I'm going to want to kill him.

"How will long-distance work between you two?" I ask. She tenses, and I take a step back. "Lo? Please don't say it…"

She shakes her head frantically. "No, no, no. I'm not leaving you, I swear. I have many plans that we will review when we're home. Matthew doesn't like it. He wants to leave his job and move to London—"

"He wants to move to London?" My brows shoot up in shock. This is huge news. If anything could convince me he's serious, this is it.

We have been begging him to move back for ages, and he would never even consider it—his job was too important.

"So this *is* serious."

"Extremely," my brother says as he rounds the corner, heading straight for me.

He kisses the top of my head quickly, then pulls me in for a hug. "I'm sorry for yelling at you, please understand that if I weren't all in, I wouldn't take a chance with someone I know you care so much about. I swear it."

"I'm sorry as well, Matty. But if you hurt her again—because I detect you're the lad who left her heartbroken last week—I hurt you. Understand? Lola is not just my mate, she's as important to me as you are, and you should know that. I've spoken about Lola for years."

"Cross my heart, she's it for me, Annabelle." He looks over to Lola with a loving gleam sparkling in his eye. He genuinely does look besotted with her.

She smiles back with the same doe-eyed look.

"You look beautiful in this color, Lo. I've never seen you in lavender before," I tell her to break up the awkward moment. It might take a minute to get used to them together.

"Lilac," she corrects. "It's always been my favorite color, and now it has a whole new meaning." She glances up at my brother again, and his eyes shine with a loving warmth I've never seen before.

"Everything good over here?" Sadie asks, peeking around the hedge and hurrying to Lola's side.

Looking between Lola and Matthew, I smile. "Yeah, we're all good now."

Sadie smiles. "Well then, in the words of my daughter, Charlie… Woohoo! Now let's go celebrate all the love."

13

Jackson

My phone dings, alerting me of a message. An instant smile stretches the width of my face, knowing it's probably Belle.

"You look like a love-sick fool." Declan laughs.

I shrug, ignoring him but not denying it, because he's right. I'm the person I've always hated, and I couldn't care less.

Queen B: Hi, lover boy :)
Me: HAHA. How's it going over there? How's my sister? An emotional wreck? I miss you and your lips.
Queen B: Which lips? ;)

I smirk. Of course that's what she says.

Me: You already know the answer to that. Both lips. Always both lips, sweetheart.
Queen B: I can't wait until tonight then! Everything is good, and

of course Sadie is a wreck. Lola and Evelyn are calming her in the room.
Queen B: So for now, instead, I'm just sitting here, sipping a delightful, crisp champagne as I stare at Nora's boobs.

I freeze on the spot, glancing up at Declan and then back at my phone.

Me: WTF?

Now all I see is Belle and Nora, naked together, and, fuck, my dick's reacting to both of them topless. Which is sick, considering Nora's tits are only huge now because they're filled with milk.

My phone dings again, and it's a picture of Belle laughing around her champagne glass, beautiful as ever, while Nora leans in, giving me the middle finger with an oversized smile on her face… and sure enough, her right boob hangs out with a small pumping device attached to it.

I bark out a laugh at the two of them and pass my phone to Declan to piss him off.

"What the feck are they doing?" he grumbles in his usual low-toned manner.

He starts typing away on my phone for a few minutes, then his eyes light up, chuckling to himself, shaking his head in amusement.

"What's going on? Show me, show me."

"What are you, five? Hold on. I'm talking to Nora."

I grab the phone anyway and look at what he's doing.

Me: It's Declan. Tell Nora she's going to be in big trouble tonight for that picture.
Queen B: Hi, Daddy, it's me. I'm so sorry I was a bad girl. Will you spank me as punishment?
Me: I've told you a hundred times to stop calling me Daddy, so because of that, and how I know you love to be spanked so much, I think maybe orgasm denial sounds about right.

Queen B: YOU WOULDN'T!
Me: Oh, I would, angel. Better yet, I will spank you… get you nice and wet, then leave you without sorting you out.
Queen B: We are not on speaking terms. BYE.

My eyes slowly rise to Declan, and he shrugs. "I was going to delete them, but you took the phone too quickly."

"Oh, it's okay, *Daddy Declan*. You have no idea how much I love soft porn." I blink my eyelashes playfully, doing everything in my power to hold back my laughter.

He stills, realizing what I've just read. "Peters… If you ever repeat that, I will literally kill you with my bare hands."

I can't hold it back. I laugh, thinking about Nora calling him daddy and him spanking her in the bedroom.

He doesn't have to kill me… I'm dead.

"What's going on?" Wills asks as he walks into the room.

Declan snaps his eyes to me. "Don't," he mouths.

I tap my back pocket a few times and waggle my brows in a silent threat, then turn back toward Wills and answer. "Not much. Declan was telling me how much he loves being a daddy now."

Declan chokes on his drink while Wills nods in agreement, not having the faintest idea what I really mean. "It's the best feeling in the world. I love being a dad."

I let out another loud laugh, unable to control myself, just as my phone dings again.

Wills narrows his eyes at me, then shakes his head, ignoring me as usual.

John: Can you meet me in the guest bedroom?
Me: In Wills's suite?
John: Yes.

"Hey, what's going on?" I shake John's hand and sit in the chair across from him.

"Trey is handled," he says, his tone deadpan.

"John, I know you're not a man of many words, but I'm going to need you to please elaborate."

"All I can say for now is he had it coming, and soon you'll find out what I'm talking about. Nonetheless, stay away. I don't want your name anywhere near that bloke. He's bad news."

I nod in agreement. "I will, I swear. After our talk, I realized how much of an idiot I'd been… Acting like a teenager, unable to control my anger. My head got the best of me, so trust me, I won't go anywhere near him."

"Good, good," he says, then looks down and reads something on his phone, back in work mode.

He's my sister's driver now, but when he first left the military, he was Wills's bodyguard and sometimes still helps with security.

"What's going on, John?"

"I need you to go grab Wills, then meet me back here. Immediately."

Annabelle

"I'm going to get in so much trouble for that text. I can't wait." Nora sighs, anxiously awaiting punishment later tonight.

"You two are fucking kinky, I love it."

She smirks. "It's only gotten better over time. You don't even want to know what we did the other day."

I pause, contemplating asking her to go on. A part of me wants to know, but when it comes to Nora and Declan, I'm afraid it might scar my image of the two of them.

I am the least prudish person on the planet, but what the two of them get up to is on another level.

"Maybe tell me when I'm drunk later at the reception. This way, when I stand across from Dec at the altar, I won't be picturing whatever it is you did."

She bites her lip and smiles around it. "Probably for the best."

Charlie comes skipping down the long corridor of the suite, holding Chloe's hand.

"Well, shit, Sadie was right. Maybe the trip was a miracle." *Wait.* "What is that dreadful sound she's making?"

Nora sits back, amused. "You haven't heard it yet? It's her new thing and worse than the *Woohoo*s. That sound would be Charlie's whistle, and you have to tell her she's doing amazing if she asks. She thinks it's the best thing in the whole world."

"I am not lying to my godchild. I'll teach her the proper way."

Sadie snorts from behind me as she walks into the room. "Yeah, good luck with that. She thinks she's God's gift to the world right now," she says, then touches my shoulder to get my attention. She smiles softly when I lift my eyes and whispers, "Would you do me the honor of helping me into my dress?"

I roll my lips, trying to hold back my emotions as I stand and interlock our fingers, following her into the bedroom.

"Oh, Sadie." I sigh, wrapping my arms around her. "It's beautiful."

Her watery eyes look up at me. "Do you love it?"

"More than love, darling. It's classic and timeless, just like you. Now, let's get you in it."

I zip up the back of her custom-made dress, then turn her around and shake my head in admiration. "Sadie Marie Peters, you are the most stunning bride I've ever seen." I kiss her cheek. "God, you're gorgeous."

Her makeup is light and natural, and her dark hair is pulled back out of her face, which would usually let the brightness of her green eyes steal the show, but not today.

Today, it's her in this dress. It is one of a kind, and it will have everyone's jaws hitting the ground.

It's an ornately patterned lace, hand-stitched with white and iridescent pearls, giving off a slight sparkle as the light hits.

It's tight-fitting, with a long train crisscrossing at the high neck to form a sort of halter. When she twirls, her exposed back peeks through the keyhole cutout, which we all know will be Wills's favorite.

On their first night together years ago, she wore a backless dress, and it's been his favorite style ever since.

"I'm marrying Wills," she says out of nowhere. "I don't know why, but it's just hitting me suddenly." Her eyes spark with a glint of excitement. "Oh, can you help me with my shoes?"

I open the box and chuckle. "Sadie, you little thief, I lent you these shoes years ago!"

She giggles. "I know. Wills loves them, so I figured I'd wear them as my 'something borrowed.'"

"Oh, that reminds me. Hold on one sec." I run into the walk-in closet where my overnight bag is stored and grab the small box for her.

"Happy wedding day, Sadie." I hand her the box, and she gasps as she opens it.

"Annabelle… oh, God, they're beautiful." She hugs me tight, holding the diamond tear-drop earrings up to her ears.

"Your 'something new,'" I say, staring at her through the mirror.

She's glowing.

"They're perfect, but this is excessive even for you, Belle. It's too much."

"Nonsense." I lightly touch her earlobes, taking them in. They're the perfect addition to the only other jewelry she has on—a small, light gold cuff with diamonds and an abstract rose, in honor of Charlie's middle name, that Wills gifted Sadie for their first Christmas together.

"Thank you so much. Not just for the gift but for always being my biggest supporter. I'm so fortunate to have you in my life."

"There is no thank-you needed," I say, holding her stare. "I'm the fortunate one, because thirty years ago, I met my other half, and I promised her I would be there every step of the way: the good, the bad, and the ugly. Today is a good day—a great day—and I'm proud to stand with you as your maid of honor." We stand there together, taking in the moment and all the years of friendship we've lived through.

Soul mates are not just for lovers.

Sadie fills my heart in a unique way, and I will always be grateful for meeting the shy American girl who grounds me. Even though I might have kept things from her in the past, just knowing she'll always be there for me is enough.

"Do you think it's bad luck that I forgot something old and blue?"

"No, you didn't," Eleanor, Wills's mum, calls from the door before she and Evelyn walk in together. She holds Sadie at arm's length, taking her all in.

"My sweet child… I have no words that adequately describe how you look or how I feel. However, I will say that you are breathtaking. My son is a lucky man."

"Thanks, Mum," she says, gazing at Eleanor with love in her eyes. "I'm sorry, I would have had you in the room with us, but—"

Eleanor shakes her head. "I understand, sweetie. You and Annabelle needed that moment alone."

"I'll give you three a minute." I go to step out, and Evelyn grabs my hand.

"You should stay. You're Sadie's sister and a part of her family, so now you're officially a part of ours too."

I still at her words. She has no idea what that means to me.

I'd never been uncertain about my friendship with Sadie before Evelyn came along. They became instant best friends, and once she marries Wills, they'll officially be sisters.

It had only been Sadie and me our whole lives, so I would be lying if I said I wasn't a bit jealous at first. But once I got to know Evelyn over the years, my insecurities disappeared. I'd been angry with myself for even thinking that Sadie would leave me behind.

We all sit, then Evelyn pulls out a small box and passes it with a shaky hand to Sadie.

She opens it slowly, and as her eyes quickly fill with tears, mine follow without seeing what's in the box. I can only imagine it's something from Evelyn's marriage with her late husband, Andrew.

Sadie lifts it, examining it closely. It's a piece of what, at one time, was probably white lace with a sliver of blue silk in the middle.

Evelyn lets out a loud sob and looks over to her mum for help. Sadie gets up and takes Evelyn in her arms while Eleanor speaks. "Sadie, what Evelyn has gifted you is something near and dear to both of us. The outside layer was a piece from my wedding dress when I married my Thomas forty-five years ago. I gift this to you as my daughter, the same as I did Evelyn on her wedding day, for your 'something old.'" Sadie smiles in thanks and holds it up to her heart.

Eleanor takes a deep breath, trying to hold in her emotions. "Your 'something blue' is the material in the middle. It was also worn by Evelyn on her wedding day. That piece is more important and meaningful than anything else. It is a piece of Andrew's tie from their first backyard wedding at age six."

Sadie scrunches up her face, trying to stop the tears.

There is not a dry eye in the room.

After a minute, Evelyn clears her throat. "It would mean the world to me if you could wear this under your dress as I did on the most magical day of my life. Maybe one day you can pass it down to the girls so that Andrew can be with us on all of our special days."

Oh my god.

"It would be my honor, Evelyn." She pins the fabric to the inside of her dress, then looks around the room. "Thanks to all of you. The family I always wanted but never knew I would be lucky enough to ever have."

Sadie hugs us all, thanking us for the hundredth time.

After a few silent moments, Evelyn lets out a loud laugh and playfully nudges her mum. "We've been hanging around Sadie too long, all of us crying like babies. We Brits are supposed to be better about holding in our emotions, and why the hell didn't we give it to her earlier? Now we all have to fix our makeup again."

There's a loud knock on the door, interrupting us, then Wills peeks his head in.

"Get out, you crazy man. You can't see Sadie yet. It's bad luck!" I scream as Eleanor runs over, trying to push her son out of the room.

It's no use. He's like a brick wall.

He ignores us both, scanning the room for Sadie. When she steps into his view, his breath hitches, and it's clear he's trying to gulp down his emotions.

"Sadie," he whispers. The two of them lock eyes as if no one else is in the room. "God, beautiful, you take my breath away."

I look at Evelyn and she smiles at me, feeling the love between them.

"Come here, baby. I need to talk to you for a moment."

Her face drops. "What's wrong? What's going on?"

He holds out his hand, silently beckoning her.

I must admit, he's worrying me too, especially when he turns toward me and calls me over.

When we walk to the door, Jack is standing on the other side.

His eyes widen when he sees his sister. "Sades, you're stunning." He kisses her cheek, then turns to me and smiles, pulling me into his side, but I can see in his smile that something's off.

"Do you trust me?" Wills asks Sadie.

She scrunches up her nose in confusion. "Of course."

"Then know what I tell you next means nothing, and I will fix it. It won't spoil the day; if anything, I think my plan is better than what we had planned anyway."

"Spit it out, Wills."

He hesitates, so Jack jumps in.

"Mom crashed the wedding. She paid the wedding planner to be placed on the guest list before we fired her, so the security guards had no idea. She's still among the guests because we don't want to make a scene."

What the fuck.

Sadie's worried eyes turn to me, then back to Wills.

I grab her hand in support, waiting to hear what Wills says—letting him lead on this.

"Why is she doing this to me?" Sadie asks the question so forlornly, I feel her pain deeply.

"Because she's a miserable cow and has always been jealous of you," I say truthfully, then turn to Wills. "What's the plan?"

"We're going to set up plan B—"

"We never had a plan B," Sadie interrupts.

"When your mum texted you yesterday, I was worried, so plan B was initiated. Jack will handle the guests and your mum. Sadie, Declan, or my dad will come to pick you up from this room in forty-five minutes. Annabelle, please help Jack, then text me when you're done and I'll meet you."

We look at each other one last time, nodding, knowing we have to move fast before this becomes something bigger than it already is.

"What a nightmare." I sigh and lean on Jack's shoulder.

We had to quickly and quietly move everyone across the street to the public gardens, and it was nothing short of exhausting.

Now we're waiting for security to escort Jack's mum out.

I'm not sure how she thought she'd get away with sneaking in.

Maybe since she was sitting in the back, she thought no one would notice her. Hoping to get snapped in a few photos so Mrs. High Society wouldn't be named a fool when the paps report her own daughter didn't invite her to the wedding.

She walks out in her pristine Chanel suit, her head held high, without a care in the world.

Then, when she sees us standing in the corner, she pauses for a split second, scoffs, and turns her head up at us before continuing her walk of shame.

Jack laughs under his breath. "Can you believe her?"

"She's a joke. Let's go and make sure she gets in the car."

Hand in hand, we follow behind her, stepping out in Place Vendôme to ensure she gets in the car that will usher her out of there.

The second we're outside, he freezes in place, and before I have a second to ask what's wrong, I see him.

Standing across the street is Jack's spitting image… *his dad.*

"Did you have something to do with this?" Jack bellows. "Is that why you've been harassing me?"

I'm not sure Jack sees it, but I do. His dad's face says it all as he walks toward us.

"Jack, let's not make a scene, okay? I don't think he knew." I pull his arm to move, but instead, he steps closer to his dad.

John is by our side in a second, but I hold him off, confident that nothing will happen.

"Hello, Annabelle."

"Mr. Peters." I nod my head respectfully.

"Don't you talk to her," Jack growls, luckily lowering his voice, then turns to me, hurt lacing his voice. "Don't talk to him, B."

I rub his arm, then whisper, "I won't, Jack. I'm sorry."

"What are you doing here?" He directs himself back to his dad. "Why are you doing this after all this time?" he cries.

The average person may think Jack is mad, but my heart is breaking seeing the hurt pouring out of him.

"I promise, Jackie—"

"Don't! Don't you call me that." He points his index finger at his dad. "You have no right, Stephen."

His dad veers back slightly at Jack's venom, holding up his hands. "I'm sorry, Jackson. I tried calling you this week. I thought she was planning something. The housekeeper called me saying she overheard your mother. I drove to her house—"

"Whose house?"

"Your mother's. We don't live together anymore."

Jack narrows his eyes, confused. "Since when?"

He opens and shuts his mouth. "That's not important right now," he says, letting his eyes linger along Jack's frame, taking in his son for the first time in years. After a few moments, he smiles sadly. "I'll let you go. I'm sorry again, I thought I would get here in time, but I was clearly too late."

"You said that's why you called this week. What about all the messages the last few months?"

His dad pauses, then shakes his head before apologizing again and walking away.

"Hey!" Jack calls after him again. "Do you know what I'm about to do?"

His dad turns to listen but doesn't answer.

"I'm about to walk your daughter down the aisle to marry the love of her life, something every father dreams of doing. Except we got stuck with a reject, so while you go home to wherever it is that you fucking live now, I will be performing one of the greatest honors of my life," Jack spits, turning quickly to hide the tears in his eyes, storming off with me by his side.

While we wait for the light to change before crossing, I turn back to see Mr. Peters stuck in place, tears running down his face.

Something is not right.

This man is not like Jack's mum.

It's clear he cares, but what I don't understand is why he hasn't spoken to his children in over thirty years.

Jack drags me to a bench, pulls me into his lap, then buries his head into my chest, taking deep, measured breaths.

"Jack?"

"I don't want to talk about it right now, please don't ask. I need a second to breathe and get in the right headspace for Sadie."

"Of course." I kiss the top of his head and rub his back in comfort.

I'll wait for however long he needs.

Jack pulled himself together as if nothing happened, walked Sadie proudly down the makeshift aisle Wills had put together in the middle of the Jardin des Tuileries, and gave away his sister with grace… even if letting her go killed him a little inside.

I think the whole "giving away" the bride part is archaic, and since I'm not as traditional as Sadie, I note that if the day ever comes for me for real, I'll be skipping that part of it.

Now Lola, Evelyn, Nora, and I stand beside Sadie in beautiful cream-colored silk gowns, all slightly different but still somehow matching.

With Declan and Jack standing by Wills, all handsome as hell in their fitted tuxedos, we watch our good friend Marco officiate the ceremony in the middle of this perfectly designed seventeenth-century garden.

The sun is shining high, everything is in bloom, and we have views of the Louvre's Baroque-style buildings and the famous Parisian ferris wheel.

This garden is also where Sadie and Wills realized they were in love.

So maybe Wills was right: Plan B turned out better in the end.

As Marco speaks, Wills's usually stoic stance cracks when he looks down lovingly at Sadie.

Afraid I'll get too emotional, I look away, only to lock eyes with Jack.

He winks flirtatiously. "Hi," he mouths, wiggling his eyebrows.

My eyes widen. "Don't make me laugh," I mouth back.

Slowly, he bites down on his lower lip. If I had to guess, he's suppressing a groan as he boldly rakes his eyes over my body.

My heartbeat picks up as I teeter back and forth on my heels, wishing away the throb that's building between my legs.

This is what weddings do to people. They make them all crazy and horny.

Well, it's probably more like sappy and lovey, but it's the latter when you're in Jackson Peters's vicinity.

Declan hits his shoulder, and my eyes widen in embarrassment when I realize he's seen our interaction.

Mortified, I look away and focus back on Sadie.

It's about time for her to say her vows and I can tell she's anxious, wringing her hands repeatedly.

Even when Wills attempts to soothe her by taking them in his hands, she doesn't stop.

Sadie opens her mouth to speak, then quickly closes it again. Her worried eyes shoot up to Wills while she covers her mouth to stop herself from getting emotional.

His stoney gray eyes meet hers as he cups her cheek. "I forbid you to say your vows. We can wait until we're in private. I don't want you upset, beautiful."

She raises one brow. "You forbid it?"

He nods with determination.

She giggles and hits his arm playfully. "Aha, that would have worked years ago, Wills Taylor, you big bully, but you can't tell me what to do anymore."

He raises an eyebrow, and her blush is instant at the insinuation.

Jack groans. "Please, none of that today."

Everyone laughs, then quickly quiets when Sadie starts to profess her love.

"Now that Wills has broken the ice a bit, I'll try my best to do this quickly before I become a blubbering mess." She smiles, then takes Wills's hands in hers and begins.

"It was right here, in this very place, the Tuileries des Jardin, where you promised a future for us." She points over to a grassy area. "It was in that very spot that I realized I was falling madly in love with you, and there was no way to stop the rollercoaster even if I wanted to. Your words stuck with me that day, especially when you said: *I hope this is just our beginning*. I believed you, and hoped that when we lost each other for that short period, you were right, that it was only our beginning, and we would once again find one another… Luckily, we did. That's when I was hit with an overwhelming feeling that my life was finally starting. *Our life*." She pauses and takes a breath as Wills wipes away her tears, and then his own.

"Never in my wildest dreams would I have thought we would be back here, getting married in front of the people we love most in the world. Especially with our two sweet little angels, Charlie and Chloe." She glances at them, sitting on Eleanor's lap. "You have given me the best gifts anyone could ask for—earth-shattering love, a found family, and most importantly, strength. You have always believed in me… and to me, that is what a true partnership is about. You are my rock, Wills, my soul mate—" She places her hand on her heart, then her other hand on his. "Our love is rare and strong, just like you. You saved me, and I will forever be grateful for the love you have shown me. You had me then, you have me now, and you'll have me forever, Wills Taylor."

"I love you, Sadie Taylor."

Her smile bursts in pure undeniable happiness. "I love you more."

"I promise you, you don't." He smirks, then kisses her, not caring that it's not time yet.

Wills does what he wants, when he wants, especially when it comes to Sadie.

"Then, now, and forever, baby," he whispers against her lips. "Although, I realized something today… forever isn't long enough."

14

Annabelle

I STAND in a delightful daze watching my best friend glide effortlessly in her husband's arms across the black-and-white-checkered dance floor.

Their moves are seamless, even though they aren't paying attention to anything but each other and the notes of their wedding song being played by the band.

Eyes locked, and often their lips as well, I can see Wills mouthing Ray LaMontagne's "You Are the Best Thing" to Sadie.

Not long after the song starts, Charlie and Chloe run out to the dance floor and join their parents, making it the most perfect first dance of all time.

Something they'll remember forever.

Despite the unforeseen challenges, today turned out better than anyone could have ever imagined. No one would say it was anything less than magical.

"Look how happy they all are." I sigh, glancing around at all my mates.

Jack and Nora stand beside me, and next to them is Declan, Lola, Evelyn, Marco, and, the newest addition to our group—Matthew.

Still so crazy to me that my brother is here with us.

Lola and Marco flank Evelyn closely, hands intertwined with hers, silently giving her any support she might need today.

I only recently learned that this is the first wedding since her own that she's attended. I can only imagine what she must be going through emotionally—wanting to be happy for her brother and new sister while battling the emotions associated with her husband's passing.

Luckily, she has all of us to turn to for help if needed.

Which is a good reminder of why we should all be thankful for the couple gliding around the dance floor. If they hadn't fallen in love, our group wouldn't be as close as it is, and our family wouldn't have formed. We'd have missed out on the genuine, lifelong friendships that have shaped us all in the best possible way.

Jack squeezes my hand in acknowledgment. "They truly are happy, aren't they? I wasn't expecting to feel this content today, but you were right. This is how it's meant to be. Wills, without a doubt, will always take care of his girls."

"He will." I rub his arm. "It's still okay that you were feeling unsure about it all, although I'm glad you're coming to terms with it."

"All right, song's over, let's get drunk!" Nora yells, interrupting us and causing Declan to close his eyes and rub his temples in frustration. "What?" She throws her hand on her hip with her usual fiery attitude.

"Jesus, Mary, and Joseph. What do you think? You barely drink, and you want to get drunk? Don't be an eejit. I'd rather not have to clean up puke tonight after my mate's wedding. That's what."

She points to Declan with determination. "Aye, challenge accepted. This is the first night I don't have little humans hanging off my nipples, milking me like a cow. So either you're in it to win it, or get lost, and I'll go have a drink with those very handsome fellas by the bar."

I choke out a laugh. "That's my brother Theo, and Nate, one of Jack's best friends."

She rolls her eyes. "Of course they are. Why couldn't I pick someone more threatening?" She holds out her hand. "You with me, Hughes? Let's go find some hot rugby players."

I smirk at her enthusiasm. "Yeah, Irish, let's do it."

Jack growls beside me, so I say, low enough for only him to hear, "It's all in good fun, lover boy." Then I wink and stalk off with Nora.

So… Nora wasn't kidding. She is on a bloody mission.

Between the tequila shots and martinis, even I'm done… and that's saying a lot since I've built up a tolerance for partying over the years.

Declan put Nora in a time-out, which has led to them fighting in the corner, undoubtedly until one of them wins.

Of course, my money is on Nora.

But I would be lying if I said I wasn't happy for the reprieve—I think I'm through with the booze for now.

My life in London consists of non-stop events, parties, and drinking. It's too much, and after spending a more laid-back week here with Jack, it's made me think I need to take a step back and hire someone younger to take over that part of the job.

It's exhausting.

I look over to Lola, then back to Matty. "She's a lightweight, don't let her have any more," I tell him. "She's already swaying."

"Fuck's sake, Annabelle." He crosses his arms. "You're bloody annoying tonight. I'm a world-renowned surgeon. I'm well-equipped to take care of my girl. Worry about something else."

His girl… still so weird.

Lola throws her hand over my mouth before I can respond.

"No fighting. I'm good, you're good. We're all good." She smiles at me, then Matthew, lingering with hearts in her eyes. She's smitten.

"Matthew," I whisper.

He must see what I see. "I promise, Annabelle, I truly feel the same about her."

He'd better.

"Hughes," Leo and Nate yell as they approach my brother, slapping him on the back.

My brother laughs, hugging them both. "God, what's it been, twenty years since I've seen you two?"

"It's been way too long. You need to come out for a New York summer in the Hamptons for old times' sake," Nate says. "Where are your brothers, by the way?"

"Definitely, would love that," Matty replies, then nods toward the corner where Theo is sitting with a girl I've never seen. "Oliver stayed home with Mum. She wasn't feeling well."

"Hey," I interrupt. "Where's Sebastian? I haven't seen him all night."

"Calling Harrison to make sure all is good at home. He's the helicopter uncle," Leo responds.

"Oh, that's sweet. Jack's the same way with Sadie's girls."

"There she is!" Jack calls. "The most beautiful bride there ever was."

Sadie comes skipping over to us, wearing a wide grin and holding out her arms for her brother.

Nate grabs her first, practically throwing her up in the air. "Sadie girl!"

"Put me down, Nathaniel!" Sadie playfully scowls, only to have Jack pick her right back up and spin her around.

"You guys are crazy." She chuckles. "Are you all having a good time? You can request any song from the band. They'll play it for you."

"Even Eminem, Slim Sadie?" Declan chuckles at their inside joke while he walks over with a smiling Nora.

Knew it, she definitely won the fight.

While everyone else is preoccupied with Sadie, I turn toward Leo. "I'm disappointed in myself. I completely forgot about the snake dick comment until I saw you guys today."

He throws his arm around my shoulder and pulls me in.

"You know, the second Jack sees you like this, he will come over and lose his shit." I chuckle.

He sniggers and shrugs. "I know. I count on it. He's always giving everyone else crap, it's good to see him squirm a bit. If you get Jackson to come to New York, I'll tell you the story."

"Leo, that's cruel. It's the worst cliffhanger. I need to know."

"I know… I have to get him there somehow, though. We miss him. My parents miss him. They were mad as hell that they couldn't come, but my dad just had hip surgery and couldn't make it. So, you get him to New York, and I'll tell you all the stories."

"Deal."

"Hands off, dickhead." Jack snakes his arm around my waist, pulling me into his side.

"Told you." I smile and lean my head on his shoulder, getting as close as possible without it looking suspicious.

Although, I guess to anyone who doesn't know us, they would assume we're a couple either way.

I've missed him all day, and after getting to spend this past week with him, I crave his touch.

"Now, now, Jackson. We don't want anyone thinking you're jealous, do we? Being that the two of you are still a secret and all."

"You lads act like childish little boys. You do know that, right?"

My eyes widen when Sadie interlocks with my arm.

Did she hear Leo?

"Come on, can we all go dance?" she asks, pulling me and Jack away before we can answer. "Leo, grab everyone else and come meet us!"

"Hi." She turns quickly and kisses my cheek. "I haven't spent much time with you. I'm sorry, but did you see the sunflower wall?"

I chuckle at her enthusiasm. Only Sadie gets this hyped-up about flowers. "It's hard to miss. Are you happy with how everything turned out? Were you surprised?"

Her eyes go wide. "Of course I was. I never know when Wills will pull these grand gestures, plus the sunflowers were such a special touch, being that they surrounded us on our first date."

The second we get to the dance floor, the music changes to a slow song and her eyes light up. "Sorry, I'll be back." She runs off, shimmying her shoulders. "Have to find my *husband* to dance with!"

Jack aggressively pulls me into his body, and I throw my arms around his neck tightly as we begin to sway back and forth to the beat of the music.

"Thank God. I've been dying to get my hands on you all night. I may pay the band extra to only play slow songs for the rest of the night."

"I know. I've missed you all day, Jack. Isn't that crazy? I don't like being away from you, that's a new feeling for me."

His green eyes flare in surprise. "Trust me. I understand that more than anyone. I've thought about nothing but you all day. I couldn't wait to see you."

"Jack—"

"B—"

We laugh quietly. "You first," I say.

"When we get back to London, we need to tell Sadie. I'm sick over not telling my sister. I understand why you thought it best to keep it to ourselves until after the wedding, but we need to prioritize it when we get home."

"I agree one hundred percent. All day, especially when we were texting, I felt guilty for keeping this secret while in the same room as her."

"Good. We can tell her when she helps us move you into my place," he states, smirking when I go still. "What? You thought after this week we'd go home and live separately? We already have busy jobs that will keep us away from one another. I don't want to have to figure out whose place we'll be at, packing bags, and whatever other shit comes along with it. It's not happening. I told you… I'm all in. And I don't need to explain again what that means to me."

He spreads his fingers against my exposed back and presses me harder into his body. "I don't like that I can't see my mark anymore. I want everyone to know you're mine," he whispers, and I smile into his shoulder.

Possessive bastard.

"Soon. You can see it when we return to our room." I wink.

He groans. "I can't even think of that right now. Otherwise, my already semi-hard dick will be standing at full attention for all to see. Tell me what you were going to say a second ago, sweetheart."

"Only that it makes me nervous that everything has changed so rapidly. I already miss your touch and crave seeing you, and it hasn't even been a whole day. How does it flip a switch just like that? Depending on a man for happiness is not my idea of normal. Then you mention moving in, and my heart starts fluttering a mile a minute, screaming, *Yes, yes, yes*. It's confusing."

"Well, I'm glad your heart's on board, because I wasn't giving you a choice." He shoots me a cheeky smirk while I poke one of his dimples playfully. "And it's not too fast. Just look at it like I do. We have always had feelings for each other, and in some ways, held back for the same reason. You, scared of getting hurt, and me, subconsciously worried about hurting you."

"And you're not worried now?"

"Don't," he warns. "You know, deep down, I'll try my damn hardest not to hurt you."

He's right.

"So you'll move in?"

My brow lifts in amusement. "I thought I didn't have a choice?"

He smiles, but it carries a serious undertone. "You don't. Because being separated at night, even by one inch, is too far. I don't want to spend any more nights away from you."

My breath catches at his words, somehow still astonished at the change between us. "You mean that?" I murmur, feeling my eyes well up.

"I mean everything I've ever said to you, more than you even know."

"Jack." I sniff, ducking my head to hide my tears.

I guess we're moving in together.

He rests his chin atop my head and rubs his thumb along the apples of my cheeks. "I want to kiss you, sweetheart. You're making this so hard on me."

"Soon, Jack," I whisper, and bury my head deeper into his chest as we move effortlessly to the music.

After a few seconds of silence between us, he says, "This will be us one day, I promise."

I lean back. "What do you mean?"

"I want to marry you properly. I want to have a proper celebration between us. You deserve it all, B."

I stare at him wide-eyed. "You continue to surprise me, Jack."

"And this will be our wedding song," he states with reverence. "It's our first dance as a real couple." He smiles, cupping my cheek, and for a second I think he might kiss me… and in that second, I don't care if he does.

Wait.

"You want an Elvis song as our wedding song?" I chuckle. "It's a little reminiscent of Vegas, don't you think?"

He barks out a loud laugh that has the people around us staring. "I didn't even think of that. Now it's even more of a reason. But no, this is a different version."

He pulls us over to Marco, mister music genius. "Hey, who sings this song? The chic version, not Elvis."

"Haley Reinhart," he tells us without thinking.

Jack moves us back to our spot, though we don't pick up our dancing. Instead, he holds me close in the middle of the dance floor. I try to move, but he tightens his grip. "I don't want to dance anymore," he mutters.

"Why's that, Jack?"

"Because this is our wedding song, and today's not our wedding."

I still, staring into the depths of his unblinking eyes. He's serious.

A warmth spreads across my chest, and my heart beats wildly at the thought of having an actual wedding song.

Jackson and Annabelle Peters.

It's a phrase I put in the back of my mind after Vegas, never wanting to get my hopes up. Now, it sounds like perfection to me.

Jack brings his face inches from mine, pressing our noses together. "'Can't Help Falling in Love' by Haley Reinhart and the words, sweetheart"—he grabs my hand, bringing it up through the tight space between us and pressing soft kisses to my knuckles—"couldn't be any more fitting."

"Jack…" I cry, my voice breaking, before dropping my head again to the crook of his neck so no one can see my tears. "I feel the exact same way."

When the song ends, I compose myself and lift off of Jack.

And I immediately freeze in place.

Straight ahead is Lola, crying happy tears with her hand on her heart, looking between me and Jack with nothing but love. Next to her is not only Matthew but Theo, too, and neither look happy… They're furious.

Well, shit.

"You're in big fucking trouble, Annabelle," Jack growls in my ear. "Last drink, then we're going upstairs."

Unable to hold back, I let a quiet giggle slip out my lips, causing another low growl from Jack.

I knew this reaction from him was coming.

We've had a few more drinks, and I realize drunk Jack is more jealous than ever. It doesn't help that I've been in the corner with London's other notorious playboy George Anderson while Jack's been stuck with Sadie for the last thirty minutes.

It also doesn't help that George and I have had playful, flirtatious banter going on for years that Jack is well aware of.

What he doesn't know is whether or not we've hooked up, and I know it's driving him insane.

George is a good friend of Wills, they played rugby together for years. He also went to school with my brother Matthew, and I've known him since I was a kid.

The flirting is just for fun; nothing more has ever happened. But I have to admit that seeing Jack suffer is even more fun.

"Last toast of the night." Jack picks up his scotch and we all follow, angling ourselves toward the bride and groom, who have two of the cutest babies asleep in their arms.

Their nanny came as a guest but also to help, though I don't think it would have felt the same if they didn't include the girls the whole time, so it's not a surprise they're still here, even if they're sleeping.

"Cheers to Sadie and Wills and their epic celebration of love. A celebration that was long overdue for two people who deserve a happy ending more than most. Tonight was one for the books!"

"Cheers!" we all sing in unison, clinking glasses. His words couldn't be any truer.

Jack scans the circle of our friends and finds Wills's eyes. "And to Wills. Someone I already admired as a father, but now as a husband, as well. Thank you for being the one my sister deserves. Congrats to the newlyweds, Mr. and Mrs. Taylor."

Everyone clinks glasses again as Wills passes a sleeping Charlie to Declan, then walks toward Jack.

He holds his hand out, then pulls him in for one of those manly hugs where they pat each other's backs and grunt. Though I can see in their eyes, especially Wills's teary ones, this means more.

The second my drink is finished, Jack's hand is on mine pulling me away from the crowd. "Let's fucking go."

"What the hell are you doing, Jack? We didn't even say goodnight."

"Everyone is drunk, passed out, or about to pass out. They don't give a shit. We'll see them at brunch in the morning."

Is it wrong that I'm excited for angry Jack to fuck me?

God, it's going to be so good.

"Ah, wait!" I put on the brakes, tugging on his hand.

He tugs back, trying to pull me along. "I'm not waiting any longer. I need you now."

I push through the door next to me and use all my strength to bring Jack along.

Shit, no lights. Where the hell are we?

"Best goddamn call you've made in your life, B. Who the hell wants to wait to get back to the room?" he mutters, lust thick in his words.

He snakes his arm around my waist, pulling me tight against him and kissing my neck, quickly realizing my dress is in the way.

"Fuck, take it off. Now," he barks.

"How can you even see right now? I'm blind as a bat." He puts his phone light on and accidentally shines it right in my eyes. "Jack. Get that light off of me."

"Shit. Sorry." He props it on a shelf. "Why are we in here?" he asks, then adjusts himself, and now I can't seem to drag my eyes away.

Why did I bring us in here again?

"Annabelle!" he snaps.

Oh. "My brothers were at the end of the hall. I haven't spoken to Theo all night, afraid he would murder one of us. So I brought us in here to hide." Which I'd thought was a good idea, but now can see from the look in Jack's eyes… it was a *great* idea.

He stalks toward me on a mission, and I back up slowly, not even caring that brooms are crashing around me.

"So you didn't come in here to fuck?"

I fake a gasp. "Absolutely not! What type of woman do you take me for?"

He does a shit job of hiding his smirk. "One who's about to get her ass fucked if she doesn't take her dress off."

"*Oh.*" I take a deep breath, my voice barely a whisper.

Jack stops abruptly, his sharp gaze penetrating me. "You like that, sweetheart? You want me to bend you over and fuck your ass right here in this dirty closet?"

I don't answer. I can't. My voice is thick, stuck in my throat.

He lets out a sardonic chuckle. "Not tonight—we have no lube. But soon. I've been dying to take you there," he mumbles, looking me up and down. "That doesn't mean I'm not going to have you. Take your dress off."

No problem. "Lock the door," I say while I unzip the side of my dress, letting it pool on the floor.

"Goddamn, you're sexy. Leave the heels on and turn around."

I don't bother telling him I was planning to leave them on whether he liked it or not. The ground must be filthy in here. But I do turn around, not hesitating even a second, sticking out my bum to taunt him.

I hear it before I feel it, the sound of whooshing in the air as his hand comes down on my behind. My body flies forward, and I catch myself on the wall.

"Bloody hell, what the hell was that for?" I cry, reaching around to soothe my poor bum. Before I get the chance, he grabs my wrist, placing my hand back on the wall.

"Don't. The sting is your punishment."

I turn my head to the side, trying to see him, but it's still dark. Though I can tell he's trying to calm himself from the sound of his deep, measured breaths.

"Why am I being punished, Jack?"

I already know the answer.

"Taunt me again with George or any other man, and it won't be the only spank you get. Now spread your legs."

"Are you not going to kiss me?" I whisper, and when he hesitates, I realize he's more angry than I thought. "I'm sorry, Jack. Honestly, I was only playing around. You're the only man for me, you know that."

He doesn't answer, but I feel the heat of his body come up behind me. A second later, he trails his fingertips along my spine, up into my hair, massaging my head.

"You're forgiven, B," he whispers against my open mouth, sliding his tongue against mine.

If this is all I got, I would be a happy woman. His kisses are perfection, and the second his lips hit mine, my whole body lights up with sparks.

Every. Single. Time.

Our kiss quickly turns frantic, his hand grips my hair tightly while my arse pushes hard into his groin, needing him inside me now.

I recognize the sound of a zipper before his fingers are at my entrance. "Fuck, you're so wet."

He slides three fingers inside, not even warming me up. It's no use anyway; I'm ready to go. "Now, please."

"You need my cock, baby? You need me to fill you up?"

I don't get a chance to answer. He pushes in in one hard, swift movement.

Oh God.

I close my eyes and bite my lip to keep from screaming out.

He holds still, buried deep inside me, trying to catch his breath. "This is going to be hard and quick, B. Sorry… I'll make it up to you later. You feel too good, and I've been dying to get inside of you all night. I'll never last."

"Oh God, me neither, Jack. If you so much as touch me, I'll explode all over you right now."

"Fuck, don't say that." He pulls out almost all the way and slams back in, then again, and again. "Belle," he moans loudly, and I have no strength to tell him to be quiet.

His hands encase my waist, pulling me hard onto his dick with every measured thrust. His hips swivel up, hitting a spot that almost no man ever finds, and for the first time in my life, I think I could come like this.

"Holy shit, Jack," I cry. "Don't. Stop!"

He leans over, trails his tongue up my back, and places an open-mouth kiss on my neck, sucking hard to make another mark.

"Oh God… B." He stands back up and continues the magical movement that has me seeing stars. "I'm going to come, Belle. You need to come soon. Are you almost there?"

He moans loudly, and I can picture his head thrown back as his Adam's apple bobs up and down his sexy neck.

"I-I don't know." I shudder. "Oh God, it feels so good, but I don't know. Rub my clit, Jack! Please," I cry.

The second his fingers are on me, I explode all over him, screaming his name, clenching hard around his dick as my orgasm rips through me.

"Ughhh… Fuckkkkk." Jack explodes a second later, hammering into me until every last drop of his come is released.

After a few long seconds of catching our breath, he wraps both arms around me, pulling me up and pressing his front to my back.

He buries his head in my neck, placing small kisses and squeezing his arms tighter around me every few seconds. As fun as that was, I wish we were upstairs, where I could hold and cuddle him back.

"You're perfect," he whispers.

"That was Belle and Jackson!" I hear Nora yell outside the door.

What the hell?

Jack snickers behind me, and all I can do is laugh alongside him while he zips me up quickly. "She better be talking to Declan and no one else."

I whip open the door, and sure enough, there stand my Irish friends. "Can you shut up, you two! Anyone could hear." I grab Nora's arm and drag her into the room, motioning for Declan to follow.

Okay, this room is a little tight for all of us, but it's better than getting caught in the hall.

I turn around, and now Jack's and Declan's phone lights are on. I can see Nora's eyes light up like a Christmas tree. "I fecking knew it!" She points between the two of us.

"Yeah, yeah. Miss fucking detective over here. Don't you say a word, Nora Buckley, or I'll kick your arse!" I narrow my eyes, and Nora laughs louder, rolling her eyes.

I might have five inches on her, but she would dominate me. There is no way I'm kicking her arse.

"I told you!" she tells Declan, except he already knows and isn't hiding it.

She sucks in a deep, exaggerated breath and pokes Declan hard in the chest. "You knew? Since when?"

"Not long. And before you get mad, it wasn't my place to say anything."

Jack interrupts us to stop the impending fight. "I asked him not to say anything. I'm sorry."

She softens at Jack's voice but still throws daggers at Declan.

"It's okay, Jackson. But why are you guys hiding? I knew something was going on."

"We'll tell everyone after the wedding, so just keep your mouth shut until then," I say, knowing she's dying to tell someone already.

"Aye, great. We all know, now can we get the feck out of this closet? I'm suddenly becoming claustrophobic," Decan says, his voice a little shaky.

I slowly open the door and when I see the coast is clear, we all exit, pretending nothing happened.

All of us get off the lift on the same floor and when Jack opens our suite door, Nora calls out our names from down the hall where she and Declan are staying.

"I just want to say, if there was anyone I was rooting for, it would have always been the two of you. I've felt something genuine between you since the second I met you. You can ask Declan."

"Aye, she truly did," Declan confirms, then swiftly pulls his wife into their room.

Jackson

As we walk through our suite, Belle's eyes light up. "Come on! It's about to start. It's our last one before we go home tomorrow." She rushes through the room, her long blonde hair wafting through the air as she runs out the doors and onto the terrace.

I follow her like the lovesick fool I am—yes, *love*. I am completely and utterly in love with Annabelle Hughes… *Peters*.

Words I never thought I would ever say to a woman besides my sister and, of course, my nieces. I've almost said it to her half a dozen times already, but something's been holding me back.

Knowing Belle needs reassurance, I don't want her to think I got swept up in the moment of our date or the wedding. I need her to understand fully that if those three words are coming out of my mouth, I mean them with a passion… along with everything else I've said to her over this past week.

So I'll wait until we're home and settled. When she knows I'm here to stay.

"We've watched this a million times. Let's go back inside. It's starting to drizzle." I wrap my arms around her midsection and place small kisses up her sensitive neck—the spot she loves, the spot I'm equally addicted to.

"Jack," she mutters. "Look, it's not just a twinkle this time. It's a full-on light show—they only do it like this once a day before it goes dark."

I smile against her skin at her enthusiasm. She's made me watch the Eiffel Tower sparkle a million times over the last few nights.

And even though I complain most of the time, I wouldn't trade it for the world. I love spending any time I can with Belle.

Glancing away from her for a second, I look at the lights. Sure, they're different, but they're still lights, and I'd rather have my eyes on her… "I see it, sweetheart." Then I turn my attention back to her.

She looks up at me and smiles. "You're not looking."

With one arm around her back, I support her neck and surprise her by dipping her low, placing a chaste kiss on her lips.

"I don't need to see them. The brightest light in my life is right here before my eyes."

15

Annabelle

IT FEELS good to be home and back in the office, mixed up with the hustle and bustle of it all. As much as Paris was a dream, being back in London calms all my anxiety and stress over work, which may seem contradictory, but I thrive on a fast-paced lifestyle.

Even wearing my work clothes settles something in me, like I can handle anything that comes my way when I wear my armor.

"Hello," I say, greeting two employees in the process of cleaning up their lunch as I go to grab a teacup. It's almost comical how their eyes widen—at the same time—as if I've never said hello to them before.

Maybe I haven't. Who knows. The chance that I haven't is high, considering Lola tells me repeatedly that I need to be more approachable.

I want this business to succeed, and unfortunately, that makes me the bad guy at times because I have no time for bullshit and chitchat.

I've said it a million times: If I were a male CEO, most people wouldn't bat an eye.

Double standards at their finest.

"Hi, Maggie," Lola says to the brunette as she walks in a few minutes after me. She gives the blonde a side hug next and says, "Mia, how's your mum?"

"She's good, thanks for asking."

The girls say their goodbyes, then Lola turns her attention to me, narrowing her eyes.

"What?" I ask defensively.

"What did you say to them? They looked like they'd seen a ghost when I walked in."

Glancing at her over my teacup, I shrug and mumble as I take a sip. "I said hi. I don't see the issue here."

She pauses, then both sides of her lips curve up as she tries to suppress her laughter. "Maybe I was wrong and you should leave the personable stuff to me and human resources."

"Why are you on my case about it? We're five years in and thriving. We promote within, and we have a low turnover rate. I don't see the problem. Are people complaining?"

"No," she huffs loudly. "I don't have all the details yet, but we've had an influx of resumes come in… All ex-employees of Victoria."

Placing my cup down, I turn toward Lola and stand in shock.

That's never happened before.

"Why? What are they saying?"

"I'm still investigating and trying to figure that out without being intrusive, but I heard shit's going down, and not only are her employees leaving, but her clients as well. It makes me nervous. That's why I've wanted you to be on your best behavior."

"Lo, just because I'm tough in the office doesn't make me unkind or unfair. I know it's hard for you because you're naturally sweet, but I didn't get to where I am today by being best friends with my employees. I like clear boundaries, and it's okay if that doesn't work for you, but it's how I work best."

She nods. "Yeah, I get it."

"So do you think that's why Victoria has contacted our clients? Maybe trying to build her business back up?"

"Makes sense, but like I said, I'm still unsure of the specifics. I'll keep my eyes and ears open and let you know what I find out," she says, then clears her throat and rocks back on her heels. "I looked at your calendar. You're done with meetings. Can we talk in your office?"

My face drops and my body tenses. "I'm not sure I'm ready to hear what you have to say, if I'm being honest."

We haven't had a chance to talk about her and Matthew, and I'm petrified—I can't do this without her.

Her name might not be on the door, but this business is just as much Lola's as it is mine. I'm worried because even though Matthew has sworn off relationships in the past, I know that if he's decided Lola's the one, he's not going to make the same mistakes again.

He'll put her first, or as best he can with his job, which means he'll want to be near her at all times… long distance won't work.

Lola doesn't answer. Instead, she takes my hand and leads me down the hall to my office, locking the door behind us. The anxiety radiating off of her only makes me that much more nervous.

We sit on my dark blue velvet sofa, which takes up the corner section of the modern space I call my office. My décor is a mix of traditional and modern, and I've always thought it adds more character. Though, right now, it feels dark and dull as the mood settles between us.

Lola's eyes are sad but clear when she speaks. "I'm not leaving you, but I am leaving this office for a while."

I raise a questioning brow in her direction, unsure of what the hell she means. She reaches over and places her hand on my thigh, squeezing lightly as she tries to calm the impending freakout she must see boiling below my surface.

"Before you jump to conclusions, let me finish. I've worked diligently on this plan and it's going to work just fine. Will it suck between you and me as mates? Yes, one hundred percent, but I need to do this for Matthew and me. So, let me explain, then we can talk about the rest."

I lean back and cross my arms. I hate the idea of giving her up to my brother.

"Okay, I can already see by that bitch-face you have going on that I should skip the small bits and just rip off the bandage." She crosses her arms, mimicking me. "I'm moving to Africa, and I'm going to commute, minimum twice a month. I'd have Zoom calls set up weekly with my direct reports. I made sure the Wi-Fi is adequate where we're going to be living and—"

"Hold on." I put my hands up. "You're going to commute from Africa twice a month. That's ridiculous. You'll be bloody knackered."

"No, honestly, I don't think I will. Matthew lives two hours from the airport, which is practically the same time it takes me to get to Heathrow in traffic. The flight is six hours, and sure it's long, but you know me, the second the plane is rumbling on the runway, I'm fast asleep. It sounds more dramatic because I'm commuting from *Africa*. People often go back and forth between New York and London or New York and Los Angeles, and it's the same distance."

I hate that my instinct is to be upset over this, because I'm so proud she's doing something for herself.

Taking a deep breath, I smile through my sadness. "I'll miss you terribly. You know that, right?"

She quickly wipes her tears with the back of her hand. "It's the only thing that's held me back, knowing I won't see you everyday. And it won't happen overnight. I still need to work on my visa and all that fun stuff."

"I'm sorry, Lo. I never want you to feel like I'm holding you back from anything. We'll work it all out in time, I promise," I say, then, "Fuck."

She startles at my sudden outburst. "What's wrong?"

"If you're not here, does that mean I actually have to start being friendly?"

She bursts out laughing. "You're ridiculous. I'll make sure to be extra nice to everyone when I'm in the office to tide them over."

"God, I still can't believe we're talking about this." I shake my head, smiling. "Not only have you finally met your match, but it's my freaking brother. You seem so happy."

She beams, that dreamy look taking over her face again. "I know.

Before we talk all about that, though, I have other news you may not like."

"What could be worse than you leaving?"

"Romeo thinks you need to go to Italy." I open my mouth, but she keeps talking. "Before you go all 'I'm too busy' on me, listen to what I have to say."

"Fine," I drag out.

"While you were in Paris, I spoke to Romeo. He told me he understands you run a business and that staying the rest of the summer would be nearly impossible. His dad's the one who's brought up how you've turned down the offer a few times already. He thinks his father was insulted, which could easily be the case. An old-school Italian man offers you one of his gorgeous homes for the summer, and you turn him down? He's our biggest client; it doesn't look good."

I throw my head back on the sofa and close my eyes in frustration. I do not have time to leave again. If I did, I would be on the next flight to Italy.

Who the hell would turn down a free trip to a gorgeous villa?

Absolutely no one.

I'm not saying no because I'm ungrateful. I've turned it down because I have enough work to last me a lifetime, and there aren't enough hours in the day to get through it.

"Lo, I just got back from a week in Paris. I have so much to catch up on. How on earth would it work?"

"I don't know, but you'll make it happen for them." She scrunches up her face and adds, "Especially because… I already told them yes."

I practically catapult off the sofa. "What?" I shriek.

"There was no other choice," she says, throwing her hands up in frustration. "They put me on the spot, and there was no way I could say no after they just signed the contract with us. You need to suck it up and go. You can make it a working trip if you want. You have that new client based out of Florence, the fashion designer! Plus, it would be nice if you touched base with Alessia, considering she got us the DeLuca project. Do whatever you need to do, but you're going." She takes a breath, then aggressively points her finger at me. "And stop complaining. Some people never get to take a holiday, let alone two in the span of a few weeks. Get over yourself."

Rearing back to avoid her finger—and her attitude—I know I can't disagree one bit.

"Okay, calm down. If you're this grumpy, you're spending too much time with my brother."

I know it's the right thing to do, but I'm still dreading the idea. Even thinking about packing for a whole other trip is making me break out in hives.

Nonetheless, I need to figure it out and see it as an opportunity. Plus, as Lola said, I can meet a few clients there. It'll be less stressful if I can use the trip to multitask. Maybe Jack can even meet me for the weekend, and we can have a romantic getaway. Sure, we just arrived home from Paris, but by the time we finally figured things out between us, we only spent two days there as a couple, and then everyone had already arrived. It was a whirlwind of chaos. We really didn't have much time to ourselves.

"When do I leave?"

She's slowly backing out of my office, not answering.

"Lola," I warn.

"They've booked a first-class ticket for you, and you leave tomorrow," she mutters.

I rub my hands down my face and take a deep breath to keep from losing my shit. "Can you come back into my office? I won't freak out, but I want to know why you're only telling me now." I get up, looking over all my work on my desk.

I need to leave soon to go to my mum's. How the hell am I going to sort this all out?

"Because we've only just finalized the details. I only committed you to a long weekend, so you can relax."

She doesn't get it. Even one day is longer than I want to be away. "I didn't even get to pick the location. They said I could stay at any of their properties."

"I picked Tuscany for you since it's near Florence. Plus, staying there allows you to learn more about the DeLuca wine. Again, consider it a work trip."

"I guess when you put it that way…"

She points to my desk. "Stop fussing with all that. I've taken care of everything. I even laid out clothes for you at home. I know how much you hate packing."

"What? You're the COO of the company, not my assistant anymore. You didn't need to do that, though I truly appreciate it."

Her phone dings as she replies, "Your assistant sucks, and I didn't trust her not to screw this up, so it was easier if I handled it. I actually sent you resumes to fill her position. You can look over them while you're in Italy." She looks down, staring at the phone intently. "Check your texts."

I grab my phone, pull up my group chat with the girls, and see an attachment from Sadie. It's a family painting of them at Wills's parents' house in the Cotswolds.

Sadie and Wills are gazing at each other as they often do, with pure happiness radiating from their faces. Charlie is lying on her back in the meadow surrounded by wildflowers beside Buddy, his paw resting on her arm. Chloe is sitting next to them, giggling and throwing the flowers in the air.

"Nora did this?" I ask, even though I can tell straight away that she did. No one I know is as talented as her.

"Yes, isn't it impressive? It was their wedding gift."

It's more than that. "Her ability to paint a picture and capture the feeling in them has always left me speechless. But wait… I thought they said no gifts? Only donations to one or both of their foundations?"

She lifts an accusing brow. "You're telling me you didn't buy anything for Sadie?"

"That's different. She's like my sister."

She leans back against the door jam, smirking. "Did you get Wills a gift?"

"That's also different. I was thanking him for taking care of my sister," I mutter, then realize the time. "Ahh, I need to leave. Call me if you need me for anything. I'm heading to Mum's to check on her, then going to Jack's to change before tonight's gallery opening."

She walks over and helps me pack up the rest of the stuff. "I asked Callie, our new senior director, to go in your place tonight. She'll email if she can make it. I've also emailed you all the details of your trip. Everything you need for work is in your inbox or the special folder I made on your laptop labeled *Italy Trip*. The hard copies you'll need are printed and are at Jack's place waiting for you."

Lola is a remarkable human. "I love you, thank you for helping." Then I add, "But wait, should I really be thanking you since you got me into this mess?"

She hugs me tight. "You know it's the right thing to do, and I promise to hold down the fort until you get home."

God… I'm going to miss her when she leaves.

"Hey, B, wait up," Jack calls from across the street.

He jogs to catch up to me, and as usual, I'm too stunned by his good looks to move.

I barely have a second to say hello before he barrels into me, grabs my face, and kisses me with reverence. Feeling just as starved as him, I press into his body, needing to feel all of him.

Has it only been one day since I last saw him?

We were spoiled in Paris, and now I crave this all the time.

Luckily we get to spend the night together once my work event is over. It will be my first night sleeping at Jack's as *our* house.

Some of my things were moved over while I was at work, and even though I still think it's fast, I'm more ecstatic than I thought I would be. If it were up to Jack, I would have moved in the second we arrived back in London.

Instead, I spent last night and this morning with Sadie and the girls, as she and Wills leave for their honeymoon tomorrow.

It would have been the perfect time to come clean to her about Jack and me, but he had work commitments he couldn't get out of, and we both agreed we should tell her together.

Now it'll have to wait until after the honeymoon. Another ten days of holding in this secret from my best friend… it's killing me.

Thankfully the girls were in rare form, still wired from the weekend excitement, so I didn't have much one-on-one time with Sadie.

"Hi, my beautiful B," Jack mumbles around my mouth, then pulls back, still holding me tight. "I've made a decision for us."

I smile at his playful tone. "Oh yeah, Jack, what's that?"

He mimics my smile, holding my stare for a moment before speaking.

I've noticed he does that often, and it's the little moments like this that don't go unnoticed by me. I cherish them more than anything because they're involuntary. He doesn't even realize his reactions.

"We're going to retire early. It's not like I can't afford to take care of us. So let's stay home together all day, every day. I hated being away from you today."

That shouldn't sound tempting because I love what I do. But… the thought of spending all day and all night in bed or traveling, enjoying the world with Jack with no other worries? Sounds like nothing short of a dream right now.

His lips meet mine again, prolonging this moment between us. easily slipping his tongue through my parted mouth, causing a deep arousal to build quickly.

"Jack," I moan, tugging at the collar of his shirt in desperation.

Why is it always like this? Needing him so badly that I can't control myself?

"I've been waiting to do that all day," he whispers darkly. "We need to get out of here."

Ahh… What the fuck are we doing? I push back and smooth down my dress.

"Can you control yourself, please? We're still standing in front of my mum's," I tease, flipping my hair over my shoulder. "And what are you even doing here? I thought I was meeting you at your place."

"*Our* place, Annabelle, not mine. And I was nearby, so I thought I'd pick you up. Should I go in and say hi?"

"Don't bother. We didn't end our conversation on the best foot."

His face is one of concern. "What happened?"

"We fought over the wedding. She should have come, and I'll be having a word with Theo and Matthew about it later. Mum was fine from the fall physically, but mentally not so much. They shouldn't have left her in London alone."

"Maybe I should go in and smooth things over, then. I've always been her favorite." He shrugs teasingly, but he's right. She's always had a soft spot for Jack.

"So full of yourself."

He laughs and grabs my arse, squeezing so tight it hurts. "Ouch." *What the hell?*

"Wear a thong with a dress like this again and see what happens to this ass of mine." He smacks it hard.

"Are you jealous someone's going to see my bum?" I whisper, and when he narrows his eyes, I pretend to lift my skirt.

His eyes darken to the darkest green I've ever seen. "I'm not even kidding. That ass is mine, and mine only. Don't test me."

"Only yours, caveman. Let's go."

I zip the side of my dress and throw on a leather bomber jacket before sitting down to put my heels on. From my peripheral vision, I notice Jack hasn't taken his eyes off me since we arrived home, causing my body to hum happily in response.

My heart has had no time to prepare for the whirlwind my love life has swiftly turned into.

No time to adjust to the intense feelings that rush over me at any given moment without warning.

Like now, something about him watching me, in his home, *as our home*, has my head spinning wildly.

I've been completely enamored by Jack's permanent smile and his proud demeanor since he walked me through the house, showing me all the changes he made for me.

I had no idea he'd worked from home half the day to make me feel as welcome as possible. He even set up my own area in his home gym, knowing how important it is for my mental health to start my day with a workout. I swear that morning workouts help my clarity and attention span tenfold.

Or perhaps it's his constant need to make sure I'm comfortable and happy with our new arrangement. As much as Jack likes to throw his weight around demanding things, he always puts me and my feelings above all else.

"It feels weird to be here like this," I say as I glance around his modern bachelor pad.

Jack and I have similar design styles, mixing old and new, making it an easy transition, at least décor-wise.

He's kept the original architectural structure of the house—the highly decorated moldings, the antique doors and handles, and the big beautiful bay window.

However, he's laid light gray concrete floors throughout the space and built a large industrial modern kitchen with dark cabinets and a mix of wood and steel running throughout the room.

The floors are followed into the bedroom, but it's mostly covered with a hand-woven gray-and-black rug. His king bed is raised on a wooden platform, inadvertently making it the centerpiece of the room, surrounded by a dark gray plush velvet headboard and mahogany bedside tables.

It's sultry and sexy, and although dark and dim, when daylight hits, this southern-facing room is bright and beautiful.

I've been here a million times before, only in a friend capacity of course, so walking through it as *our* space feels different.

"Why, if anything, you should feel right at home. You've been here more than my sister," he says, mimicking my thoughts.

"Well, that's just it. It feels like I'm visiting you. I wonder how long it'll take to feel like I live here."

He removes his watch and it slips from his fingers, falling to the ground. "Why don't we get a new place?" he says nonchalantly.

"What? Why? You love this place."

Jack's always been proud of the home he's built, which is why it was easy for me to move here. Plus, it doesn't hurt that it's three times the size of my place.

"I bought this house so long ago that I'd make a profit if I sold, and you definitely will make one on your flat. Then, we can start fresh and pick the exact area and style of home we both want."

"Really?" I ask, still surprised, yet thrilled at the idea.

My flat was only ever supposed to be an investment, but I stayed longer out of convenience. It would be nice to sell it and move on finally.

Start a new chapter with Jack.

He bends down to grab his watch. "Why not? It sounds like the perfect plan."

"Okay, I'm excited. While you're down there, can you help me with my shoe?" I ask, wiggling my foot in the air.

He doesn't hesitate. He turns and crawls toward me.

"Jack," I chuckle, arching my brows mischievously. "I like you on your knees."

He rolls his lips, hiding his devilish smirk as he bows his head, continuing his crawl.

Stopping in front of me, he lifts my foot and uses his chest for support as he fastens the clasp of my gold Saint Laurent heel. He runs his fingertips up the inside of my leg, following his path with light kisses.

"My love," he whispers against my skin, kissing the inside of my ankle with an open mouth and drawing small circles with his tongue before biting down.

My body instantly fills with butterflies at the endearment, though simultaneously, my sex clenches at the feeling of his tongue dragging along my skin.

"You are my Queen B, and I'd get down on my knees for you any day of the week. You deserve all my praise, Annabelle."

"Jack," I gasp.

He can't say things like that right before I need to leave, because now I'm stuck, too consumed by his presence to move, especially

16

Jackson

FUCK!

"Belle," I scream up the stairs at her retreating form, seconds after she bursts through the front door like a wrecking ball.

I turn toward Anna. "You need to leave. Please don't ever show up here uninvited again," I say, escorting her out the front door and locking it before she even has a second to respond. Women's tears are one of my weaknesses, so it kills me to throw her out of the house like I have zero compassion for someone I've known for over twenty years.

But when it's between Belle and anyone else, Belle will always come first. Plus, I need to haul ass upstairs; she's probably packing her shit as we speak.

God. Fucking. Damnit.

I take two steps at a time, and sure enough, she's in the middle of the closet, throwing her belongings in a suitcase.

She's not leaving me over this. I won't let her.

"It's not what you think. Nothing happened, B, I promise," I cry in desperation. I can already see that she isn't going to let me explain; her walls are up and securely locked.

when his fingers travel up and over my sex, rubbing lightly against my center.

"As I thought, soaked right through your panties," he murmurs, his fingers brushing over my clit.

"Oh God." My voice quivers. But just as fast as he started, he stops.

"What the hell, why did you stop?" I cry.

He leans over, laces his fingers through my hair, and pulls my body forward to suck on the sensitive part of my neck, using his free hand to pinch and pull my nipple.

"You'll go to your event tonight buzzing with a need for me, soaking wet. Each time you take a step, you'll be reminded by how much you want my fingers on you." He pinches my other nipple. "You'll think of my tongue on your clit, and my dick filling this needy cunt."

"Jack," I moan in desperation. "Please."

His lips travel up my neck to whisper, "No. Now go to your event while I stay here, naked in bed, stroking my thick cock, waiting for you. When you get home, I want no words. I want you to undress in front of me silently. Then it'll be your time to crawl to me… right to my dick. You'll impale yourself without warming up. I want you to feel the burn, each inch of me entering you."

God, he's so freaking dirty. I love it, but he can't be serious about waiting. I need him now. "If I'm your Queen B, then I command you to finish what you started."

He lets out a sardonic laugh. "If you're my queen, am I not your king?"

"Ah, you poor, deluded man," I say, patting his cheek. "You, my sir, are just my lonely servant whom I call upon in my time of need." I widen my legs to emphasize said *need.*

Jack stands and takes my hand, hastily pulling me up. "Nice try." He swats my arse. "The quicker you are tonight, the sooner you're home with me."

"Fine. I won't forget that you teased me." I narrow my eyes. "And all your plans sound amazing, so don't accidentally fall asleep on me. I want to talk about this weekend with you."

I'm going to plan something extraordinary for Jack if he comes to Italy. He put in a great effort for us to have a spectacular time in France, then accommodated me with open arms here in his London home. I want to do something for him to show my appreciation.

"Of course," he says, offended. "You think on our first night together in our home I would fall asleep without you?"

I smile softly. With just one sentence, he has me going from sexually frustrated to melting at his words. I give him a chaste kiss so I don't get sucked into staying longer. "See you later, Jack."

I look back before I enter my waiting car and find him casually leaning against the door frame, arms crossed, watching me go. I'm not at all surprised—I felt the heat of his stare the second I walked out of the house.

"Hurry home to me, sweetheart," he calls as he waves me off.

"Sir, I'm so sorry. Are you able to turn around and bring me home?" I ask my driver.

This is brilliant news for me. Callie's other event ended earlier, making her able to take my place at the gallery opening, so I get to go home and spend tonight with Jack.

"No problem, love. The house I picked you up from in Kensington?"

"No, I live—" I cut myself off, forgetting I live with Jack now. "Yes, I recently moved, sorry. Kensington is perfect."

"Thank you," I call as we pull up, getting out as fast as my four-inch heels will allow.

As I put the key in the door, I see Jack through the bay window, talking passionately to someone. I hope he's on the phone and no one's here. Declan often stops by, but it's late, so I'm hoping he's home with Aoife and Agnes, his twins.

Not that I don't love Dec, but the whole ride I've thought about

nothing other than surprising Jack, ordering some crappy food, relaxing, watching a movie, then taking him up on what he promised me earlier.

Declan's not really in the mix of all that.

Before I even open the door, though, I realize it's not Declan at all.

My stomach drops, and a cold foreign sensation drifts over m body, causing goose bumps to scatter in the most uncomfortable way.

I begin to shake, so I brace myself on the door as the fearful image build in my mind.

The glimpse of Father and my disgraced aunt.

My boyfriend of many years, Trey.

And now Jack… with his arms around Anna, in our house, as s cries into his chest.

I bow my head as my breathing picks up. How could he? Not on does he invite another woman into our home the second I lea but *her*?

Fear and anger knot inside of me. It's the first goddamn night, a this is how he chooses to prove his loyalty to me.

I stop the impending tears by clenching my jaw and taking de measured breaths.

He doesn't get my fucking tears tonight.

I pull back my shoulders and stand up tall, taking one more bre in an attempt to calm myself.

Though, there's no use.

I'm like a bomb ready to detonate, ready to fucking explode.

when his fingers travel up and over my sex, rubbing lightly against my center.

"As I thought, soaked right through your panties," he murmurs, his fingers brushing over my clit.

"Oh God." My voice quivers. But just as fast as he started, he stops.

"What the hell, why did you stop?" I cry.

He leans over, laces his fingers through my hair, and pulls my body forward to suck on the sensitive part of my neck, using his free hand to pinch and pull my nipple.

"You'll go to your event tonight buzzing with a need for me, soaking wet. Each time you take a step, you'll be reminded by how much you want my fingers on you." He pinches my other nipple. "You'll think of my tongue on your clit, and my dick filling this needy cunt."

"Jack," I moan in desperation. "Please."

His lips travel up my neck to whisper, "No. Now go to your event while I stay here, naked in bed, stroking my thick cock, waiting for you. When you get home, I want no words. I want you to undress in front of me silently. Then it'll be your time to crawl to me… right to my dick. You'll impale yourself without warming up. I want you to feel the burn, each inch of me entering you."

God, he's so freaking dirty. I love it, but he can't be serious about waiting. I need him now. "If I'm your Queen B, then I command you to finish what you started."

He lets out a sardonic laugh. "If you're my queen, am I not your king?"

"Ah, you poor, deluded man," I say, patting his cheek. "You, my sir, are just my lonely servant whom I call upon in my time of need." I widen my legs to emphasize said *need*.

Jack stands and takes my hand, hastily pulling me up. "Nice try." He swats my arse. "The quicker you are tonight, the sooner you're home with me."

"Fine. I won't forget that you teased me." I narrow my eyes. "And all your plans sound amazing, so don't accidentally fall asleep on me. I want to talk about this weekend with you."

I'm going to plan something extraordinary for Jack if he comes to Italy. He put in a great effort for us to have a spectacular time in France, then accommodated me with open arms here in his London home. I want to do something for him to show my appreciation.

"Of course," he says, offended. "You think on our first night together in our home I would fall asleep without you?"

I smile softly. With just one sentence, he has me going from sexually frustrated to melting at his words. I give him a chaste kiss so I don't get sucked into staying longer. "See you later, Jack."

I look back before I enter my waiting car and find him casually leaning against the door frame, arms crossed, watching me go. I'm not at all surprised—I felt the heat of his stare the second I walked out of the house.

"Hurry home to me, sweetheart," he calls as he waves me off.

"Sir, I'm so sorry. Are you able to turn around and bring me home?" I ask my driver.

This is brilliant news for me. Callie's other event ended earlier, making her able to take my place at the gallery opening, so I get to go home and spend tonight with Jack.

"No problem, love. The house I picked you up from in Kensington?"

"No, I live—" I cut myself off, forgetting I live with Jack now. "Yes, I recently moved, sorry. Kensington is perfect."

"Thank you," I call as we pull up, getting out as fast as my four-inch heels will allow.

As I put the key in the door, I see Jack through the bay window, talking passionately to someone. I hope he's on the phone and no one's here. Declan often stops by, but it's late, so I'm hoping he's home with Aoife and Agnes, his twins.

Not that I don't love Dec, but the whole ride I've thought about nothing other than surprising Jack, ordering some crappy food, relaxing, watching a movie, then taking him up on what he promised me earlier.

Declan's not really in the mix of all that.

Before I even open the door, though, I realize it's not Declan at all.

My stomach drops, and a cold foreign sensation drifts over my body, causing goose bumps to scatter in the most uncomfortable way.

I begin to shake, so I brace myself on the door as the fearful images build in my mind.

The glimpse of Father and my disgraced aunt.

My boyfriend of many years, Trey.

And now Jack… with his arms around Anna, in our house, as she cries into his chest.

I bow my head as my breathing picks up. How could he? Not only does he invite another woman into our home the second I leave, but *her*?

Fear and anger knot inside of me. It's the first goddamn night, and this is how he chooses to prove his loyalty to me.

I stop the impending tears by clenching my jaw and taking deep, measured breaths.

He doesn't get my fucking tears tonight.

I pull back my shoulders and stand up tall, taking one more breath in an attempt to calm myself.

Though, there's no use.

I'm like a bomb ready to detonate, ready to fucking explode.

16

Jackson

FUCK!

"Belle," I scream up the stairs at her retreating form, seconds after she bursts through the front door like a wrecking ball.

I turn toward Anna. "You need to leave. Please don't ever show up here uninvited again," I say, escorting her out the front door and locking it before she even has a second to respond. Women's tears are one of my weaknesses, so it kills me to throw her out of the house like I have zero compassion for someone I've known for over twenty years.

But when it's between Belle and anyone else, Belle will always come first. Plus, I need to haul ass upstairs; she's probably packing her shit as we speak.

God. Fucking. Damnit.

I take two steps at a time, and sure enough, she's in the middle of the closet, throwing her belongings in a suitcase.

She's not leaving me over this. I won't let her.

"It's not what you think. Nothing happened, B, I promise," I cry in desperation. I can already see that she isn't going to let me explain; her walls are up and securely locked.

"I would bloody hope not, you arsehole!" she shouts at the top of her lungs, aggressively trying to zip her bag shut.

I don't understand. "If you know nothing happened, why are you leaving me?"

She whips around at lightning speed and jabs her finger into my chest. "I'm packing for Italy. I have a work trip. Not that it's any of your fucking business. But let me explain something to you, Jackson Peters." She makes sure to sneer my name as she pokes at my chest, stabbing me with her nail with every word. "If you ever disrespect me like that again, I will never speak to you again."

"Belle, I promise she showed up here unannounced. I had no idea she was coming. It was poor timing." I reach out to hold her only to have her hit my hand away.

"Don't you dare touch me." Her eyes conveying the fury within her. A look I've never seen before.

She picks up her bag to leave. "Wait, Lola said Italy was tomorrow. Where are you going?"

"Plans changed. I'm leaving on the eleven-thirty flight tonight." She tries to move past me, but I step in front of her, stopping her from leaving.

We need to talk about this.

Struggling to get around me, her blue eyes blaze furiously. "Night one, Jack. Just think about that. Night fucking one, I walk in to see *her* in *our* house. How many times will I come home to find one of your fuck buddies here? Maybe I should line up and wait my turn next time."

Fuck. "Belle, I'm so sorry. Please let me explain, and maybe you'll—"

"No." She shakes her head. "I have no time and need to get the hell out of here." She runs around me, down the stairs, and right out the front door.

"That's it? You're just leaving?" I call out, not caring that it's late and my neighbors will hear me.

She doesn't look back but says, "I need time to think. I'll talk to you."

"Think about what? Us?" This was a goddamn misunderstanding; I don't understand why she can't stay and talk about this like an adult. Not even that, I want to hold and comfort her because although she's furious with me, I don't miss her hurt and pain radiating off her.

"Everything. I need to think about everything," she says, low enough that I almost miss it, then gets in the car without looking back.

My heart plummets to my stomach the second she closes that door. Why does it feel like she's closing it on us… on our relationship?

Night one.

Her words play on repeat in my head, her fury and pain of her emotions flashing before my eyes. All her worries and insecurities unfolded the first night we were back in London.

Belle's right. How did I let this happen, and how did it spiral so quickly that I couldn't hold on and stop the impending catastrophe?

From such a minor mix-up.

This is precisely what I didn't want to happen, I continuously promised her my past couldn't touch her, yet I lied.

Night one.

Night fucking one.

Belle is my life, my love, the one I will protect with every inch of my being, so if she needs time to think, to collect her feelings, *fine.*

But I won't let her leave me, leave us. I told her I was all in, and I don't take that lightly.

Declan stops abruptly at my office door, his face twisting with confusion. "What are you doing here?"

"I work here, fucker. What do you think?" I mutter, annoyed I'm being interrupted as I review a new contract before sending it off to legal.

"I was sure you would've followed Belle to Italy. You're almost worse than Wills lately."

Lola was kind enough to let me know when Belle landed safely in

Italy late last night, but I haven't heard one word from her. "Nope, I'm stuck here in gloomy London with you."

He crosses his tattooed arms. "What did you do?"

I shake my head, annoyed at the whole situation. "I don't want to talk about it right now."

Belle had every right to be furious last night, but that doesn't make it right for her to run out on me like that. After sharing so much in France, you would have thought she'd be more open to telling me what was happening in her head, or at least let me explain why Anna showed up.

Am I sorry she felt betrayed and humiliated even? Of course.

Am I also pissed off that she ran?

Without a doubt.

The buzzer on my phone goes off, bringing me back to reality. "Hi, Millie, what's up?"

"Wills is asking to see you and Declan."

"Sure, we'll head over there now," I reply, then look up at Dec. "Why is he in today? Isn't he leaving for their trip soon?"

"Aye, I thought so too. Let's find out what he wants."

"You look good," I say to Wills as we enter his corner office. "Relaxed, like you've already checked out."

"I feel it. I thought it would be more of a production leaving the girls with Mum and Dad, but they did well. I'm just happy we can leave in peace."

He gestures to the chairs in front of his desk for me and Declan to sit. "They love your parents. They'll be fine. Are they staying in London or returning to the country with them?"

"Half and half… which reminds me. Do you think you can stop over today to make sure the girls are being good? Mum never tells me. I don't want them taking advantage of her."

"Of course, no problem. Will you tell me where you're taking my sister on your honeymoon, or is it still a surprise?"

He shoots me a cocky grin, and I can already tell he's proud of himself. "We're going to Peru and Argentina."

I sit up taller, thinking I might have heard him wrong, and judging by Dec's face, he's thinking the same thing. My sister and Belle have traveled all over the world together, it's a passion of theirs, so I know Sadie will be thrilled. But Wills doesn't seem like someone who'd honeymoon in South America.

He's more of a "let me relax in the Maldives" kind of guy.

"Peru? Wait…"

He nods. "It's Maria's seventieth birthday. Sadie has been saying for the last six months that she wishes she could celebrate with her." He shrugs. "So I'm taking her to Peru for the party, then we'll head to Argentina where we're touring the wine region."

He's got to be kidding me. Sadie is going to lose her mind with excitement.

Maria was our nanny from the day I was born and was like a mother to both Sadie and me, even coming out of retirement to help Sadie with Charlie when she was a newborn.

Sadie spent every spare second she had with Maria, and I can tell you now that this will be one of the best surprises she's ever gotten.

"Does Maria know?"

Wills shakes his head. A dual surprise. It's going to be epic. "You did good, Wills. Can you make sure to video it for me?"

"Of course." He glances at his watch. "I only have a few minutes left. I'm here to talk to you guys quickly before we leave for the airport. Sadie's waiting in the car with John downstairs," he says, passing both Declan and me a thick packet.

"What is this?" Dec asks, already flipping through the pages.

Wills takes a breath that catches my attention. His earlier laid-back demeanor has changed to one of nervousness.

He leans back, swiveling his chair back and forth. "Jackson, you're now my brother by marriage, and even though you're one of the biggest pains in the arse I've ever met, I'm proud that it's finally official. I've considered you both brothers for a long time now. And Declan, what started as me taking you under my wing as a young rugby lad quickly turned into a brotherhood that I cherish deeply." He looks between us. "Not only am I lucky to have two mates who are family, but also the best business partners around. Charlotte's is thriving, and I hope soon we can say the same about The Social Club. So I thought it fitting to share The Taylored Group with both of you."

I sit stunned, completely bewildered at the idea. The Taylored Group is his baby, and he wants to share it with us?

When he realizes both Dec and I are in shock, he continues, "The name would stay the same. I would own fifty percent, and the two of you twenty-five each." He pauses, looking between us. "Unless you don't want it?"

I don't answer. I get up, walk around his desk, and shake his hand. He stands and takes me in a hug before I say, "Thank you for trusting us to work beside you in the business you take so much pride in. It's an honor, truly."

"Aye," Declan says, squeezing Wills in a tight hug. "Accepting this offer is a no-brainer and, like Peters said, an honor."

We sit back down, and I can't help myself from joking, "So this means I can boss you around now since I own part of the company."

"You're not the fucking boss, dickhead. I'm still the majority owner."

"Same thing." I shrug, holding back my smirk. He's already about to freak out. It's so fucking easy to rile him up.

"It's not the fucking same thing," Wills spits.

I can't help but push him over the edge. It's my favorite pastime. "Tomato, tomahto."

"Will you just shut the fuck up and take this seriously?"

I smirk.

"You know he's doing this on purpose. Why the hell do you let him get to you, you lunatic?" Declan asks, unable to hold back his laughter.

"Does this mean you love me? It does, doesn't it?" I ask, batting my eyelashes.

Wills looks at Declan. "You need to shut him the fuck up, or I'm going to kill him."

"Just admit it. You love me and can't live without me. You want to work with me forever now."

"Okay, you two gobshites, enough. Since we're all talking about good news, I have some myself," Declan announces as he sits up taller.

"After the unfortunate death of Archie's grandmother, we have officially started taking steps to adopt him. Because he's been like family to us already, we hope the process is quick and painless for Archie as he adjusts to his new life."

I turn toward Wills, whose face instantly mimics my pride and happiness for Nora and Declan. This time Wills gets up and walks over to Declan, holding him in a long embrace, celebrating adding another to *our* family.

Wills and Declan run The Taylor Foundation, a charity that funds an after-school program for underprivileged children who want to play rugby, now recently extended it to soccer, and tennis.

Soon after they opened the foundation, Declan began mentoring a young boy named Archie, and they quickly formed a tight bond. When he met Nora, it was no different. He spends most holidays and birthdays with the Buckleys and as such he's gotten closer to the rest of us too.

Last month, his grandmother, who was his legal guardian, passed away from a heart attack, and Nora and Declan were awarded the privilege of being his foster parents. They could have just left it at that. Many foster parents keep older children in their care for years without taking the step toward adoption, and considering Archie will be eighteen in four years, it would have been understandable.

Though, it doesn't shock me for even a second that they want to make it official, even though they already care for Declan's sister who has cerebral palsy, as well as their five-month-old twins.

Archie is meant to be a Buckley.

"Congratulations, Bucks. Let's grab a pint at the pub to celebrate before you go home?" I could really use a drink after last night.

Declan shakes his head. "Can't. Although this is good news, today has been tough for Nora. It would have been her mum's fiftieth birthday today."

Ah fuck, Nora must be a mess today. "I'm surprised you even came in."

"She's painting in the park with Maeve, and I was going stir-crazy, so I came in, but you know what—" Declan mumbles and stands in a rush.

"You're leaving early, and you're going to see her now?" Wills finishes.

"Aye, I need to get to my girl."

The second Declan is out the door, my phone pings, and I take it out of my pocket so fast I fumble it, trying to see if it's Belle, but disappointment fills me when I see it's my sister.

"Sadie just texted, you left your phone in the car, and she says your time's up. You need to leave."

I walk him out and stop him before he gets on the lift. "All kidding aside, Wills. Thanks for today. I needed some good news."

He pauses and gives me a good once-over, narrowing his brows. "You doing okay?"

I shrug. "Been better, but I'll figure it out."

"All right, if you need anything… Call Declan, not me." He smirks. "I'll be preoccupied, if you know what I mean."

The doors close before I can respond. That fucker's dead when he gets home.

"Hi, Mom," I call out as I walk through Wills and Sadie's house.

"We're in here, Jackson." Eleanor's voice drifts from the kitchen.

I walk down the hall where she's cooking up a feast and kiss her head. Eleanor is one of those moms with something freshly baked or brewing on the stovetop no matter the time of day. She reminds me a lot of Mrs. Morales, Seb, and Leo's mom.

"Up, up. Up, up," Chloe says repeatedly until I lift her out of her highchair, kissing her and cuddling her close to my chest—her favorite thing.

"Are you having fun with Nan?" I ask, and she nods against my chest. She's so much like my sister, it's uncanny. Quiet, shy, and sensitive.

So unlike *her* sister, which reminds me… "Where's Charlotte?"

"Drama class. She won't be home for an hour. Here," she says, sticking a spoonful of something saucy in my mouth.

My taste buds instantly dance in my mouth with delight. "Holy crap, what is that? It's delicious."

Eleanor smiles proudly. "Thai basil fried rice with marinated chicken. That trip we took to Thailand inspired me."

"Well, I'm glad I stopped over at dinnertime. I'm starving." I rub Chloe's back and she snuggles closer. "All's good with the girls? Charlie's not giving you a hard time?"

She huffs loudly. "I'm assuming Wills made you stop over? He forgets Charlotte is Evelyn 2.0, and I can handle her just fine."

I look over the stove and quickly open one of the other lids, groaning at the sight before me. "Is this fresh bread? You know that's my weakness. Maybe I'll stay with you all week instead of going home."

She slaps my hand with her spoon. "Hands off, and I'm not sure your new roommate would appreciate you staying."

Caught off-guard, I turn to face her, completely surprised by her comment.

"Don't give me that look. Mums know all, like how something's wrong, so sit down and talk to me about it."

I don't hesitate. I sit, still stunned. "Were we that obvious?"

She laughs sarcastically, sounding so much like Wills. "Jackson, you've been obvious the entire time I've known you, so it was no surprise I recognized the shift the instant I saw you two together this weekend." She makes me a plate of food, places it in front of me, then continues, "But you should know by now that we're one big family, and you can't hide anything, like how you're now living together. Nora told me this morning."

I try to put Chloe down, but she's like a koala hanging on, so I eat around her. "We haven't told Sadie and Wills yet. We'll tell them the second they get home… Well, as long as we've worked out everything between us," I mumble around my food. If she's going to be here cooking like this all week, I'll have to double up my sessions at the gym.

"Explain what's going on, and I'll help the best I can." She smiles softly, leaning back, giving me her full attention.

So I do. I tell her everything from our past to our present, not leaving out one single detail. If I trust anyone besides Belle and my sister, it's Eleanor.

When I'm done talking, she nods toward my food. "Finish that up, because you're leaving."

I hesitate, blinking in bafflement. "What do you mean?"

"Men," she huffs, then picks up my plate even though I've taken two bites. "You bloody lads don't have a clue, do you?"

She wraps up my bread and puts the rest in a takeaway container. "Here." She thrusts it into my hand and takes a now sleeping Chloe out of my arms. "You're going to go home, pack, and get on a plane to Italy."

I protest, but she stops me. "Before you tell me she wants her space because she said she needs to think, you're wrong. Annabelle is very similar to me in ways—strong-willed and sometimes too prideful for her own good. She doesn't need any more time in her head. She's had the last thirty-odd years for that. What she needs is you, Jackson."

I mindlessly stand up. *Am I going to Italy?*

The second Belle left, all I thought about was running after her, following her until she got it through her head that it wasn't what it looked like. It's not in my nature to sit back and let things play out. However, considering I've never had a girlfriend in my life, I was trying to be reasonable and respect her wishes.

Eleanor guides me toward the front door, then lowers her voice and speaks in a gentle tone. "You love each other, and although I respect your thought process, sometimes it's okay to assert your dominance. A little push won't hurt." She tugs at my shirt, so I lean down for her to kiss me goodbye. "Make the best of it, Jackson. These are the best times of your life, young and in love—nothing will ever compare."

17

Annabelle

I WANT TO GO HOME.

Not one part of me wants to be here, plain and simple. There is no use for me when I'm physically unable to enjoy myself. The only thing on my mind is Jack and how childish I acted, letting my fears get in the way and not letting him explain when I knew the second I saw him that nothing happened. *You have to let go of your fear.*

Still, I couldn't control myself in the moment, and I'm completely mortified over it.

Scared of future incidents where my emotions play a bigger role than anything else, letting my insecurities once again rear their ugly head, incapacitating me as a rational human.

So, needless to say, it's been the longest thirty-six hours of my life, and now Jack's not answering any of my calls, texts, or emails.

Not that I blame him one bit. Except it's still unlike him; even if he's angry, he usually would answer or at least message back to ensure I was okay.

I'm sure after my little performance, he'd go back to ignoring me, but still, he's a gentleman first over anything else.

I hug my knees to my chest, taking in the spectacular view I'm barely appreciating—the green-manicured rolling hills, rows upon rows of vines, and tall, neatly groomed Cyprus trees lining the winding road leading up to the limestone villa.

God, this is a freaking dreamland, and I'm sitting here moping like a loser.

"Buongiorno, bella," Romeo calls as he walks up through the olive groves, and I internally sigh, wishing him away.

Romeo picked me up from the airport, arrived yesterday with breakfast, and today he's giving me my first lesson on winemaking, which normally I would be ecstatic about, but my less-than-stellar attitude hinders everything I attempt to do.

Luckily for me, Romeo has picked up on my bad mood, so there's been no excessive flirting, just business. I appreciate that greatly since I wouldn't have been able to turn him away, considering he's the son of one of my biggest clients.

"Good morning." I wave, forcing a smile. "I didn't see you pull up. Where did you come from?" I ask.

He points past the olive trees. "Beyond there is a pool you must use. It's an instant stress reliever surrounded by dozens of lemon trees, and I promised Mamma I would bring some home, so I used our private road and parked there."

"Ah, I see, sneaky." I will definitely be taking him up on the pool idea, though I'm not mentioning that, because I have a funny feeling Romeo's lack of flirting would change the second I put on a bikini.

"Come, I will show you our family's history," he states proudly, a genuine smile on his face.

This is something I admire greatly about the people of Italy. The pride for their country's history and fierce love for family is unmatched. I've never come across it before in all my travels.

"This is your first time to this property, si?" Romeo asks.

"Yes. I've only been to your parents' house. But I prefer it here if I'm honest." I smile, knowing Romeo will never tell them.

"I agree. To me, this is real Tuscany. I love that we are building our name up so people worldwide can sample the love we put into our wine, but here"—he gestures around the property—"is where my ancestry lies, where my great-grandfather started it all. I feel at home here."

The DeLuca family property, where most of the wine is produced, is spectacular but designed in a more modern style.

Here you feel like you've stepped back in time. It's giving me a sense of how it was many years ago because, believe it or not, although I work closely with Lorenzo, Romeo's dad, he shares more about the modern techniques of winemaking and what sells the wine now, not how it was when they started.

In the future, we need to add more of their family's history and show that they started from nothing and built their empire from hard manual labor.

Buyers will eat it up.

I follow Romeo through vines over the next hour or so, and he explains to me about the different varietals being grown in the area, the surrounding region, and what makes Tuscan wine different from others.

It's all so fascinating, and it's the first time I've enjoyed myself since stepping foot in Italy. "Tell me a fun fact about Italian wine, Romeo."

"A fun fact," he mutters while tapping his temple. "Ah yes, I've got one." He smiles. "In Italy, there are around two thousand varieties of grapes, but only about three hundred and fifty are used and authorized."

"Geez, that's a lot. How many do you have here at this property?"

"Sadly, we lost many vines due to age, but all of them are the same varietal of Sangiovese, which is indigenous to Tuscany. My great-grandfather planted these seventy-five years ago. It's why we don't use them—they don't produce great wine anymore—but it is a part of our family's history, so we try our best to keep it as long as possible."

"Wow," I murmur, running my hands along the tops of the vines, in awe of everything I'm learning.

"I'm happy to share more information about the wine, but this is not my favorite part of the property. Would you be interested in trying our olive oil?"

I perk up at the idea. "Yes, please. I didn't know you produced that."

"The olive trees are said to be around five hundred years old." He places his arm around me to maneuver me around some branches. "Come, I'll show you."

"Get your fucking hands off my wife," a familiar growl penetrates the air.

My head shoots up, and I'm taken aback, in complete shock. "Wh-what are you doing here, Jack?"

Romeo takes a step back. "I wasn't… Wife?" Romeo looks at me, scared shitless, and I roll my eyes. Grow a pair, will you?

"Don't listen to him, Romeo." I turn toward my husband. "Jack?"

He ignores me and steps up, towering over Romeo, who is built like a Roman God, yet Jack's anger radiating off him is even scaring the six-foot-five Adonis.

Jack laughs. "Of course your name is Romeo. How cliche." He fakes a wave. "Adios."

I cover my eyes in embarrassment. "That's Spanish, you bloody idiot."

"Great, I don't give a fuck. Let's go, Belle. Now," he says through a clenched jaw, pulling me back toward the main house, leaving Romeo standing amongst the vines.

"You're acting crazy, Jack. What the hell are you doing?"

"Crazy? Oh, you've haven't seen anything yet, you hypocrite," he screams.

I look around, embarrassed. "Can you keep your voice down?"

"Oh, don't start your fake manners shit now. I'm so mad—no, I'm past that, I'm livid, and it's healthy to yell a little. To let it all out, so don't tell me not to scream, or I'll really lose it."

He stops in front of a car that I presume he rented, places both hands on the roof, and bows his head, taking deep, labored breaths.

After a few silent minutes pass, he turns, dropping his hands to his sides, forming a clenched fist, all while shooting me a venomous glare that has me stagger back from the unfamiliarity of his eyes.

"So let's get this straight, Annabelle." He steps closer. "You run out on me, leaving me like yesterday's trash, to come here and spend time with him? Instead of talking to me, you're in fucking Italy laughing and smiling, having a grand ol' fucking time. Meanwhile, I'm sick to my stomach over what happened."

I quickly shake my head. "It's not what it looks like." The second the words are out of my mouth, we both know I fucked up.

This is exactly what Jack said when Anna was over and I didn't give him a chance to explain, so why should he grant me the courtesy to do so now?

Jack closes his eyes and takes a second to himself before walking closer, kissing my forehead quickly. "We have a lot to work on, Belle. We both have had years to engrain shitty habits into our systems when it comes to relationships. So this will only work if we fix things *together,* and give each other a little grace. Because this won't be the last time we fuck up, far from it. But if we don't start working together from the beginning, we never will." He walks back toward the car, opening it to get in, and I start to panic.

"Please don't go, Jack," I cry.

"In Paris, I didn't pressure you. I stood back and let you figure things out, but now I choose me. I'm going for a drive, and when I'm back later tonight, it will be your choice if I stay or go… for good."

What?

I watch him get in the car.

I watch him pause, look at me, and turn the engine on.

Then I watch him drive away, and I'm still standing here like a statue.

Until it hits me.

I'm not waiting for tonight.

I jump up and down, waving my hands, but he doesn't see me, so I run inside, grab my phone, and dial his number.

He picks up on the first ring.

"Come back," I cry. "Please come back."

He hangs up without saying a word, then one second later, he's flying down the gravel path and wrenching the door open, allowing me to fly into his arms.

"Jack," I cry, whimpering into his shirt. "I'm sorry, I'm so sorry," I scream as a gut-wrenching sob leaves my mouth. "I choose you… us. I'm so sorry."

What the fuck is wrong with me?

I don't even recognize myself… Get your shit together, Annabelle.

"Come on, sweetheart, let's go inside." He picks me up, and I tightly wrap my arms and legs around him as he carries me into the house.

"Upstairs to the right," I mumble into his neck.

He sits on the large armchair in the corner of the room, keeping me tight against him as I snuggle on his lap.

"Can you explain to me what the hell is going on? There's something wrong if I'm the voice of reason, Belle. Where's my strong, confident queen? The one who would have kicked Anna's ass, not run the other way?"

I shake my head into his chest, too embarrassed to explain and hating the feelings that took over me the other night.

He pushes me to sit and wipes any leftover tears lingering on my cheeks. "Talk to me, Belle."

I sigh, rather sick of talking about our feelings but knowing they will hang over our heads forever if I don't explain.

"When I walked up to the house, I saw Anna before I entered and it triggered something I've never experienced before… flashbacks." I pause to regulate my breathing. "That's never happened to me, Jack. All these memories started to flood my mind, and it was then that I realized something that scared me so much I left…"

Jack rubs my arm in encouragement. "What did you realize, B?"

"If something happened to us, it would break me. If anyone in this world could do it, it would be you, Jackson. Not my dad, not Trey. You're the only person I care enough about to cause real damage, and it scares me more than anything. I like to be in control of my own life. Insecurities are for the weak, and I pride myself on my strength.

I don't know why I'm letting this suddenly take over, but I'm scared."

"Annabelle," he whispers. "I don't ever want to hurt you, sweetheart. I told you I would have never pursued you if I wasn't ready, if I wasn't all in." He sighs, and I can hear the slight annoyance in his voice. "Do you not trust me?"

"It's not you, Jack." *I'm the fucked up one.* "I'm going to do better. I promise."

He maneuvers me so I'm facing him straight on. "I will never betray you, B, nor will I ever leave, no matter what happens, as long as you talk to me about it. But, if *you* ever leave me again, I won't chase you. I know that's not the romantic gesture you want to hear, but I've never held anything back from you. I put it all on the table, and if you choose to run without talking it out or considering my feelings, I'm done. This is it. No turning back, sweetheart."

Look at Jack sticking up for himself.

"I know."

I really do.

Because who the hell would continue to put up with this shit?

I wouldn't.

Wordlessly, he stands and walks us over to the bed, lying me down in the middle, then crawls on top of me, kissing me quickly before pulling back.

"I don't know when things got so complicated between us, B, but I'm fucking sick of it. Can we please go back to Jackson and Annabelle, the badass dynamic duo?"

Smiling at his sudden enthusiasm, I nod.

"Aren't you sick of being in your head? I sure as fuck am. I'm done with letting things get in our way… Let's finally do it with nothing between us."

I raise a brow. "That sounds similar to the plan we had for after Paris."

He rolls his eyes and smirks. "What the fuck did we know? This time, we'll mean it."

When my smile turns up a notch, he drops down and kisses me hard against the lips.

"Tell me you want me, Belle."

"Always."

I have always wanted him.

"Say the words," he demands.

"I want you."

"Tell me you need me."

"I need you."

Always needed him. Always will.

He pauses, his lips still pressed against mine. "Tell me you love me."

My breath catches, but I don't hesitate even a second longer. "I love you." I sigh. "So much."

He cups my cheek and lets those beautiful eyes penetrate mine. "I'm so in love with you, Annabelle *Peters.* I might have taken longer to catch up and realize what I wanted in life, but rest assured, it has always been and always will be you." I trace his dimple as he continues, "We are going to have an amazing life together, and as much as I hate that it took me this long to get my act together, I am eternally thankful that I finally did. Because you, sweetheart, are the best thing that has ever happened to me."

"Jack," I cry.

God... this man.

"We may not have had the proper wedding or exchanged the perfect vows, but right here and now, I promise you everything. Everything good in this world is yours, and I'll go to whatever lengths to make sure of it."

With a wide grin, I push his fallen hair out of his eyes and speak my truth. "You are what's good in the world, Jack, and I have you. And in having you, I have everything I'll ever need."

He dips his head, letting his lips dust over mine. "How about this?" He grinds into me. "Is this cock of mine what's good in this world?"

I roll my eyes but don't deny the deep ache that immediately grows inside me. "You're ruining it." We both laugh before his lips open in a silent invitation.

The kiss is not rushed or crazed. It's slow and completely erotic, causing my body to burn quickly with pleasure.

Rocking against his erection, I silently beg for more as our tongues glide together in a perfect dance. Then, without disconnecting, he rolls over so we face one another, hitching my leg over his waist, and slides his hand under my dress, slowly caressing from the top of my spine down to my behind.

My heart is pounding in my chest. I can barely breathe from the anticipation.

Fuck.

He feels perfect against me, even over our clothes, and I can feel my release building fast.

I could come just like this. With every movement, every swipe of his tongue, my sex throbs with need for one thing: *him*.

Embarrassing or not, I can't stop it.

I love sex, always have and I reckon I always will, but it's different with Jack.

I don't just love it. I crave it. I crave him.

I pull back and drop my head to his chest, trying to regulate my breathing as his fingers slide under my panties, over my bum, to my entrance. His breath hitches when he feels my arousal. *I* can feel how wet I am from how easily his fingers slide against me.

"Oh God, Jack," I moan. "I—Fuck. I want you inside of me when I come."

He pushes two fingers inside me, stretching me, pumping me with vigor, only causing my orgasm to reach me faster.

He pushes in a third finger, and with every pump, he brings his fingers all the way out to glide over my clit.

Hold it.

On the last swipe, he hovers over my clit, rubbing with all three extremely wet fingers.

My mouth hangs open. There is no fucking holding it.

I cry out as my hips buck against Jack's hand, riding out my orgasm as my body quivers.

"You have no idea how much you turn me on. Fuck, you're so hot," he mutters as he drags his finger along my sensitive area, up and over my backside.

My eyes flare as I look up at Jack, wondering what he's thinking.

"Take me there," I whisper.

He pauses, and I feel his dick jump in excitement through his trousers. "Now?" he growls.

"Yes," I plead as he enters me with a finger. I'm not sure what's come over me, but I want him there. I want him to have been inside me in every way possible.

"Whose ass is this?"

"Yours, Jack. All yours." I push back onto his finger, causing it to sink deeper.

He curses something unintelligible under his breath, then stretches me with a second finger. It's tight and it burns, yet I welcome it easily.

"Naked, Jack. We both have too many clothes on."

Based on his deep growl, he's reluctant to glide his fingers slowly out of me. His eyes are bulging as he stares down in awe at the sight.

His face alone is a turn-on.

So bloody sexy.

We start to undress when he pauses, slightly deflating. "We have no lube."

I roll my lips and scrunch my face, "I might."

"Why the hell would you have lube in Italy?" He spits.

"I was curious about some internal needs if you know what I mean. I thought I could practice myself."

He laughs, "So you're telling me, when we were angry, packing like a mad woman, you had time to pack a dildo and lube?"

"Priorities, Jack. Priorities." I giggle, then grab the lube.

He cups my chin, so I look him right in the eye. "You don't practice without me, understand?"

"Yes, sir," I snark.

He bites his lip, a certain sparkle in his eyes as he rakes them over my naked body before shaking himself out of it. "How do you want it?"

I look down. Just the sheer size of Jack is intimidating, so I'm not sure it matters the position.

He's huge, like really fucking big.

It'll hurt either way, considering it's been a while since I've done this.

When I don't answer, he gives me one more assessing glance, stopping at my boobs, and I can see it in his eyes. He wants to touch them; he always wants them in his hands.

It doesn't matter where we are or what we're doing, he's either touching them or staring at them.

He's obsessed.

He shakes himself out of his daze and smiles darkly before grabbing my waist and flipping me over, taking charge of the situation. His breathing is labored, echoing through the otherwise quiet room. I know he's lost all restraint and is totally in his element.

I love that I get him like this, all worked up and hot for it.

It only turns me on that much more.

He leans down and presses small kisses along my spine. "I love you," he whispers, more to himself than to me.

Will I ever tire of hearing him say those words?

Never.

When I feel his fingers on me, I look between my legs and watch him collect my wetness, dragging it up to my behind, then wetting his cock and working himself up for a few seconds.

If I weren't already bent over, I'd be weak in the knees from the sight. Everything Jack does is such a turn-on that it's almost too much to handle.

"Like that, sweetheart? You like watching me touch myself?"

I have no words to answer him with when he nudges himself against my opening, but we both know the truth—of course I like it.

I love it.

"Touch yourself, baby. I need you more open than this," he croaks, sounding pained, only in the best way.

Without any hesitation from me, my hand is on my clit. Soon after, I begin to soften, and the tip of him slips in.

Shit, that burns.

He holds my hips still. "You're in control, B. Push back and take it slow. I'm too crazed right now to take over."

Turning him on turns me on, and by his loud, deep moans, I know Jack's in all his glory. So I try to quickly move back and forth, dismissing the pressure and pain I feel.

His hands continuously squeeze my hip bones, assisting my every move. My bottom lip stays secured between my teeth as I bite down with every soft thrust.

All while simultaneously trying to forget the sheer size of what's currently inside me.

Jack's support is not cutting it anymore. I stop touching myself and place my other hand on the bed, bracing myself for what's to come.

He starts to take over, and he's bottomed out in no time. I drop my head and close my eyes to block the burn.

"You okay?"

"Mmm. Give me a second."

Quicker than I thought, the it begins to fade, so I reach back and squeeze his hand in a silent gesture, telling him that I'm ready.

He pulls back, starting slowly as his cock slips in and out of my tight hole. He's being measured and considerate, but I want him to lose control.

I want this to be the best thing in his life without worrying about being careful.

"Harder, Jack," I whisper. "Right now, give it to me."

His grip on my waist tightens and he pulls me back with force, slamming me down on his cock. "Fuck, yeah," he grits. "So. Fucking. Good."

I've never felt pleasure like this before. With every fiber of my being, I know it's because it's Jackson.

We begin to move in sync… His pumps are deeper, rougher. My whole body is on sensory overload.

He pushes between my shoulder blades and I fly forward, tearing at the sheets for something to hold on to as he really starts to give it to me.

His fingers slide from my hip to my sex, and that does it. I'm done for.

A deep burn starts from my toes and takes over my body. "Jack," I scream for what seems like forever as the most intense orgasm rips through me relentlessly.

"Oh, fucking hell," he groans deeply. "Do you know how fucking hot it is to take my wife like this?"

Wife.

"You. Are. My Wife," he bellows through the room, slamming into me once more as he releases inside me.

His breathing is ragged, and when it finally slows, he flips me over and brings us nose to nose.

"You're mine. My wife, my life. It's me and you against the world, sweetheart."

My wife. He has no idea what his words do to me.

The Freddie Mercury-loving playboy who, unbeknownst to him, has been the center of my life and dreams since I was thirteen years old is now mine.

All mine.

We slump over and I kiss his jaw. "And you're my husband, Jack," I say, hunching my shoulders, realizing I've never called him that to his face.

"Hey," he whispers to grab my attention, wiping a few left-over orgasm tears. "I'm not perfect, but I promise you, Annabelle, I'll be worth it."

"Jack," I whisper, "All that matters is that you're perfect for me, and that's exactly what you are."

He cups my cheeks. "I love you, B."

"I love you too," I whisper, then kiss his full lips, lingering there and thinking how it still amazes me that I have Jack here with me.

All the women of New York and London can sod off. He's mine now.

"You know, you didn't correct me when I said Peters earlier. Will you change your name?"

I never thought I would, but it sounded good when he brought it up in Paris, and even better after he told me he loved me.

"Don't overthink it, B." He pulls me in closer. "It wasn't conventional, but you're mine, my wife. You don't have to take my last name for me to know that. I know how progressive you are, so as long as you accept that we're only going forward *together*, I'm good with it."

I pause, thinking it over.

Something strong and carnal overtakes me. "I want to be a Peters. I want to share the same surname."

He growls under his breath. "If I weren't fucking exhausted, I would be taking you again right now for that."

"Caveman," I tease.

We lie in comfortable silence, holding each other tightly. Ridiculous as it is, I can't help but let my mind wander to thoughts about Anna.

Not one inch of me thought anything was happening between them, though now I want to know what was going on.

Why was she in his arms?

Why was she crying?

I know I should drop it, leave it in the past and move forward, but I also know myself and won't stop until I have answers.

"I feel you thinking. What's going on?" He pulls me closer to his chest.

I contemplate trying to forget it, but ultimately, my insecurities win. "Please don't get mad. I'm not upset anymore, but I do wonder why Anna was in the house and why she was crying."

He stills beneath me, making it clear he doesn't want to talk about this. But I know Jack, he'll tell me, knowing *I* want to talk about it.

"She showed up unannounced, upset to hear we were in a relationship. Not because it was you—" he cuts himself off. "Well, maybe because it was you." I pinch his side, and he laughs. "I always told her I never wanted more, that I was never interested in anything but a fling."

Oh.

If I were a better person, I'd feel bad for her.

She's probably been pining over Jack for years, sticking around hoping he'd change his mind.

"You're not going to ask about Romeo?"

"Nope, I realize now he's not a threat to me," he says confidently, then quietly starts chuckling.

"Why are you laughing?"

He shakes his head in disbelief. "I'm thinking how I said *adios* like an idiot." He laughs again. "I was in a different headspace, raging like a lunatic."

I laugh along with him. He *is* an idiot.

Him saying that reminds me that I'll have to apologize, because not only was Jack in the wrong, Romeo is still the client, and it was completely unprofessional.

"Did you have plans for later, or would you want to go to dinner in Siena?" he asks. "It's maybe twenty minutes from here, and I've never been. If we're here in Italy, we might as well take in some of the sights."

"Yeah, a date night with my husband in Italy sounds amazing." I yawn. "Right after a nap, I'm bloody knackered."

My phone pings and we both groan at the idea of moving. I could let it go, but with Lola holding things down at the office and me staying in the DeLuca home, I should get up.

"What is it? You have a smile on your face."

"Alessia emailed me. She wants to host a wine tasting for us tomorrow, not far from a town called Arezzo." I look it up quickly. "It's also only about twenty or thirty minutes away, just in the opposite direction."

"Us?" he questions.

I smirk. "I was always going to ask you to meet me here, but then shit happened… you know."

"Alessia is your client who got Sadie her first place here. Marco's cousin?"

"Mmhmm."

"Well, it all sounds amazing, and I'm happy to do anything as long as I have some time to work in the morning. This villa is insane, by the way." He glances around the rustically decorated room.

"Brilliant, I'll let her know." I email her back, and then it hits me again that we're in Italy.

Screw the nap.

Let's go for that swim.

18

Annabelle

MUSIC PLAYS from somewhere in the villa, so I follow the sounds of—you guessed it—Queen, and find Jack in the kitchen, cooking us an early lunch.

He's half-naked with a towel strung around his waist as water drips from his dark thick hair, still damp from the shower we took together.

It's a serious sight to behold and every woman's wet dream.

I'm the luckiest lady.

He starts swaying to the music as the beat picks up, and I watch in amazement at how every toned muscle in his back moves and bulges as he dances along.

"I can feel you staring," Jack calls over the music, turning with a broad, genuine smile stretching his face, holding his hand out for me to take. "You look beautiful." He spins me only to quickly bring me back into his chest.

"And you look very naked." I tweak his nipple, and he smirks. "We need to leave in thirty minutes for the wine tasting."

"I'll be ready. I wanted to feed my girl before we left." He lifts the spoon for me to taste.

"Mmm, that smells amazing. What is it?"

"Fusilli with pistachio, ricotta, and fresh herb pesto. It's a recipe I've been wanting to try, so I figured, hey, *when in Italy*."

"This is delicious, Jack. I thought it would be heavier, but it's the perfect lunchtime pasta." I lean over and kiss his lips in thanks.

I still can't get over what a fantastic cook he is… who knew.

As I turn to take a seat, I pause, noticing something on the counter that I haven't had in ages. "Bloody hell, I forgot about these cookies." I rip open the bag and take a bite, moaning as the deliciousness hit my tongue. Gocciole Chocolate Chip Cookies are one of my favorites, and I'm mad at myself for completely forgetting about them.

When I was younger, my brother Matthew always brought me home souvenirs when he was traveling, and one year, while in Italy, he forgot, so he ran into a random store on the way home and grabbed them, and I've been addicted ever since.

"I saw them at the airport and they reminded me of you."

I still, cookie midair. "You bought them for me?"

He narrows his eyes. "Who else would buy them?"

"I don't know. Maybe the DeLucas, since they had the whole house stocked," I answer, still in shock. "How did you know I liked these?"

"Remember when you and Sadie were in college and you went to Italy that one summer? I met you in Positano, and you ate a bag a day… You loved them."

I take another bite to hide my emotions. I think I need to start taking Gingko Biloba because I remember nothing, yet Jack remembers the type of cookie I ate eighteen years ago.

He turns up the music. "This is my song for you."

Huh?

I listen closely to "You're My Best Friend" by Queen playing through the speakers, instantly making me melt into a puddle.

"You've always been one of my best friends, now more than ever."

"I'm your best friend?" I ask with a smile, shamelessly wanting him to confirm.

He gives me a funny look. "Of course you are. What a stupid question." He sits and passes me my bowl.

"Didn't your parents teach you that no question is ever stupid?" I freeze the second it comes out of my mouth. *What the fuck is wrong with me?* "I'm sorry, Jack. I didn't mean that."

"Never thought you did, sweetheart. I've had a lifetime of getting used to shitty parents. One little mention about them doesn't hurt."

I place my hand in his lap and squeeze his thigh in a silent thank-you for letting it slide.

It was a shit thing to say to someone in his position.

"You know, you're my best friend too, Jack."

He doesn't turn toward me, but his lips curve. "I know."

"What?" I squeal and slap his thigh. "How do you know it's not just your sister who's my best friend, huh?"

"I know you better than you know yourself. Plus, Sadie and I practically count as one. We share the same DNA."

"Good point." I laugh.

"Don't tell Bucks, though. He'll be upset," he says, placing his fork down. "Shit, I left my phone out by the pool when I went for a swim this morning. I was supposed to forward him an email."

"I'll grab your phone while you get dressed. What's the email? I'll send it."

He leans over and kisses my cheek. "Thanks, sweetheart. It came in from Millie around seven this morning, and it's labeled "Investment Report/Second Quarter."

I take the last bite of my pasta and stand up to leave. "Can you grab my straw Loewe bag?"

"No problem. I'll be ready in ten, let's meet at the car."

Where the hell is his bloody phone?

Aha. Of course, it's under his wet towel.

Men.

Without an issue, I find the email and forward it to Declan, but when I close out his email, what I see is appalling.

Two hundred and fifty tabs open, and almost half his apps are running.

No wonder his phone is constantly dying and we're always on the look-out for an electrical outlet.

Note to self—buy Jack a portable phone battery.

While I walk back to the front of the villa and wait for Jack, I start to close out unnecessary tabs. Like his twenty-five Amazon tabs… How many times do you need to open a tab to buy no-show socks?

For a so-called billionaire, he needs to utilize his personal assistant more often.

Swipe… swipe… swipe… Wait.

What the hell?

I go back and open up his notes app, seeing a page labeled "Annabelle Louise Hughes/Peters."

My hand flies to my throat as I hurry over to the small table and chair in the corner.

Oh. My. God.

1: Favorite Ice Cream: Mint Chip, Chocolate Sprinkles (she pretends they are rainbow)
2: Favorite Color: Purple
3: Favorite Movie: Exorcist (a girl after my own heart) Pretends it's Clueless for Sadie.
4: Hates frogs- petrified!

I laugh through my happy tears, thinking about how stupid I was.

I'm no longer scared of frogs, but that one summer—it had to have been maybe 1999, if that—when I was swimming in Sadie's pool, the biggest frog I'd ever seen jumped in, landing right on my head, and we couldn't get it out.

It was traumatizing.

5: Obsessed with the perfume Light Blue by Dolce and Gabbana (updated part ten- Favorite Perfume: Le Labo Santal 33)
6: Allergic to Kiwi

7: Weirdly ticklish on the inside of her elbow

I can't believe my eyes right now.

I skip ahead and scroll all the way down to the bottom. Then scroll back up, then back down. *Holy shit.*

Jack has one hundred and fifty-two things listed here about me.

All my likes, dislikes, important information… it's all here. He must have started this when I was a teenager and kept it up until now, because the new ones are information he learned in Paris.

151: Prefers Pinot Noir (for now)
152: Still loves espresso, but also lavender honey lattes.

Though I'm well aware this is snooping, I have no intention of stopping. He has things listed that I barely remember about myself, or have purposely forgotten, like number twenty-seven. On of my most terrifying memories.

27: Sucks at surfing/hates sharks. Not a great day for Belle

"The water is bloody freezing, Sadie! Maybe my English blood is not cut out for this," I scream over the guys cheering me on.

"Don't be such a wuss," Nate calls from the nearest surfboard.

"You're the only one with a full wetsuit on. I think you'll survive." Sadie laughs as she paddles out further.

"Okay, Annabelle." My surf instructor waves his arm to get my attention. "You'll be fine. Let's acclimate ourselves and get comfortable sitting on the board."

"Okay." That seems easy enough.

I look back to my friends. They're all sitting on their boards too, waiting their turn for the next big wave, I suppose.

"You're doing great, Belle!" Jack calls from shore.

Jeez, I must not be that far out if I can still hear him, yet I feel like I'm miles away.

I think I prefer the sand to this. I'm freezing, and every time I feel

anything move around my feet dangling off the board, I internally freak out.

Yesterday, I made the mistake of screaming bloody murder when seaweed grazed my leg. Now I'll never live it down.

"When you feel comfortable, I want you to go from sitting to the lying position we practiced yesterday."

I give my instructor a thumbs-up and follow his lead. We practice a few times, and I start to feel more confident.

Jack is waving and clapping every time I make even the slightest move. I've not even popped up yet, and he's acting like I rode the biggest wave of the day.

Suddenly the lifeguards are blowing their whistles to evacuate, and everyone rushes to move ashore.

What the hell is going on?

"Follow me. We need to get out of the water."

"Why? What's going on?"

The instructor doesn't answer, but he paddles past me, waving to me to follow. I look around, panicked.

Where are my mates?

What's going on?

Sadie, Nate, and Leo are farther away, but I see they're paddling fast toward the shore.

"Annabelle!" the instructor calls, snapping me out of it and getting me paddling.

He points behind me, and I have no clue what he's trying to say. I can't look anywhere but straight, but before the thought is even out of my mouth, I'm knocked over into the water.

The current pushes my body around violently, and I can't get my bearings. Desperately, I claw at my ankle to where my board is attached, trying to get ahold of it, but I have no luck.

Finally, the waters go calm, and I'm able to pop back up, gasping for air, but the second I do, I hear someone scream, "Shark."

"Shark?"

Oh my God.

Oh my God.

My arms flail around, and I can't find my board.

Someone needs to help me.

Another wave comes out of nowhere and I'm dragged back under.

My arms move as fast as possible, but I'm not moving. It's as if I suddenly forgot how to swim. Panic sets in quickly, and I don't know what to do.

My head pops up to get a breath, but I still can't move.

Help!

Where are the bloody lifeguards? I don't want to die out here in the middle of Montauk, I'm not even in my own fucking country.

A pair of arms wrap around me, pulling me close to their body, swimming us toward the shore.

Thank God.

We make it back safely, and I'm pulled onto the sand. I have no strength to move, but I open my eyes, and my favorite shade of green stares down at me.

"Annabelle," Jack's voice breaks while pain laces through his eyes. "Are you okay?"

I nod, unable to talk.

There's a good chance I'm still in shock.

A lifeguard runs over, and Jack starts to lose his mind.

"Where the fuck were you?" he bellows, causing the beachgoers to go silent.

"Jackson, man, calm down. We saw you had it."

"Calm down? Are you fucking kidding? I waited minutes for you to react, and you weren't paying attention. You can kiss your job goodbye."

Sadie is at my side, tears running down her face. "Annabelle. Are you okay? I'm so sorry... So, so sorry."

"You're sorry because I forgot how to swim?"

"No, because I forced you to try surfing. I should have known my posh English bestie would do better on land." She's trying to make a joke, but her pain-stricken face says otherwise. She leans down, hugging me tight.

"All right, now that the shock has worn off, I'm utterly embarrassed and need to sit up or get the hell out of there."

"Let's go home. We can't go back in the water anyway," Nate says from beside me.

I almost forgot. "There was really a shark?"

Sadie shrugs like this is normal. We don't have bloody sharks in London.

Jack stops his attack on the lifeguard, and without another word, he picks me up and holds me close to his body, not letting me even attempt to walk.

His legs must be burning walking through the sand while carrying me. Plus, we still have a long walk to the car. Though, he's still not entertaining my protests to walk myself.

He turns to Nate. "My keys are in my back pocket."

"You're going to let me drive your precious car?"

"Consider it your lucky day."

I'm too stunned to say a word. Jack doesn't allow anyone besides Sadie to drive his car , and even that's a stretch.

Jack buckles me in, then jumps in next to me while Sadie gets in on the other side.

His arm reaches around me, holding me close to his chest. Never once on our fifty-minute drive back to Southampton does he let me go.

If anything, his hold only gets tighter over time, as he occasionally kisses my forehead and strokes my wet, messy hair.

"Belle?"

Startled by Jack's voice in the distance, I throw down his phone with a shaky hand and sit still as a statue until he comes into view.

Once again, I'm struck by his gorgeous, muscular frame stalking over to me while my emotions are a mix of elation and fury… unsure if I want to kiss or kill him.

The list is one of the sweetest, most thoughtful things I've ever come across, but I've also come to the conclusion that Jack has loved me for quite a while, and that bloody bastard took all these years to finally do something about it.

Thankfully, his outfit choice breaks me out of my thoughts so that I can, for now, think of something else.

"Yeah, you're going to need to change immediately."

He looks down, confused. "What, why?"

"I appreciate the fashion-forward look, but either put some compression shorts under those linen pants, or we're not going wine tasting."

His lips turn up, and he swings his hips so his penis swings back and forth.

"Are you even wearing briefs?" I cry.

"Of course, but when you're blessed with a big dick like me, it can't be helped."

"Jackson," I warn, trying my hardest not to smile.

"What?" He walks up and grinds himself into my arse. "You. Love. Big. Dicks, and you cannot lie."

"Oh my God!" I burst out laughing and try to run away from this man. Why does his brain even work like this?

He catches up to me, spinning me around, biting my neck. "Are you jealous someone will see my cock, B?"

"Yes," I huff, not even trying to deny it. "Women are worse than men."

"Oh please, I doubt that."

"Men have zero brain cells when checking out a woman. It's like they go stupid, standing there with their mouths open and eyes wide. We women are crafty. We can stare discreetly, tracing the outline, imagining what it would look and feel like—are you a grower or a shower? Especially from someone as gorgeous as you. All of this happens without you even knowing. So I'm not going to be with you like this unless you want me to kill off all the women in our path."

He bites his lip, smirking down at this dick. "I'm a grower *and* a shower."

"Oh, you wanker, go change, will you."

Jackson

Belle leans into me, whispering dreamily, "It's beautiful here, isn't it?"

"It is," I confirm, glancing around the picturesque scenery before us. The sun is starting to set over the rolling hills, the twinkling lights shine above us, threaded through an ancient trellis filled with climbing vines of roses.

The long table, filled with scattered candles, is occupied by Alessia's friends and family, who have been nothing but welcoming. We've laughed, drank, danced, and eaten for hours, and when I say we ate, I mean *we ate.*

Fresh fruits, cheese, and meats—never in my life have I seen that much prosciutto. Let's not forget the focaccia and arancini balls from Alessia's nonna. There is no doubt I'll be recreating those in the future.

"I was going to set up a wine tasting for us, you know. I wanted to do something special, but I'm not sure I would have done it justice. Today has been like a scene out of a movie."

I squeeze her shoulder and lean over to kiss her head. "It's the thought that counts."

She tips her chin up in a silent request, and of course, I oblige happily. I'll never tire of kissing her plump, heart-shaped lips.

With my mouth pressed against hers for a moment longer than acceptable at a table with others, she lets out a low moan, trying to deepen the kiss. It kills me to reject the idea, but there is no way in hell I'm sharing her sounds with anyone else. Everything about her is mine, no one else gets to hear my favorite noises.

She screws up her delicate features and attempts to whisper, only to slur slightly, "Why won't you kiss me?"

I've been waiting for the wine to hit her.

After the top-notch wine tasting earlier, we stayed well past the end as the day switched from informal to no fucks given.

If I thought the food was free-flowing, it had nothing on the wine. Bottles line the table, some with vintages dating back years, some unlabeled. And it doesn't help that Alessia fills our glasses the second it hits below the halfway mark.

So the slur of Belle's voice makes complete sense. "Because I don't share. I don't want these horny Italian fuckers to get a glimpse of you turned on," I growl.

Her eyes flare with the same gaze she has in the bedroom, causing my dick to harden even more than it already has.

"Oh." She pauses and angles her body toward me. "Maybe we can step away for a second. I'm suddenly craving something… delicious." She licks her lips.

Note to self—don't get Belle drunk when you have nowhere to fuck her. Your dick will thank you later.

I run my fingertips down the side of her face, loving how she melts into my touch and how my fingers burn under her blush. "Later, you'll get all the kisses, all the touches." I continue my path down her clavicle. "Wherever you want them."

I break my own rules and let my fingers glide down her cleavage.

We stay like this momentarily, lost in each other, until Alessia clears her throat. Belle dips her head, laughing, while I lean back, annoyed at being interrupted.

Alessia smirks and raises the wine bottle.

This is going to be a long night.

Belle's too distracted as she gets in the back of the car, so I lean over and buckle her in. We're with Alessia, following her friends to the local bar. The second Belle heard dancing would be involved, she was rushing to leave.

"Ugh," Belle groans and throws her phone back into her bag.

"What's wrong, sweetheart?"

She deflates, then leans back into the seat, closing her eyes. "My brothers, especially Theo, won't stop messaging me. I'm going to have to explain Vegas and how everything started."

"Leave that to me, I'll handle it."

"Jack—"

"No. You're my responsibility now, and I want to ensure my intentions are clear. We both know that their issue is with me."

She leans her head on my shoulder, which I take as a victory. Thankfully, she didn't fight me on this. It's something I wouldn't have given in to.

After about ten minutes of driving, Belle pops up and screams, "Pull over!"

"What, why?"

She points to something in the distance, but I can't make out what it is. Alessia directs the driver to pull over and we quickly get out of the car, following Belle down one of the small alleyways of the old city.

"B, what the hell?"

She runs back when she notices we're not keeping up and pulls us forward. "Trust me. It's going to be great."

We finally reach our destination, and I don't need to ask her what we're doing here. I know her better than anyone.

Before turning to Belle, I glance up at the historic chapel, taking in the beauty of the architecture. It sits on the hilltop, granting you a stunning view of Tuscany. Even in the dark, it's still breathtaking.

Reaching out, I pull Belle into my chest and wrap my arms tightly around her, overwhelmed by the emotions I feel for her.

Belle tilts her head up, smiling, and the warmth of it echoes in her words. "Do you want to marry me again, Jackson Peters?"

I never thought of myself as a romantic or even an emotional man, but when it comes to Belle, my feelings seem to continuously pour out of me like the wine we had earlier. I guess one would say that's a sure sign of my unconditional love.

I pull her harder into my chest, then lean down to bite her neck. "The answer will always be yes, my beautiful B."

"I think it's a sign I wore white tonight. Don't you agree?"

"Doubtful," I say dryly, and she playfully hits me, causing us both to laugh before we enter.

We interlock our fingers and pause at the doorway, taking in the grandeur of it all. I wasn't expecting this small chapel to be so magnificent. I lift her arm and kiss the inside of her wrist, letting my lips linger.

"This is a little fancy for what I had in mind."

"Only the best for my girl," I state, then gesture to continue down the aisle where Alessia stands to fake-officiate us.

Belle trips, and I catch her before she face-plants, reminding me we've had a lot to drink tonight. "Careful," I warn.

"Sorry." Belle shrugs, quickly regaining her balance, and practically bounces with excitement the rest of the way down.

When we reach Alessia, Belle raises her hand to stifle a giggle.

"This was all I could find." Alessia laughs, holding up a bible. "It's more official with a book, no?"

I shake my head at the ridiculousness of it all. "It would help if it wasn't upside down."

"Oh." She flips it quickly and clears her throat, causing her and Belle to lose it.

"Are we ready?" I ask, breaking up their cackles so we can get on with it. I'm currently imagining a little old Italian priest rushing toward us, yelling to get out, so it's better if we act quickly.

When the girls settle, Belle and I turn toward one another, and suddenly, the air calms around us and all is right in the world. This is exactly where I'm supposed to be at this moment in time.

I reach up and cup her face, rubbing the apples of her cheek. "I love you," I mouth.

She gulps down her emotions and wipes a rogue tear. "You have no idea how much that means to me, and how much I love you back. I've been waiting my whole life for this."

Now I'm the one holding back my emotions.

"Okay, you two. Less sappy. We have dancing to do."

Belle's smile is infectious, and her bright blue eyes are full of life as they stare back at me.

Alessia's words go by in a complete blur because I'm so lost in my Belle trance.

It still amazes me how my life has turned out after all these years, coming full circle with the one I was always meant for. Maybe

Alessia's right and it's a bunch of sappy bullshit, but I can't ignore the feeling of being whole again. Belle has always been a part of me, and now as my wife, the woman I love, she's fixed me, believed in me, and loves me back wholeheartedly.

"I now pronounce you husband and wife"—Alessia pauses dramatically—"again."

"Again," I whisper, but before I kiss my bride, I unzip my back pocket. Belle thinks I wore these pants because they were stylish, but I wore them for the practicality of keeping something safe.

"Oh my God," Belle cries, covering her mouth as a soft sob escapes her lips. "Jack. What? How?"

I slip the diamond wedding band, which I've held safe for the last few days, onto Belle's slender finger. When we returned from Paris, I ran to the jeweler, knowing it was the right time.

I packed it for Italy, knowing this was it for us. If she finally let go like I knew she would, I wanted to make sure our life in London started on the right foot—her as mine, as my wife, not just on paper but in every sense.

Looking down at the ring on my beautiful wife's finger, I understand why rings are so symbolic, or at least for me and Belle. We've finally come full circle. There's no turning back now.

"Jack?"

I look up, and both Belle and Alessia are standing there with tears running down their faces. "I bought this ring in London. I thought if we had a second alone today, giving it to you in the vineyards of Tuscany would have been romantic. We didn't have a chance, which thankfully worked out, because here and now is the exact right time."

Belle rolls her lips, trying to get ahold of her emotions. "I love it so much. Thank you, Jack. Will you wear a band if I get you one?"

"It would be my honor, sweetheart. I want everyone to know you're mine as much as I want them to know I belong to you."

Belle throws herself at me, and I barely have a second to catch her, but when I do, her lips crash against mine while Alessia yells, "You may kiss the bride," from somewhere in the distance.

Her kiss is desperate as she aggressively takes my lips. Our mouths open in a rush, our tongues gliding against one another, and it feels like nothing but home. She starts to melt against my body, so I hold her tighter, growling into her mouth when her hands slide through my hair, pulling at it in despair.

"Okay, okay, not so much a 'church kiss' anymore, you two," Alessia calls, laughing at our need for one another.

I always want her, I can't help myself.

We disconnect slightly, panting heavily, smiling wide, and I know this is it… it's the beginning of everything.

The good, the bad, whatever it is. I'm ready for it with Belle by my side.

"Now we really have a reason to go dancing. We need to celebrate!" Belle calls, and she's right. It's time to have some fun.

19

Annabelle

I THROW my arm around Alessia and cheers her with my gin and tonic. "Thanks for hosting us. It turned out to be a brilliant day," I scream over the 90s music blasting in this small-town pub.

"Cin, cin, Annabelle. I'm glad our working relationship has turned into a great friendship."

Alessia was one of my first clients and she's been invaluable to my business ever since. Her family owns one of the oldest textile companies based in Milan and Florence, and she was recently named CEO, which has not been easy for her in a male-dominated industry.

The Italian businessmen have been less welcoming, and we often bond over the hardships of running a business.

She introduced me to the DeLucas and the many fashion houses I work for, including the up-and-coming fashion designer who attended the wine tasting tonight. I was lucky enough to squeeze in a small pitch for her, since the Italians take their time off seriously and there was no other work-talk allowed.

But I will most definitely be following up the second I'm home.

The fashion world has always been my main focus, and I hope one day I have the ability to focus solely on that and get rid of the athletes.

I bump her side to get her attention again. “Sooo,” I drag out, “I remember you telling me the DeLucas are best friends with your parents so you often went on holiday with them as kids. Has anything ever happened with Romeo?”

The second the words are out of my mouth, an instant blush fills her cheeks.

“Shut up. It has, hasn’t it?”

“Nothing serious, just teenagers fooling around.” She shrugs, but something tells me that’s not the whole truth, so I keep my eyes on her until she says more. “It’s nothing, we tried dating in our twenties, but he didn’t want anything serious. Romeo is like a typical Italian man, he loves women, and women love him. So, when we were younger, that was more appealing to him than anything serious with me.” She tries to play it off, but I can still see it affects her.

“He seems like a good lad. Maybe things will be different now that he’s older. Look at me and Jack. I’ve told you about him in the past. Something clicked finally, and we’re making it work.”

Her frown turns to a genuine smile. “We’ll let the many women of Italy have Romeo, but I have to say, I’ve not seen a man so obsessed with a woman before. Jack loves you very much.”

Now it’s my turn to smile, matching hers. “He does, and the feeling is mutual.”

“It better be,” a familiar voice growls as he hugs me tightly from behind. Jack’s manly smell invades my senses as he buries his face in my neck. “Time to dance, sweetheart.”

I hand my drink to Alessia, then turn back to Jack. I’ve been waiting to dance with him all night. “You don’t hold a flame to my dancing skills!” I yell as I shimmy my way onto the dance floor.

His eyes are locked on mine, sparkling full of excitement as his cheeky smirk turns up, popping his dimples on full display. In slow motion, he takes off his blazer, making a show of it for everyone to see.

“Strip teases don’t count, lover boy!” I roll my hips to the music, hitting the beat with precision.

I throw my head back, letting my long hair run down my back.

God, I love all these songs. They remind me of my younger days.

I'm just warming up, but as the tempo increases, so do my moves, and I almost forget about Jackson. *Almost.*

He takes one, two, three steps onto the dance floor, loosening the buttons on his shirt and piling on the dramatics.

Women to our left cheer him on, yelling sentiments in Italian, boosting his ego even more.

He glides smoothly with his arms spread and ends it with a turn, coming face-to-face with me.

Not missing a beat, he grabs my hips and slams us together.

"Sweetheart, you know I don't like to lose. I'm the better dancer, and I think we all know it, especially my fan group over there." He nods toward the group of old Italian women ogling him, and then grinds his hips into me.

Unable to contain my laughter, I let it out in his face, then gesture toward Alessia. "It seems like my admirers are a bit more attractive."

Jack turns his head, instantly becoming serious. "If they look at you for a second longer, there will be serious issues. It took all my restraint during dinner not to reach over the table and knock the one guy out."

I pat his chest. "Now, now, you promised you were done with all the violence and I'd get the old Jack back."

"Sorry, B." *He shows no signs of remorse.* "I'll have to break a promise if someone disrespects my wife. I won't be able to control myself."

"All right, enough crazy, more dancing," I whisper seductively, running my hands up and down his chest.

"You feel good in my arms, B," he whispers back as we move as one to the music, our hands exploring every inch that's acceptable for the public—and maybe sometimes not—unable to get enough of each other.

"Well, you feel good as my husband," I counter, and he lets out a low growl as he bucks his hips into me. "You like that, Jack? Being my husband turns you on, doesn't it?"

"Fuck yes, it does. I love the fact that you're mine and only mine."

He grabs my arse hard and pulls it close to his groin, still moving our hips side to side, keeping up with the beat of the music. "We need to get out of here so I can fuck my wife. You want that, don't you, sweetheart? You're ready to go home, to feel me inside you… to have me claim you as my wife again." His lips kiss my neck, and my eyes involuntarily roll back into my head.

"Yes, dancing is overrated. Let's go home," I moan as he discreetly reaches up and cups my heavy breast. He takes my lips and kisses me hard before we reluctantly pull away, only to find an amused Alessia standing there holding tequila shots.

I smile sheepishly at Jack and say, "I guess shots are in order first."

"Come on!" Jack grabs my hand, pulling me away from the house. "You're walking very slowly, Mrs. Peters."

"No shit, I'm drunk and need a bed. Where are we going?" I mumble, then laugh out loud as he nearly falls over his own two feet.

"I want to make love to you in the vines." His eyes sparkle with mischief.

Oh… I like the sound of that.

Wait.

"No. No. This is my client's house. We can't do that here, Jack. We need to stick to strictly bedroom sex." I try to pull him the other way, but he's determined, and when he realizes what I've said, he pauses.

I think for a split second that he may have stopped because he realized it's wrong to do this here, but his eyes say something different.

He's turned on.

"Good, let my good friend Romeo see so once and for all, he can back off my girl," He pulls me into his chest. "You understand, don't you sweetheart?"

"I do, Jack," I moan as he runs his hand over my sex.

"That's what I like to hear, B." He brushes his lips along my jaw. "I'm afraid if he doesn't get the point, I'll be attending every meeting with you."

I let out a small chuckle that turns into another loud moan. “That's unreasonable. I have many good-looking male clients.”

Back and forth, I feel the outline of his fingers perfectly through the thin material of my dress. He cups my breast with his free hand. “These are mine.” He caresses them for a moment, then taps my heart. “Mine.”

“Yes,” I grit with desperation as my legs buckle from the intense pleasure radiating through me. “Jack, more. Please.”

Heat pools in my core, and suddenly, my drunk body is extremely turned on, though now it feels more like a punishment than anything else with the way he’s withholding.

“I’ll give you more when you realize nothing comes between us. Not work, clients, friends… nothing and no one. I’ll trample over every meeting you have if it means keeping everyone in check. I’d be stupid to think they aren’t all ogling you, but it also makes me murderous that anyone gets a glimpse of this sexy body, this perfect mouth.” He kisses me lightly. “Your tranquil eyes that have me bound to you.” He kisses me again. “Tell me.”

“I’m yours and only yours.” I bite my lip, not caring if there are potential cameras, because when Jack looks at me like this… like I hang the moon… I lose all ability to think straight.

“Tell me more. Tell me what I need to hear,” he demands as his fingers work quicker.

When my legs turn useless, he lays me on the ground between the rows of vines, lifts my dress, and pushes my knickers aside. “I need more,” I beg again.

“But I love exploring you, running my fingers through, feeling the wetness pool between your legs, knowing I’m the cause of this.” His words hit my core, and my body reacts the only way it knows how when Jack’s fingers are pressed against me.

“I’m going to come,” I cry, but he pulls back one second before my pleasure hits. “Why would you bloody stop?” I yell.

“Because…” His hand finds my center again, this time tracing around my lips, where it’s just enough to tease but nowhere near enough to put me back over the edge. My hips buck up shamelessly, trying desperately to make contact with his fingers. "You never told me what I want to hear."

"What do you want to hear?" I yell, frustrated. "That I love you? That I've always loved you? That I will love you and tell you so every single day for the rest of my life?" I gasp when his fingers move to my center. "Because I do. I love you. I love you. I love you. I love you. I love you. I love you," I chant repeatedly as pleasure overtakes my body, tingling through every possible inch. "I love you. I love you. I love you," I keep screaming, opening myself to him, exposing my only weakness but my biggest strength.

Somehow amid my outburst, Jack has unzipped his pants and is now positioned to enter me. "I need to feel you. I need every inch of us to be connected right now." He pushes in, and the second he enters me, combined with his fingers working me to perfection, shuddering cries leave my lips as my orgasm bursts through my body.

He lets out a guttural roar through the dark night as I pulse around him. I can feel myself contracting, squeezing him tightly, and I can only imagine it's driving him insane.

Reaching up, I grab onto his shirt so he'll come closer, then take his face in my hands to finally kiss him. The second our tongues touch, dancing together, his hips slow, sliding in and out of me as we savor each other.

I cling to him desperately as we kiss for what feels like forever.

He pulls back, our chests rising and falling together as we try to catch our breath. It's been like this every time, completely in sync.

Jack reaches around and lifts my hips, and his eyes darken as he hits a new angle inside me.

Oh, bloody hell, that feels good… like, really fucking good.

Jack's jaw goes slack, his eyes hooded as he picks up the pace. His eyes scan my face, then travel down my body, and I see it the second he realizes that holding me up doesn't give him access to his favorite things in the world.

My boobs.

He leans over and grabs my jumper and his trousers, rolling them up to push under my hips.

"Smart."

He smirks. "I know. I needed to feel these tits bouncing in my hands." He squeezes them tight, almost painfully. "I still need to make you come like this." He tweaks my nipples between his fingers, causing my breath to catch. "You think we can do that, sweetheart?" He leans down and licks my swollen nipples that are trapped between his fingers. My sex clenches, and his smirk deepens. "I think you like that idea. I think you'll come one day without my dick or fingers on your clit. I think my tongue and teeth"—he bites down—"on these thick pink nipples will be enough."

"Yes, oh… Jack. Fuck," I murmur while his thrusts pick up, quickening his pace.

From the look on his face, he reluctantly lets my breasts drop, swollen and heavy with need. He leans down and quickly pecks my lips before placing his hands on either side of my head, straight-armed, holding himself up to really let me have it.

In and out, slamming into me, he's just as lost to the pleasure as I am, moaning loudly between his deep breaths, the sound guttural and so fucking sexy, turning me on like never before.

My body is moving as best it can in the position when I feel it… the familiar build, that deep burn creeping through my body.

My face screws up in disbelief as Jack rotates his hips over and over, pumping into me hard and deep, slapping our bodies together.

I'm going to come… from sex.

"Jack," I cry.

"I know, baby," he pants. "Squeeze me and let it go. Come all over my cock, Annabelle." His face is a mix of pain and pleasure as he enters me with force. "Fuck. Yes," he screams as I throw my head back and cry out as a full-force orgasm rips through me, taking over everything in me.

I'm crying, shaking, and screaming.

This is like nothing I've ever felt before.

I look up until our eyes connect. Locked together and unable to move, we share a raw, emotional moment before Jack screams out, following me as I feel his cock jerks and warmth fills me deep.

After a few seconds, he drops to my side, pulling me close, crashing his lips to mine. Despite his roughness, our kiss is soft and tender.

My body is tired and limp, feeling overwhelmed and completely bare. I open my mouth and a small whimper escapes as I whisper another, "I love you."

"I love you, and I've got you, sweetheart," he whispers, squeezing me tight.

For many years, I stayed away from Jack, trying to protect myself, thinking he was no good for me. Who knows… maybe he wasn't then, but now, we're finally free to live happily.

We lie in each other's arms quietly for another few minutes until we hear a sound in the distance.

"What the fuck was that?" He leans up, looking around, but it's too dark to see anything in the distance. Then we hear it again, a mix of squeals and grunts echoing through the property.

Jack pops up and pulls me with him. "We need to get the fuck out of here."

I look down and giggle. "It might be rather hard for you to walk like that." I point down, and he laughs as he tucks himself back in and pulls up his trousers.

We're at the edge of the property, walking quickly back to the house, away from the noise, when I turn and see it.

Wild boars.

Jack stills, his eyes flickering to me with pure terror lacing through them. "B. What the fuck do we do? These things are vicious."

"It's fine. Let's just keep walking," I say, just as one of the boars growls at our sight.

"Annabelle!" he screams, and I double over in laughter. He has no idea the DeLucas just fenced this area due to the overpopulation of the boars.

"This is not fucking funny." He tries to pick me up and run, but I'm squirming and laughing too hard.

I can barely breathe. "There's a fence," I finally get out.

He stills, puts me down, and looks through the next opening, shaking his head, deciding it's not enough. "These things look fucking angry. They're going to break through any second and fucking eat us."

I raise my eyebrow. "Hmm, I'd rather you eat me."

"You're a sick fuck, you know that, Annabelle Peters? I'm about to die, and you're thinking about me eating your fucking pussy?" he cries, yanking out his hair.

Drunk, scared Jack is bloody hilarious, and I still can't get a handle on myself.

"But what a way to go… death by pussy. I'll engrave it on your headstone."

He can't help himself now. He's laughing along with me. "What the fuck is wrong with you?" He laughs harder, pulling at my hand to bring me closer. "You're crazy, you know." He nips at my bottom lips, trailing his hand down to my bum, momentarily forgetting about the boars before they start up again.

"Oh fuck no," he cries and scrambles back. "Look at them, lined up there. They look like fucking rhinoceros. Not pigs."

"There's a first. Rhinoceros-sighting in the depths of Tuscany."

He picks me up again and swats my arse. "Not the time to be a smartass, Annabelle Peters. Not the fucking time."

Jack picks up his pace, and I yell, "*Run, Forest, Run.*"

He turns his head and bites into the flesh of my arse. "You're going to fucking get it when we get back."

"Am I alive?" I croak, reaching out for some water. "Where's the bloody water?"

"Be quiet," Jack moans, throwing a pillow over his head.

"You be quiet, Mr. Let's Get Some Wine and skinny-dip. Why the heck did we think that was a good idea?"

Jack dry heaves. "Don't even say the word wine ever again in your life."

I chuckle, but it barely comes out. My throat is too dry and hoarse.

"This is your fault. Get me some water," I demand, then take in the room, realizing what a disaster it is.

All the lights are on. There are crisps scattered all over the bed, parts of the blanket are wet— clearly we never dried off after the pool —and one of Jack's socks is hanging off the fan.

The fuck?

"My fault? It wasn't the tequila shots or hours of wine drinking that did it?" He leans up, rubbing his eyes. "Fuck, is the room spinning or is it just me?" he cries, then bursts out laughing when he looks at me.

"What?" I get up to use the loo, and what I see in the mirror is traumatizing. "Oh. My. God," I scream, then hold my head as a throbbing pain thumps in my temple.

Jack walks up behind me with a glass of water. "Puts a whole new meaning to your morning Medusa hair, doesn't it?"

I chug the water, then slap him on the chest. "Shut up, Jack!"

Besides my hair being a complete rat's nest, it's no longer blonde. It's green from the bloody chlorine in the pool. I have an event to go to for work tomorrow when we return to London. What the hell am I going to do?

Jack passes me another water then wraps his arms around my waist, resting his head on top of mine while looking at me through the mirror. "Could be worse." He shrugs. "I almost died last night."

I narrow my eyes. What the hell was he talking about?

Oh…

"Death by pussy?" I smirk.

He closes his eyes and shakes his head. "And you say I'm addicted to sex. No, Belle, not death by pussy. Death by wild boar," he says dryly.

"Don't be dramatic." I walk over, sit on the toilet, and start to pee.

He stands there in shock, then quickly turns up his lips.

"What?"

"You're peeing in front of me. We've hit a new level of intimacy."

I roll my eyes. "Only you would be excited about this. I'm going to die if I don't have more water. Can you get me some?"

"Sure. I'm going to make coffee to try to feel human again. Do you want one?"

"No, thanks," I reply.

He pauses at the door and turns back slowly. "A memory just hit me. The best fucking memory," he growls.

What is he talking about?

"You came on my dick last night, didn't you, B? All from penetration. I got you to orgasm for the first time that way."

I should act surprised, but I've been waiting for him to bring this up. Honestly, I'm amazed it took so long. I thought he would have been reciting it in his sleep.

"Yeah, yeah. You're amazing, lover boy. Now, can I pee in peace?"

He fist pumps and exits the bathroom, whistling, completely chuffed with himself. I won't boost his ego, but it is pretty impressive, and I hope to practice it many times in the future.

My laptop rings with an incoming FaceTime from Sadie. I check the time and realize it must be the middle of the night for her in South America if it's early here. I'm worried something may be wrong.

I glance outside where Jack is sitting with his cappuccino, reading the paper, taking in the outdoors on our terrace. It looks like he's not even halfway through reading, so I hope he stays out there while I answer this call quickly.

"Hi, darling. What's wrong?"

Her eyes widen. "What's wrong with me? What the heck is wrong with you?"

I laugh, completely forgetting about my appearance. Luckily I put on a nightgown when I went back to bed. "The effect of an over-chlorinated pool."

"Jeez, you scared me. I'm not used to seeing you looking like—" She waves her hand around. "You're in shambles."

I lean back to get comfortable. "Trust me, I scared myself when I looked in the mirror. So, will you tell me why you're calling me in the middle of the night on your honeymoon? Where are you?"

"We're in Argentina now. We arrived late tonight. It's been the trip of a lifetime so far, but that's a story for another time. I can't sleep." Her face falls, and she looks away in the distance for a second. "I need your advice, Annabelle," she whispers solemnly.

My stomach twists, not liking the tone of her voice. "What's wrong, Sadie?"

"Are you going to judge me if I tell you I've been speaking to my dad since the wedding?" My face must give something away. "I knew it." She looks down, forlorn.

I glance to ensure Jack's still outside. "No, darling, it's not that. I'm just taken aback, and I wasn't expecting that at all." I pause, contemplating how to say this. "I need to tell you something that happened."

"He told me about the wedding, B, and I believe him. My intuition tells me I need to talk to him. I'm not sure what's going on with him, but something seems different."

I close my eyes, hating being in the middle of this. I don't want to betray Jack, he's my husband now, but Sadie's right. I tried to say this to Jack, but he wouldn't have any of it.

I've even brought up his dad a few times since, but he dismisses the idea of talking about him altogether.

But I saw it in their dad's eyes while in Paris… something was different.

"Did your dad tell you I was with Jack while everything went down?"

"He did. He told me everything. I think." She shrugs. "From your face now, it doesn't seem like you think I'm crazy."

I try to discreetly check on Jack again. "You're not crazy. I saw something similar when I stood there. Jack was in such a rage that he only saw red, but I saw remorse and even longing for his son. Jack would kill me if I said this, but I felt bad for him. I don't know what it was, but it pulled at my heartstrings."

"I know… He wants to meet."

"I'm not giving your dad a pass for what he did, but I'm wondering if there might be more to the story. He's clearly nothing like your mum. Wait, what?"

"Shh," she whispers, looking back into her room. It's clear she's keeping this from Wills. Not that I blame her. I have a feeling he'd put a stop to all this if he knew.

"He's asked to explain himself, and I've decided I'm going to hear him out. He can't hurt me anymore, but after all these years, I still want answers. So he's coming to London, and we're going to talk."

"The fuck you are," Jack roars behind me, ripping the laptop from my hands. "Over my dead body, Sades. Not in this life or any other are you meeting that piece of shit!"

Jack's chest is heaving wildly as he stares at his sister.

"Jackson?" Her voice rises. "Why are you in Italy with Annabelle?"

I don't miss the accusatory tone of her voice and neither does Jack, so he quickly glances over to me, shooting me an apologetic look. After all this, keeping it a secret so we can tell her together in person, we're going to have to do it over the phone while she's in a different country.

But he tries to distract her anyway.

"I'm not kidding, Sadie. After all he's put us through, not to mention what he let mom do. He doesn't get a pass."

"What the hell is going on?" Wills's voice booms through the computer. I can't see the screen, but I can only imagine his confusion at all the yelling.

Sadie ignores him. "Jackson, I'll ask you again. Why are you naked in Italy with Annabelle?"

Jack closes his eyes and takes a deep breath before walking to where I'm still in bed. He positions it so that we're both in the picture, then hangs his arm over my shoulders.

I widen my eyes. "Surprise?"

20

Annabelle

Sadie narrows her eyes. "What do you mean, *surprise*?"

"Again, what the hell is going on out here?" Wills asks as he walks over to Sadie, lifts her, and places her on his lap.

He looks between us, confused, but clearly catches on much faster than his wife.

I look at Jack for guidance, unsure who should speak first. He nudges me in the leg, but I sit still and silent, nervous to hear their reaction.

I'm suddenly feeling sick with guilt over keeping our relationship a secret, let alone our marriage.

Jack must feel the tension radiating off of me, so he speaks first. Thankfully he got the clue, because I'm not usually one lost for words.

"The surprise is, Belle and I are together," he says, lifting my shaky hand to kiss my wrist.

I could have done short and to the point. I thought he'd give a little more.

I look between Jack, Sadie, and Wills.

Wills is a statue and Sadie's in shock, her eyes unblinking and wide like a deer in headlights.

"Like *together*, together?" Sadie whispers.

I nod. "Yeah. It's not that we wanted to keep it from you, but we wanted to ensure it worked out before telling you all and risking screwing up our friend group. It's not the same as meeting a random bloke at the pub. Your opinions matter to us."

For a while, everyone's quiet until Wills rubs Sadie's back, spurring her on.

"I… I think I'm in shock, sorry." She pauses. "For how long?"

The air drains from my lungs. Another question I've been dreading answering.

Jack opens his mouth to speak, but I squeeze his hand in a silent plea to let me explain this part.

He may be her brother, but a friendship like ours, which is more like a sisterhood, is meaningful in different ways. This is one of those things that should come from me.

"Why is it so difficult to answer the question?" Sadie's voice starts to rise, sensing something's off.

Wills glares between the two of us pointedly. He's not happy to see Sadie upset, and by the way Jack tenses beside me, neither is he.

If I don't spit it out, this will only get messier.

"Well, we officially started dating in France, but—"

"Oh, so this is new? I mean, I don't like that you kept it from me, but I always knew if you both settled down, it would be with each other. At least, I had hoped that would be the case. Wait, you got together in Paris? When you were there helping out with our wedding?" She smiles brightly at Wills. "I love that. Isn't that a great story, baby?"

My heart breaks at her optimism, knowing I'm about to break hers.

Wills doesn't answer, his eyes locking on mine instead. "What else?"

Fuck's sake.

"Do you remember last year, when Nora was testifying for the court case in New York? And how Jack and I were in Vegas beforehand?" Wills starts to shake his head and pulls Sadie into his chest.

Sadie scrunches up her face, confused. "I do…"

"Keep going," Jack whispers.

"Well…" I let out a nervous laugh. "Jack and I got a little drunk and… we might have gotten married in one of those Elvis chapels," I spit out.

It doesn't hit her right away, but when it does, her face quickly falls.

"You're married?" she whispers, hurt lacing every syllable.

"Sades," Jack pleads. "Please don't be upset. It's not what it seems. We never mentioned it because we weren't together. At first, we thought it was a drunken mistake. We were seeing other people, but then—"

"We started dating, and we realized how much we love each other." I look up at Jack, hoping Sadie can recognize the love that passes between us like I often see between her and Wills. "So we decided to stay married. This is it for us. We both realize how stupid we've been over the years and are committed to making this marriage work. I know it's not a fairytale story, but it's our story, and to us… it's perfect."

"I understand." She clenches her jaw, smiling through it, and I can see she's holding back tears. "I'm happy for both of you. Who knew I would gain two sisters-in-law in a matter of weeks?"

"Sadie." I let out a sigh. "We're so sorry. We never meant for it to go on this long. Then the wedding happened, and we didn't want to take any attention away from you."

"It's fine," she snaps, and her lip starts to quiver. "I'm truly happy for both of you. I love you." Her voice breaks as Wills shuts off the screen and kills the call.

I turn and bury myself into Jack, and he holds me tight as we sit in silence. I can't help thinking of the pain we've caused one of the most important people in our lives.

"This is my fault," I mumble into Jack's chest. "I'm so sorry."

He pulls back, confused. "What do you mean it's your fault? We're in this together."

"I asked you to keep this a secret in Paris. Sadie would have understood if we'd told her when this first started. I don't like upsetting her."

"Annabelle," he chastises. "I'm a grown man. If I wanted to tell people, I would have talked to you about it. I agreed with all the reasons you wanted to hold off. I still agree with you." He kisses my head. "She'll get over it. Once she calms down, we'll explain it in more detail. She'll be ecstatic. She's just upset that the two people she's known and loved the longest did something monumental without her. You would be upset too."

"I know. It doesn't make it easier, though."

"Declan and Nora eloped," he reminds me.

I nod. "They did, but that's nowhere near the same. They told us the same day, and we got to celebrate with them. We've kept this a secret for over a year. That's where we went wrong."

Both our phones ping with a message and the second I check it, any reassurance I felt leaves my body.

Wills: Really fucked up.

"No," Jack announces loudly. "You know what? They hid their relationship from me. So how the fuck is this different?"

My shoulders sag. "Jack, you can't compare the two."

"Maybe you can't, but I can. When they found out Wills knew me, they still kept it from me. And I know they did that so they could work things out between them before the shit hit the fan. It's the same fucking thing, B."

When he puts it like that… he makes sense.

But it's still not exactly the same.

I let out the deep breath I've been holding in. "All right, we have a few hours left here. Let's go to town, eat off this hangover, then go home to London. We'll figure it all out then. I don't want to end the trip on a sour note."

Sitting in Jack's lap as we wait for the car to bring us to the airport, I'm reminded of how fortunate I am to have visited two beautiful countries with Jack this past month.

Although the situation with Sadie has put a slight damper on the morning, we've tried to make the most of it.

We enjoyed a lovely lunch sitting in the piazza, overlooking the medieval town, local to us. Then we did a little shopping, and I bought the most stunning painting from a local artist that I left as a thank-you to the DeLuca family.

Being here the last few days, I've realized what a blessing it's been to get away. Paris never felt relaxing. I was constantly working, even though I tried my best to put it aside. Not to mention figuring things out with Jack.

Finally letting loose in Italy meant we got to enjoy our newfound happiness. It's a shame we can't stay longer. Hopefully, in the future, they offer the house again.

From a distance, we see a car turn down the drive. I stand, thinking it's the car service, but when I hear the familiar roar of the Lamborghini engine and recognize its owner, I quickly turn toward Jack, begging him to behave.

"What the hell does he want now?"

I squeeze his hand in a silent plea. "It's his house, remember that, Jack. And he's a client. The client part is the most important."

"I'm not a savage. I'll act professionally."

If Romeo weren't pulling up, I'd laugh aloud at his ridiculous statement.

"Ciao," Romeo calls as he walks over to us.

I wave, praying that this chat goes okay. I'm still mortified at what happened the other day. "Romeo, I'm so glad you stopped over before we left." I push Jack toward him. "We wanted to apologize for the other day. It was completely unprofessional, and—"

He cuts me off by waving a dismissive hand. "Bella, you're forgetting I'm Italian. Passion and possession is what makes up the Italian love language. There is no sorry needed. I've only come to apologize to your husband." He turns to Jack. "I love many women, but that does not include the married ones. I wanted to apologize for overstepping. I had no idea she was taken. You have my word, man to man, that our relationship will remain purely professional."

Jack sticks out his hand, and Romeo graciously shakes it. "I appreciate that, Romeo. Belle and I are navigating a new relationship, and I sometimes get a little carried away."

"As long as you trust one another, a little jealousy never hurts anyone." We all let out a small laugh. I'm thankful it's been taken care of, one less thing to think about when I'm home. "I heard you two had a fun day and night yesterday."

"Oh, did Alessia tell you?"

He blanches ever so slightly, and I might have missed it had I not been fishing for that exact response. Since my discussion with Alessia yesterday, I've been curious to find out more about their relationship so I wanted to see if I could get a reaction out of him.

"Alessia and I don't speak anymore." He gulps, and I have to hold back any facial reactions. That was not what I expected him to say. "Rosella called this morning, and she told me the two of you spoke. I let her know all the wonderful things you've done for us, and she promised to follow up with you."

"Romeo." I hug him quickly before Jack freaks out and we're back at square one. "I appreciate that more than you know. Fashion is my passion, and I hope to work with more designers in the future. Thank you for putting in a good word."

"I only spoke the truth," he says, gesturing to the arriving car. "Back to London then. I would love to get dinner with both of you if you're interested. I'll be there in a couple of months. Maybe you have some single English friends for me?" He smirks.

I pat Jack on the back. "I'm sure Jack here has a few from the old harem he can share," I kid.

"Funny, B. We'd love to host you, Romeo. I own two clubs in London where I'm sure you'd have a good time." Jack shakes Romeo's hand again and we say our goodbyes, thanking him profusely.

We're about to step into our waiting car, so I wave one last time. "*Arrivederci*!"

Romeo smirks and calls out, "*Adios*!"

I laugh while Jack covers his face and gets in the car. "Mortified. That's all I can say."

On our drive to the airport, we stare out our windows in awe like we haven't been here all weekend. But the view never gets old.

Jack reaches over and interlocks our fingers. "We're making amazing memories, sweetheart. Perfect stories to tell our kids one day."

I freeze and try to pull my hand away. Why did he need to bring that up right now?

"Jack," I whisper. "Can we talk about this when we get home? I've told you before that I don't want kids. Is this going to be an issue?"

"I know you love your job, but we can make it work. I can retire early."

"It's not that, Jack." I glance at the driver. "This is not a discussion for right now, but it's not because I'm a workaholic, I promise you. I —" I stop myself, shaking my head. My trauma is not something I want to talk about in the back seat of a car.

Jack must sense my anxiousness. "Forget I said anything. We'll talk about it another time." He lifts my hand and kisses each fingertip. "Everything will work out."

I hope so… I hope he understands my decision and why I've kept it to myself all these years.

Otherwise, our blissful bubble will pop.

For good.

One Week Later

Jackson

"Are you serious?" Belle mutters, annoyed, throwing herself onto the ground.

I bend over to catch my breath. "Don't be a sore loser," I tease.

On the mornings when she's not doing Pilates, we've been running together before I head to the gym, and I've never let her win. It's killing her and her competitiveness.

She narrows her eyes. "You could have finished last this one time, for fuck's sake. It would've been the gentlemanly thing to do."

I bite my lip to hide my smirk, follow her to the ground, and crawl on top of her.

Sweaty or not, she's sexy as hell.

I kiss her cheek and neck with an open mouth, slowly trailing my lips down until I reach her beautiful breast that clings to the material of her white shirt.

I bite her nipple and smirk when she moans. "Oh, sweetheart." I bite her other nipple. "There will only ever be one time I finish last in life, and that's in the bedroom with you."

"Bloody hell, Jack. You can't say things like that when I need to go to the office." She tries to swat me away, but I catch her wrists and hold them over her head.

"There's always time." I grind my erection into her and bite her nipple again.

She's breathing heavily and her eyes are closed, so I know I've got her right where I want her.

"Take it inside, you gobshites," I hear the familiar Irish brogue call from across the street. I throw up my middle finger and carry Belle inside before she changes her mind.

When we got home from Italy, we put both of our places on the market, as we discussed. They sold quicker than we expected, so we're temporarily living in a house Declan is remodeling across the street from his own. It's not ideal, but good enough for a few weeks until our new place is ready.

"Jack, I need to leave soon," she protests weakly as I begin peeling her clothes off. When she starts to help, though, I know it's a done deal.

This will be quick and easy, considering we had a warm-up earlier this morning, and I'm not talking about our run.

We've been completely insatiable. It's almost like we're making up for lost time.

I grab Belle's legs and spread them wide, glancing down at her pussy that's already glistening with need.

Fuck yeah.

I push in slowly at first, then quickly pick up my speed.

We're moaning each other's names, lost in complete ecstasy, and it never fades until the very last drop of my come enters her.

Decline.

"I'm sitting right next to you. I can see you declining my meeting invite," Belle spits.

Here we go again.

"You're quite snippy for someone who just had sex… twice."

"Jackson," she huffs. "Can you be serious?"

I give an uninterested shrug. "I don't need a calendar invite to speak with my wife."

She slams her hands against the table and stands up, dumping her latte down the drain.

"Then fucking talk to me, Jack. Tell me to my face right now that you don't want kids, and it will never be a discussion. Otherwise, we need to talk. You're only dismissing me because you don't want to hear my truth."

She's right. It's the last thing I want to talk about.

I realized quickly that I made the wrong assumption about why Belle doesn't want kids. For the last week, she's been begging and pleading that it's important and that she needs to talk to me about it, so I'll admit I'm scared to hear her reasoning.

So instead of talking, I've been distracting her with lots of sex—not that she's complaining—and plans that include outdoor activities.

I know I can't put this off forever. I *do* want kids, and I'm not getting any younger. They might have been a far-off fantasy for most of my life, but that was only because I was single. I've always known that kids would be part of the equation if I finally found my match

I sip my coffee and sigh. "Fine, Annabelle. Tonight."

She pauses mid-step. "Oh… uh. Okay. Considering it's a Saturday, I think I can work from here after my last meeting."

"Your brother is back in the gym today, so I'm finally sparring with him. Then I can be home."

Her head twists at lightning speed. "Oh God, don't provoke him. Please. He's been more high-strung than ever."

"I can handle Theo, don't worry."

I block an uppercut. "Can you calm down, you cocksucker?"

"Me?" Theo roars and throws a right hook that I quickly duck under, thanking my lucky stars that my stealth movements are on point today. Theo's on the warpath. "You don't do monogamy. You're known all around as London's premier fuckboy, and I'm supposed to trust you with Annabelle?"

"Luckily for you, it's not the nineteenth century. She's her own woman, making her own choices." I get in one quick jab when he gets annoyed.

"Fuck off, you cunt. You're the last bloke I want around my sister." That fucker gets me below the belt and I buckle over in pain.

"Ease off, you two," the gym manager yells from his desk, giving me a second to stand and retreat to catch my breath.

"All right, we've been at this for a while. Can we get out of the ring and talk like civilized adults?"

Theo's raging and trying to catch his breath, so I use the break to duck out of the ring and grab my water bottle. Call me a pussy for running away, but I'm not in the mood to die today.

He stalks after me, demanding answers, and I don't blame him. I know how the outside world sees me, but he's known me long enough to know that I'm true to my word and wouldn't fuck around on Belle.

"So that's it, there's no fucking discussion. You're with my sister? End of?"

"End fucking of, Theo. We're not goddamn teenagers, and we're both capable of making decisions, not to mention she's fucking older than you." I take a breath. I need to stay calm, otherwise he's going to fly off the handle more than he already has. "Listen, Hughes. I respect you and your whole family. I've known you most of my life, so I wanted to tell you to your face, even if you guessed it at the wedding. Do you truly think, after all this time, I'd pick Belle just to fuck around on her? Not to mention how much that would hurt your mom?"

My words must resonate, because he softens, leaning back in his seat.

"Why now?"

I give an impatient shrug. "Because it finally clicked. There's no science behind it. I love Belle, and she loves me." I can see he's still struggling. "People change, Theo. Look at Matthew. He swore off women, and now he's moving Lola to another country to be with him."

He shakes his head. "Can you believe that shit?"

"I would've said no if you'd asked me last year, but now I understand. I would do anything for your sister."

He holds my stare. "Don't fuck this up."

"Not planning on it." We sit in awkward silence until I ask, "How's your mom?"

He blows out a frustrated breath. "Hanging in there. Seeing Dad wasn't easy on her, but she's taking it day by day. She's taken a liking to Wills's mum, which has been a healthy distraction, so let's hope it stays that way."

Me too.

"Oh, before I forget." I reach into my gym bag and pull out a stack of papers. "My sister printed these for you a few weeks ago and I completely forgot to give them to you. I don't know which dogs are still available at Amelia's Angels, but based on the information you gave Sades, she thought one of these dogs would be the best fit for you to adopt."

He flips through as I pack the rest of my stuff up. For the first time since getting together with Belle, I'm dreading going home. I almost wish I were back in the ring with Theo getting my ass beat.

"Peters," Theo calls. "She acts strong, but be gentle with her. She has a lot going on in that head of hers."

I walk into the house to find Belle sitting in her loungewear, a large blanket wrapped around her and a cup of tea in her hand.

This isn't going to be good.

"Sit," she whispers and pats the chair in front of her with her free hand.

My stomach is twisted in knots as I walk with a heavy foot toward the chair. I had hoped she would still be in the office, but it's clearly not my lucky day.

"I think it best if I just jump right in."

"Probably best," I say dryly, not purposely wanting to sound like a dick but my nerves about this conversation are getting the better of me.

She places her teacup down and wraps her arms around her legs in a protective hold. "I want to start by telling you this is not easy for me to say, and I hope you keep an open mind. I see the anguish in your eyes anytime I try to talk to you about it. I know you'll be upset, but please consider the bigger picture. Things are not always black and white."

I give a curt nod, unable to speak.

"I've kept something from you, and I'm beginning to think it was a mistake. But I was only a teenager, listening to my mum, and scared. Then, as time went on, I saw no reason to hurt another person with what I went through. It wasn't until we got serious that I realized you needed to know, and maybe you should have known all along."

I lean my elbows on my knees and hang my head in my hands. "What is it, Annabelle? What should I have known?" I whisper in despair.

She sniffles, trying to rein in her emotions. "In my first semester at

Cambridge, I had an ectopic pregnancy," she whispers. "A miscarriage."

My head snaps up. "What? A miscarriage?" *Wait…* "Your first semester…" I trail off, doing the math in my head.

When I meet her tear-filled eyes, it hits me.

"I had a miscarriage with *our* baby, Jackson."

21

Annabelle

JACK STILLS, letting the words sink in. "Our baby?" he whispers in complete shock.

I watch his face as the words take over, processing them in his own time. When he finally stands, I follow his movements, unsure of what to do until he speaks again.

Should I explain what happened, and why I kept it to myself?

Tell him what I went through?

I don't know. I'm at a loss here. I had it all planned out, but nothing prepares you for pure devastation.

Jack starts pacing, his chest heaving as he tries to calm himself down. "I don't understand, Annabelle. I don't understand," he yells.

"Jackson," I whisper. "I—"

"You what?" he bellows. "We had a baby?" His voice catches and tears pool in his eyes. I try to swallow the lump that lingers in my throat. Instead, I choke out the sob I've been holding back, his tears pushing me over the edge. "I… We had a baby?" he repeats.

He sits back down, so I follow his lead and position myself across from him. He rocks back and forth, grabbing at his hair in despair. It's breaking whatever whole pieces are left of my heart to watch him like this.

After a moment, he runs his hands down his face and mumbles, "Explain."

I pause, forgetting my words as the emotions and memories flood my vision.

"Annabelle," he grits, growing impatient. "Start from the beginning."

I grab my quilt and bunch it up in my hands for security, then take a deep breath to calm myself. "Ten weeks after I gave you my virginity, I found out I was pregnant while at Cambridge." I pause again to collect myself. One sentence in and I'm already struggling.

This was one of the most challenging times in my life, so trying to replay something I've suppressed for nineteen years is not easy.

"I don't understand why you wouldn't call me. It's me, Belle. Me —" He jabs a finger to his chest.

"Please, Jack," I beg. "Let me finish, because this is not the story you probably have in your mind." He finally sits back, and I take that to mean he's ready to hear the rest. "I had an IUD, and it was typical that I would miss a period at times, so I didn't think anything of it. Then one night, I woke up in severe pain. I couldn't move, I had no idea what was happening, and I was rushed to the hospital."

His face falls. "What?" he whispers.

I look down and clench my jaw, breathing through my nose. "I was bleeding internally and had something called a ruptured ectopic pregnancy. The egg never reached the uterus, and the baby started developing in my fallopian tube. When I got to the hospital, they rushed me into surgery, performed a laparotomy to stop the bleeding, and had to remove one of my fallopian tubes," I choke out. Finally, I let the tears go. "There was no chance of survival for the baby, and if I hadn't gone that day, I would have died alongside him."

"*Him.*" He sucks in a breath.

I shake my head, wiping the tears. "It was too early to know. I-I always just called the baby him."

His tormented eyes find mine. "God, Annabelle, my heart is

breaking for you and what you went through. We lost a *baby*. I could have lost you…" He blows out a breath and shakes his head like he can't believe it. "But the pain rippling through my body right now is taking over, and I'm not sure I can stop it. Why would you do this to me… to us? Why wouldn't you tell me? Did you honestly think I wouldn't have been there for you?"

"I wasn't thinking straight—"

"You weren't," he spits.

I stare at him and continue, "No, I wasn't. But I was young, so young, and had just undergone emergency surgery, only to find out I had a baby inside me that wasn't alive. You were at university with your mates. Why would I want to burden your life too? The devastation was too much to handle for even one person."

"Because—" He breaks off, and from how he says that one word, I can hear that his emotions are quickly turning to anger. Not that I blame him. He doesn't know how else to express his hurt, and if I have to be his punching bag for now, so be it. I'm the one who caused him this pain, so I deserve the punishment. "It wasn't your call, Annabelle. Out of all the fucked-up things you could do, you kept this from me? And the fact that you thought it would be a burden blows my mind. When have you ever been a burden? Not one fucking time in thirty years." He walks over to the bar and slams back a scotch. "Tell me," he grits out. "Who was there to care for you after you lost our baby, since it wasn't me or I'm assuming my sister?"

"Mum, only Mum. No one else knows."

He stiffens, and I can see the wheels in his head turning, calculating when this would have taken place. "*Your mom*? The woman who was in a deep depression at that time? The woman who only a month earlier couldn't move you to Cambridge because she was in such a state? That mom? Or maybe the mom who left you stranded at the airport because she was so drunk she forgot to pick you up after your month-long holiday in the States?"

"Enough, Jackson."

He's breathing heavily through his nose. "Enough? Enough? I had a fucking baby, and you're telling me *enough*?" He throws his head back and roars in anguish, "Whyyyy?"

"I'm so sorry."

Why did I listen to Mum? She told me he would feel obligated to take care of me, to be bound to me since we shared a loss.

How fucking stupid of me.

I wasn't thinking straight then, and when I finally moved on, I felt it was too late to tell Jack. To dredge up all the painful feelings again.

What did I know at seventeen years old?

"I feel like I don't even know you. You've put something between us that I would have never imagined in my whole life. I need to leave. I can't look at you right now."

Panic starts to set in. "Please don't go."

He whips around. "Tell me, did you mourn our baby?" he yells, tears pouring down his face.

God, he's so hurt. "Do you think about him at night? Wonder what he would be like?" He points at me with a shaky hand. "You took that from me. Nineteen *years*. I had no fucking idea, and now I mourn my child. I don't care if he was one week or twenty weeks… my child died, and I didn't fucking know."

I have no other words, because he's right to be upset.

"Fuck this." He storms into our bedroom and aggressively pulls down his luggage, causing half his clothes to fall everywhere.

"You're leaving me?" I gasp in horror. This can't be… he can't leave me.

His eyes narrow and he instinctively takes a step back. I've never seen Jackson with such venom in his eyes, especially directed toward me.

"Did I say that, Annabelle? Did I say I was leaving you? I said I was leaving… meaning getting out of this fucking house, because I'm suffocating and I need space." He throws a random mix of clothes in his luggage and haphazardly tries to close it, but the zipper won't budge.

"Motherfucker!" He punches the bag, then lifts his eyes, still filled with tears. "You've ripped my heart out, Annabelle."

I bow my head to hide my quivering lip before I speak. I don't deserve penance, so there is no reason he should see my guilt.

"I'm sorry I didn't tell you, Jack. I don't know what else to say. Anything that comes out of my mouth now will sound like an excuse."

"I'm sorry you didn't tell me too." He pauses in front of me and lifts my chin, glaring into my eyes. "Because your unspoken words have caused us the most hurt."

The pain laced through his words stabs at my heart, and I have no one to blame but myself. My only hope is that somehow he forgives me.

Even though I caused this, it doesn't mean I'm not just as heartbroken, so I follow after him, and with each step, my sobs get louder.

What if he doesn't come back?

He swings open the front door, and there stands Sadie and Wills, wide-eyed and motionless.

Fuck.

Jackson

Fuck.

I completely forgot I invited my sister over to clear the air. They must have just got home from their honeymoon.

This is the worst and best timing possible.

Best because I'll need a ride somewhere, since all I see is red at the moment and I'm in no condition to drive. Worst because I have zero interest in talking about what happened, and I know my hand will be forced.

"What's going on?" Sadie glances back and forth between our pain-stricken faces.

Belle tries to talk, but chokes on her tears. Everything tells me to turn and hold her, but I can't.

Not yet.

I turn to Wills. "Can you drive me somewhere?"

He takes in the scene and looks at Sadie for guidance.

"Go, I'm staying here with Annabelle." She moves toward her best friend, placing an arm around her to hold her close.

Although I'm livid, I can't help but feel relieved she'll have someone here to comfort her if it can't be me.

"We walked. Give me the keys to your car," Wills says. I throw them to him and we walk out silently. I climb in the passenger seat and we drive off, the house disappearing from view.

"Any particular destination?" he asks me after a few minutes.

"Nope."

"So are you going to tell me what the hell that was back there?"

I lean back on the seat and close my eyes. "Do I have to?"

"Probably, before the end of this car ride."

Turning my head I look out the window as the city moves by in the blink of an eye. Everything still goes on, even though I feel like my life is at a standstill.

I didn't know it was possible to feel completely numb while hurting so badly. I can't wrap my head around anything I'm feeling.

A near-fatal situation for Belle, a fatal one for *our* baby.

A rush of agony hits me, and for even more torture, I take my phone out, opening a file with pictures of a younger Belle and me.

What would the baby have looked like?

I throw my phone on the car floor. Why the hell am I doing this to myself?

Running my hands down my face in frustration, I let out a loud breath. God, what was she thinking keeping this from me?

The car stops and I realize Wills has parked in front of The Swan. "Let's go. You can tell me over a pint."

He places the drink in front of me, and I take a large gulp before getting into it.

"Belle was pregnant," I say before giving him the whole rundown of what happened. "And I don't know what to do. I want to be with her, comfort her. For fuck's sake, she almost died. But I also want to throttle her for not telling me she was pregnant with my child."

"This is fucked," is all Wills says.

No shit, Sherlock.

"I'm just so angry, so hurt. I can't see the light at the end of the tunnel. She took something away from me that I can never get back."

Wills stays silent, not responding to anything, letting me play out everything myself.

My thoughts and words are all over the place. I have nothing to say.

After another drink, the pub door opens, and a familiar face walks in. "You told him?" I ask Wills, who nods in response. "Thanks."

My two best friends.

Declan pats my shoulder before taking a seat. "How are you feeling?"

"Like I'm missing someone I never knew existed."

Their faces fall.

"It'll all work out," Wills sips his beer.

"How? Will I get over this hurt?" I look at Declan for my answers.

"Is your trust broken? Will you leave her over this?" he asks.

Thinking on it for a second, I answer honestly, "No… to both."

"Then you need to go home. Sleep in another room if you have to, because—*fuck*. Can you imagine what she went through as a teenager? And now to bring up all the old memories of it? She must be going through some shite."

"What about me and what I'm going through?" I don't want to sound like a petulant child, but do my feelings of being left in the dark not count?

"Aye, no one's saying you shouldn't be hurting or even mad at her, mate. I think, though, if you go home, even if you don't speak, she'll feel the support." He pauses. "No one can pretend they know what it's like being in your shoes or Belle's, but I do remember being seventeen."

Annoyed, I ask, "And all the years after?"

They both shrug.

He passes me his phone, and it's a text from Nora.

Pip: This isn't good, Dec. Belle's in bad shape. If he doesn't fecking come home to his WIFE (did you know they're married?!), we'll

stay with her. She shouldn't be alone. I'm gutted for her… Can you imagine losing one of our babies? Then the operation? No wonder she doesn't want to have kids. We're holding Agnes and Aoife all night, I don't care if we keep them up.

"I'll go home," I mutter and pick up my glass. "Well, let's cheers to our baby." Their faces drop as they somberly hold up their glasses. "Rest in peace, baby Peters."

Annabelle

My head rests on Sadie's lap that's now soaked from all my tears as she strokes my hair, trying her best to comfort me.

I know deep down that I don't deserve this kind of consoling.

She should be with her brother.

"Goddammit, Sadie," I mumble as I raise my head to look at her. "Be mad at me. I've kept secrets from you. You're the one person besides Jack I should have shared my world with. I was a coward. So stop it, be angry. I can take it," I cry.

Her smile is sad as she sweeps the wet strands of hair from my face. "My sister soul mate, I am upset, yes. But I won't be angry, and I won't kick you when you're down. We'll work through this together." She maneuvers my head into a better position and strokes my cheek. "Close your eyes and rest. You need to calm down."

"I'm not one of the girls. You don't need to treat me like a child."

She chuckles lightly. "Fine, you look like dog shit. Now rest so you can get rid of those bags under your eyes. Is that what you wanted to hear?"

I smile, unable to control the small chuckle that slips through my lips. It feels nice to be happy for even a second. "Yes, darling. That's exactly what I needed. I love you."

"I love you too. And Belle, my brother loves you even more. He always has. He just needs time."

I glance up into her eyes and see the truth behind them. "I hope you're right, Sadie," I whisper before closing my eyes.

Never would I have thought I could sleep in a time like this because in the darkness all I see is Jack, our baby, and the pain I've caused the people around me by keeping this secret.

My body can no longer take the pain though, and I'm forced into a fitful sleep.

"Annabelle, wake up," Sadie's soft voice echoes in my ear.

I'm already up. "You thought I could sleep through her ranting?"

Nora pauses mid-tirade. "Sorry," she says, cringing. "I didn't mean to wake you. My emotions are getting the best of me right now. How are you? Do you want something? Water?"

I nod, and then ask Sadie, "What's she going on about?"

"I think she's feeling very passionate about what's going on. Jackson's currently on her shit list."

She leans down and kisses my head. "How are you feeling?"

"Guilty."

Perhaps I should feel more, but the tears have run dry and all the other emotions have disappeared. Only guilt has lingered, and it's eating me alive.

Sadie quietly sighs. "For not telling Jack?"

I draw circles on her knee, thinking about what I would do differently, if anything at all.

"Guilty because I'm not sure that I would tell him if I had the opportunity to go back in time, knowing what I went through. It was so traumatizing, I blocked most of it out. As an adult, of course, I know I should have told him. I have a lot of mixed thoughts. I feel sick to my stomach about the path I chose, but being so young, with only the guidance of my unhinged mum, I'm not sure the outcome would have changed."

"How did I not see something was going on with you?"

Because I lied to you. "Do you remember when I was heartbroken over the military guy?"

"Uh-huh."

"There was no military guy… There was no heartbreak. I used it as an excuse."

She huffs. "I still should have picked up on it."

"We were freshmen, living in two different countries. We talked, sure. But FaceTime wasn't a thing back then, and phone calls can be deceiving."

Nora walks in holding a jug of water and some cold compresses. "You need these for your eyes. They're very swollen." She takes my hand and pulls me into a sitting position. "Drink first."

"You're being very motherly," I kid, trying to lighten the dark mood I've put over all of us.

She smirks. "Only because I'm mam now. You know I don't have a maternal bone in my body, otherwise."

"Where're Evelyn, Marco, and Lola? I'm surprised they haven't barged in yet," I say.

Sadie smiles. "We're a nosey gang, aren't we? Ev is in New York for that meeting with Leo, and Lola and Marco are in Nottingham for a floral show I asked him to attend."

"Oh yeah, I forgot."

"Stop pacing. You're making me dizzy," Sadie tells Nora.

She stops and places her hands on her hips. "While you're talking, trying to distract her, I'm here trying to get over your brother leaving." She picks up her pace again. "He's no longer my favorite. In fact, he's down at the bottom of the fecking list."

"Don't be mad at him. He's upset. He'll come around… I hope," I say.

"He will." Sadie squeezes my hand to reassure me. "But I won't lie and pretend I'm not mad he left too. If Wills and I hadn't come over, he was planning on leaving you here, upset like this. That puts a bad taste in my mouth."

Nora points to Sadie. "See? Even the sister agrees. You made a mistake almost twenty years ago, so what? We all have."

"He's mourning our baby, Nora. It's not fair to be angry with him. Let him process it the way he wants."

Sadie ducks her head. "But he should still be here for you."

"Exactly. If your forty-year-old husband can't deal with his emotions, he can sod off."

"You want to say that to my face, Nora?" Jackson booms as he walks in.

"Watch it, Peters," Declan growls.

Fuck.

I glance at Jack, who looks as bad as I feel.

What did I do to us?

"Whatever, I'm going to sleep." He walks to the side of the house where the guest rooms are. It's not that I expected him to sleep with me, but it still hurts.

At least he came home… That's a good sign, right?

"I'll be right back," Sadie whispers, jumping up to follow her brother.

Jackson

"Sades." I exhale heavily. "I'm not in the mood. I'll call you tomorrow." I continue my path down the hall to the one guest room that has bedding.

Sadie's footsteps don't falter behind me, following me into the bedroom.

I do my best to ignore her, done with talking for the day.

"I'll stay here all night if I have to, so it's probably best you just get it over with and talk to me."

I drop my head in frustration, but I don't want to take it out on my sister. "What else is there to say? You know all the facts. Nothing has changed in the last couple hours."

"True, but I don't know how you're feeling. Is it not okay for me to check up on my brother after what he's gone through?"

I shrug. "I'm fine."

"Are you, though? Are you truly fine?"

What does she think?

Narrowing my eyes, I answer, "No, I'm not fucking fine, Sadie. Last week I was in Italy having the time of my life with my wife.

Someone I thought I knew everything about. Someone I trusted wholeheartedly. She betrayed all of that."

"I understand you're upset—"

"How could you understand what I'm going through? It's not possible."

She walks around me, her finger pointed in my direction. "Don't take it out on me, Jack. I'm only trying to talk."

I gulp down my unease. She's right.

"Sorry."

"Think about the big picture, Jackson. You share everything. Do you honestly think she would purposely keep this from you to hurt you?" I go still. "Yes, I know the two of you are closer than you let on. I'm not stupid. Tell me what hurts the most."

"I don't know," I tell her honestly. "That I missed out on being a dad, and if I stay with Belle, we'll never have a baby."

She takes a seat in the corner of the room and crosses her arms. "You didn't miss out, Jack, because there was no baby. You're making it sound like she aborted the baby or gave it up for adoption. She went through a horrific—not to mention traumatic—time in her life with no one by her side." I open my mouth, but she stops me. "Don't give me the crap about her not telling us. Unless you've been pregnant, you don't have an input. Being pregnant and giving birth is hard enough. Your hormones are all over the place, you're unstable at times, and you don't know how to control your emotions. That's how I felt when I gave birth to two healthy babies. Annabelle—" she cuts herself off, choking on her words. "She never gave birth. She was told that a baby growing inside her would never mature into anything and that they would need to remove it from her body. On top of discovering that she almost died, they also informed her that they'd need to remove part of her reproductive tract. That would be shocking to anyone, let alone someone who had just gone through what Belle did."

My stomach drops at the horror of it all.

"Maybe this is my punishment for fucking around all my life, for being a player and never caring about anyone other than myself."

"Maybe, or maybe you have nothing to freaking do with it." She raises her voice. "And let me add, you don't put a timeline on when people overcome and heal from the hardships in their life. Get a good night's sleep, mourn your baby, but wake up tomorrow and talk to your wife." She shrugs. "Or don't. Maybe no more words are needed, but support her and comfort her. Comfort each other." She wipes her tears. "Be the brother I know, because that woman out there is not my best friend. She's trying to act strong for you because she regrets the choices she's made. But I can see she's replaying it all over in her head, and I'm afraid she'll eventually fall down a dark hole if she lets the trauma she buried deep come back up again." Sadie walks to the door and stops. "My heart breaks for you both. Was she wrong for keeping it to herself after all these years? Yes. But people make mistakes, Jackson, and sometimes they don't even realize they're making them when it's to protect themselves."

A wave of sadness overwhelms me, and I drop my head to hide my emotions.

After standing in the same spot for a few minutes, I walk lifelessly to the bed and take my sister's advice to mourn, so that tomorrow hopefully we can try again.

I cry for our baby.

But more than that, I cry for Annabelle.

22

Annabelle

THE WIND effortlessly sweeps through the tall grass while the butterflies feed off the foxglove that grows between the blades.

Somewhere the birds chirp happily as the early morning dew disperses in the air and the city comes alive.

What must it be like to be free of feelings?

To have no worries or responsibilities?

I sip my tea and try to quiet my brain, taking in the stunning scenery before me until I hear the daunting sound of his footsteps throughout the house.

I've come to dread the sound. It means he's leaving for the day and I won't see him again until this time tomorrow.

It's been a few days since I exposed my secret, a few days since I broke Jack's heart, yet we haven't discussed it once. He wants to, he's tried even, but it's too much too soon for him to wrap his head around it all.

He hasn't left me, though, which I take as a good sign.

I won't force him to talk. He needs to come to me when he's ready.

Though his quietness only worries me more, because he's going through the days emotionlessly.

Not that I'm any better. I hid my phone and haven't checked my messages since Sadie and Nora left that first night.

Sometimes denial is easier to deal with than anything else.

My back is to the door so I only know he's here from the different sounds I've started to recognize his shoes make. I lift my teacup. "Fancy a cuppa?" I ask like I've done every morning, waiting for him to bite.

But just as he has the past few days, he says, "I'm leaving for the office, don't wait up—"

"I know, Jack… you'll be late." I sigh.

I feel him hesitate. "I have a meeting in St. John's Wood, near that bakery you love. Would you like me to grab anything for you?" *He's trying.*

"Sure, whatever you think I'd like. Thank you, Jack."

When I don't hear his retreat, I glance in his direction but swiftly turn back when I see his lifeless green eyes taking in my disheveled appearance.

It's why I sit facing the garden every day. I can't bear to see his eyes any way but sparkling. It's his best attribute. Even when he's having a bad day, he can always see the best in everything.

Not anymore.

I've dimmed his light, but I'll be here to help spark it back alight when he's ready.

When the door closes and I know he's gone, I allow myself a small amount of tears. Some perhaps from exhaustion since I'm bloody knackered. I haven't been sleeping well, and when I finally manage to shut my eyes, it's time to get up so I don't miss Jack leaving for work.

A few tears are shed for Jack and the strain I've put on our relationship. But the rest is for our baby, who, although I've mourned before, I'm now mourning all over again alongside my husband.

When the tears dry, that's my sign to start my day of doing nothing. I tried to go to the office the first day Jack did, but I couldn't expose myself to the public yet.

Trust me when I say I'm a walking disaster.

Heading inside, I walk right to my makeshift bed—*the sofa*—and turn on the telly. I can't bear sleeping in our bed alone knowing he's on the other side of the house, so I've been camped out here until we figure everything out between us.

Before jumping back into *Downton Abbey*—which reminds me of Jack and our time in Paris—I check my emails on my laptop. I ignore the ones from everyone except Lola, who flags anything I need to attend to urgently.

I may be useless in the office, but I won't leave her completely hanging. Working remotely has been effective so far, and it's good practice for when she leaves for Africa.

It's also put my work-life balance into perspective.

When I think back about the importance of it all, I have to wonder why there's so much pressure put on work.

Sure, we need money to survive, and personally, I thrive in that atmosphere. But the way I acted when I was preparing to leave for Italy—bloody *Italy*—for the weekend, as if London would implode in my absence, is no way to live.

I'll always make it work.

I'll always catch up on what I've missed.

What I can't get back or make up for are the memories, the ones taken for granted until times like these where I'm lying here, depressed and alone, sleeping in the same pajamas *yet again*, never washing my hair or face, and ignoring my friends and the world around me.

Once my husband's ready to talk, I'm going to make sure he knows how committed I am to having a better handle on my priorities—with my happiness and his being at the forefront.

It's something I think we both can work at.

But for now, since he's *not* ready and I'm exhausted, I would prefer to sleep away the day so I don't get lost in my horrific thoughts.

I lay my head on the pillow, cover myself with my quilt, then briefly pause, wondering why this feels different. I sit back up, and then it dawns on me.

Jack changed my sheets.

I drop my head, and if I had more tears to cry, they'd be pouring down my face. This shouldn't surprise me, because this is Jack.

The man I love.

Even while he's upset with me, going through what I don't need to imagine is one of the toughest times emotionally, he's still taking care of me.

If he let me, I would care for him too, but I know how Jack works. If he can't talk yet, these acts of kindness are his way of showing me it will all be okay.

I press play on *Downton Abbey* and eventually let my eyes close. And because of Jack's sweet gesture, I drift into a peaceful sleep rather than the nightmares filling my head recently.

"Bugger off," I grumble as I try to snatch my blanket back.

Wait, what?

My eyes shoot open to find Nora standing over me, staring daggers.

"What the hell are you doing, Nora? I was sleeping."

She crosses her arms, annoyed. "Aye, you don't think I knew that, considering I just woke you up? I've been sitting here watching your show for the last six hours and you haven't even budged. It's one o'clock, and you're getting up for some lunch."

I snuggle into my pillow, not wanting to leave. "I'm good. I have some food in the refrigerator."

"The curry I saw there four days ago when I was here last? Thanks, but that's just wrong." She shakes her head, looking disgusted. "Up you get." She grabs my arm.

"I'm not leaving the house. I'm sorry you wasted six hours sitting here. Why were you even here for six hours? Where are the babies?"

She starts cleaning up my rubbish and folding my extra blankets. "They were here most of the time. You were out like a light. They're back home napping."

I sit up and cover my face, groaning loudly. "I'm not in the mood."

"Too bad. Now go shower. You smell disgusting." She pushes me from behind to lift me off the couch. "You know what? You can shower at Sadie's."

This is the last thing on earth I want to do. Why is she pushing me?

What if Jack comes home early and I'm not here?

"Nora," I say, my voice breaking. "I don't want to leave."

Her face drops, but she masks it quickly. "Too bad." She pulls me toward the front door, bends down, and puts on my shoes. I have no strength to fight back, so I let her. But why the hell is she being so bloody bossy?

Nora, at times, can be rough around the edges with her feisty attitude, but she's taking it to a new extreme, and if I weren't a walking zombie, I'd say something.

Today though, I'm useless.

She walks me out, opens the car door, and buckles me in, then swiftly walks around to the driver's seat.

I yawn and rub my eyes. "God, couldn't you give me a second to drink some water? I feel like I'm still sleeping."

She starts the engine and drives off, ignoring me.

The second we're out of view from the house, her whole demeanor softens and she takes my hand in hers. "I'm so sorry for being forceful back there, Belle. It was killing me inside to push you around like that when I know you're hurting, but I knew it was the only way to get you out. How are you?"

I look down at my mismatched outfit. "Not great. I'm exhausted."

She squeezes my hand then rubs small comforting circles along my skin. "I think one day around us will help. You're so tired because you're oversleeping, your body is going into shock. It's used to you being on the go at all times."

Maybe… Who knows?

"Who will be at Sadie's, Nora? I'm not fit to be around people."

"It's just the three of us. You've been worrying us by not answering, especially Sadie."

My heart plummets at the idea of hurting anyone else, and I know my sensitive Sadie has probably been just as distraught as me and Jack.

She pulls up in front of Sadie's house. "Why didn't we just walk?"

She raises an accusatory brow. "You would have walked when I could barely get you in the car?"

"Fair point."

The front door whips open and Sadie's standing there with a giant smile stretched across the width of her face. "Hello, welcome to the Taylor residence."

"Oh my God, you're an eejit." Nora laughs.

Sadie bounces on her feet. "I know, and I don't even care how corny I am. I'm telling everyone I see on the street that I'm a married woman now."

"She's not lying. It's fucking embarrassing," Wills says as he walks out with the girls.

"Daddy!" Charlie screams, making Chloe giggle in Wills's arms.

"Sorry, princess. I'll put money in the jar."

"You should do it twice since you said it *and* yelled the bad word." She rests her hand on her hip, popping it out to one side.

So much attitude.

Where she comes up with this stuff is beyond me.

When she spots me, she shrieks and drops everything she's holding to run into my waiting arms.

"Auntie Belle." She hugs my neck tight. "Where have you been? I've missed you."

I squeeze her against my chest and lift my eyes to see Sadie's tear-filled ones match mine. "I'm sorry, love. Auntie Belle wasn't feeling well. I had to stay away this week."

She pulls back to cup my cheek before planting a wet kiss. "I'm happy you're allllll better now. Guess where I'm going?" She eagerly widens her eyes.

"Where are you going?"

"Daddy's office!" She bounces in my arms. "I see Daddy all the time though, so I'm going to hang out with Uncle Jack. I miss him too. Was he sick?"

I gulp down the lump in my throat. "He was. So you give him a big kiss for me, okay?"

Since I can't kiss him any other way.

"Okay, I will." She leans in, kisses me again, and then jumps out of my arms. "Bye-bye."

"Guess the boss says it's time to go," Wills mutters as he leans down and kisses my forehead. "You okay?" he whispers, and I shrug, not wanting to get upset again.

I give Chloe a quick cuddle for an extra shot of serotonin before they leave, then turn to Sadie standing with her arms open wide. I involuntarily lean into her hug, not realizing how much I've needed human contact.

"Don't shut me out, Annabelle," she whispers, sadness filtering into her words.

I don't answer, because what's there to say? I didn't have the mental capability to talk to anyone.

I still don't.

"Come on. I've made lunch."

"This seems excessive for lunch, no?" I stare down at the large spread taking up half of her kitchen.

"I figured you weren't eating properly." She eyes me up and down, looking for any sign of malnutrition, but it's impossible to see under my oversized joggers.

We each make a plate, then we head out to the garden where she's set a table filled with stunning bouquets on top of floral linens.

Never an absence of flowers in this house.

We sit silently until I'm mid-bite and look up to find both Nora and Sadie staring at me. "What?"

Nora reaches over the table and squeezes my hand. "We don't need to talk about it in detail, trust me, between the two of us"—she gestures between her and Sadie—"we have a lot to catch up on. But forgive us for caring, Belle. If we let you sit there stewing over your thoughts any longer, what type of friends would we be?"

Sadie frowns. "Are you okay? Have you talked to Jackson at all?"

I drop my head and play with the napkin in my lap. "Not really. We're like two ships passing in the night." I sigh. "But that's okay.

He'll be ready when he's ready. And I'll be there for him, no matter how long it takes."

"How are you?" Nora asks. "Mentally, have you been replaying old memories? It's okay if you have."

"Is it normal? It's not so much the memories, it's the nightmares." I exhale heavily. "How have you dealt with them all these years?"

Her eyes search mine. "I'm so sorry, Belle. I wish I could tell you they get better, but I don't have the answers you're looking for. Mine took over ten long years to stop, and I still get them at times. Though if I had to make an educated guess, yours will go away once you work things out with Jackson."

"I hope," I mumble, leaning back. "Other than the nightmares, I've blocked out the surgery completely. I do let myself think about the baby though, and while it makes me sad, it was so many years ago that I've had time to heal. Jack, on the other hand, is what worries me most."

"He'll need time, but you'll get through this," Sadie says.

"You're sure?"

Because I'm not sure they're right about that.

"Yes," they both speak up.

I drop my shoulders and let some of the stress wash away for now. I must admit, sitting out here with the sun in my face, side by side with my mates, feels good.

Even if it's a temporary feeling, I'm going to try my best to enjoy it.

"Since you've dragged me out of the house, tell me all the things."

"Okay, I'll start." Sadie smiles proudly. "Wills met Sebastian at the welcome party, and they struck a deal that Tournesol would be the main restaurant in Seb's new London hotel."

My eyes widen in excitement.

Tournesol is a restaurant Wills opened with a chef friend in memory of Sadie when he thought he'd lost her years ago. It's now one of London's premier restaurants, so it's a smart business deal on Seb's part.

"The hotel won't open for at least two years, but they're going to do a test pop-up at one of the other locations here in the meantime."

"That's bloody brilliant, congratulations. I'm so happy for you both." I turn to Nora. "Anything new with you?"

"Tons, but most importantly, I saw Jameson on a date the other day. He says it's an old colleague, but they seemed awfully close." She waggles her brows playfully.

"You love the gossip, don't you? And will you give that guy a break? I'd be quitting if I were him."

"He loves me."

"Doubtful," Sadie mutters.

Jameson is one of Nora's bodyguards. She has a complicated past, and for safety reasons, she's decided to keep two bodyguards with her, especially now that she's a mum.

"Nora, you *bliksem* enough with my personal life," Jameson calls from over the fence.

God, how do I always forget they walk the perimeter of the house and have trained ears? I must be so used to it by now that it barely phases me.

"You live in England now. No one knows what your South African slang words mean around here." She covers her mouth to hide a giggle when Jameson walks away, cursing. "And you work for me. Stop calling me names," she yells after him.

"Please fire me already," he calls back, and we all smile at their interactions.

He doesn't mean it. They really do love each other like brother and sister.

"All right, Aoife and Agnes will be up from their nap soon. I'm going to head home," Nora announces.

My whole body tenses when I realize our day is nearly over, meaning it's time to face Jack… or not, since I won't see him again until tomorrow.

I had a lovely time catching up with my mates, but returning to reality seems like the worst thing ever. I would love to say that today snapped me back to life, but I know the second I walk back into the house, I'll fall right back into my depressed state.

As if my body is already sensing the doom, my shoulders have slumped and my overall mood has quickly changed.

Sadie puts her arm around me and places her head on my shoulder. "It's all going to be okay."

"If you say so," I murmur.

"Ready?" Nora asks.

I shake my head. "I think I'm going to walk."

"If you're sure?"

"I am." I hug her goodbye and whisper, "Thanks for caring, Irish."

"I'm always here for you." She hugs me back, then Sadie and I walk her out.

"Before you go, I need to tell you something," Sadie says, wringing her hands nervously.

I narrow my eyes. "What's up? You're already making me nervous."

"Dad called," she mutters uneasily.

Keeping my face passive is hard, but I try my best. I want to hear her honest thoughts, and if she thinks I feel one way or another, she might change her opinion.

"I'm going to meet him, I've decided. He's coming this weekend." She scrunches up her face when my eyes go wide.

"Does Wills know?"

"Yes, we've been talking about it since the honeymoon. He thinks I should do it, and that even if nothing comes out of it, I'll at least find some closure on that part of my life."

"Well, if it means anything, I would do it if I were you. Especially after seeing him in Paris. Will you tell Jack?"

She takes a deep breath. "I will, yes. He's going to lose his shit, but I should give him the option to come if he wants. I think it would be good for him too. My only worry is that it's too much all at once—the baby, and now our dad."

It's exactly my thought.

"Let Wills talk to him. Jack only wants to protect you from getting hurt, so if he sees Wills is on board, there's a better chance of him agreeing."

She bumps my hip with hers. "You're very smart."

I let one side of my lip turn up. "I know."

We kiss goodbye, and I promise not to ignore her anymore. Even though I have no idea what tomorrow will bring, I'll try my best to keep my promise.

"Wait!" Sadie calls after me once I'm halfway down the street. "I almost forgot." She hands me a piece of paper with a highlighted line on it.

"What is this?"

"It's a copy of a note you once wrote to me, and that there," she says as she points to the bit highlighted, "is what I want you to remember. I love you." She hugs me tight and then returns to the house.

Please don't let anyone erase your spirit and sparkle that makes you, you.

Jackson

"Where are you?" my sister snaps down the line.

I narrow my eyes at her attitude. "Hello to you, too. I'm home early, and I was wondering if Belle was with you. What's with the attitude?"

"I know you're hurting, Jack." *All right, get right into it.* "But I thought you would take my advice and try to comfort each other."

"I have no clue what you're talking about."

She huffs, annoyed. "Belle just left; she's walking home. Meaning she'll be there any minute. But I can't tell you how hard it was for me to look at her during lunch. I felt sick to my stomach at how, in only four days, she's changed, only going through the motions, not truly living.. How are you sitting there, looking at her and not caring? Do you not want to work this out? Because if you don't, then tell her. Otherwise, she'll wait forever for you."

"You're wrong," I snap. "My only concern is her. It has only ever been her." I breathe heavily, trying to collect myself. "You don't think it's killing me? Belle's welfare has always been my top priority, even when we were younger. I attempt to talk to her every morning, but I'm afraid to say the wrong thing because I'm still hurting, too, Sades." I pause. "I'm not as mad at Belle as I am that our baby didn't live, that Belle almost died, that her mom made her keep this from us, and that I can't take care of both of us right now. So I'm afraid if we talk, I won't be able to express myself without fucking it all up."

The line goes quiet, then I hear her sniffle. "Consider easing back into it. Maybe watch a movie? I don't know, but don't wait too long, or else too much damage will be done."

I hear the front door open. "She's home. I'll talk to you tomorrow."

Belle gasps and takes a step back. "I'm sorry, you scared me. I wasn't expecting you home." She bows her head and walks past me, but not before I get a good glimpse of her.

The deep, sunken circles around her eyes, the pale, lifeless color to her skin… All because I can't man up and comfort her when we're both hurting.

A pang of guilt stings my insides. I'm the cause of this.

I told her I would always take care of her, and the one time we should be together, mourn together, I shut her out.

What have I done?

That's not how my queen B should look, especially mine.

She grabs a bottle of water and retreats back to her "bed" where she turns on the television. And again, I say nothing.

Just go in there.

Instead, like a coward, I turn the other way and leave her.

Maybe tomorrow.

Two days later

Knock, knock, knock.

"What the hell?" I look at the clock. It's late. Who the hell is here?

I open the door and Wills is standing there with his arms crossed, ready for battle.

"Sadie is losing her goddamn mind. Why haven't you called her back?"

I shake my head and can see the second he notices Belle, because his face falls and he looks back at me with concern.

Two days later and we still haven't talked properly. I tried, I promise, but then my anger started to simmer, so I knew it wasn't the time.

It wouldn't have been fair to her, but right before Wills interrupted us tonight, I was planning on taking Sadie's advice to suggest a movie.

"I think I broke her," I whisper.

He palms his face and shakes his head. "You didn't fucking break her, but grief and sorrow can be debilitating, especially when left alone to your own thoughts." He shoots me a pointed look. "This isn't why I'm here, and it's probably not the best time with all this shite going on, but it's happening."

"What's happening?"

"Sadie is meeting with your father… tomorrow."

I step back, thinking I must be hearing things. "Excuse me? What the fuck are you talking about?"

The thought of Sadie in a room with that guy tears my insides apart. I can't believe she's going through with this.

"You're allowing this?" I hiss.

He inhales a deep breath. "I didn't like the idea at first, but she needs this, and frankly, so do you."

"Why the hell are you just telling me now?"

"So that you don't overthink it." He pauses, "Ev's still in New York, so we're using my old place at noon. Be there for your sister… but also, for yourself."

23

Jackson

BY THE TIME I wrapped my head around the bomb Wills dropped on me, I'd missed my opportunity to spend time with Belle since she turned off both the lights and television, which was my cue to go to sleep.

Except sleep never came.

I'd been tossing and turning all night, thinking of the woman I love more than anything in the world and how I could have handled this week differently. Something my sister said about how we can't put a time limit on a person's healing process has been stuck in my head, and if I were in a better frame of mind, I would have thought more about it days ago.

Instead, I let us both suffer.

What am I waiting for? What if this takes years for me to get over?

What if I never do?

Am I just going to shut Belle out because of it? Instead of getting help and working through it with her?

The last few weeks of our relationship have shown me that communication is key, and if we talk to each other, we can work through anything. The old saying that two brains are better than one rings true in this situation, and I'm disappointed I let it get this far.

I'm also disappointed that for the first time in my life, I feel like I've failed *myself.* I'd like to call myself an honorable man that keeps his word, but while lying here tonight, I can't help thinking about the promises I haven't upheld.

I swore I would always be her friend no matter what happened, and I failed. I watched my best friend fall and didn't even attempt to catch her.

In Italy, I vowed that if she told me her truths, we would get through them, and instead of doing that, I turned my back on her.

That's not the man I want to be.

I never want to be like *him*, my dad… The other reason for my insomnia.

I slam my head back on my pillow, frustrated that my sister and Wills put me in this position. I want nothing to do with the man that gave up on us so long ago, and I can't wrap my head around Sadie wanting to either.

My phone buzzes, breaking me out of my thoughts. As I sit up and read the text that's just come in from our New York group chat, I realize I've missed a few and scroll back to catch myself up.

Leo: I just got the best head. Top fucking notch.
Seb: How the fuck are we brothers? Keep that shit to yourself.
Leo: Holy fuck, Nate.
Leo: She's engaged.
Nate: Who is?
Leo: Maddie Grace.
Leo: Hello?
Nate: Don't fuck with me.
Seb: Mason just confirmed… Shit. I'm sorry, man.

Well, fuck.

Maddie is the one who got away, and Nate's been obsessing over her for years, especially since he's the reason she left.

This is going to fuck him up real bad.

Me: I didn't even know she was dating someone. I'm so fucking out of the loop.
Seb: Why are you up?
Me: Can't sleep.
Seb: Everything good?
Nate: Who the hell cares if everything is good with Peters?
Nate: What am I going to do?????
Nate: FUCKKKKKK
Nate: FUCK FUCK FUCK
Nate: Where does she live? Still in Georgia? What's this fucker's name? How did they meet?
Nate: And why didn't anyone fucking tell me it was serious? You were supposed to keep me fucking updated… What kind of brothers are you?

Nate Davenport has left the group.

Me: Leo, you cocksucker. Couldn't you have waited to tell him in person, for fuck's sake? You need to go over there right fucking now before he does something stupid.
Seb: I'm already on my way.
Seb: Leo, get the pussy out of your face and get to Nate's. NOW.
Seb: Jackson, you good for now? I'll call you tomorrow to check in.
Me: It's fine, just make sure Nate doesn't lose it. Bye, fuckers.

Clarity. That's the only word that comes to mind at this moment.

Nate losing Maddie has made me further realize that life's too short to sit back and wait.

Jumping out of bed with a new mission, I splash water on my face and head downstairs, not caring one fucking bit what time it is. I need my girl.

The second I round the corner, I come to a screeching halt when I hear soft whimpers from where Belle's sleeping.

Crap.

I stalk over, put my arms under her soft form, and carry her toward our bedroom.

"Jack?" she whispers.

"Yeah, sweetheart. It's me." I swallow the lump in my throat. "Time for us to go to bed."

She sags with relief before wrapping her arms around my neck in a punishing grip. "Oh, thank God," she rasps.

I won't let you go, B. I'm here now.

With each step up toward our room, the heaviness and pain that's weighed me down all week dissipates, and the feeling is liberating.

After laying Belle down in the middle of the bed, I climb in behind her, wrap my arms around her center, and bury my head into her nape, breathing her in. How I went even one day without my beautiful B and her intoxicating scent is a mystery.

We've settled into a surprisingly comfortable silence when I decide to break it. "Annabelle, I'm sorry, sweetheart. I didn't handle myself right."

She moves forward enough to tilt her head my way. "Don't even try it, Jackson Peters. Only one person in this room needs to apologize, and that's me. We both know it."

"Turn over," I mumble, holding her hair up so it doesn't tangle while she maneuvers herself. "I think we have a lot to work through, and it's not going to happen overnight, but just because I was angry with you doesn't mean I should have abandoned you."

She cups my cheeks and grins. "As hard as this has been, I knew we would be okay."

I pull her into me and brush my lips against her forehead. "How were you so sure?"

She bows her head and chuckles lightly into my chest. "Please don't be angry with me, but I might have snooped on your phone."

I furrow my brows and wait for her to explain..

"I may or may not have found your notes about me," she rushes out, hiding her face. "Don't be mad, it was an accident… well, the first time."

"Annabelle," I warn with zero malice behind it.

"I found it first in Italy when you asked me to send an email, but then I caved and snooped on your phone this week while you were showering. I needed to know if you added anything, if you still cared, and when I saw you did, my hope was restored. Why else would you keep adding to a list of all my favorite things if you were planning to leave?"

I'm shaking my head, but I'm not upset in the slightest.

"You're not mad, are you? Because I find it quite endearing, really."

"I'm not mad, sweetheart," I tell her honestly.

When we fall silent, she asks, "Do you want to talk about anything or ask me anything about it all?"

I have a million questions, but I don't think bombarding her is the right move, so I ask the one that's been burning me alive. "Your stance on no children: is that because you don't want them, or you can't have them?"

She stills beneath my touch. I'm sure I've struck a chord, but we'll need to get it all out in the open eventually, so it's best to start somewhere. She must agree, because she begins, "I can have them with strict monitoring or even IVF, but I don't want them, Jack. I would be a nervous wreck that something would happen, and I don't think that would be good for me or the baby." She pauses and takes a deep inhale. "I'm sorry. I know how much you've always wanted to be a dad. I've never considered it, but perhaps we can adopt or go through surrogacy."

Although I'm sad that I won't ever get the chance to see Annabelle pregnant, her mental and physical health are what's important to me.

Maybe we're only meant to be aunts and uncles. Who knows.

"Don't be sorry. Having you alive in my arms is more valuable than anything else, and the only thing set in stone is that we end up together. The rest we'll figure out along the way."

"I love you, Jack."

"Me too, B."

She snickers. "You love *you* too, or you love me?"

"Well, obviously, I love myself." I laugh. "But I love you more than anything else."

Sighing contentedly, she eases into my hold and within minutes, falls into a deep sleep.

My only wish is that I could join her, but the news of my father's presence here in London still weighs on my mind.

To go, or not to go?

Annabelle

"Our first morning back together and you're showering without me. That's a punishable offense," Jack jokes.

"Oh no, you don't," I say as I push him back. "I need to get ready and get dressed, Jack."

He reaches out and grabs a palm full of my arse as I walk by, squeezing tightly. "Fuck, it's been too long since I've touched you. I want to spend the day with you. Don't go to work."

After I put on my robe, I brush my hair and watch Jack through the mirror to see how he will react when I tell him what I'm doing today.

"We're okay, right, B? I know it'll take time, but everything will work out."

I smile softly as I glide the brush through my long hair before pulling it into a slick bun. "We're as perfect as we can be, Jack. I'm not getting ready to go to work. I'm going to Evelyn's with Sadie and Wills to meet your father."

He stops mid-scrub and sets down the soap. "What did you say?"

"I'm not forcing you to go. I thought about it for a second, but you need to be the one to make this decision. I'm going because Sadie asked us to be there to support her."

He holds my stare, then huffs loudly and continues his washdown. "Well, I'm not going. I've decided he can fuck off."

"Okay. I figured as much," I say absentmindedly.

This was a fifty-fifty gamble. Jack needs to go today; he can't go the rest of his life wondering what the hell happened with his dad.

Option one was I demand that he goes, but he's a prideful man, my Jack, and forcing him would never have worked.

The only way I know I stand a chance is with option two: reverse psychology. If I nonchalantly give him the reasons he should go—like supporting his sister—he'll think he made the choice himself.

"It would probably be too many people in his face anyway, and I'm sure he has a lot to say after thirty-five-plus years of distance," I announce as I walk out to change.

Soon after, Jack's behind me, clanking his stuff around and acting like a child. "If he wants to talk, he should have to deal with however many people it takes."

"You're right." I step into my new Victoria Beckham trousers. "I wasn't thinking. Sorry, darling." I kiss his cheek as I reach for my blazer.

Walking back into the room, I feel him hot on my heels. "What is this outfit?"

I look down. "What do you mean? It's new. You don't like it?"

"Like it? I'm about to bend you over the bed and fuck you into tomorrow."

I smirk. "I'm wearing wide-legged trousers and a bodysuit."

"Your so-called bodysuit is a tank top showing side boob, and you know it turns me on when you're dressed all CEO-like," he says, adjusting his growing erection.

Fuck.

I take a deep breath and turn away so he can't distract me. It's been days… *days* since we touched each other, and it's killing me just as much as I can *see* it's killing him.

"Well, I feel like this is a meeting I'm stepping into, so this outfit seems appropriate." I shrug into my blazer to cover my "side boob," then bend over to put my shoes on.

Jack's behind me, pulling me into his dick, grinding himself between my cheeks. "Just stay here. We have a lot of making up to do."

"I won't be long." I swat him away, but not before grinding back into him, torturing us both. "I know it's a lot for you to handle after the miscarriage. I get it. I can always relay anything he says back to you. But"—I pause dramatically—"I really want to be there for Sadie."

I walk to my side of the bed, put my gold hoops in, and then pick out the rest of my jewelry, sliding on both rings I got in Italy.

"It's not a-fucking-lot, Annabelle. I—" His voice breaks, and his eyes connect with mine. "I don't know what to think anymore. This whole thing is fucked."

"Jack," I say softly. "Please get dressed and come with me. Not only for answers and closure for yourself, but to support your sister. Don't do something you'll regret." I take his hand and squeeze lightly. "You have a pretty great track record going; you've been there for her your whole life."

He stands silently for a few more seconds before wordlessly turning and sauntering back into the closet, where I hear the movement of his hangers.

I'm proud of him for making the right choice.

We leave the car and walk up to Evelyn's building. "I haven't been here since Wills lived here, have you?"

"A few times, but not much. Ev usually comes to one of ours, and now I wonder why since hers has the best views."

"Mr. Peters, a pleasure." Wills's old doorman shakes Jack's hand. "Ms. Annabelle. It's been a long time, *too long*. I hear congratulations are in order?"

I look at Jack, and he's just as confused as I am. "I'm so sorry. What for, exactly?"

"Well, for getting married, of course. Congratulations, Mr. and Mrs. Peters." He smiles brightly, and instantly I match his enthusiasm.

Mrs. Peters… Mrs. Jackson Peters. Holy shit.

I hitch my shoulders and squeeze Jack's hand. "You're the first person ever to call me that, thank you."

He tilts his hat. "My pleasure. I wish you both a lifelong marriage full of love and happiness." Jack shakes his hand again and thanks him before pulling me toward the lift and punching in Evelyn's private code to access the penthouse.

"My wife," he murmurs, lifting my chin to kiss my lips. "Saying that'll never get old."

Entering the lift, we interlock fingers and Jack's hand starts to tense the higher we climb. "Are you okay?"

He takes a deep breath."I don't know."

As the doors to the lift open, we're struck with the sight of Sadie, Wills, and Jack's Dad, who looks like he's aged ten years since we last saw him in Paris.

We embrace Wills and Sadie, and I smile politely at Stephen while Jack ignores him completely.

"You okay?" I whisper to Sadie, and she smiles enough that I know she's holding up. I nod and let Wills handle her as I move to stand beside a very *not okay* Jack.

"Maybe it's best we all sit down and get this moving along," Wills announces as he watches his brother-in-law pace the room.

The four of us sit huddled together as a visibly tight unit, with Stephen on the couch across from us.

"Dad, why don't you start by telling us why you're here now, after all this time," Sadie says with a shaky voice.

Stephen sits tall and takes a deep breath. "If it's okay with you all, I'd rather start at the beginning. It will make more sense that way. Of course, interrupt me with any questions."

We all nod, encouraging him to begin.

"If you didn't already know, I met your mother at Princeton our senior year. She was beautiful, smart, and I was completely enamored with her. Thinking back on it, I'm sure part of it was that I got caught up in the fact that she liked me. I mean, the rich girl with a trust fund whose last name was on our finance building liked *me*, the poor boy from Brooklyn who was there on scholarship and got kicked off the rowing team for smoking pot. A whole year went by, and everything was perfect. She was nothing like her catty friends or stuck-up family, and I knew one day I would marry her." He shakes his head and continues, "How stupid must I have been? She was the one who brought it up first, so she wasn't happy when I told her I was excited to marry her, but that I thought we should wait. I wanted to travel the world before making my debut in corporate America."

I look around and see even Jack's eyes are glued to him, eager for the next part.

"After informing her of my plans, I invited her, of course, but she blew me off, and soon after, everything changed. She set me up to get caught for possession of cocaine, linked with someone who had just overdosed the day before. She knew that because I had a record of marijuana, it would stick, plus her last name meant everything at that school… and with the police."

"Oh my God," Sadie whispers. "Why would she do that?"

I want to add that it's because she's an evil fucking bitch, but I keep my mouth shut.

"Because she needed a husband when she graduated, not a year later. It was the only way for her to gain access to the rest of her trust. In addition, since she was an only child, her father stipulated that she must marry a man with an Ivy League education to take over the business since, of course, they wouldn't allow a woman to do it in those times. So she played me, and when it didn't fall into place as she thought, she blackmailed me. Go to prison, or marry her."

Jack stays quiet, but his grip on my hand tightens into a harsh squeeze while Sadie's starts to sweat profusely in my other hand.

"So, why are we here now?" Wills asks, getting right to the point.

He is not a patient man.

Their dad leans back and drags his hand down his face. "I had no choice. I married her. My family was poor; we had no money or connections. There was no way to fight back. She became a complete psychopath, and we lived separate lives until about four years later, she threatened to tell her father about "our" scheme. At this point, I respected her father. He was nothing like your mother, and I didn't want him to know anything. In exchange for her silence, I promised to give her two kids." He looks between Sadie and Jack. "I'm so sorry. I thought I could protect you."

"You fucking didn't," Jack finally snaps. "You made it so we were alone in that house, moving around it like a shadow and letting Mom treat Sadie like she was garbage, verbally abusing her constantly."

Stephen's face drops. "What?"

"Oh, don't act stupid now. You've had years of that already."

I squeeze Jack's hand. "All right, calm down."

Stephen nods. "I truly didn't know, but that doesn't make it right. I knew she wasn't kind, but I didn't realize how bad it was. I thought I was taking the brunt of it."

Sadie sucks in a deep breath. "What does that mean?"

"Well, I guess that leads to why I'm here now. When Jackie—sorry, *Jackson* was born, your mother wanted nothing to do with him. She wanted kids for the persona alone. So, I vowed to be everything for Jackson—the mom and the dad. I was trying to figure out how to leave without her family coming after me. Before I could leave, she demanded a second child. I put up a fight, but she had the upper hand, so I gave in and she got pregnant with you, Sadie. After you were born, her behavior shifted again. Your mother was jealous of my relationship with the two of you and started to threaten terrible, terrible things." He leans his head back, taking a deep breath, and wipes a few tears that have started forming.

"W-what terrible things?" Sadie asks.

"I don't even want to say."

"Just go on. If we're here listening, tell us the facts," Jackson utters.

"I'm so sorry," he says, looking between his two kids. "She threatened to hurt you, beat you, and on more than one occasion, said she would send you where no one would ever find you and tell the world you were kidnapped."

Oh, God. I look between my two favorite people—Sadie's head is buried in Wills's chest, and I can see Jackson is holding back all his emotions.

"Then what?" I prompt.

"What else was I to do? I was locked into this life, but I didn't want either of you to suffer unnecessarily at her hand, so I did what she said. I stopped talking to my own kids, pretending they didn't exist. I tried to talk to you in secret when you were younger, but she found out. She took all her anger out on me. I wasn't the type of man to hit back, and it wasn't just physical abuse, but mental and emotional too. Over time, it wears on a person. I couldn't leave, because if I did, I knew she would take it out on you both. And I couldn't get us all out, because she threatened to go to court and show them everything she'd been fabricating against me. She once threw herself down a flight of stairs, took pictures, and then went to the hospital claiming her *husband* 'didn't mean to do it.' Taking you would have given her even more ammunition. She's an evil, manipulative person. I'm so sorry. I thought I was doing what was best in a lose-lose situation."

I put my arm around Jack and lean my head on his shoulder. "I'm so sorry," I whisper, and he gives me a slight nod.

"Can I ask why you didn't leave when your children got older?" Wills asks while holding a sobbing Sadie.

"I did. She found me."

Jackson

My stomach is in knots as I listen to my father's story.

I see a broken, abused man, but I also still see the father who hurt me. And I hate myself for that. Because if I can't get over this, I know I was hurt more than I ever realized.

Belle mentioned before that it might be too much all at once, and while I know she was saying it to goad me into coming today, I can see the truth behind it now.

I glance behind Belle and reach for my sister. "You okay, Sades?"

She shrugs, not even trying to act strong, and I don't blame her. This story is more fucked up than I ever thought possible.

"So she found you, then what?" I ask, wanting to get on with it. I need to hear the rest and get out of here.

"She didn't find me… the men she hired did." *Fuck.* "I still don't know to this day if she hired them to scare me or kill me, but they beat me within an inch of my life because of your mother. She had to have been scared I would finally talk. The day I returned was the day I broke, and for many years after, I was her punching bag. I knew then that the two of you, Jackson and Sadie, were better off without me. It's why I didn't come sooner, and the only reason I can offer you now is all because of the housekeeper. She forced me to leave."

"She helped you?" Sadie asks.

"Yes, right after your daughter was born. She saw it was killing what little light I had left in me to pretend I didn't have a granddaughter. So, one weekend, while your mother was away, I came downstairs to a man standing in the kitchen. I assumed your mother hired a hitman and thought, *This is it. I'm finally dead.* But no, it was Mariana's son, the tech wiz. He told me he could loop the cameras, allowing me to leave without her knowing. There was no way your mother would guess the housekeeper could do something like this since she looked down on her employees like the terrible person she was. She would assume I hired someone to do it." He takes a deep breath. "So I left, paid cash for a small place, and started seeing a therapist. Before your grandfather died, I spoke to him and told him everything. He believed me, and it devastated me to know I could have just gone to him all those years ago. I know it sounds simple, and even when I say it aloud, I ask myself why I didn't do things differently. But when you're enduring daily mental and physical abuse, it screws with your thought process. I didn't come here for your pity or forgiveness, but after years of therapy, I am finally in a place to tell you the truth. Even if what I did in trying to save you made you think I was a monster in the process, I need you both to know that I never stopped loving you. Not for one second of my life."

Sadie sobs into Wills, and Belle looks at me through tear-filled eyes. "I'm here for you, Jack," she whispers, and I'm so grateful to have her by my side.

Sadie gets up finally and hugs our dad. I knew she'd have no issue moving on from the past, but I'm struggling.

When they break apart, I speak up. "I'm sorry for what you went through, and I appreciate you protecting us while putting your life on the line to ensure *we* lived. I'm also sorry that we didn't see any signs to help you as we grew up. I—"

Dad cuts me off, "There's no way you could have ever known. Her abuse was very calculated, always ensuring that the physical harm was untraceable."

I nod in understanding. With no more words left to give, I glance at Wills and he shoots me an understanding look that I should go. I know my sister will have more questions, things I can't hear yet.

I stand abruptly, and Belle's right there with me.

"Again, I'm sorry you went through that, and I'm thankful you told us. I'm going to need some time to process everything that was said today."

His eyes—green that match my own—stare at me with so much emotion. "I understand, and if today is all I get, that's okay too. I need you to know I love you. It's all I care about, all I've ever cared about."

I hesitate before deciding to walk over to him. He stands and I hug him quickly, not knowing if it'll be the last hug I share with my dad or the first of many to come.

Still undecided.

As Belle and I are about to enter the elevator, he calls out to me, "I'm proud of the man you've become. I've been following you for years. Congratulations on all your success."

The ride home is silent, but the second we cross the threshold of our home, I'm on Belle, kissing her, touching her.

"Jack, what are you doing?"

I kiss her hard against the lips. "I need this… I need you. Please, sweetheart."

She pulls back and stares into my eyes. She must see whatever she's looking for, because she says, "Okay, Jack. Anything you need."

24

Annabelle

IT STILL SURPRISES me anytime Jack picks me up effortlessly and carries me up the steps. I'm slim, but my height alone must make it difficult.

He drops me on the middle of the bed and stands over me, trying to regulate his breathing.

Slowly licking his lips, a subtle grin tugs at them as his eyes bore into me, sparkling with mirth.

And from that look alone, I get a flashback of a cheeky young Jack, and it's a stark contrast to his presence here in this room.

Now he's all man.

Sexy as hell and completely full of himself, but still the most caring man I've ever known.

And he's all mine, the way I've always dreamt of it.

His suit-clad body climbs onto the bed, and I can't help but let out a shaky breath, not from nerves but from anticipation.

I've missed my husband.

I need his hands on me now, but first… "Jack, wait," I stop him. "I know you need to escape, but are you sure you're okay?"

"Belle," he growls. "Right now, I only care about getting lost in you, nothing else matters. You okay with that?" He smirks, and I poke at one of his dimples.

"Love these. And yes, I'm beyond good with it."

"That's what I thought," he murmurs against my lips. "I'm going to take my time tonight. I want to taste every part of you, especially here," he says as he rubs against my sex. "I've missed my tongue between your legs."

How does he get me like this, panting like a dog in heat in under two seconds?

"Clothes off, Jack. Too many…" My voice trails off as he cups my cheeks, encasing them in both hands as he swipes his thick tongue through my mouth, exploring and gliding, causing me to shiver in pleasure and my skin to break out in a sheet of goose bumps.

My toes curl as our kiss turns desperate, as though it's been a lifetime rather than a matter of days since we've kissed.

I guess to us, two people utterly insatiable for one another, this time apart *did* feel like a lifetime.

I grab at his hair and kiss him, matching his desire as I lose complete control. I love his mouth; if this was all we did, it would be enough.

He's an amazing and passionate kisser.

The best.

"Naked… I need you fucking naked."

"I know," I snap. "I already bloody said that."

He raises one brow and snickers as he reluctantly sits up. "Sexually frustrated, are we?" He shrugs off his suit jacket and gets to work unbuttoning his dress shirt. I almost fall off the bed, but instead, I sit there, drooling.

Holy shit, my husband is fucking hot.

"You looked good in that suit," my voice rasps. He loves when I wear a power suit, but if he only knew the things I think about when he's dressed like he's ready to take over the world...

It does something to a girl.

He shrugs off his shirt, and I'm struck speechless.

Jack's olive skin is tanned to perfection from the few short days in the Italian sun, enhancing his broad chest and muscular abs. I trace the light dusting of hair and watch as he slowly unzips his pants, pulling out his dick. Of course, it's already hard, thick, and beating angrily, waiting to be touched.

He wraps his hand around himself and begins to stroke his cock, putting on a show, knowing how much this turns me on.

Starting with slow, even tugs, he soon picks up the pace, working every muscle in his forearm. His hand glides over the head and smears the pre-come down. With every stroke, every touch, I feel it on my skin.

We're connected in every way.

The sensation creeps up my legs, stopping at my center, causing a deep throb to radiate through the rest of my body. I let out a slight shiver to keep from touching myself, but it does nothing to stop this euphoric feeling coursing through me.

My eyes snap back up when he moans my name as his labored breaths pick up.

Our eyes connect, and I gasp at the intense feeling ricocheting through us.

The way his emerald eyes darken with longing as they penetrate my soul reminds me of how much he wants me.

It's the look of desire.

Of lust.

But also love.

"Why are you still fully clothed?" he barks, getting my attention.

I bite my bottom lip, grinning. "I was momentarily too stunned to move," I say, then begin to undress.

Slowly, of course, because the second they're off, I know Jack will either melt into a million pieces or fuck me into oblivion.

The latter being my preferred choice.

"Holy. Fucking. Shit. Annabelle." He scoots forward and trails one finger along my clavicle and down my sternum. "This is all for me."

Not a question.

"Always," I breathlessly say. "Do you like it? I thought you might need something special after today."

I'm wearing a cupless bra, which I'm sure he's beginning to realize I've been wearing underneath my shirt all day.

Lace circles around my breasts, pulled tightly along my breastbone and fastened around my neck, still giving my large boobs the support they need while simultaneously leaving my nipples and areolas on full display.

The stars of the show, according to Jack.

"Best goddamn gift." His thumbs lightly brush over my sensitive buds before tracing and cupping my breasts. "I'm a lucky guy," he says as he leans forward and flicks his tongue against my hardened nipple. "What do you have on below?" He pushes my pants down and shakes his head. "Fucking bare," he growls.

I caress my boobs. "I wanted to accentuate these for you. Now what are you going to do with them?" He pushes me back and I land on the pillow. "Jack," I laugh. "Easy."

"*Easy* is not in either of our vocabularies tonight. I changed my mind, fuck taking it slow." He unstraps my heels and pulls my trousers off.

He runs his hands up my legs, rubbing torturous circles on the inside of my thighs before trailing his fingers back down. "Everything about you is fucking perfect."

No one is perfect, yet the emotion in his words tells me he means it.

"This is new," he mumbles to himself. "I can't decide what I want to do with you. I need to do all the things, but deciding what comes first is driving me insane. It's what you do to me, baby." *He's right there with me.* "I'm burning with desire, even though you're right here and so fucking touchable, I feel lost. I want to fuck your tits in this bondage-like bra, but staring down at your wet cunt, glistening against the light… Oh fuck. Are you kidding me right now?"

His words only amp up what was already coursing through my body, causing me to clench my sex, and I know he catches the movement.

He reaches forward and swipes his fingers through my slit. I begin to roll my hips, needing more of him. The urgency is building quicker than ever before.

He rubs the pads of two fingers against my clit, massaging in a way that feels like a small vibration.

"Oh… Jack, ah," I gasp.

He does this to me with every word, every touch. Nobody has ever made me feel so free, like I'm flying high.

He's better than skydiving or any fucking vibrator in the world.

With just the tip of his fingers grazing my skin, this man has me feeling wild.

He enters me with two fingers and starts pumping me with relentless power, not easing up even when I cry out.

"Look at you, riding my fingers. Your greedy pussy wants more," he says as he adds a third, but I don't want to come like this today. I need more of *him*.

I reach for him. "I want to touch you." He doesn't listen. Instead, he slides down my body, but I quickly cross my legs. "I want to touch you, I said."

He aggressively pulls my legs apart. "Too bad you don't get to make the decisions in the bedroom, do you?"

"Please." I bite my lip and demurely bat my lashes.

He pauses, his face in between my legs, so close if he sticks out his tongue, he'll touch my clit. My breathing is ragged, and I'm clenching every muscle to stay still. If he sees my pulsing clit or how greedy I am for him, there's no way he'll let me touch him.

After what feels like forever, his face lights up and he rolls over on his back.

"Sit on my face," he demands.

"What?" I pause.

I'm experienced, sure. But I've never felt comfortable suffocating a man with my pussy.

But… it's Jack.

"Did I stutter?" He laughs darkly. "Sit facing out so you can suck my dick."

Oh.

Well, that's more my speed. Without another second of hesitation, I crawl over to him.

"Ah, my queen is so desperate, she crawls to her peasant boy." He chuckles, and I roll my eyes at his terrible attempt at a joke.

"Funny, *lover boy.*"

I lift my leg and straddle him. His hands grab my hips to swiftly pull me back against his waiting mouth, and I have to catch myself when I nearly tumble forward.

But I could care less.

I could have face-planted, and still my mouth would've remained open and in awe as he swipes through my soaked center, quickly turning naughty as his tongue trails up to my arse.

"Suck my dick, Annabelle," he growls against my tight hole. The vibrations shoot an intensely pleasurable pulse through me, causing me to push back into his face.

He chuckles sardonically, then really lets me have it while I do my best to hold back until I get into a rhythm. Otherwise, I'll be coming all over his face in a matter of seconds.

Doing this is just as much of a turn-on for me as it is for him. Any pleasure I can elicit from Jack is a win in my book.

Leaning down, I part my lips and open wide to take him all in one go. He hits the back of my throat and lets out a loud animalistic roar that echoes in the room. "Goddammit." He squeezes the globes of my arse and lifts it slightly for better access to my clit.

He pushes and pulls my body against his waiting tongue. My body's rocking quickly, the bed even moving at Jack's strength, making it almost impossible to suck him off.

I push my pleasure to the back of my mind for a split second—I'm not a quitter. Steadying myself, I match his speed, bobbing my head along his length and simultaneously jerking the base in a swivel motion.

My cheeks, stretched to the hilt from his girth, go concave with every pass, allowing my tongue to lick the underside of his shaft.

Jack's hands are running up and down the backs of my legs, and my body shudders from the combination of his tongue against my clit and the loud moans he's letting loose.

The way his hands feel against my skin is almost more of a turn-on than anything else. How he rubs my body, sometimes squeezing my thighs tightly when I take him deep, it's a measurement of his pleasure too.

Oh fuck.

I suck hard one last time, lingering on the head of his dick, and flick my tongue through his slit, just like Jack's doing to me.

Oh God.

I can't breathe.

The head of his dick pops out of my mouth, and he lets out a string of curses just as I start to moan, feeling the burn creep up my spine.

"I'm going to come," I cry, tears burning the backs of my eyes.

I hold on to Jack's thighs and push back onto his face as he grips me tightly, shaking his head side to side against my center.

HOLY. FUCKING. SHIT.

"Ahhhh." I fall forward as Jack sits up, still with my hips in his hands, suspending me in the air.

I look back with my cheek pressed against the mattress and see his face buried deep between my folds, sending me right over the edge.

My body starts convulsing, and with each breath, I let out an ear-piercing scream as the orgasm hits me like a never-ending freight train.

The second I finally stop, Jack's flipping me over, and I'm scrambling up to finish my job, but instead, he shakes his head. "Need you," he chokes out, pulling me up and slamming me down on his dick without warning.

"Fucking *fuck*. Jack."

His jaw is clenched and his nostrils flare as he holds my hips down, allowing me a moment to adjust.

And by a moment, I mean a second.

Then he picks me up with force and slides me up and down to meet his hips thrust for thrust with precision, hitting that new-to-me, toe-curling spot. Once, twice, three times as he uses me for his pleasure.

Within seconds, his head is thrown back, groaning my name, and somehow a miracle happens: he fucks another orgasm out of me.

"Oh my… ah." My muscles tighten around his erection, squeezing every drop left inside him. I fall onto his chest and his arms swiftly embrace me as I snuggle into his neck.

Both of us breathing loudly as we try to get a handle on ourselves.

"You did it again," I mumble against his skin.

He's rubbing small circles on my back, chuckling into the side of my head. "Trust me, I know. I'm keeping score."

I playfully hit his chest. "Don't be daft. You are not."

"I'm going to start, trust me, because I wasn't even trying this time. That's how good I am."

"Idiot." I giggle and let out a loud yawn, causing Jack to follow suit.

I roll off his chest and wiggle my body in a silent plea for a cuddle, swiping my unruly hair away from my face.

Without a word, Jack sits me up and braids my hair, using the elastic from my wrist. Then he lays me down and silently wraps my body with his.

"Mmm." I sigh groggily as I slowly wake up from my nap.

Holy crap, am I having a wet dream?

I groan loudly as another intense feeling of pleasure shoots through my core.

Can girls have wet dreams?

"Who knows, but this isn't one," Jack says breathlessly.

My eyes snap open. "Wh-what's going on?" I moan as arousal thumps through my body. "Oh bloody hell, I feel like I'm going to come."

Instead of Jack's usual position behind me, I'm flipped facing him, and his mouth is around one of my nipples, sucking and biting so pleasantly hard.

"I told you you could come like this," he snarks cockily. His eyes roll back as he lets out a loud, guttural moan.

I look down, and… oh shit, that's hot.

Jack's lubed up, his free hand surrounding his thick cock, wanking himself off next to me.

He's getting off, on *me* getting off.

And it might be one of the hottest things I've ever seen in my life.

He leans back and switches nipples, this time using his fingers, tugging and pinching with perfect pressure.

My eyes are on Jack as he works himself over with long, strong strokes, pre-come dripping from the end.

I reach out and swipe my thumb over his slit, spreading his come around his tip.

"Jack," I whisper, and his hooded eyes find mine. "I'm seriously going to come soon. I want you."

"You have me, baby." He tips his head back, and all I hear is the sound of the lube slapping against his dick with each tug.

If this isn't an aphrodisiac, I don't know what is.

His fingers tighten on my nipple, and my body starts to shake.

I can't believe this is happening, though all I can think about is his dick in his hand and how I want to help him.

I lean up on my elbow and reach out, placing my hand over his, and together, we stroke up and down. His eyes snap to mine, breathing deeply, and just from that, I know he's close.

"I'm… I'm… Jackkkk."

I'm done. The sight of this alone sends me over the edge.

With quick movements, Jack pushes our hands off of him, lifts my leg high into the sky, and slides inside of me, pumping quickly as we both come in a rush.

"Kiss me," he demands.

I press my lips to his and he grabs the back of my head, pushing us together as we kiss for what feels like a lifetime.

The best life there ever could be.

"I love you," he whispers.

I smile against his lips. "Me too."

He pinches my bum playfully and pulls back slightly. "How did that feel?"

"My nipples are sore"—I rub my poor little nubs—"but it was intense. Powerful. I was clenching down below but from nothing. It was strange… a good strange."

"That, on top of your jerking me off, was fucking wild and one of the hottest experiences. Everything we do drives me wild."

"Good." I kiss his lips again. "I'm closing my eyes now because your crazed sexual appetite is tiring me out." I smirk and turn over to cuddle back into my spot.

"Good morning, my beautiful B." Jack kisses my nape as my eyes flutter open.

I can feel his dick harden against my bum, so I move forward and away from him. "Don't even think about it. You woke me up five times, Jack. Five. How are you even alive right now?" I groan, feeling exhausted. "And how is that thing still hard? You're not a young lad anymore, you know."

He pulls me back and growls, sucking at my neck and marking me once again, I'm sure. I've never had to wear so many high-necked shirts or jumpers before.

"I need you again. It was the first thing I thought about when I woke up. Your tight, warm pussy wrapped around my dick." He grinds into me.

He's so filthy.

I stand my ground when I see the time, even though my body is screaming *Yes.*

Does no part of me realize I'm no longer a spry, twenty-year-old woman?

With a lot of strength behind me, I push Jack off of me. "We need to get up and get ready. It's already too late."

"I'm lying in bed all day and never moving. When you're done with whatever it is you're doing, come back home to me here… naked."

I open my phone and throw it to him, my email app front and center.

His eyes snap to mine, and a huge genuine smile stretches across his face. He jumps out of bed and runs around the front to pick me up, twirling me around in circles.

My laughter is loud and boisterous, just as happy as Jack's.

"We get to go see our house today," he sings. "*Dear Mr. and Mrs. Jackson Peters, congratulations*," he repeats the opening line of the email from our realtor.

"What voice was that?" I chuckle.

He narrows his eyes. "The voice of a cocksucker. I'm telling you, if that little fucker even looks at you—"

"Okay, okay, a little too possessive for first thing in the morning. Let's take it down a notch."

"Never possible when it comes to you, B." He kisses my cheek, then lets me down. "Come on, let's shower and go see our new home."

"And do some shopping," I call. "It's been a week. I think a new Chanel bag is calling my name."

He chuckles. "Whatever you want, sweetheart."

Our hands are intertwined as we walk out of our dream house. We received the lucky news when we arrived earlier that we can move in on Friday, and I think it's perfect timing with everything going on.

Before leaving, we stop on the pavement and glance back at our beautiful home in one of London's most prestigious neighborhoods.

It's the perfect fit for us both. The original architecture has been retained to suit the typical Victorian-style of the surrounding houses. Its white façade stands tall, lined with beautiful foliage and a small cottage garden as you walk in.

The inside has been updated in a contemporary style, with additions like a basement cinema room—perfect for when our nieces and nephews come over—and a wine cellar.

Aside from the interior decorating that Evelyn has already started on, only minor changes need to be made.

It's hard to believe that this home where we'll start our life together could be the same one we end it in. Though, it's exactly where I can see us spending the rest of our days.

"Thank you." I place my head on Jack's shoulder. "I never imagined I would have a life like this, and it wouldn't have been the same with anyone but you."

He pulls me into his side and kisses my forehead. "I was just thinking the same thing."

"It's getting late. Let's go to Sadie's," I say, reluctantly turning away from our home.

Sadie's outside in her front garden pruning her roses when we approach the house. When she sees us, she lights up and runs toward her door, screaming, "Wills, come here, baby."

She turns and puts her hand over her mouth, desperately holding in her laughter. It's nice to see her happy after yesterday.

Sadie can sometimes get down on herself and it takes a while for her to snap back.

We walk through her secret garden-like walkway, and I see Jack beside me, mimicking his sister's resistance to hold back his laughter.

Wills walks out and looks around. "What's going on?"

Jack puts out his hand, and Wills shakes it halfheartedly. "Jackson Peters, your new neighbor. I wanted to introduce myself formally."

Wills looks across the street at the sold sign, then back down to Jack and me. "You must be fucking kidding me." He turns to Sadie. "Please tell me this is a sick joke. I already see this arsehole at work. Now he's going to live right over there?" He points at the house.

"Nope, not a joke." She bites her lip and bounces on her feet excitedly. Sadie's the one who sent us the listing. She thought it would be perfect for us to be closer to the girls, and Declan and Nora are within walking distance too.

Sure, Jack loved the idea that it would piss off Wills, but ultimately, we truly loved the house. We looked at many, and I only had to walk into one room to know it was the one.

"Un-fucking-believable." He looks at Sadie. "You're in big trouble."

She shrugs, then hugs Jack. "It's going to be great, don't be so grumpy about it. Let's go in and have a celebratory glass of wine or two. The girls don't get home until tomorrow; they're still in the countryside with Eleanor."

Since it's beautiful out, we take our wine into their back garden. We've been lucky in London this summer. It's been dry and sunny for the greater part of it. Though, I wake up every day expecting our typical rain to return.

Jack hangs his arm around my shoulder, and when I turn, smiling, he places a chaste kiss on my lips.

"Okay… wow. I'm still getting used to this." Sadie smiles. "I always wanted this for the two of you, but it's something else seeing it in person."

"It shocks me sometimes too." I laugh and look at Jack. "After all these years, who would have thought it?"

"Literally everyone," Wills says dryly.

We all ignore him while Sadie takes my hand and frowns. "You don't have an engagement ring?"

Jack's face drops, so I grab his hand for reassurance but look at Sadie as I speak. "This band has more meaning than an engagement ring would. Remember, we kind of jumped that step." I laugh. "It would have no significance for me. This is the only ring I want." I smile and twirl my ring around on my finger.

It's the truth.

After catching up and again apologizing to Sadie profusely for not telling her about our secret relationship, we get updates on the girls and hear all about their honeymoon.

We also get suckered into a housewarming party next month.

If Sadie wants to plan it all, she can be my guest. I'm more of a night-out-for-drinks-and-dancing kind of girl, but a catered house party… That's all her. And she'll enjoy doing it.

I turn toward Wills. "Do you want to help me with another round?" I say, gesturing to Sadie and Jack. "We should give them a minute."

"Yeah, good idea."

"Hmm, a compliment from you. What is this world coming to?"

He grumbles something Wills-like under his breath, and it makes me smile. Things are finally falling into place, and it's all starting to feel normal again.

Jackson

When Wills and Belle walk away, I take my sister in my arms and hold her tightly against my chest before we sit down at her favorite garden table.

"How are you doing?" I ask.

"The better question is how are *you* doing, Jackson? I'm worried after you ran off yesterday."

My face falls. "Sades, I'm sorry. I just needed time."

She takes my hand and places it on her lap. "I didn't mean it to come off like that. I'm sorry. We all process things differently. I don't blame you for leaving."

"You seem better than I thought you would." There are fresh tears on her face, but I surmise those are from our hug.

She takes a deep breath, and I see her contemplating her answer. "Last night was tough for me. I kept replaying his story on a loop, and then I'd start getting worked up over our mother. I know you've always hated her more than me, but now… there's no question. I despise that we both came from her, honestly." She wipes a few tears. "What a terrible life he lived… for us."

I bow my head, ashamed. "I could never in a million years imagine it, and I feel badly about that. But I'm also someone who figures shit out, so it's hard for me to wrap my head around him waiting this long to talk to us."

She nods in understanding. "I believe you'll come around."

"I don't hate him," I whisper. "That must be something, right? I'm not heartless, but I'll need time with this, Sades."

"Will you be upset if I pursue a relationship with him eventually? I already know I want to." She shrugs. "I told him I would be open to a session with him and his therapist."

I squeeze her hand. "Never. You do what's best for you. I'll deal with it, and I'm sure it'll all work out over time." I pause. "You know I hate quacks, but after you had so much success with Dr. Esposito, I think me and Belle should see one. To talk over what happened with the baby, her keeping it from me. I could probably benefit from talking about Dad, too."

She smiles softly. "I'm proud of you. Therapy isn't easy, but when things hurt so deeply that you can't see the light at the end of the tunnel, it helps. And other times, it's nice to have an objective person give their opinion." She looks back quickly. "He hates to admit this, but therapy was healing for Wills. After all these years, he still blames himself for the attack, so we sometimes do Zoom calls with Dr. Esposito. I bet she would meet with you. You know her already, which might make you feel more comfortable."

I don't promise anything, but I agree to taking her number.

Sadie and I might be on different paths with our relationship with our dad, but supporting one another is something we've always been good at.

"You know, you're looking amazing. You're glowing. The honeymoon treated you two well." I smile, and she tries to hide her flinch, but I catch it. "What is it?"

"Nothing." She sips her wine.

"Sadie, I'm not kidding around. Tell me," I demand. I see it written all over her face. She's hiding something.

"I'm pregnant," she whispers.

"What?" I hug her tightly. "That's amazing. Congrats! Why are you looking like you're about to throw up, and why the fuck are you drinking wine?"

"Oh God, I was so nervous to tell you after finding out about the miscarriage. I was going to wait, but I'm crap at lying to you." She lifts her drink. "Non-alcoholic wine."

She glances back at Belle through the kitchen window, and I see the uncertainty on her face. "She'll be just as excited as I am, I promise. You should tell her." I hug her again. "Another niece to add to the mix. I can't wait."

"Or nephew."

I shake my head. "Nah, it's a girl. Wills only makes girls."

She leans on my shoulder. "You know how we always joke that Nora's life could be made into a movie? After yesterday, I think ours gives hers a run for her money."

I huff out a laugh. "No doubt."

25

Annabelle

I LEAN against the door frame and watch my husband in his designer jeans and custom shirt, wrapped in a Freddie Mercury apron, while Queen blasts through the speakers.

He looks bloody ridiculous dancing around, singing into his knife, but hey… whatever makes him happy.

I laugh when he taps his feet quickly to match the beat of "Don't Stop Me Now."

"I can't believe you wore that when Chef Odette was here," I call, causing him to stop mid-spin.

"Aha, there she is, my beautiful B." He smiles, then turns back and finishes cutting his vegetables. "And of course I would. No one disrespects Freddie in my house, even my wife." He points the knife in my direction.

"Easy there." I smirk.

I saunter over and kiss his cheek while stealing a few cucumbers that will hopefully hold me over since Jack is a stickler about the food for tonight.

After a month's delay, it's finally our housewarming party, and Jack surprised me this morning with Chef Odette's arrival from Paris.

It was a lovely surprise. Jack set it up so we could finish our cooking class, and then he hired her to stay for tonight's party. He was excited to cook tonight, but there was no way he would be able to cater to all the guests. He's taken it more seriously since Paris, but he's still learning.

Even with knowing Jack all these years, it's been a welcomed surprise finding out what a romantic he is.

Placing the knife down, he tugs me by the waist and kisses me hard against my lips. "Hi." He kisses me again. "How was your call?"

I push back a few strands of his dark hair as we sway to the music. "It went brilliantly. I'm set to leave for California next month with the DeLuca family."

His face drops, and he returns to the food he's been preparing.

I furrow my brows in concern. "What's wrong?"

"Nothing." He shrugs sheepishly. "I don't particularly love the idea of you being away for a whole month. I'm going to miss you. But I know it's selfish after all the work you put into building this client relationship."

The bell rings, breaking up our conversation. I rub Jack's shoulder and promise it'll be okay as I go to open the door. A delivery man stands there holding a large box and a clipboard for me to sign. "Hello, what do we have here?"

"No idea, love. I've only been hired to deliver the parcel."

I sign the paperwork then check the label, my eyes widening in excitement when I see it's something I bought Jack two months ago.

Talk about perfect timing. I have a special surprise for him tonight, and this will be the icing on the cake.

God, I'm so bloody happy this came.

"Hey!" Sadie yells. "Help a girl out." I laugh and grab the flowers from her hand.

"Darling, we have no more room in the house. It's like the bloody botanical gardens."

She waves me off. "No such thing. What's that?" She looks down at the box.

"I was just calling Wills to help with it. Can you ask him to bring it downstairs for me without Jack seeing it? It's part of his surprise."

"On it." She follows me into the house, and I place the flowers on the table.

"I'm going to finish my makeup since everyone will arrive soon. Do you need anything else from me?" I ask.

"No, go get pretty, and I'll come get you when people start arriving."

"Please." I flip back my hair. "I'm already pretty. No more help is needed." I laugh playfully.

She rolls her eyes. "You've been hanging out with my brother a little too much."

"Truth." I blow her a kiss and get ready for our party.

If I weren't already pathetic enough about the two of us, I'd be skipping two by two up the steps.

But I'm keeping my cool… *or at least trying*.

"There the lass is, my favorite troublemaker." Declan kisses both my cheeks.

"I've been a good girl lately. No trouble from me." I wink.

"What kind of good girl?" Nora waggles her brows.

Declan grumbles something, walking away, and we both laugh. "Hi." I kiss her hello, then take Aoife in my arms. "They're getting so big, soon they'll be walking."

"Don't remind me. Here—for you and Jackson." She hands me two gift bags.

I peek inside the small one, but I can't see anything, and it's hard to open with the baby in my arms. "What is it?"

"We thought you could both use a nice spa retreat after a stressful few months and no honeymoon. It's only an hour away. Dec and I went there after the babies were born."

"Thanks." I swallow, starting to choke up. "You didn't have to."

"But we wanted to. The second bag is just two perfumes I made for both of you. They're different, but complement each other perfectly." She gives me a meaningful look, and I push the rising emotion down further.

"Hanora," I cry. "Thank you." I hug her tightly, squishing the babies until they whine.

We walk into the living area where all our guests are enjoying a pre-dinner drink. I turn to Sadie. "I thought you were coming to get me."

Her eyes widen. "Shoot, sorry. Pregnancy brain is kicking in already." She stops a waitress and grabs a glass of champagne for me. "Cheers, Annabelle. The house is beautiful, and I know it's a reflection of the life you and Jackson are building. God, I still can't believe you're my sister-in-law. It's what I always hoped for."

"Yes, cheers," a smiling Lola announces, followed by Evelyn and Marco.

"Oh." I jump. "You scared me," I squeal as Jack wraps his arms around me and places his head on top of mine.

"Dinner's almost ready," he announces. "Everyone take your seats, please."

"Can I speak to the two of you?" John asks as we step into the hall. "Sadie and Wills. You, as well."

"No problem." We follow him into Jack's office and anxiously await what he has to say.

"It hasn't hit the news yet, but I suspect it will come shortly, so I wanted you four to be the first to know." He hands us his laptop, and my eyes almost bug out of my head. It shows Victoria and Trey arrested and led into a police station.

"What the hell is this?" Wills asks.

"Who cares? Whatever those two evil people did, they deserve it," Sadie spits out.

It's not every day my Sadie has any type of venom laced in her words, but these are people she hates more than maybe even her mom.

Jack interlocks our fingers when we read the rest of the article that's yet to be released.

"Insider Trading" is labeled in large letters across the top.

"Holy shit," Jack blurts out.

"What the hell happened?" Wills asks John.

"These two have been dating, and Trey found out from a lawyer who works at the company that a huge lawsuit was looming. They miraculously both sold their stocks before it happened."

"Fucking idiots." Wills laughs. "They deserve this and more. Hopefully they get convicted and go away for a long time."

"I second that," I say.

Fuck Trey and all the terrible shit he did to me.

And fuck Victoria for messing with Sadie and Wills's life.

I don't even care so much about her stealing my clients. If they want to leave, let them. They'll come crawling back, and I'll double my fee.

We all thank John for having our backs and then join our guests for dinner.

Despite the size and difficulty of fitting everyone in the one area of the house I wanted to use, Sadie did a beautiful job.

She asked me what theme I wanted, and I requested a Tuscany one.

At first, I thought Parisian, but Tuscany—where Jack gave me my wedding band—felt more appropriate.

She decorated the rented rustic tables with candles, small olive trees, and potted rosemary plants that line the table with lemons stacked between them. She might have gone overboard with having our gardener plant cypress trees, but she was in her element and we weren't about to stop her.

I look around at all our guests, loving the mix of them all. There's Mum and her new mate Eleanor, who we have to thank for Mum's speedy recovery, and Wills's dad surrounding the kids.

Besides the typical crew, there's Matthew and Theo. Of course Oliver is missing in action. Nora's bodyguards, Jameson and Max, sit with us as friends today, next to Archie, their foster child, Agnes, Nora's nan, Maeve and Penny, her nurse, who has also turned into a friend.

And scattered around are our new neighbors, employees of Charlotte's, and a handful of our cherished clients.

It's bound to be a great night.

"You know your pregnancy is messing up my party vibe tonight," I joke with Sadie.

"Tell me about it," She huffs and drinks her diet coke.

I turn toward Jack and smile wide. "Today is perfect."

He lifts my wrist and kisses the inside. "I love you," he says softly.

I let out a sigh of happiness and stare into those mesmerizing green eyes. "Same. Always, Jack."

After a long but delicious dinner paired with too many glasses of wine, Jack and I stand to give a toast.

I lift my drink. "Bear with us, but it's been a while since we've all been together, and we have a few things to celebrate tonight. First and foremost, cheers to all of you who have supported us individually and as a couple. Having a group of badass friends and family is what it's all about."

"Auntie Belle!"

"Sorry, Charlie, love. We can say bad words at the fun house, remember?"

She shrugs her little shoulders. "Okay."

Everyone laughs, and we cheers one another.

Jack tilts his glass toward his sisters. "Congratulations to that spunky one's mom and dad for expecting their third baby girl. Sadie, you're an incredible mother. I'm so proud of the woman you've turned into. You're an amazing role model for my nieces."

Jack leans down and hugs his sister.

"Two babies are coming," Nora announces, pointing between her and Sadie.

"What!" I squeal. "Oh my God."

"It's still early days. I'm right behind Sadie."

I smile warmly at Nora and Declan and whisper congratulations before turning back toward our guests. "Cheers to Nora and Declan."

"Now to Jack and Declan for becoming part owners in The Taylored Group. I know it killed Wills to give up some control, but the three of you are a formidable trio."

Shouts ring through the house as I turn toward Jack. "I'm so proud of you, Jack."

"Thanks, sweetheart." He leans over and kisses my cheek.

"Last but not least"—I turn toward my Lola girl—"Lola, my sounding board. The one who keeps me in check and who is like a younger sister to me, has finally found the man of her dreams, my brother, Matthew. The man who raised me into the person I am today. And obviously, I'm pretty great, so he did a good job." We all laugh. "In all seriousness, they both deserve happiness, and I want to wish them the best on their new journey together in Africa."

Everyone clinks glasses, but Nora and Declan stand up as we sit down.

"If you don't mind, we'd like to make an announcement," Nora states.

"Fuck's sake, you guys love the sound of your own voices, don't you," Theo mutters, and Nora narrows her eyes at him.

He doesn't want to go head-to-head with her, no matter his size. He'll lose every time.

Declan palms the back of Nora's neck and pulls her close to him, her eyes watering, which is rare. She's not a crier like Sadie and me.

"This morning, Declan and I received some of the best news of our life." Her eyes search the crowd. "Archie is officially our son. He's officially a Buckley."

Roars of happiness boom through the room as we surround our friends with hugs and kisses, sharing tears of joy.

I knew today would turn out perfectly.

While everyone's still occupied, I grab Jack's hand and pull him toward the basement, wanting to show him my surprise.

"If you wanted a little action, we could have just gone to one of the six bedrooms we have upstairs."

Ignoring him, I keep walking through to where I'd told him I was designing my office. He knew I didn't want him to see it until I was done, but I've had something else up my sleeve all along.

Pushing open the doors, I yell, "Surprise."

Jackson

What?

My head is on a swivel, taking in the room. When did she do this?

"Annabelle," I whisper, trying not to let my emotions get the best of me.

I take her in my arms and kiss her all over. "I love it, B. This is beyond incredible. God, Belle, I don't even know what to say." I look around the room, the one she designed for me.

A "man cave" filled with an abundance of Queen memorabilia, records framed on the wall, some even signed, and holy shit—

"Is that…"

"Freddie Mercury's signed manuscript of 'We Are The Champions.' I thought it was only fitting." She raises a brow playfully.

I'm at a loss for words. Every square inch is filled, including a vintage record player.

This must have taken so much planning and cost her a fortune.

"How did you get it all?

She chuckles. "I was flipping through a magazine for a client and saw that an auction was happening for Queen. What are the odds? I dragged Lola to Sotheby's auction house with me, but you'll have to ask Lo about the rest. She said I was mad trying to bid for everything."

I laugh at the thought. I can imagine my girl taking charge there.

"It's incredible and so thoughtful. Thank you, sweetheart." I take her in my arms and sweep my lips against hers. "I think I'm in shock," I mumble.

She pulls back and cups my cheek. "You do so much for everyone else. It's time someone spoils you. So, thank *you* for always caring for me, your sister, your nieces, and all our friends. You're the one everyone turns to, and I want you to remember I'll always be the one *you* can turn to."

I drop my head to her shoulder and take a shaky breath. "You can't make me cry. Bucks will never let me live it down." I laugh.

"Come on, let's get back upstairs. We can come back later and you can fuck me while looking out at all the weird shit you love." She grins and pulls me upstairs.

It's the middle of the night and we're partying like we're young with no responsibilities or care in the world. The music is blasting, and Belle's on the couch dancing with Lola.

Sadie and Wills's nanny took all the kids across the street, though Sades probably should have joined them. She's been sleeping in the corner for the last three hours.

I have no clue how Nora's still up; Sadie never had any energy in her first trimester.

I put my arms out and Belle jumps in them easily.

"Mmm, you smell good, lover boy." She kisses my neck, then slides to the ground to continue dancing.

"The staff was sent home hours ago. I'm going to go inside and finish cleaning up."

"Okay." She winks, then shimmies her tits in my face. "Come back and play after."

Fuck.

"What's going on here?" I stand at the entrance to the bedroom, taking in the scene.

The lights are dimmed, casting a glowing shadow throughout the room, and from the lack of response, my voice echoes throughout.

Belle is curled in the middle of the bed, her favorite blanket wrapped tightly around her, while my sister is snuggled up close to her, fast asleep.

Nora, Evelyn, and Lola sit against the headboard on either side of them, and Declan, Wills, and Marco sit off to the side of the room.

Walking into a scene like this makes you think, *How close is too close for friendships*?

"Did everyone lose their ability to talk?"

"We're christening our new bed on our housewarming night." Belle winks.

"You're right. That's exactly what's about to happen in ten seconds. I know Bucks and Nora are kinky as fuck and would love to see the show, but I don't share. Out. Now, fuckers."

Wills picks up a sleeping Sadie who doesn't so much as flinch, and everyone else heads out.

"Hey, Lo, sleep here in one of the guest rooms. When he had to leave earlier, I promised Matthew that you wouldn't go home alone."

"Okay." She yawns. "See you in the morning."

Once everyone's out of the room, I stalk over to my wife. "I hope you're not tired."

"Never for you." She grins.

I lie on the bed facing her, taking in her beauty as I stroke her face.

"Tonight was a success."

"It was like a true fairytale." She leans in and kisses my dimples. "You've always been my fantasy, Jack."

"Sweetheart, who needs a fantasy with a life like ours?"

"You're a smooth talker, Mr. Peters."

"I know I joke around a lot, but I hope you know I mean everything I say to you. You are my life, B. You've opened my eyes to love and to a future I thought was so out of reach that I never even dreamed of it."

"Oh, Jack," she whispers, gulping down her tears.

"Now, if you want to live out a real fantasy, get on your hands and knees, Mrs. Peters." I smack her ass, and she laughs loudly.

"With pleasure." She sighs.

Reaching over, I dim the lights and quickly glance at our original Vegas wedding bands framed beside the bed.

It's a reminder that no matter our journey or the obstacles thrown our way, we were always leading to the same finish line together, hopelessly in love and happily married.

EPILOGUE

Six Months Later

Jackson

Why is it so bright in here? I rub my eyes and open them to see Belle smiling.

"I thought you said I could sleep in for my birthday?"

She tries to push me off the bed. *What the hell?*

"We have an appointment in one hour. You're not going to want to miss this." She pushes me toward the shower.

"I don't even get a birthday blowjob. What kind of marriage is this?"

"There's no time, darling. Hurry up!" she snaps.

I'm standing in Chelsea, staring at a sign that's almost unbelievable to my eyes.

Dr. Sara Hampton
Obstetrician-Gynecologist

Belle snakes her arm around my waist and leans her body into me. "I've been keeping a secret," she whispers.

"Are you pregnant?" My eyes bulge, darting between her and the sign.

She grins with a look of contentment. "No, but hopefully one day."

"What are you saying, Annabelle?"

"I'm saying that without you knowing for the last six months, Dr. Esposito and I have been putting a plan into place where I feel safe to have a baby. We've been working through my fears and found the best doctors in London to work with. We spoke to them together, and they all assured me that, under supervision, we could try naturally for a baby. Of course, being in my late thirties, my age may be a factor, but besides that, it's safe for us to start trying. Happy Birthday."

"B… Sweetheart."

I don't want her to go through any unnecessary stress for me. We're happier than ever, and we don't need to change a thing.

"Look at me, Jack." I turn my face toward her willful one. "I know what you're thinking. But I want this, and I put a lot of work into figuring out the logistics. Unless you've changed your mind?"

"Of course not. You know how I feel about having kids." I look back at the building. "You're sure about this?

"I am, truly. I want to have your baby, Jackson Peters."

I bite my lip to hide my grin. "I'm not sure whether it's okay that I'm turned on by that statement… but I am."

"That's because you're a horny bastard."

I laugh loudly. "Okay, B. Let's try to make a baby."

Annabelle

Eight Years Later

Here we are, eight years later, with our closest friends and family in Taormina, Sicily, lounging on the beach overlooking Mt. Edna in post-marital bliss.

I was done with weddings. We've had six more fun, fake ones during our travels, but Mr. Romantic needed something real, and I love him for it. So, we settled on a vow renewal in Italy.

It might not have been where I fell in love with him… that was the summer I became a raging hormonal teenager, spying on him in his boxer briefs through a crack in his door, dancing and singing along to Freddie Mercury.

But Italy is a beautiful country for many reasons, and it gave us hope for our future years ago, making it all the more special now.

"Mummy? Where's Daddy?" I pick up my sweet Emmeline, our rainbow baby, and sit her on the lounger with me.

"He'll be right back. He went to get us some water."

Her eyes scan the beach, and when she sees Jack at the stand, she relaxes, snuggling into my side. She's a daddy's girl through and through, never wanting to leave Jackson's side for even a minute.

Jack and I had to overcome a lot once we started trying for a baby.

It took us almost two years, a few rounds of IVF, and still, nothing worked. Then, one day when we least expected it, I got pregnant naturally.

It was one of the happiest and scariest times of my life.

Pregnancy put a lot of stress on our marriage, friendships, and my overall mental health. Even with a therapist's help, it took a lot out of me, and unfortunately, I took it out on everyone who came in contact with me, including Jack.

My anxiety was through the roof when I did fall pregnant, especially when it came closer to my due date. If I had gas pains, I would make Jack call our doctor in the middle of the night.

The first time the baby kicked, we were rushing to the hospital.

So, for both of our sanity and after years of suffering through a "negative" test result each month, we eventually decided Emmy is our angel. She is enough.

One and done.

"Hi, Charlie," Emmy whispers as her older cousin approaches us. Emmeline is infatuated with Charlie, and it's the sweetest thing ever.

My itty-bitty niece is now a hormonal teenager driving her parents up the wall.

She's told Wills she has a boyfriend, which, of course, Sadie and I already knew about, and I thought he was going to have a heart attack right there and then.

"Hi, Em." Charlie smiles and holds out her hand to her wide-eyed cousin. "Do you want to come down and build sand castles with Aoife and me?"

Emmy's eyes light up and she nods enthusiastically, pausing only when she sees Jack.

"Don't worry, baby. Daddy won't go anywhere. You go with your cousins and have fun."

She thinks about it for a second, ultimately disregarding me, then runs up to cuddle Jack's leg, climbing it like the gymnast she is.

"Hello, my littlest love." Jack kisses her.

She gives him a quick cuddle before running off toward all her cousins. "Charlotte, watch her by the water!" I yell after them.

She rolls her eyes, annoyed I'm telling her how to babysit her cousin. "I know, I know."

"Waters and Aperol Spritzes, wife."

"Why do you keep saying *wife* like we just married for the first time? We've been married for ten years."

"Feels like the first time all over again." He smirks.

I raise my eyebrows and give him a blank look. "Really? Because we were blackout drunk in Vegas, and I know you don't remember one minute of that wedding."

He taps his head. "Don't you worry, B, it's up here somewhere, and one day it'll come back to me.

"I don't know about that, old man. Soon you're going to lose your memories.

He scoffs. "I'm forty-eight, not eighty-eight."

We both turn to the sound of our daughter's happy squeals echoing around the beach as Matthew throws her up in the air to Theo, who then takes off toward the water.

"Nooo, Uncle Matty, save me!" she yells, but Matthew does the exact opposite. He picks up his son and follows them into the water.

"I love that kid."

I turn toward Sadie, who's walking up beside us.

Me too.

"Isn't it funny how your firstborn is more like me than anyone else, and mine is like you," I say.

She chuckles. "Yes, but at least yours has my DNA. No clue where Charlie gets it from." She reaches over, stealing my drink.

"That has alcohol in it!" I grab it from her lips.

She rubs her pregnant belly with my fifth niece. Wills begged for years for one more kid, and when he finally got it, it was another girl. Not shocking whatsoever.

"One freaking sip won't do anything. Do you know how hard it is to be on this beach with you all, dying of heat stroke, while you're partying it up and having fun?" I smirk at my dramatic soul sister. "Everywhere I go, it's an army of us just kicking back and having fun. Then there's me. I'm about to roll over on the sand and pretend I'm a beached whale."

"Oh please, stop complaining. At least all your girls are well-behaved. Our four boys are absolute maniacs," Nora says as she approaches, double-fisting margaritas.

I smirk, thinking how Sadie's going to lose her mind.

"How about you both stop complaining? It's not like any of yours were 'oopsie' babies. You planned on them. There'll be eleven between just the two of you, plus Archie. Eleven, that's just too many."

They both grin, knowing I'm right and that they wouldn't change it for the world.

While checking on Emmy, I only notice Charlie and Clara, their third daughter. "Where's Chloe and Claire?"

"With Dad." She turns toward Jack. "Inviting him was nice of you. I know it meant a lot to him."

Jack's relationship with his dad has been rocky, but it's better than nothing. It will never be perfect, but it's good enough for him to be here, and that says enough.

Suddenly over the beach club speakers, the music changes to a slow song, causing everyone to groan.

The second I hear the song, though, I freeze and turn toward Jack, already teary-eyed.

His hand is outstretched. "It's finally our wedding day."

"Can't Help Falling in Love" by Haley Reinhart plays out over the beach as I take my husband's hand and he pulls me into his chest.

We glide the best we can through the sand, singing the lyrics of the song I waited nine years to dance to. "You make me the happiest man alive, Annabelle Peters. Thank you for being my wife."

I drop my head and cry the happiest tears. "Your words always hit just right."

"Mummy and Daddy, may I dance with you?"

Jack leans down and picks up our sweet girl, placing her between us.

She frowns. "Why are you crying?"

"Because I love you and your daddy so much that I can't control my emotions. They're happy tears, I promise you."

She hooks her arms around us and kisses our cheeks. "Well, I love you too. Both of you."

I look at Jack smiling at Emmy, then at me. "And I love you," he says.

"Always." I kiss his lips, and that's the truth.

I will always love this man.

Like I always have.

The End.

AFTERWORD

Thank you so much for reading. It means the world to me to have your support.
If you enjoyed reading Secret Lovers, please consider leaving a review!

Don't forget to check online for other releases and my website for my newsletter and updates.

Read on for an excerpt from London Lovers

ALSO BY J R GALE

The Taylored Men Series

London Lovers (Wills and Sadie)

Destined Lovers (Declan and Nora)

Secret Lovers (Jackson and Annabelle)

Novellas

Lilacs and Lovers (Lola and Matthew)

The Bonded Brother Series

Coming Soon

ACKNOWLEDGMENTS

First and foremost, many thanks go out to the incredible and selfless T L Swan. You're an inspiration, and I wouldn't have written these words without your guidance.

To my fellow Cygnets, your continued support, wisdom, and reassurance mean the world to me.

L.A. Shaw and Katherine Jay, I'm lucky to have met you through this community...cheers to figuring it all out together.

Elle Nicoll, you're a saint for listening to all my messages—I love the routine we've created for ourselves.

To Sara, the best PA and friend out there. Thank you for listening to me waffle all day, every day, and indulging in my crazy ideas. Your support from day one has been invaluable. I appreciate it and you beyond words! xx

To my betas, Kathryn, Sara, Jaclyn, Lizzy, Danielle, and Andi, thank you is not good enough to express my appreciation for the time and commitment you gave my characters. Your words and support over those few months made this book what it is today.

Lizzy, thank you for going over and beyond to help edit. You are truly a lifesaver, and I'm so thankful you've joined the team and that I've gained another lovely friend.

To my family, Michael, Mom, and Dad. Thank you for always supporting my crazy ideas and ventures. And, Michael, for dealing with my very late nights and becoming a hermit for months at an end.

Last but not least, to you, the best readers around.

Thanks for being the biggest part of everything I'm doing and for choosing to read Secret Lovers. Always remember, this is not possible without you.

J R Gale xx

ABOUT THE AUTHOR

J R Gale is a contemporary romance author obsessed with the happily ever after.
She is a native New Yorker, residing in New York City with her husband and rescue pup, Cali.
When she's not thinking of your next alpha book boyfriend, you can find her traveling the world—romance book in hand.

LONDON LOVERS EXCERPT

Chapter One

Sadie

Finally! The wheels hit the ground, and I'm instantly bouncing in my seat. Anticipation runs through me, excited for what's to come. But it's taking freaking forever to get off this plane.

It's been eight hours since I've left Manhattan and eight hours since I left my old self behind.

Now, I'm excited to get the hell away from New York and to start my annual girls' trip.

But I'm especially excited to see my best friend, Annabelle—it's been almost one year since I've seen her last, the longest stretch since we have been kids.

Finally, the seat belt light switches off, and all the passengers jump up to grab their carry-on bags. Lining up, eager to head off the plane.

"Bienvenu en France," the stewardess kindly welcomes me as we disembark the plane, and I thank her.

"Merci beaucoup," in what I can only hope sounded French.

I walk out onto the tarmac, waiting for the shuttle to bring us to our terminal, and that's when I'm hit with that familiar feeling I always get when I arrive at my final destination.

It's that buzzing energy and eagerness you feel from other travelers excited to start an adventure.

I take a minute to check out my new surroundings, and almost everyone looks the same. Eyes wide, backs tall, heads high, smiles wide. No matter where you land in the world, everyone does it. It's the magic of traveling.

For some, it's the excitement of starting something new, maybe a honeymoon or a well-deserved holiday they've saved for. But, for others, it's a feeling they've escaped whatever it is they are leaving behind. And, unfortunately for me, it's the latter—the cheater ex-boyfriend and parents who aren't worthy of holding the title.

An hour later, I finally exit the customs area after getting stuck behind the loudest New Yorkers known to man. Not exactly the way I envisioned this starting. But I'm off to retrieve my baggage, where Belle should be waiting for me.

"Sadie, darling, I'm over here!" she screams across the baggage claim, waving her hands like a crazed woman.

She isn't hard to miss. I spotted her instantly, along with half of the airport.

I'll never know if people are staring because she's screaming or because of Belle's looks. She must have been a model in her former life; Tall, blonde, and perfect—inside and out.

Growing up, we spent every summer together, and all the boys fawned over her, giving her the unfortunate nickname of "BB" or "Double *B*" for Bombshell Belle. Luckily the only time she ever hears that now is if my brother is trying to piss her off.

I walk over to where Belle is still waving her arms. I love this girl with all of my heart, but I can already see her enthusiasm is at level one hundred. And, after my long overnight flight, I'm not exactly ready for it.

The saying "opposites attract" is not just about romantic couples. It applies to best friends too.

Annabelle has that larger-than-life attitude. She's a busy bee, Miss Popular, career-driven, and all around good person with a strong backbone. On the other hand, I tend to be more reserved and shy. I probably could use a little of Belle's charisma in some instances.

That's what this trip is all about, breaking all my bad habits of letting everyone walk all over me and finally doing what's best for me. Although I don't love being the center of attention, I am still a strong, independent person. I just lost my way a little, and I am finally set to be back on track with my life.

And, with Belle by my side, I know it will happen. She is the only person in the world I want to be right now, my bestic and sister soul mate. The best support person you'll ever need in your life.

"I've missed you so much," I mumble into her hair.

"Oh, Sadie. I've also missed you so much. I can't believe it's been so long."

"Please, Annabelle, don't start. If you cry, I cry."

I need to go into this trip with good happy vibes.

I've felt terrible that I canceled going to London to see Belle and my brother for Christmas. Instead, I was suckered into staying for my mother's charity luncheon, her charity banquet, her charity cocktail party, and who knows what other event she made me attend for appearances. *But no more.*

"Right, right, well, let's get your bags and make our way to the hotel. Our driver is waiting right out front."

We drive a short distance to our hotel located on the Cote d'Azur in a small town called Antibes, located somewhere between Nice and Saint-Tropez.

Initially, I rented a country home right outside Avignon, where I could reset, think things through, and try to understand how I let myself get steamrolled by my family and Colton, my ex, time and time again.

But unlucky, for me, lucky for Belle, the house caught fire a few months ago, and Annabelle insisted on staying here. Which now isn't looking so bad, after all.

We enter the property down a long, tree-lined driveway, barely making out the hotel in the distance. This place is top notch, I can already tell. But then again, I did not expect anything less from Annabelle.

We might have grown up "upper class," but I try to live a more reserved lifestyle. Belle, on the other hand—not so much.

The bellhops walk out to meet our car while the hotel staff waits with champagne and warm towels.

"Welcome, you must be Ms. Hughes," the one attendant says to Annabelle.

"Yes, and this is my friend, Sadie Peters."

"Welcome, please let us take your luggage while my colleague Jacques escorts you to reception to check in."

I pinch Annabelle's side and raise my eyebrows.

Jacques is gorgeous, and if I know Annabelle, she will jump right on that.

"Jacques," she purrs. "What a beautiful French name. Where are you from?"

Paris pronounced Pa-ree in his beautiful French accent

I walk away to explore the hotel before catching Annabelle go into full flirt mode.

And, wow, I am lost for words. This hotel is beyond gorgeous.

After you pass through the two massive front doors, the reception area is entirely open, greeting you with the most spectacular view of the Mediterranean Sea.

The lobby is done mainly in sleek white marble and glass walls, adorned with huge flower arrangements of orchids, white roses, and I definitely smell jasmine somewhere. White-and-beige linen curtains blow from the sea breeze, giving it a relaxing but romantic feel. This place is perfect.

I make my way over to the beautiful lady waiting for us to check in. *Geez, do they only employ good-looking people here*?

I look down at my overnight flight outfit, realizing I probably should have freshened up and changed at the airport before arriving at the hotel.

After giving our information to the front desk attendant, Annabelle wanders back over.

"Holy shit, Sadie!" she whisper-screams.

"What? What's the matter?"

"Did you see who's here?"

"Who?" I ask, turning my head, looking to see someone familiar.

"Well, knowing you, you probably were more worried about the decor and floral arrangements than paying attention to anyone else."

I roll my eyes. "Oh, shut it, Miss I Need To Flirt With Every Man I See."

"Well, don't look now. But Wills Taylor and three other extremely good-looking, probably also rugby players, are standing over to our right, about to check in."

"I have no idea who Wills Taylor is, Belle," I say in a huff.

She knows everyone and their mother. Why would I expect anything different now that we are in the South of France?

I slowly move my head to check out this Wills Taylor she is talking about, and holy hell, she wasn't lying.

There are four massively huge, very attractive men over on the other side of the hotel check-in area. Usually, the big muscle type is not my cup of tea, but no one can deny how good-looking these men are. They are all dressed perfectly in crisp summer suits and loafers, but one of them is just that much more handsome than the others. He looks like he should be in an old Hollywood movie, the James Dean of our time, but with a very muscular, athletic body. It's hard to move my eyes away. It's like I'm glued to him. But just when I go to turn back to Annabelle, he slowly turns to me, and his eyes catch mine.

Oh god, this is like a bad car crash, where I can't look away. He slowly lifts one side of his mouth with a too-sexy smirk, and I can feel the heat of embarrassment spread through my body.

"What the hell?" Belle snaps me out of my gaze. It's also when I realized I've been holding my breath.

"What's the matter?" I widen my eyes and act surprised.

"I just told you not to look, and you were staring right at Wills. Now he is staring right over at us. Actually…"

"Actually, what?" I snap a little too fast.

She raises her eyebrows slightly and says, "He's staring at you, and he just tapped one of his mates. They are both looking at you right now."

"You need to get your eyes checked, Belle. I'm standing next to you, and I'm in yoga pants and a T-shirt. Let's go. Our room is ready."

I start to head toward the elevator, not waiting for her. I need a shower and a glass of wine to relax in our suite. I can't be thinking of any guys.

"What does that mean? You're standing next to me?" she huffs once she catches up.

I roll my eyes at her. "It meant nothing, just that you're standing here dressed like we're about to go out to a garden party, all perfect and beautiful, and I look like I just did an hour of hot yoga."

I press the elevator for one of the top floors where all the suites are located; we are sharing a two-bedroom suite that Belle says is "to die for."

As the doors are closing, I catch another glimpse of this Wills she keeps going on about, and my stomach drops. He really is strikingly handsome, all serious and mysterious looking. But fortunately, the doors shut before I could think any more about him. I am here to turn over a new leaf, not troll for men.

"Sadie, are you even listening?"

"Huh? No, I zoned out for a minute, sorry. What were you saying?"

"That you need to stop being so hard on yourself—you are your own worst critic. You're beautiful even with yoga pants on. Plus, I would die for your bum." Belle laughs and pinches my behind.

"Okay, okay, enough about me. Our room is here, number 1414."

We walk inside, and again the beauty of this place has me lost for words.

Our bags are already up here, and the porters must have opened all the windows so we could smell the fresh sea breeze. We walk through the white-and-gray marble foyer that leads to the balcony.

Holy crap, this is bigger than some New York apartments. We have a small dipping pool overlooking the sea, a dining room table, lounge chairs, and a small bar area. We could probably stay here the whole vacation and never leave.

"Wow, Belle, you did good. This place is amazing. This is the exact place I need to be right now."

She settles up next to me, leaning over to give me a side hug. "I'm glad you're happy. You deserve this trip more than anyone. But I know you're exhausted, so go jump in the shower, take a power nap, and get ready so we can relax, catch up, have some drinks before dinner. Woo!"

"Take it down fifty notches until I get that nap, crazy!" I laugh as I head toward the shower.

"Love you, too!" she yells.

I find my room, and holy crap, it's filled with multiple bouquets of flowers. Well, there goes the no-crying rule because the tears are already streaming down my face. I know this is Annabelle's doing. I walk over to the small arrangement next to my bed with fresh lavender and read the attached small card.

My darling Sadie,

I think each of our paths is already set for us when we are born. We may not understand the whys and reasoning behind our journeys yet, but we will all go through things in life that set us up for what is meant to be. You have already overcome some obstacles that have only made you stronger. So, please don't let anyone erase your spirit and sparkle that makes you, you.

You are the most selfless, kindhearted person I have ever had the pleasure of knowing in my life. What comes next for you on this life journey will only bring you happiness and love. I know it. So please embrace whatever comes your way next. I am so proud of you. You deserve it all.

I love you.

Your sister soul mate,
Annabelle

Now sobbing, I take the note and store it in my bag to avoid losing it.

Between Belle and I, we have more emotions than a romance novel. But I don't know what I would do without her, always knowing exactly what I need to hear. People could only wish to have an Annabelle in their lives.

After I shower and nap, I stroll out to the balcony where Belle is relaxing, sipping some champagne. I walk over to her and hug her tightly. She kisses my cheek, and I whisper, "I love you."

"I love you, too, Sadie."

We sit there hugging for a minute until Belle decides it's time for more champagne.

"A toast is in order!" she shouts. "Cheers to the almost birthday girl. Let's make this trip the best one yet. Sleep all morning, beach all day, drink, dance, and have sex all night!" She clinks my glass.

I hit my hand to my forehead and laugh. "I am not having sex all night, or sex at all. You're lucky that I'm agreeing to party, *sometimes*."

"Sadie, you need to let loose on this trip. Why can't sex be in order? The way Wills was staring at you made it very clear he would be interested. It just so happens, I think I know one of his friends. I'm going to invite them out tomorrow night if I have the chance."

I ignore her and continue to drink my champagne. I feel a blush creeping up and butterflies in my stomach. The feeling I got when Wills just glanced over was something I am certainly not used to.

But he looked like he would be all too consuming and a little intense for my liking. I practically roll my eyes at myself.

Yeah, right, Sadie, you liked exactly how he was looking at you.

I ignore those thoughts and stare out over the balcony. I take in the view before me, thinking about what this trip means to me. Belle and I take a few weeks' vacation every year, but tomorrow, I turn thirty and I promised myself I would start doing what was best for *me* now.

I am finally going to open my own floral design shop, it's something I've dreamed about my whole life. I want to volunteer more and travel even more.

Belle has been trying to get me to move to London for some time now, and honestly, it isn't the worst idea. A place to start fresh. Plus, my brother, Jackson, lives there, and I miss him a ridiculous amount. So I know it's the right move, I just need to woman up and take the plunge.

Besides being close to Annabelle and Jackson, the other major perk of moving would be to distance myself from my parents and our toxic relationship.

The other reason would bc I wouldn't have to see Colton anymore. Since I caught him cheating, he has tried to get back together numerous times, claiming it was only that once.

But little does he know—I know the truth. It's been going on for more than six months, and honestly, I'm not sure I even care. Which tells you… I'm done.

I clearly didn't love him anymore, and it took an unfortunate circumstance to show me that. At the end of the day, I was more embarrassed than heartbroken with what he did.

He was what my parents always wanted, a rich boy from a high society family with strong political ties. We met when we were twenty-four and were good friends first. Both of us were so carefree and enjoyed many of the same interests. I did love him. But he grew to be everything I hate about the social circles our families run in. Caring more about status and appearances than me.

Annabelle tops off my champagne, not saying anything. She knows when I just need to process things by myself.

Maybe it wouldn't hurt if I let loose this trip and lived untroubled like Belle? I know how to go out and have a good time. It's just not my priority like her. Plus, I don't have many friends in Manhattan that I enjoy letting loose with like I do with her. Since she lives over three thousand miles away, it's easier to have quiet weekends with a good book and wine. On occasion, a nice dinner, or if I'm forced, my family drags me to events to be "seen."

So, to let loose and have "Annabelle type of fun" is just not second nature to me.

But maybe it's time to set out and try.

"Let's go shopping tomorrow, Belle. I think I need something sexier and more birthday appropriate if we aim to go out dancing tomorrow night."

She couldn't whip her head faster toward me, clapping her hands like a little kid.

"YES, YES, YES, let's do it! When we head down to dinner, I'll ask the concierge where the best shopping is. And on that note, let's go inside so you can get ready for dinner," she says as she tops us off with even more champagne.

I'm jet-lagged and now tipsy. We better leave soon. Otherwise, I'll be passing out again.

I'm finishing up my makeup when Belle comes into my room looking freaking gorgeous.

"Belle," I moan. She always does this. "You said we were getting drinks and dinner at the bar downstairs—nothing fancy tonight."

She looks down at herself and smirks. "You know me, fancy is my middle name."

"I'm almost done, and to be clear, when we get downstairs, I want no more talk about me. I only want to hear about you—you can catch me up on this new guy you're dating."

"Dating is too serious of a word. I'm not tying myself to anyone right now."

Of course, she's not.

"Done! Let's go."

My stomach rumbles loudly as we leave. It's only now I realize I haven't eaten since the plane ride.

We make our way to the hostess stand to get seated for dinner. I'm still in awe of the decor in this hotel. The beach theme continues throughout but adds different elements as you explore.

The restaurant reminds me of beach meets Paris, all-white flowing linens, but high ceilings and beautiful moldings. The bar is a white marble with brass hardware fitted with mauve-colored velvet chairs. I think I need to recreate this at home somehow. It's classy, simple, yet super sexy all at the same time.

The hostess is an attractive young girl—*shocker*—and not the friendliest. Nevertheless, she's giving Belle the once-over, and I can already tell this will be an issue.

"I am sorry, but we are very backed up tonight. So, you will need to sit at the bar and wait," the hostess says in a short, clipped voice.

"Well, that's not good enough. How long will it be? We traveled all day and have a reservation for right now," Belle explains.

"Madam, I do not know. You need to move to the bar now. I have other customers to help."

"Annabelle, let's just get a drink first, then eat." I hate confrontation.

"Fine." She glares at the hostess. "One drink, then our table better be ready."

We walk off to the lounge area near the bar. "Don't get all worked up," I warn.

"She just hit a nerve. She kept looking me up and down. It was as if she just decided right there and then that they were busy and we couldn't sit."

We switch from champagne to some slightly dirty martinis. I can already predict most of our drink orders—champagne, wine, martinis, and lots of spicy margaritas.

"So… spill the tea, Belle. Starting with this new man of yours."

We may talk every day and get caught up with each other. But it's just not the same as an in-person gossip sesh.

"Ugh. He is not my man. I am still a single woman. But I think there is potential there. I met him through a coworker of mine. His name is Trey."

"Trey?!" I spit my drink out, laughing. God, why am I laughing? That's so mean. But I can't help it, I can't stop. "Trey has to be listed as one of the top ten douchiest names, right?"

I cannot see Miss High Society Annabelle with a "Trey."

She starts laughing now too. "I know it's terrible, isn't it? But he is rather handsome, so it makes up for his name."

I take a deep breath. "Okay, okay. Sorry. Tell me more. Give me the rundown."

"He is older by a few years and very close to his family. Which, by the way—they have a house in the Alps, so now we have a ski house if this works out. He is an only child, lives in Mayfair, has many good-looking friends for you, and he's a barrister." She takes a deep breath. "He's just over six feet, so tall enough for me, which is crucial."

Belle, being probably around five feet ten, needs someone tall, no question about it.

"He has more of a runner's body, but still muscular, dark hair, light eyes, light skin. Proclaimed foodie. No faults so far, except he works a lot. And he lives a lifestyle a little closer to yours." She winks. "Probably better off since I am always out and about at events and openings all around London for work and fun. If we both lived a similar lifestyle, it wouldn't work."

Belle is in public relations, which suits her perfectly.

"Well, even though I will probably never be able to say his name without laughing, I am glad you're happy and giving this guy a try." I smile at her softly.

"You've been killing it at your job, and now you have someone that seems just as successful. Who, hopefully, won't feel threatened like other men in your past."

"Boys, Sadie, not men. Too emasculating to date a woman that's more successful than them."

She chuckles and adds, "Plus, they all had small dicks. I can't work with that."

She is too much. I'm laughing hard again—god, I've missed this girl. At least my abs are getting a workout tonight.

We finish our martinis when I feel someone's eyes on me. I turn to the bar and spot Wills's friends all standing ordering drinks, but I don't see him.

But for some reason, I just know he's here somewhere. I'm getting the same feeling I had when we were in the lobby. So I take another look around when a deep voice whispers in my ear, sending a shiver through my body.

"Looking for me?"

I slowly raise my eyes. Jesus, he is freaking hot. His gorgeous gray eyes bore into mine, and he raises an eyebrow in question.

"Huh?" I hear him chuckle a little. Jesus, I can't even put together a sentence.

"I asked if you were looking for me? I saw you looking over at my friends. Then it seemed like you didn't find what you were looking for."

So smug.

"I, um, no. I was looking for the waiter to order another drink," I say.

Belle's eyes are as wide as saucers right now, and I am trying to telepathically tell her to jump in here and say something.

"Wills Taylor." He reaches his hand out for mine.

I extend my hand to him, and he kisses the back, leaving his lips there a little longer than expected.

"And you are?" he says in his posh British accent.

"Sadie. And this is my friend Annabelle."

He doesn't even glance over at her. This is very intense. *He is very intense.*

"Can I buy you ladies another round?"

"No," "Yes," Belle and I say in unison.

"Yes, please." Belle beats me to it.

"Okay." He chuckles. "I'll be right back." He drops my hand. I hadn't even realized he was still holding it. But the second he lets go, I feel an instant loss.

What the hell is that all about?

"Holy shit, Sadie! That was freaking hot. I told you he wanted to devour you."

What do I even say to her? She's right. He looked like he wanted to eat me alive, right there and then.

I glance back to the bar and catch a glimpse of Wills talking with his friends. He's in the perfect position for me to see him full on now.

He's wearing a different suit than earlier and has undone a few top buttons for a more relaxed feel. His chest is broad, where you can see the outline of his muscles and a dusting of very light-brown hair. But his legs, holy hell! The way they fill out his suit is just, wow.

I think Belle mentioned he played rugby, and I can see it now.

I realize I'm staring, so I slowly turn my eyes back to a very smiley Belle. "Don't start. That was too intense. I could barely form a freaking sentence," I mutter.

"That's because you're turned on. Look at you—you're beet red."

"I am not," I deny. But I know I am. I can feel the heat radiating off me. And I can't help but reach up and touch my face to confirm. "I was just taken by surprise, that's all."

"Well, I don't believe that one bit. Anyway, Wills is coming back over now, with his three friends."

I jolt up and fix my dress and hair quickly.

I think I hear Belle murmur, "That's what I thought." But I ignore her. I can't have her in my head right now.

All four guys make it to our table with our drinks. Wills hands me mine.

"Thank you, Wills," I whisper and look down at my drink. His stare is too intense for me.

"Annabelle Hughes, it's lovely to see you. How are your brothers?" I hear one of Wills's friends ask Annabelle.

Now, I remember she mentioned she may have known one of his friends.

"They are trouble, as usual." She laughs.

"George, this is my best friend, Sadie Peters. We are here on holiday for the next few weeks."

George walks over and kisses both my cheeks.

"It's a pleasure," he says.

Behind him, Wills is staring daggers into the back of his head. What the hell is that about?

"Seems like you met Wills. These are our friends Leo and Declan. Lucky for you girls, we are also here on holiday for a few weeks." He winks, and I shake the other two's hands, introducing myself.

Leo and George seem like fun boys. Declan seems just as intense as Wills but with a gentler side. I'm getting this feeling that there is more to him than meets the eye.

"Anna, it's been so long since I've seen you. I'm surprised I recognized you," George states.

"Ah! Anna, I haven't heard someone call you that in a long time." I laugh, and she glares at me. She would rather be called Double *B* than Anna. Not sure what her hang-up is, but she's hated it for as long as I can remember.

"You've known each other a long time?" George asks.

"Yes." Belle smiles over at me. "We have been best friends for twenty-five years."

Wills still hasn't said a word since walking back here, but I can feel his eyes on me. I don't chance a look because I'm afraid I'll start drooling or do something equally as stupid.

"Why don't you ladies join us for dinner?" Leo chimes in.

"No can do, boys. The first night is always just Sadie and me. No matter where we travel, it's our rule. Just her and I." She grabs my hand and squeezes lightly.

We made that rule when we were teenagers, as our life got too busy. Whenever we saw each other, throughout the years, the first night was always to catch up and just spend time together.

"But I have an even better invitation," she adds. "Tomorrow, it's Sadie's thirtieth birthday, and we are going dancing. Meet us at the club after dinner? I can send you the details, George."

They all nod.

"See you boys tomorrow, then!" Belle giggles and blows kisses to the guys as they walk off like she's known them for years.

Wills is still beside me, so I finally look up as he leans down toward me. "Good night, Sadie, until tomorrow, beautiful," he whispers, then kisses my cheek with a slightly open mouth, lingering there for a second.

I'm speechless. Again.

What the hell was that*? And why did I want to turn my head so my lips could feel his open mouth?*

Made in the USA
Middletown, DE
19 March 2024